KYLE FIELDS

NO ROOM TO LIVE

No Room To Live

ISBN-13: 978-1-963102-16-1 (Paperback)
ISBN-13: 978-1-963102-45-1 (Hardcover)
ISBN-13: 978-1-963102-15-4 (eBook)

Cover Art by Cedar Sanderson

Published by Defiance Press and Publishing, LLC

Bulk orders of this book may be obtained by contacting Defiance Press and Publishing, LLC at: www.defiancepress.com.

Public Relations Dept. – Defiance Press & Publishing, LLC
281-581-9300
pr@defiancepress.com

Defiance Press & Publishing, LLC
281-581-9300
info@defiancepress.com

PROLOGUE

Waimea, The Big Island of Hawai'i
03:10 Hawaiian Standard Time (HST), 26 January, Many Years Ago

They came in the middle of the night. It was standard procedure.

Leilani Damonati was sleeping peacefully in her crib when the hands reached around her and placed her in an infant transporter.

Her mother was also sleeping peacefully in the next bedroom. The *tranqgun* had done its job. She would stay that way until midmorning when Leilani's grandmother arrived to babysit.

Of course, by then, it would be too late. Leilani would be over 730,000,000 miles away on her way to the place they called the Orphanage.

PART ONE
SOON

CHAPTER ONE

"**N**ice night," First Officer Kuparr Winston said as he glanced through the Central Pacific Airlines 777 windshield after closing the flight deck door. Puffy clouds, illuminated by the full moon, stretched to the horizon thirty thousand feet below. Underneath the windshield, five large screens displayed a multitude of information, emitting a soft glow into the dark flight deck. He focused on the second screen from the right, which displayed their route of flight as a vertical magenta line interrupted by several waypoints. They were still well west of the International Date Line, but where they were going, it had just become today. In fact, it had just become this year.

Captain Lydia Kahananui glanced up from the left seat. "Yes. It's beautiful." She jotted down the aircraft's estimated time of arrival at the next waypoint on a paper copy of their flight plan. "We're logged in with Nadi Control, three minutes ahead of the flight plan, and two thousand pounds up on the gas. Get any sleep, Kup?" Her long black hair was pulled into a tight ponytail, and she wore a purple-and-blue scarf in lieu of a tie. A red hibiscus sat above her right ear; it had been a rough divorce. Somehow, the flower always made it through Australian and US agriculture checks.

"Slept like a rock," Kup said as he sat down in the right seat and placed his coffee cup in the cupholder to his right. "I might have had too much fun with my mates from uni last night." He adjusted his seat for his six-foot frame. "I reckon one of these days, I'm going to realize I'm not in my twenties anymore."

The long layover had allowed him to spend New Year's Eve watching the fireworks over the Sydney Harbour Bridge with some old friends, followed by brunch at his parents' house the next day. By the time they had departed Sydney at 5:00 p.m. on New Year's Day, he was worn out and thankful he was the *bunky*, slang for the additional first officer required on long flights. He had had the first break in the 777's bunk and would sit in the flying first officer and captain's seats during their breaks. For takeoff and landing, he sat in the flight deck's jumpseat. James Carmichael, the flying first officer, was just starting his break. Lydia would take the last one.

The center console sat between the captain and first officer seats and contained the throttles, fuel control switches, three more displays, and an assortment of other controls, switches, and buttons. Kup glanced at the display that indicated they would land in Honolulu at 15:44 Greenwich Mean Time, or 5:44 a.m. Hawaiian Standard Time, on New Year's Day. Thanks to a quirk in the International Date Line, it seemed like they would land before they had taken off. At least it appeared that way on the Central Pacific website.

Lydia scrolled through a series of screens on the center display that monitored various aircraft systems. "Well, even after all these years, I still struggle to fall asleep in the bunk. I think I'm a little claustrophobic. What time is your flight home to Kona?"

"Seven."

"Are you and your wife going to party it up tonight since you missed New Year's Eve with her?"

"Hardly. Kahea's planned a quiet evening at home for tonight. I'll be drinking zero-alcohol beer—spousal support. We just found out last week that she's pregnant."

"Congratulations. Is it your first?"

"Yeah. Our plan is to get all the little ankle biters out of the house by the time we both turn fifty, so the clock is ticking."

"Well, my kid left the house, and then he—"

A warning horn sounded as the autopilot disengaged. Lydia pressed the button for the left autopilot on the glareshield panel just below the windshield. The warning horn stopped when the left autopilot re-engaged.

"That's weird." Lydia glanced at the center display to see if any system malfunctions were indicated. "Huh ... nothing. I don't get it. You didn't bump anything just now, did you?"

Kup took a sip of coffee as he stared into the night sky. "No, but what the hell is that?"

Several orange specks of light spun about themselves in the distance above and to the left of the 777's flight path.

The warning horn sounded again as both the autopilot and autothrottle disengaged.

Lydia pressed the button for the left autopilot. "What the hell is what, Kup?"

The warning horn continued to blare. Lydia pressed the switch for the autothrottle, but it would not re-engage. The right autopilot was equally disobedient. "What is going on with the autopilot and autothrottle?" She silenced the warning horn. "Kup, take the aircraft while I try and figure this out."

Kup put his coffee in the cupholder and placed his right hand on the yoke and his left hand on the throttles. "Okay, I have the aircraft, but you need to look at this thing."

A high-low chime announced a message from dispatch in Honolulu.

Kup's eyes remained fixed on a spot in the upper left of the windshield. "That's not an airplane."

"What? What are you talking about?" Lydia glanced down at the message from dispatch displayed on the center console.

KONA AND HILO AIRPORTS ATTACKED

ALL OTHER HAWAII AIRPORTS CLOSED TO

PLANNED ARRIVALS NOT YET AIRBORNE

AIRBORNE AIRCRAFT CURRENTLY

ALLOWED TO CONTINUE

POSSIBLE DIVERT TO NADI OR PAGO PAGO

MORE DETAILS AS THEY BECOME AVAILABLE

"What?" Lydia shook her head. "What is going—"

"Lydia, look out the windshield. Ten o'clock high. There's a bunch of weird lights."

Lydia looked up through the windshield. "Oh, shit."

What had been an unusual cluster of lights now appeared as a triangular gray object with orange lights at each corner. It was descending as it crossed from left to right and appeared to be tumbling end over end.

"You don't think it's going to hit us, do you?" Kup asked as he advanced both throttles forward. The airspeed was ten knots slow.

Lydia shook her head. "No, it's moving in the windshield. It should pass over us."

Kup's eyes shot to the screen displaying the engine parameters, where multiple indicators were decreasing. "The engines, Lydia—the engines are rolling back. I think both engines have flamed out."

"Huh?" Lydia glanced down at the engine readings as the 777 decelerated. "Nice night, my ass," she said as she reached across the center console, switched both fuel control switches to CUTOFF and then back to RUN, and pressed the RAM AIR TURBINE button on the overhead panel. In theory, a small turbine should have automatically extended into the airstream to provide additional hydraulic pressure and electrical power in the event that both engines failed. The button was a backup.

"Start a driftdown to flight level … two-five-zero for now, Kup. Slowdown to—"

Every display went black. Although the full moon provided enough light to see inside the flight deck, every light and illuminated switch was now dark. The sound of the airstream rushing past the fuselage diminished, and the low clouds on the horizon began rising in the windshield.

Kup pushed the throttles to the forward stop as he pulled back on the yoke.

"Crap!" Lydia said. "Now we've lost all electricity? Descend, Kup. We don't want to get too slow."

"Too slow? How am I supposed to know what 'too slow' is?"

"Wing it, Kup." Lydia fumbled with her iPad, which contained all the flight manuals. It remained dark.

Loud pounding noises came from the other side of the flight deck door.

"My iPad's broken, Kup. Try yours."

Kup put his left hand on the yoke and reached over to his iPad with his right hand. Despite multiple attempts to unlock it, its screen remained black. "Same for mine."

The pounding on the door intensified.

"I've still got nothing from the throttles," Kup said.

The aircraft jolted upward and to the left.

"We're climbing? Lydia, we're climbing!"

The tumbling gray object no longer moved in the windshield.

"How can we be climbing with dead engines?" Kup said as he pushed the yoke forward. "And … are we vibrating?"

Lydia stared at the object in the windshield. "Turn away from it, Kup. Turn away from it!"

"I'm trying. The controls aren't responding." Kup turned the yoke to the left and the right. He pushed it forward. He pulled it toward him.

The object grew larger in the windshield.

Between poundings on the door, a female voice screamed something about the lights. It sounded like Manu Keller, the lead flight attendant.

The triangular object filled half the windshield.

Lydia turned her head to face the flight deck door. "Brace command, Manu. Brace command, now!"

CHAPTER TWO

"*Hauʻoli Makahiki Hou*, Governor." Senator Leilani Damonati beamed up at Governor Brian Kupule through her black square-rimmed glasses. She had much to celebrate tonight; however, the new year would likely be anything but happy for the governor of Hawaiʻi.

The band played "Hawaiʻi Aloha" as trade winds breezed through palms planted along the edges of the rooftop garden of the Hawaiʻi Convention Center. Leilani's age-appropriate red evening gown fluttered in the wind.

"Same to you, Senator," said Governor Kupule as he pressed his champagne flute against Leilani's. *"Okole maluna."* His sockless black Italian loafers reflected the lights from the stage. His muted navy Hawaiian shirt and long pants exemplified the formality of the event.

The New Year's Eve party was a Who's Who of the state's political elite. Leilani was the most elite of them all and the most powerful by far.

Many of the elites and not-so-elites there had been discussing the *rumors* about what had happened in Iceland and Texas. Leilani had anticipated some of this; disinformation was difficult to control. There were just too many people with too many opinions.

"Leilani, did you see a flash of light toward the southeast right at midnight?" Governor Kupule asked. "People have been asking me about it."

"I saw fireworks, Brian. Lots and lots of fireworks." Leilani noticed Luka Hill waving at her with his right hand from a far corner of the rooftop, openly displaying his *birth defect* for all to see. His left hand held a plate stacked with every available pupu from the buffet. He was her partner—in more ways than one. "Excuse me, Brian. Luka needs me for something." Her short, piston-like legs propelled her squat fiftyish body across the floor. Her black pageboy haircut rocked back and forth.

Luka's bright-orange Hawaiian shirt, combined with his almost seven-foot height and platinum-blond hair, acted as a beacon to guide her through the crowd. The oversized shirt also hid a physique containing only trace amounts of body fat, even though he was many years older than Leilani.

"Luka, what is so important?" Leilani asked as she strained her neck. "And put your damn hand in your pocket."

Luka looked around them. "There is an issue we need to discuss. There is a problem."

"Okay, what kind of problem?"

"The Hawai'i *Command Ship* is missing."

"Missing? I don't understand. How can it be missing?"

"There was a malfunction of the *Quantum Transubstantiater* aboard the Hawai'i Command Ship. Although it performed nominally on the Big Island, its operation caused systemic malfunctions in the ship's navigation, EMP, and tow beam. The crew lost all control. They entered the atmosphere somewhere over the South Pacific. We've lost all contract with them."

"Contract?" Leilani looked around her. "Luka, your people's command of their technology is as shitty as your command of English. How long will it take for a replacement ship to get here?"

"It could be a couple of days or a week or two. Command is working on it."

"A week or two? But we can't move forward until then." Leilani stepped back from Luka as the band stopped playing "Hawai'i Aloha" halfway through the song. She noticed Governor Kupule was surrounded by three of his aides. All three were talking on their cellphones.

All around her, everyone was either talking, looking at their phones, or both.

"Luka, I should have known your people would find a way to screw this up."

"It gets worse. They may have hit an airliner."

CHAPTER THREE

Northeast of Vanuatu
21:30 VUT, 1 January

Kup stared into the black abyss below. Beneath him, Captain Lydia Kahananui's arms and shoulder-length hair streamlined upward as her descent accelerated. The muted glimmer from the metal wings attached to her uniform shirt faded to black. Two small bubbles wobbled as they floated upward from her mouth. The feeble light from the moon surrendered to the miles of black ocean below, and she vanished from view. He couldn't abandon her—even though she was probably already dead.

Kup filled his lungs with air and dove. With each kick, the ocean became darker, as silent as it was black. Other than the increasing pressure in his ears, he had no indication that he was even descending. He swung both his arms, searching for Lydia in the void.

He kicked harder. The pressure in his ears morphed into an excruciating pain that seared across his eyes. His arms flailed back and forth in an improvised search pattern. A wad of hair got caught in his left hand. He grabbed the hair and glanced toward what should have been up. A dim light on his right side caught his eye.

He moved his right hand along Lydia's chest, searching for the inflation tab of her life vest. His legs were cramping, and he needed air.

Kup yanked the inflation tab, and with a loud whoosh, Lydia shot toward the faint light. He squeezed his nostrils together and gently blew. The sharp pain in his ears subsided.

He kicked toward Lydia and the faint light.

His head popped above the water, and he gulped salty air as he looked to his left toward the nose of the 777. The slide raft from the forward right door jutted from the fuselage past the nose. It appeared to be empty. No slide raft was attached to the forward left door, but people were crawling onto the slide raft at the door in front of the left wing. Several people stood on the left wing, and the image of the full moon reflected off wet aluminum below them. Voices screamed. Other voices were yelling. Some voices cried.

There were no lights of any sort. There were no fires. There was no spilled jet fuel.

Lydia and First Officer Johnny Carmichael bobbed beside him as the wind blew small bits of spray onto their expressionless faces. Kup had been able to inflate Johnny's life vest just after he had pushed him through the shattered windshield. He hadn't been as lucky with Lydia's life vest.

Kup grabbed Lydia and Johnny, one in each hand, rolled onto his back, and began kicking toward the left wing. His legs started cramping again, but he kicked through the pain.

"Help me," somehow came out of his mouth. "Can somebody help me?"

The forward door on the left side of the Central Pacific Airlines 777 was half open. Behind him, unseen voices yelled instructions while others begged for help. Seawater went down his windpipe, and he began coughing. His head slammed into metal. A hand grabbed Kup's shirt as Lydia's and Johnny's limp bodies were hoisted beside him. Hands reached around his armpits and lifted him onto the wing.

Kup staggered onto his feet. His shock of wet black hair dripped salt water onto the soaked collar of the short-sleeved uniform shirt, clinging to a chest defined by several years of triathlon workouts. His stomach began to heave.

The windows along the fuselage were still above the water. The vertical stabilizer, adorned with a pikake flower overlaying the Hawaiian Islands, towered over them. People clambered into the inflated slide rafts from the doors in front of and behind the wing and the door at the tail. The forward door by the nose, however, was still half open and did not have a slide raft attached to it.

Kup looked down at Lydia and Johnny and began shaking. The moonlight illuminated Johnny's gray USAF Reserve T-shirt, soaked with blood flowing from multiple cuts across his face and neck. A two-inch shard of glass extended from underneath Lydia's left captain's epaulet.

Kup spit a mixture of bile and saltwater.

With his wet blue sweatpants clinging to his body, a gray-haired man kneeled, placed two fingers under Johnny's right jaw, and shook his head. He moved to Lydia and did the same.

The man eyed Kup's wet uniform. "You're one of the pilots?"

Kup nodded as he wiped his mouth with his left hand and glanced at his blank smartwatch.

"What the hell happened?" asked the man.

"We saw this thing. It looked like a ..." Kup heaved as he grabbed both his knees.

"Saw what? What did you see?" asked the man in the blue sweats.

Kup heaved again, ejecting a mass of stomach bile from his mouth. He walked along the wing toward the fuselage and reached for clean water to rinse his face and mustache.

"Kup! Kup! Over here. I need your help." Manu Keller, the lead flight attendant, was waving at Kup from the doorway in front of the wing. Her waist-length black hair had somehow remained in a bun, though she had multiple cuts across her forehead. The water had risen above her knees and was touching the bottom of her navy skirt. "Kup, a slide raft accidentally opened inside the cabin between the forward galley and the flight deck door. Cheryl is trapped up there!"

Kup jumped into the water and climbed onto the slide raft attached to the open doorway in front of the wing. Once at the doorway, Manu stopped the flow of exiting passengers long enough for him to enter the cabin.

Kup walked into the mid-cabin galley, out of the way of the stream of passengers sloshing their way out of the jet.

"I couldn't deflate the slide raft," Manu said. "I looked for the deflation valve, but it's a jumbled mess up there. I had to come back here and assist with the evacuation. You've got to get Cheryl out of there, Kup."

"Did you try cutting it?" Kup wiped his face with his right hand. The water was halfway between his knees and his waist.

"With what?"

Kup's eyes darted around the dark cabin as passengers rushed by him. "Where are the first aid kits?"

"They're already loaded on the slide rafts."

"All of them?"

"Yes, of course."

"Damn. I need something sharp to cut the raft open. How about the knife on the slide raft?"

"We might need that later to cut the mooring line of the slide raft."

A middle-aged man knocked Kup down. When he resurfaced, Manu was holding a corkscrew in her right hand.

"You could try this," she said. "I forgot I had it in my pocket."

Kup fumbled with his hands along the floor, trying to stand. "That will have to work." He stood, grabbed the corkscrew with his left hand, and began wading upstream against the stragglers from the first-class cabin, who were struggling with their carry-on luggage. As he entered the now emptied first-class cabin, his right foot slid on something cylindrical, and he fell backward into the water. His right hand brushed up against a wine bottle. He stood once again and continued sloshing his way forward.

In the dim light of the fuselage, the inflated slide raft appeared as a colorless blob. It completely blocked the opening between the bulkheads on either side of the left aisle. In fact, it bulged into the left aisle past the first row of lie-flat first-class seats. The right aisle was similarly blocked.

Kup felt along the slide raft for a valve.

"Please, somebody help me!" said a female voice from the other side of the slide raft.

"Cheryl, this is Kup. I'm going to get you out! I've got to deflate this thing."

"Kup, hurry, please! The water's rising. I'm stuck."

"Keep raising yourself into the air pocket."

"I can't raise up any higher." Cheryl began choking. "The slide raft is holding me down. Please don't leave me behind, Kup."

"Cheryl, I won't abandon you. I will not leave you behind."

"Kup, I … Kup. Please."

Kup began pushing the sharp point of the corkscrew into the stiff, rubber-coated fabric of the slide raft, but the water made it difficult to get any leverage. He bore down on the corkscrew with all his weight, and it punched through. A small jet of air shot through the water when he pulled the corkscrew out. Kup repeated the procedure and made a second puncture.

"I punched two holes in it, Cheryl. It's deflating. I'll be there before you know it." *We'll be underwater before this thing deflates enough.*

He walked back down the aisle to the last row of lie-flat seats and submerged himself.

A minute later, he surfaced and smashed a bottle of merlot against the metal edge of the bulkhead that separated the first-class cabin from the economy cabin.

He returned to the slide raft and jammed a jagged edge from the bottle into one of the small holes he had created. Bearing down on the broken wine bottle with his full weight, he began sawing the slide raft back and forth.

The rubber-coated fabric tore several centimeters, and the water frothed around him.

"Cheryl, hang on just a little longer."

The water was just below Kup's chin when he felt the slide raft soften enough to move it.

"Cheryl? I'm not leaving you!" Kup tilted his head to keep water out of his mouth. "Try to move the slide raft out of the way!" He tossed the wine bottle and pushed the mostly deflated slide raft upward and to the side. He held his breath as he crawled along the aircraft floor.

A flaccid hand brushed his left cheek. Kup grabbed the hand and towed Cheryl toward the forward left door. He released her, opened the half-open door the rest of the way, and pushed her through. Following her through the doorway, he inflated her life vest, and she shot to the surface. While treading water, Kup placed two fingers underneath her jaw on the right side. "Oh damn … no."

A flotilla of six slide rafts drifted away in the distance. "Hey!" Kup yelled. "Don't leave us! Over here. Come back!"

Several heads turned. Multiple people paddled with their hands, but the flotilla continued drifting away with the wind.

Kup slammed his left fist into the water. "Bloody hell. Come back!" Seawater splashed onto Cheryl's face. Her hazel eyes appeared to gaze at the night sky above. Her blond hair was slicked back from her forehead and bobbed in and out of the water.

The forward left door, the tail, and the bottom of the vertical stabilizer were now underwater. The rising water sliced the image of the Big Island on the Central Pacific logo in half. The 777 was sinking tailfirst.

Kup stared at the flotilla as it drifted farther and farther away. "Come back! You can't leave us behind. You can't … leave." *Oh bloody hell, I need a slide raft.*

Kup swam around the nose of the 777 to the right side. The slide raft, still attached to the forward right doorway, was now pressed against the sinking fuselage and blocking the doorway.

I've got to go back in there from the other side.

He swam back around the nose to the submerged forward left door, pulled himself through the doorway, and worked his way through the deflated slide raft to the doorway on the right. His hands slid across the bottom of the doorway, and he pulled back the Velcro strap holding the slide raft release handle. The deflated slide raft seemed to be everywhere, and he needed air.

He yanked on the cloth handle, and the end of the inflated slide raft detached from the fuselage and shot to the surface.

As he pulled himself through the doorway, a wad of rubber-coated fabric wrapped around his left thigh. The harder he pulled, the tighter the deflated slide raft constricted.

Kup looked at the ocean surface and the end of the inflated slide raft half a meter above him.

CHAPTER FOUR

Honolulu, Hawai'i
01:15 HST, 1 January

Leilani stormed onto the open-air walkway of the twenty-seventh floor of her condominium building before the elevator doors had fully opened. Luka followed her.

Their neighbor, Janey Takiguchi, stood in the open doorway of her condominium, leaning on a wooden cane she gripped with her right hand. "Senator! Senator!" Janey scrambled onto the walkway, clutching an iPad in her left hand. "Senator, did you see what happened to the Big Island? It's just horrible."

"Auntie …" Leilani eyed the lights of a helicopter flying low over the Ala Wai Canal. "You do realize those are just unconfirmed rumors?"

"Oh, it's true, Leilani. There's a video. The airports are gone, and all the ships have run aground inside the harbors. They say the harbor floors are only a few feet deep now. I've never seen anything like it. Do you or Luka have any family on the Big Island?"

"No, we do not."

Luka said, "But I—"

"We do not have any family there." Leilani glared at Luka. "My mother was from Waimea, but she's dead."

"Who did this, Leilani?" Janey asked. "People are saying it was aliens. You must know something. You are our senator."

"Would you mind going ahead to the condo, Luka?" Leilani asked. "I have something I need to discuss with Janey."

Luka nodded and walked past them to Leilani's condominium.

Leilani glanced left and right. "Auntie, what I am about to tell you, you must promise not to tell anyone. It's a matter of national security.

Can you promise me that?"

"Yes. Yes, of course, Senator." Janey nodded several times. "I won't tell anyone. I promise."

"Well, okay. Certain people at the highest levels of our national intelligence agencies have told me that the attacks on Iceland, Galveston Island, and now the Big Island are all the work of the Russian Government."

"No—the Russians? Again?"

"Yes."

"Oh my. It's a little scary, you know. The Big Island is not that far away."

"Now, don't worry, Auntie. I can assure you that our nation's resources are on this. We're developing a plan to counteract the Russians as we speak."

"Oh, good, Senator."

"Now, remember, Auntie—this is our little secret, okay?"

"Oh, of course, Senator. Good night, and *Hau'oli Makahiki Hou*."

"Good night, and … yes, Happy New Year to you as well." Leilani walked past her. *Dipshit. Russia will be all over her Facebook page within minutes.*

Leilani opened the screen door of her condominium and walked through the hallway. Doorways along the left wall led to the guest bedroom, powder room, and master bedroom. Photos of her with various VIPs lined the other wall. The hallway opened to a living room lined with sliding glass pocket doors along its entire length. The opened pocket doors led to a lanai, and trade winds jostled the fronds of a small potted palm in the corner of the living room. An open kitchen bordered by a kitchen bar with two barstools was on the left side.

Centered in the living room was a glass coffee table. Centered on the coffee table was a floating hologram of downtown Honolulu with a few notable differences. A gleaming green building stood in the spot currently occupied by Iolani Palace. Once built, it would rise to a projected height of one kilometer and would be the tallest building on Earth. A building in earth tones stood where the Hawai'i State Capitol should have been. It was planned to be five hundred meters tall. Where the Prince Kuhio Federal Building currently sat, a sky-blue building stood. Its planned height was two hundred fifty meters. Hawai'i's past would be erased and replaced. The rest of the world would follow—unless it didn't.

Leilani threw her black purse onto the brown granite kitchen bar.

Luka chewed on a Spam musubi as he filled two flutes with champagne. "When did your mother die?"

"How in the hell would I know? Your people didn't implant that bit of knowledge in my brain, but then again, maybe they didn't know. Maybe they didn't care."

"And your father?" He handed her a flute of champagne. Except for his two thumbs, his fingers were all the same length. "What about him?"

"Some Italian tourist. One of those one-night things. Your people gave me his last name."

"But your mother was ethnically Japanese."

"Yes." She glanced at her champagne. "I don't feel like celebrating."

"So, you are a *Mixed?*"

"Yes. All of us *Stolings* are, and all of us Stolings are unable to reproduce. Your people made sure of that. But enough of my past. Let's talk about your people's screwup." Leilani glanced at her watch. "Phase Two should have begun by now in Iceland. We should be celebrating right now, but instead, let's talk about this airliner your people may have hit. What flight was it?"

Luka shrugged. "What would it matter?"

"What would it matter? Luka, what if it was just a near miss? What if some passengers saw the Command Ship and are about to land somewhere and engulf the internet?"

"It would be just another UFO report. Easily debunked."

"What if one of the crew saw it, Luka—someone credible, not some nutjob with a tinfoil hat? A viral video like that could overwhelm us. Our servers are practically overheating right now trying to stamp out all the disinformation just from tonight's three events, and stuff is getting through."

"Well, there is something else I need to tell you."

"Something else?"

"Yes. I received another message while you were talking to Janey. The *Peace Squad* was aboard the Hawai'i Command Ship."

"The Peace Squad?"

"Yes."

"But we are vulnerable without the Peace Squad."

"Yes. That is true, and a replacement Peace Squad could take a couple of weeks, maybe a month, to get here."

"A month?" Leilani slammed her champagne flute onto the kitchen bar. "Everything will have to be put on hold, Luka. This could jeopardize all our plans and the entire operation."

"Leilani, the Hawai'i Command Ship is just missing. Command hopes to begin search operations within the hour. Hopefully, it will be located intact, and the Peace Squad is okay."

Leilani walked onto the lanai and gazed at the twinkling lights of Waikiki. "This city was promised to me. This nation was promised to me. This planet … this whole damn planet is supposed to be mine one day." She turned around and faced Luka. "I have done everything your people told me to do. If the experiments fail … if they all fail, your people will move on. We both know that. For you, it would be just a transfer, a whole new planet to fix. I don't have another planet to go to, Luka."

CHAPTER FIVE

Reykjavík, Iceland
12:00 Greenwich Mean Time (GMT), 1 January

"**T**he helicopters are everywhere. It is like the end of the world." Hildur Einarsdóttir stood beside a large picture window that straddled the entire length of the functional yet sterile hotel room. She sipped coffee as she gazed at the street below. A thick brown robe exposed her muscular calves but hid the large bruise on her right thigh. Years of hiking had kept her figure lean. The sun intensified the sheen of her shoulder-length straight blond hair, which hid a bruise on the back of her head.

The room shook as a fighter jet flew overhead.

Trevor Ringlund looked up from his smartphone and glanced out the window. "Well, I guess Article 5 of the NATO charter has kicked in." Trevor's platinum-blond curls pushing out from underneath his Taos Ski Valley baseball cap contrasted with the olive-colored skin of his neck. With his height pushing two meters, he could easily pass for an Icelander, or at least an Icelander who'd just returned from a tropical beach.

That night, they had welcomed the New Year by watching the Northern Lights beside the Old Harbor. The evening had been magical until the dancing greens and purples of the night sky were obliterated by a blinding white light. When Hildur's vision returned, she was lying on her back, looking up at a container ship heeled over at all the wrong angles. The ship was in the process of rolling on top of her. Trevor yanked her onto her feet, and they began running. Once out of harm's way, they stopped and turned around to face the ship. A loose, rolling car tire from a damaged container slammed into her, and she had fallen backward onto the ice-covered asphalt.

"I do not understand what is happening," said Hildur. "There is nothing about this on the Icelandic news stations. They have said nothing of what has happened here, yet my phone is full of texts and emails from people around the country. The airports have all been destroyed, and the major harbors are unusable. People are saying the same thing happened to Galveston Island in Texas and the Big Island of Hawai'i."

Hildur handed her phone to Trevor. "Watch the video someone posted of the Coast Guard ship from last night. I remember seeing this very ship."

Trevor pushed the Play button. The video showed several people in uniform trudging through knee-deep water beside the keel of a ship. The keel was completely out of the water at a forty-five-degree angle. Fifty meters past the Coast Guard ship, a tender lay on its side. Slack chains extended to the top of an anchor that extended half a meter above the water.

"How does the harbor floor rise up underneath the ships?" Hildur asked. "And why is this video not on the news?"

Trevor shook his head. "Who do you think could have done this? The technology is so incredible." He handed Hildur her smartphone and returned his attention back to his own.

"I do not know … I do not think the government knows. They are scared we will run out of food and supplies. I think they are trying to hide it from us."

"Well, one way or another, Hildur, I'm stuck here and soon to be homeless. Icelandair canceled my flight, and the hotel is kicking me out tomorrow."

"You can stay with me at my house in Vík." Hildur took another sip of coffee. "We can go back to the ice cave—just the two of us."

A low-flying Icelandic Coast Guard helicopter shot past the window. The beating of its rotating blades reverberated through the room.

"Is that thing going to land on top of us?" Trevor ducked his head. "Anyway, that sounds wonderful and a lot more fun than a physics conference in Stockholm. I'd love to go back to the ice cave again." He smiled. "I will need to call my boss at Los Alamos and tell him I won't be at the conference, though."

"Okay. Tomorrow, after you check out of the hotel, I will take you back to Vík with me. But for now, I am hungry. Let me take you to my second favorite restaurant in Reykjavík. It is beside the harbor. Do you like to eat the fish?"

"I love fish." Trevor chuckled.

A half-hour later, they entered the hotel lobby. To their left, three-meter-tall windows were interrupted in the middle by a glass revolving entry door. The wall in front of them contained a large screen displaying a virtual fireplace and a sitting area consisting of off-white Nordic-inspired furniture. The right wall contained the reception desk and the entry to the restaurant.

Behind the reception desk, a slender brunette woman looked up from her computer. "Mr. Ringlund, may I please speak with you about your reservation?"

Trevor froze.

"It is okay, Trevor," Hildur said. "I need to call and check on my father. He is visiting my aunt and uncle in Grindavík. I will make my call while you speak with the front desk." Hildur walked toward the sitting area.

Trevor sighed. "Okay, great." He walked over to the brunette and looked back at Hildur, who was sitting on a couch as she spoke into her cellphone.

The brunette woman said, "Mr. Ringlund, you were going to let us know about canceling your reservation after tonight. Have you reached a decision?"

Trevor turned his head and faced the woman. In a hushed voice, he said, "Yes. Please cancel my reservation. I"—he turned and saw Hildur across the room still on her cellphone—"will check out tomorrow."

"Very well." The brunette woman typed on her computer for several seconds. "I have updated your reservation to check out tomorrow instead of next week. Have a pleasant day, Mr. Ringlund."

"Thank you. You have a—"

"Trevor, you must still check out tomorrow?"

Trevor jumped at Hildur's voice behind him. He turned and faced her. "Uh, yes. I'm checking out tomorrow still. Let's go. I'm hungry."

They passed through the hotel's revolving door and began walking down Vesturgata. The air was crisp, and the sky was cold and blue. Around them, the stoic residents of Reykjavík walked—and ran—in every direction. Most of them were carrying around empty shopping bags. Since it was New Year's Day, most stores were closed, and mobs of customers filled the few that were open. A policeman stood at the front door of a supermarket to limit the number of people allowed into the store as police sirens came and went in multiple directions.

"How's your father? Is he okay?" Trevor asked as he reached for Hildur's right hand.

"Yes, he is well, but he gets lonely. My mother died of cancer two years ago."

Trevor nodded.

"And your parents? Are they both still alive?" Hildur asked.

"I was put in an orphanage when I was just a baby, so I don't know if my biological parents are still alive."

"Oh. Trevor, why did they put you in an orphanage?"

"That, I don't know."

"And where was this orphanage?"

"Orlando. It was in—"

"What is this?" Hildur stopped as they rounded a corner.

They had come upon a famous hot dog stand. The line stretched almost thirty meters and wrapped around a corner intersection. At the midpoint of the line, two women were punching and screaming at each other in Icelandic.

Hildur put her hand over her mouth. *"Fjandinn!"*

"What is that, Hildur?"

"Damn. I said damn." Hildur shook her head. "I have seen nothing like this before. Not here."

Trevor was a little less shocked.

"I do not want to see this, Trevor. Let us move on."

Further down Tryggvagata, the harbor came into view. Several kayaks and small johnboats traversed back and forth and seemed to be ferrying crews from the ships lying on the middle of the harbor seafloor. Elsewhere, people in drysuits sloshed beside exposed keels.

To their right, a container ship overhung a snow-covered parking lot. The containers aboard the ship sat at a precarious angle on the deck, and several had already fallen onto the parking lot. A group of fifty or sixty people had formed around the parking lot and ship, and the police had set up a barricade. A Coast Guard helicopter flew fifty meters over their heads, heading toward the middle of the harbor.

Hildur pointed to a squat red-roofed building ahead on the left side of the street. "Here we are at the restaurant, Reykjafisk. It is quite good and has an excellent view of … what *was* the harbor."

"Well, there should be plenty to watch today," Trevor said.

They got drinks at the bar and sat at a table with a view of the listing container ship butted up against the parking lot.

Trevor reached for his Gædingur Stout on the table, which was shaking back and forth. "Are we moving?"

Hildur's martini shook in her hand. "It feels like a tremor. We have them all the—"

The restaurant jolted. Trevor's eyes bulged. Hildur said, "Okay, that was an earthquake. Like I was saying, we—"

A crackling noise followed by the screeching of bending metal sounded throughout the restaurant as container after container slid off the deck of the listing ship and onto the parking lot. Loose snow shot up into the sky.

"Oh, shit." Trevor pulled his beer away from his mouth.

Hildur stood up. "The earthquake must have made the containers fall from the ship."

The mob of onlookers fell back from the police barricade but started breaking through as the snow settled, revealing several open containers. Boxes of televisions, vacuum cleaners, and coffee makers spilled out onto the parking lot.

Several containers still dangled from the ship's deck as the mob overran the barricades and spread out over the crumpled containers on the ground. Some onlookers had brought bolt cutters and were breaking into the unopened containers. After yelling at the mob to get back behind the barricade, a lone policeman blew his whistle. The whistle was ignored, as was the policeman.

"I cannot believe my eyes," Hildur said. "The people are ignoring the police. It is like anarchy here today."

Box after box of flat-screen televisions and space heaters were on their way to their new forever homes when two white SUVs with blue stripes and "Lögreglan" on the side pulled up alongside the barricades. The boxes scattered along with their new owners. One man in a yellow sweater, however, didn't scatter. He also wasn't holding a box. Instead, he held a bottle full of a clear liquid in his right hand. The bottle had some cloth sticking out of its top.

Trevor said, "That guy … in the yellow sweater …"

One of the white SUVs erupted in flames. A policewoman jumped out of the driver's seat. Her arms were on fire.

"No!" Hildur slammed her fists against the window. "This is not happening."

The second SUV caught fire.

Hildur slumped down in her chair. "We are a peaceful people. I …"

The sound of helicopter rotors shook the restaurant. Seconds later, five men wearing black berets, steel-gray uniforms, and black combat boots scrambled out of an Icelandic Coast Guard helicopter in the parking lot next to the restaurant. Each man carried a submachine gun as well as a Glock-17 pistol. The helicopter took off and flew over the harbor.

Hildur said, "Guns? They have machine guns?"

Their twenty-something bearded blond waiter approached their table, transfixed by the scene unfolding outside. Trevor glanced at the waiter and looked back outside. "Who are those guys, Hildur?"

"I do not know."

"The *Víkingasveitin*," the waiter said.

"The Viking what?" Trevor asked.

"The Viking Squad. They are part of the police," said the waiter as he glanced down at Trevor. "You would call them a SWAT team. I have read about them, but I have never seen them before. But I had never seen a lot of things until today."

Hildur shook her head. "I feel like I woke up in a different country this morning."

The waiter nodded. "Yes, people are saying things could become bleak for us. We only produce about fifty percent of our own crops."

"But your country has so much geothermal energy," Trevor said. "Can't you build more greenhouses? And you've got plenty of fish and sheep around."

"We are now apparently too busy setting police cars on fire to go fishing," Hildur said as she gazed through the window.

Multiple hands hurled glass bottles in various directions. Cars, buildings, and people erupted in flames.

Repetitive flashes accompanied repetitive blasts of machine gun fire.

Glass shattered and flew across the restaurant. Five meters away, an empty table burst into flames. Trevor and Hildur fell to the floor beside their table.

Glass shattered and flew above their heads.

The waiter slid down the wall beside them.

"Get down!" yelled Trevor, grabbing the waiter's right hand and yanking him to the floor.

A two-centimeter shard of glass protruded from the waiter's right cheek.

"Are you okay?" Trevor asked. "Do you need a doctor?"

The waiter reached up and removed the glass from his cheek. "*Guð hjálpi okkur.*"

Trevor turned to Hildur. "What did he say?"

"God help us."

CHAPTER SIX

Kup was tired but wired. He sat on the floor of the slide raft with his back against a tubular air chamber about two feet in diameter. Cheryl's rigid body occupied a spot five feet away. Her eyes seemed to fixate on him.

He couldn't stop thinking—about Cheryl, about Lydia, and about Johnny. If Johnny hadn't been such a jerk and insisted on sitting in the right seat for the ditching, Kup would be dead right now. Of course, that would mean Johnny would be the one sitting in a raft in the middle of the South Pacific with dead Cheryl. He wasn't sure which fate was worse right now.

There were other questions as well. What exactly was the object that they had almost hit? Why had they lost everything electrical aboard the jet? Why had the engines quit? How could they have been climbing without power? It was like the jet had been possessed. Christine, the evil car, had transformed into an airliner.

Seconds from an imminent collision, the tumbling UFO had gone dark, and they had regained control of the aircraft. The 777 had become a giant, cumbersome, heavy glider, but it was a glider at least they could control—somewhat. With a complete loss of electricity, the fly-by-wire flight control system, with its multiple redundancies, was inoperative. Instead, they were left with a few mechanical cables that controlled a spoiler on each wing and a manual trim tab on the elevator. The spoilers were meant to control the 777's roll, and the trim tab would control its pitch. The mechanical backup was designed as a last-ditch redundancy to allow for straight and level flight while the electrical system was recovered. Their flight path, however, was neither straight nor level, and the entire electrical system was fried.

Johnny had eventually joined Manu at the flight deck door, and they had both pounded their fists against the door until Lydia had unlocked it manually. Lydia briefed them both on what had happened, and Manu returned to the cabin to prepare for the ditching. Johnny insisted on taking the right seat for the *landing*. They did the best job they could. Lydia kept the wings somewhat level while Johnny kept their airspeed somewhat constant as they descended toward the moonlit clouds below. At about fifty feet above the water, Johnny began trimming the 777's nose upward to slow their airspeed. Then the vibrations started again. The jet banked right, and the right wingtip slid under the water. The jet's nose pitchpoled into the face of a swell.

A wall of ocean and windshield slammed into Lydia and Johnny; they never had a chance. Kup sat in the jumpseat behind Johnny, and Johnny's body effectively shielded Kup from the torrent of shattered glass and water.

Holding his breath, Kup had tried to open the flight deck door, but it wouldn't budge. He had somehow managed to unbuckle Lydia and Johnny's seatbelts and shove them through the busted windshields. The tightness in his lungs had begged him to just swim to the surface, but he couldn't leave them behind.

Kup heard a loud whoosh as a whale exhaled somewhere near the raft, and he scanned the surface for the blow.

It seemed to be getting brighter out.

His eyes eventually landed back on Cheryl. She was looking at him again, even though she obviously wasn't.

He turned away and faced the brightest point on the horizon. The sun couldn't be rising already, but it was hard to tell with his fancy smartwatch indicating nothing. He pulled his cellphone out of his pocket and made a final attempt to bring it to life. The black screen sealed its fate, and he tossed it over the side of the raft. He frowned as he rubbed his hands over the tube of the slide raft, which seemed to be vibrating. *No. Not again.*

A dim orange light glowed above the horizon as the raft bobbed over a large swell. Multiple fins sliced through the water as they headed toward the glowing light.

The raft had been drifting with the wind, but it slowed and eventually stopped. It then began moving upwind toward the distant glow.

The raft topped another swell, and the glowing object became visible. The triangular object Kup had seen only hours before in the air was headed straight for him. It appeared to be only twenty to thirty meters above the ocean's surface.

Kup's heart began pounding against his chest as the raft sped over the crest of a swell and slid down into the trough. Spray shot over the front of the raft, dousing him. His entire body shook as if he was having some sort of epileptic fit.

Kup pulled himself onto the side of the slide raft as it crested another swell. The triangular object in the sky began tumbling end over end a few hundred meters away. He grabbed the lifeline strung along the side to steady himself.

The raft shot up the side of another swell and launched into the air. The tumbling object passed overhead twenty meters above his head. The slide raft, Kup, and Cheryl's body drifted upward for several seconds.

Then they began falling, and Kup watched Cheryl's body fall into the water. A split second later, he also fell into the water. The lifeline he clutched stopped his descent.

The raft started moving, and he strained against the drag of the water to pull himself forward. His arms ached. He just wanted to let go.

Something slammed into his left hip, and his hands released their grip on the lifeline. He began moving sideways to the right, and his arms and legs flailed against the drag of the water. The pressure in his ears became painful as the water became colder. The jaws gripping his left hip embedded multiple teeth into his skin.

CHAPTER SEVEN

Galveston Island, Texas
06:34 Central Standard Time (CST), 1 January

The cold, wet end of Michael Phelps's nose pressed into Jerry Morgenstern's neck at 6:34 in the morning.

Jerry opened his eyes. A Weimaraner sat next to Michael Phelps. Jerry focused on the embroidery of the Weimaraner's turquoise collar. *What the … oh, yeah. Daisy. Her owners are probably ...*

Jerry began replaying the previous night in his head. The phone call from the Westheimer Senior Center had interrupted his law firm's New Year's Eve party. His mom had fallen and was being rushed to Hermann Memorial. He had just taken the onramp for the Galveston Causeway toward Houston when he was blinded by a white light. When his vision returned, he was lying on his back, looking at the bottom of a car door. His boots were lodged on the doorframe of his Tesla, which had mated with a Honda Civic. He started placing his fancy new plastic business cards under the windshield wipers of all the wrecked cars—there had been a dearth of serious aviation accidents lately—as he walked along the causeway toward Houston. He dropped all his business cards when the causeway and a red Chevy Tahoe atop it both abruptly ended at the shoreline. The Weimaraner had been strapped into the backseat of the Tahoe. There was no front seat; the front half of the SUV was gone. Its sheet metal was cut in a perfect line, and the same was true for the part of the causeway that extended over the water. The concrete and steel ended abruptly with a flawless, smooth edge.

The Weimaraner had whimpered when their eyes met. No one had answered the phone number embroidered on the collar next to "DAISY."

Jerry rubbed Daisy's chest. "You had a rough night last night, didn't you, girl," Jerry whispered. *Shit, who am I kidding? A lot of people had a rough night last night. I guess a lot of people are gone. We're lucky we're not gone, too.*

Michael Phelps moaned his Chewbacca imitation. Breakfast was always at 6:30—always.

Jerry sat up in bed and yawned. *There's no way I'm going back to sleep now. I might as well feed you two.*

Jerry planted his feet on the floor and eyed the scale sitting in the corner of the bedroom. Gail was snoring on the other side of the king-size bed. Michael Phelps's light-golden eyes followed Jerry's every move.

Jerry stood on the scales. He had somehow added another five pounds to his five-foot-ten thirty-eight-year-old frame. He shook his head as he pinched his right love handle through his lucky maroon Texas ATM T-shirt. The shirt had become a silly but ongoing source of friction with Gail because of the multitude of holes it had developed. It was his one deviation into slovenliness.

Michael Phelps, who had just turned five, belted out another Chewbacca moan. Starvation seemed imminent. Then again, for a yellow lab, starvation always seemed imminent.

Jerry walked downstairs with his cellphone and sat down at the sky-blue kitchen table, which matched the exterior paint of the house, and sat in an alcove off an expansive modern kitchen. All the bedrooms were on the third floor. A garage occupied the ground floor and had a twelve-foot-high ceiling in preparation for the inevitable hurricane.

Glasses rattled as several fighter jets flew over.

Jerry glanced through the kitchen window at the Catalina 45 sloop behind the house in the boat slip. The maroon ATM flag near the top of the mast fluttered. A light breeze ruffled the fronds of the thirty-foot-tall Queen Palms dotting the backyard, which faced west. Across the bay, mainland Texas sat low, green, and pancake-flat several miles in the distance. Several cranes stood in the shallows. Michael Phelps would change that—after breakfast.

Jerry called the hospital to check on his mother. The nurse reported she was doing fine; they planned to release her later that morning. Michael Phelps put his left paw on Jerry's leg while Daisy sat in the corner of the kitchen, shaking.

The voice of a familiar broadcaster from NNN, the National News

Network, streamed into the kitchen from the living room. Jerry got up from the kitchen table, and Michael Phelps started trotting toward the utility room. When Jerry walked into the living room, Michael Phelps froze and groaned once again. His food dish was not in the living room.

Cindy sat on the couch, crying. The previous night, Gail had pulled her blond hair into two tight pigtails and adorned them with red ribbons. On television, NNN was replaying scenes from New Year's celebrations across the world.

Michael Phelps trotted over to Cindy and put his face in her lap. He let out another loud Chewbacca groan. A daily regimen of dog-paddling thousands of yards as he patrolled the bay behind the house kept him at a lean sixty-six pounds despite his voracious appetite.

Cindy slid off the couch and stood up. "I'll feed you, Michael Phelps. I won't let you die of starvation." Cindy wasn't the baby of the family. She was older than Michael Phelps by two years and was serious about her responsibilities as his elder.

"Sweetheart, what are you doing up so early?" Jerry said.

"I couldn't sleep anymore, Daddy. I keep thinking how we're all going to die of the Russians."

"Oh, Cindy, we're not going to die."

"But, Daddy, the attack last night! Everyone on my phone keeps talking about the Russians. They attacked Galveston. They blew up the airport, and there's a cruise ship sitting on its side at the port. I saw it on Instagram." Tears poured down Cindy's cheeks. "They got the causeway and the bridge over San Luis Pass too. You almost died last night, Daddy."

She slumped onto the couch. Michael Phelps jumped on it and began licking her wet face.

Cindy wrapped both arms around Michael Phelps and squeezed. "And poor Daisy." Daisy shuffled over to her and Michael Phelps.

Cindy sniffled. "The people on Facebook are saying we're going to run out of food. The Russians cut off the island we're on. Nobody can bring us food. We're going to starve and die."

Jerry walked over to Cindy. He leaned down and kissed her on the forehead. "Sweetheart, you can't believe everything on the internet. There are a lot of false rumors floating around. People will say anything. It's called disinformation. Just watch NNN if you want to know what's really going on."

"But we can't leave the island. We can't see Grandma, and they can't get food to us. We're going to die of starvation. This lady on Facebook said so."

"There will be food, Cindy. Plenty of it. I'll show you. Why don't you go to the utility room and feed Michael Phelps and Daisy? I'll grab my wallet, and we'll grab some stuff for sandwiches at the grocery store for our sailboat ride this afternoon. How does that sound?"

"Okay, I guess." Cindy wiped her eyes and trotted off to the utility room. Michael Phelps trotted alongside her while Daisy brought up the rear.

A text message from one of Jerry's neighbors popped up on his phone. It linked to a website that reported the attacks were the work of the Chinese Government. Jerry read the entire article and shook his head. *I thought the FTA was supposed to stomp out crap like this. No wonder Cindy's upset.*

The Federal Disinformation Act had established the Federal Truth Administration. The Federal Communications Commission had become the FTA, trusted with the additional responsibility of protecting the people of the United States from the disinformation occurring in all the various forms of media in the United States. The FTA had been successful with the various forms of broadcast media; however, there was still much work to be done with social media.

Jerry walked into the utility room and jingled Gail's car keys. Jerry's Tesla was still in the queue to be towed from the causeway. Michael Phelps glanced at the keys before gulping down his last three pieces of kibble.

Jerry opened the side door and took a deep breath. The air was thick and salty. Cindy walked into the utility room wearing a burnt-orange T-shirt, green shorts, and bright pink Crocs.

"Daddy, we're almost out of dog food."

"Okay, we'll get some at the store." Jerry glanced at the thermometer mounted on the outside wall. "Sweetheart, don't you want to put on a sweatshirt? It's a little chilly out there this morning."

"No, Daddy. The thermometer says sixty-two, and Mommy says I don't have to wear a sweatshirt unless the thermometer is less than sixty."

Jerry rolled his eyes as Cindy walked out the door.

Michael Phelps and Daisy were both sitting at attention in the utility room.

"Come on, you two," Jerry said. "Let's go get some kibble."

Michael Phelps bolted through the doorway. Daisy paused and looked behind her for a split second but then followed Michael Phelps out the door. Both dogs made a detour by the pee tree. Michael Phelps eyed the four cranes standing in the shallows until Jerry opened the right rear door of Gail's Mercedes SUV. He cocked his head toward the open door and then back at the intruding cranes.

"Come on, boy," Jerry said. "You can take care of them when we get back."

Michael Phelps hopped into the backseat but continued staring at the cranes.

Daisy stopped at the car door and sat down. She looked up at Michael Phelps and Jerry.

Jerry dropped to his knees in front of Daisy. "We both saw something last night, didn't we, girl?" He began stroking her neck. "It's okay. Come on. Hop in the car." Jerry pulled Daisy into the back seat, and she laid down next to Michael Phelps, who began licking her ear. Jerry scratched his head. "Canine PTSD?"

"What's canine PBSD, Daddy?" Cindy strapped herself in the front seat. "Is that what soldiers have when they come back from a war? Are we going to have a war, Daddy?"

"It's PTSD, sweetheart, and, no, we're not going to have a war. I promise." Jerry closed his door, and the foursome headed to the grocery store to buy dog food and deli sandwiches.

Halfway into town, they saw a column of smoke rising in the distance. An orange-and-white US Coast Guard MH-65 helicopter flew low along the beach, heading northeast, parallel to their route.

Cindy watched the helicopter for a while and turned her head forward. "What's that smoke, Daddy?"

"Somebody is just burning some trash or something." Jerry debated turning around.

"There are police lights ahead, Daddy. Do you think we just got attacked by the Russians again?"

The traffic ahead slowed to a crawl as they approached a burning gas station on the opposite side of the road. Cars jammed the pumps despite the building being on fire. A quarter mile in the distance, a firetruck sat with its siren wailing. Cars blocked both lanes of traffic as they jockeyed for position to enter the gas station.

"Why doesn't the firetruck put out the fire, Daddy?"

"I don't think he can get to the fire, sweetheart. Those cars are blocking the way."

"Why are they blocking the way?"

"That's a good question. I don't know, sweetheart. Maybe the traffic is just bad."

A policeman stood in the middle of the road, trying to clear the traffic so that the firetruck could get to the burning building. Cars jammed the pumps and the entire parking lot of the station.

Jerry rolled down his window as he approached the policeman. "Officer, what's going on?"

The policeman pulled his whistle out of his mouth and turned to Jerry. "Somebody held up the gas station and made the attendant turn on all the pumps. Then they set the building on fire. I guess word got out about the free gas. You just have to pump it next to a burning building." The policeman blew his whistle and motioned for a red pickup truck to move.

Multiple fistfights had broken out as people fought for a position at the pumps.

The sound of another helicopter grew louder as a UH-60 Black Hawk emblazoned with "Duty – Honor – Texas" on the side landed in the shopping center parking lot across the street. Ten soldiers from the Texas Guard hopped out wearing Kevlar vests and helmets and carrying machine guns and bullhorns. The leader of the group announced that everyone must vacate the premises.

Jerry looked for a way out of the mess, but cars filled both lanes of traffic. "Cindy, I need you to close your eyes for me."

Cindy's eyes remained glued to the scene outside the windshield.

A second helicopter, an AH-64 Apache, approached from the west and hovered over the gas station pumps, then backed away and angled itself so that its twin machine gun turrets were pointed straight at the people pumping gas.

Cars began backing out of the gas station parking lot and clearing a path for the fire truck to inch forward.

A brown SUV sped past them on the right shoulder. Something flew out of the SUV, and a police car sitting in the left median burst into flames. The brown SUV continued down the right shoulder, and several seconds later, the firetruck itself was burning.

The Apache helicopter climbed several feet and flew over the road in the direction of the brown SUV.

Jerry ducked his head down. "Oh, shit."

"Daddy, that's a bad word."

The soldiers took positions around the station's perimeter, and the cars jamming the parking lot began to disperse. The charred fire truck pulled into the gas station.

Jerry's phone was lighting up with text messages about a burning gas station and the governor's declaration of martial law on Galveston Island. He shook his head as he turned around into the other lane. "Let's just go home. We can get food later."

"Okay, Daddy."

Jerry looked in his rearview mirror. "God help us."

CHAPTER EIGHT

Northeast of Vanuatu
01:00 VUT, 2 January

Another fin, illuminated by the full moon, sliced through the water five meters away. It was headed in the same direction as Kup, who was hunched over the side of the slide raft. His hands clutched the lifeline attached to the sides. The multiple puncture wounds around his left hip oozed blood.

Kup had stopped counting the fins after number twenty-six. All were racing toward the large, semi-submerged triangular object ahead, which was now about two hundred meters away. Multiple floodlights shot skyward from the object, which had large orange flotation balloons attached at each of its three corners. Kup could see bodies moving about on the top. These bodies appeared to be holding some type of weapon. Beams of light shot out from these weapons into the water in multiple directions. *These people—they can't be human. Nobody has this kind of technology.*

Kup squinted. *What are they shooting?* The vibrations shaking his head had become violent tremors, making it difficult to see in the moonlight. His left hip began to ache.

Something bumped into the slide raft from the right side. Kup looked into the water on the right side as a flash of light shot overhead. A fin slammed against the side of the slide raft, and water sprayed over him.

Kup looked forward as a flash of light hit one of the flotation balloons on the UFO. One end of the triangular object began sinking into the water while the other two corners remained above the surface. As the UFO heaved over, bodies slid into the water. Floodlights that now shot diagonally through the water illuminated their white skinsuits.

Other bodies, more streamlined, darted through the water below and beside them. Some of these streamlined bodies slammed into the side of the UFO itself; others turned their attention to the frantic bodies struggling to tread water on the surface.

The night erupted into a chorus of intermittent screams. A few seconds later, the screams were silenced. Beams of light shot through the water in every direction in a feeble attempt to interrupt the feeding frenzy underneath the surface.

His entire body shook.

Kup was fifty meters away when he heard a final scream and saw a beam of light impact a corner of the UFO. An explosion followed, and the UFO broke into four pieces. The floodlights extinguished, and three of the four pieces began sinking into the black water. The one remaining flotation balloon began to deflate, and the fourth chunk of UFO slipped into the ocean.

The vibrations that had been pounding Kup's body stopped, and the slide raft began drifting with the wind. Kup, however, continued shaking.

The only sounds were the wind and Kup's heavy breathing. The feeding frenzy was now several hundred meters underwater.

An orange light appeared from under the water and rose to the surface. Moments later, a clear capsule launched out of the water ten meters in front of him. It shot up thirty meters, stopped, and fell back into the water. The capsule bobbed in the ocean and began sinking. The orange light in the capsule illuminated a tall man whose eyes were locked on Kup. The man started screaming, "Help me!" Water had already risen to the waist of his white skinsuit.

Kup eased himself onto the side tube of the raft. A dark, streamlined shadow shot between Kup and the sinking capsule. He eased himself back to the center of the raft.

The man in the capsule pounded on the transparent walls with his palms. His four main fingers were of equal length. "Please. Save me. Please!" The water was up to his chest. "I am unable to open the door."

Kup eased back toward the edge of the slide raft. The capsule was only ten meters away, an easy swim. *He can't be human, not with this kind of technology. And those fingers?* He looked down at the bloodstains on the raft from his injured hip. *I can't do this. I will die. He's not even human—he can't be.*

Inside the now submerged capsule, the man's platinum-blond hair floated above his head. His eyes remained fixed on Kup as he continued pounding on the side of the capsule. Air bubbles wobbled out of his mouth.

Kup shuddered as he took a deep breath, slid off the end of the slide raft, and began swimming toward the capsule. He opened his eyes underwater and scanned the dark water for even darker shadows. Except for the orange light from the capsule, there was only blackness, but he knew they were lurking nearby. They had to be.

As he approached the capsule, the man inside pointed to a small orange oval on the outside and placed his left palm against the side of the escape pod. The man screamed something unintelligible, and bubbles escaped from his mouth.

Kup placed his left hand on the orange oval, and the clear doorway of the capsule slid open. Kup pulled the man out of the capsule, rolled him onto his back, and placed his right arm across the man's chest. Kup began swimming upward but struggled. The man was heavy—too heavy for his size.

They breached the surface. Kup gasped for breath. "Kick, dammit! You weigh a ton!"

They sank below the surface. Kup kicked underwater. It was the hardest ten meters of his life.

He saw the slide raft at the surface two meters above them, and he kicked toward the surface.

The slide raft was now only half a meter above them.

Kup reached for the boarding stirrup, a small strap that hung down into the water from one end of the slide raft. He missed, and they began sinking.

Kup kicked as hard as his cramping legs would allow. They ascended and were now only twenty centimeters below the boarding stirrup.

Kup grabbed the boarding stirrup with his left hand and pulled himself to the surface. He took a deep breath.

The strange man's head was still underwater.

Kup pulled the man's left wrist up to the boarding stirrup with his right hand.

The man grasped the boarding stirrup and pulled himself to the surface. He threw up a mouthful of water and gasped for breath. "I will drown."

Kup pointed to the boarding handle on the top edge of the slide raft. "Grab this handle, or you *will* drown! I can't hold you any longer."

The man grabbed the boarding handle.

"Now stick your foot in this boarding stirrup and hoist yourself up."

The man hoisted himself onto the slide raft and looked back at Kup. "I am okay!"

Something bumped Kup's left thigh. "Well, I'm not!" He grabbed the boarding handle and made multiple attempts to stick his left foot into the boarding stirrup.

The man pointed toward the water beside Kup. "There is a shark beside you. You should get out of the water as soon as possible."

"No shit. Help me, dammit!"

The man reached down and pulled Kup aboard. "Now, also, you are okay."

Kup rolled over onto his back. His chest heaved up and down.

"Thank you for saving me from the water," the man said. "We cannot swim. The explosion aboard my ship damaged the escape pod." The man wore a small blue backpack. His white skinsuit revealed a tall, thin physique of extremely dense muscle and bone. "You have done a great thing for *Society.*"

"Society?" Kup struggled to catch his breath. "Bloody hell, what do you weigh, mate?"

The man glanced at the blood oozing from Kup's left thigh. "A shark has injured you. I must repair your wounds. You have caused inequity between us." He pulled the backpack off his shoulders.

"Inequity?" said Kup as his breathing began to slow.

"Yes. I must resolve the inequity between us. It is Supreme Law. I cannot disobey it."

"Disobey it? Who in the hell is going to punish you out here on this raft? And what's up with your fingers? They're all the same length except for your thumb."

The man glanced at his fingers and then at Kup's hands. He shrugged as he pulled out a rectangular device about the size of a cellphone. "I am obviously not the same as you." He placed his right thumb in the center of the device. "But I have been told this device works equally well on your species." The device glowed a dull orange.

"You've been told ... wait, wait, wait ... species? Are you ... what is that thing? Are you going to use it to kill me?"

The man placed the device over a puncture wound in Kup's hip. "Of course not. That is forbidden."

"Forbidden by whom?"

"Society."

"Society? Whose society do you keep talking about?"

The device glowed red.

Kup clenched his teeth. "Whoa, whoa, whoa. What are you doing to me?"

The puncture wound disappeared. The device returned to orange.

"That didn't hurt." Kup stuck a finger through a hole in his uniform pants. "The cut in my skin … it's gone. It's like nothing ever happened there." Kup unclenched his teeth. "That's amazing."

The man nodded as he moved the device to the next puncture wound and repeated the process. "You are lucky. The bite radius is not so big. The shark—it must have been not so big."

"Yeah, I feel so lucky right now." Kup watched another wound disappear.

The man shrugged and continued using the device on Kup's other wounds.

Kup sat up on his elbows. "So, the thing in your hand … it heals wounds instantly? And your ship. Who on Earth has technology like that?"

"No one."

"So, you really are a—"

"Yes."

"Yes? But you look like us. I mean, mostly. You're not exactly what I was expecting."

"Evolution takes similar paths in similar environments. What exactly were you expecting?"

"I don't know exactly what I was expecting—maybe some big, bulging eyes and gray skin?" *I know I wasn't expecting three-ton Johnny Spandex.*

"You confuse me."

"*I* confuse you? You just threw the proverbial alien cat amongst the Earthly pigeons, and *you're* the one that's confused?"

"Yes."

"I'm the one who should be confused—and terrified—right now. I'm the one who should have all the questions. Like, what the hell happened to my airplane?"

"A systemic malfunction occurred aboard our Command Ship. Unfortunately, your aircraft flew too close to us and became affected by the electromagnetic pulses as well as the tow beam. We—"

"Electromagnetic pulse? You hit us with an EMP? No wonder we lost everything! Why did you hit us with an EMP? What did we ever do to you?"

"It was not intentional. As I said, it was a malfunction, and you flew too close to us. In order to avoid a collision, we had to shut down all systems and perform a …"

"Reboot?"

"Yes. A reboot. We recovered control of the Command Ship just before impact with the ocean. We attempted repairs. Our sensors spotted your raft, so we flew toward you to investigate while we tested the ship's systems. Unfortunately, our repairs failed, and the malfunctions reoccurred. We tumbled into the ocean. Then the sharks came. I believe the EMP was attracting them and causing their frenzied behavior. Unfortunately, we were not able to shut down the malfunctioning EMP due to the violent impact with the ocean."

"The EMP attracted all the sharks?" Kup shook his head. "I reckon you attracted every shark within ten kilometers."

"Possibly. I do not know. It was not something we anticipated."

Kup nodded. The strange *man's* vulnerabilities calmed him; his heart rate began to slow. "So, what should I call you? You got a name, mate?"

"I am the Warden. It is my service to Society."

"The Warden? The Warden of what?"

CHAPTER NINE

Honolulu, Hawai'i
07:00 HST, 1 January

Leilani slammed the door against its backstop as she walked into her office on the eighth floor of the Prince Kuhio Federal Building. Noa Kim, her Hawai'i-based chief of staff, stood in front of a mirror adjusting his over-gelled jet-black hair. He had the tan and compact body of a surfer, although he had never surfed a day in his life. He had the look of a local, but his English was refined, not pidgin. He had been born in Lihu'e, but his childhood was spent in a place very far away from Kaua'i.

"Anything unusual about any airliners this morning?" asked Leilani.

Noa turned to face her. "Central Pacific Flight 855 was supposed to have landed here from Sydney over an hour ago. They're saying the plane just … vanished."

"Vanished? Like our Command Ship vanished?" Leilani asked.

"They still haven't located it?"

"They located an escape pod beacon on the bottom of the ocean. Luka says they're concentrating the search in that area, but the Hawai'i Command Ship is most likely a total loss. All aboard are most likely dead. The only consolation is that if there was a midair collision, then the passengers aboard the airliner are also most likely dead."

"About that … I'm not so sure there was a collision."

"Why is that, Noa?"

"The Automatic Dependent Surveillance-Broadcast system, or ADS-B, aboard CPA 855 suddenly stopped transmitting its position over SATCOM. My sources gave me the exact time this occurred. Coincidentally, the Hawai'i Command Ship sent a reboot signal seconds after the ADS-B stopped transmitting CPA 855's position."

"So, what does all this mean, Noa? What do you believe happened to the plane?"

"Well, *we* know the plane may have encountered the Command Ship's malfunctioning tow system, which would have ensured a midair collision. *We* also know it may have encountered the Command Ship's malfunctioning EMP. If so, it would have shut down the plane's electrical system, explaining the sudden loss of ADS-B signal and why there was no distress call. The Command Ship's subsequent reboot, possibly meant to disable the tow system and avoid a midair collision, would have allowed the pilots to regain control of CPA 855; however, the aircraft's electrical system would have remained inoperable. If the plane ditched and sank intact, there would be no distress signal and no debris field. It would have effectively vanished."

"Ditched and sank intact?" Leilani looked across the room through the expansive window on the opposite side. The bow of a massive cruise ship pointed at her from the cruise terminal across Ala Moana Boulevard. "Noa, what are the chances there are survivors aboard the airliner?"

"Ditchings are rare, but there have been several successful incidences of airliners ditching through history."

"I see. Well, you are not exactly brightening my day, Noa. With the delay in the timeline because of the missing Hawaiʻi Command Ship, it is critical that we control the narrative during this period. We cannot afford for a bunch of survivors to start blabbing about an encounter with a UFO, and it would be especially harmful if one of the crew reports the encounter."

"I understand," Noa said. "When will a replacement Command Ship for Hawaiʻi arrive?"

"Luka said they were not sure, but hopefully soon. Unfortunately, the Peace Squad detachment was aboard the Hawaiʻi ship. The entire operation is vulnerable at this point. We have no protection without them. We cannot allow our plans to become public knowledge. It could provoke a political response."

Noa nodded. "Is there anything we could do to preemptively discredit any potential survivors, any crew members in particular, in case they are found?"

"Yes. Brilliant minds think alike, Noa. Or maybe Stoling minds think alike."

"Thank you, Senator. I'll obtain the passenger list and do some background checks."

"And I'll take care of the crew. I assume that Susan Kupule will know some of them. I'll call her. Hopefully, she's not too hungover to talk on the phone, and hopefully, Central Pacific hasn't fired her yet. Brian had to pull some significant strings to get them to hire her as a flight attendant."

"Just like he pulled those strings to get you to hire Gretchen?"

"I wouldn't call them strings, Noa. It was simply a transaction. He needed a job for his nitwit daughter; I needed some element of control over the governor."

Noa nodded.

"You know, between those two, Brian should never have been allowed to procreate."

"Well, it's too late now, Senator," Noa said as he walked out of the office.

Leilani punched a button on the intercom sitting on her desk. "Gretchen, can you please get your sister on the phone for me? I'd like to discuss the missing Central Pacific flight with her."

Gretchen Kupule's sheepish voice replied, "Yes, Senator."

Forty seconds later, Susan Kupule's voice streamed over the speakerphone. "Uh … hello?"

"Susan, dear, this is Leilani Damonati. *Aloha kakahiaka.*"

"Uh … good morning to you, too, Senator." Susan yawned. "What— is everything okay? Did something happen to Gretchen?"

"Gretchen is fine. I apologize for calling you so early on New Year's Day, but I need some information. Did you know any of the crew on Flight 855?"

"Flight 855?"

"Yes, my dear. I'm sure you've heard that it's missing."

"Missing?"

"Yes, it should have landed here this morning around six, but they lost contact somewhere northeast of Vanuatu. I assumed you had heard."

"Shhh, I'm talking to a senator—they're in the kitchen. Sorry, Senator. This is awful news."

"Yes, my dear, it's terrible. I'm trying to gather some … information on the crew. You know, in case the press asks me about them. It would be helpful if I could humanize them somewhat. Did you know any of the crew?"

"Well, I don't know. I'll need to check the company's website. Oh my gosh—give me a second."

"Of course, my dear."

The sound of a clicking keyboard came over the phone. "Manu Keller was the lead flight attendant. I'm not a fan. But, yeah, I've worked with all the flight attendants that were aboard."

"And the pilots?"

"Hold on a sec ... Kuparr Winston? What an asshole. Lydia Kahananui—kind of a bitch, but whatever. Johnny Carmichael. Flown with him once; seems okay."

Leilani jotted the words "bitch" and "Lydia Kahananui" on her notepad. "Why do you say she is a bitch?"

"Oh, I don't know. I get the feeling she thinks she's better than me. She's a big captain, and I'm a lowly flight attendant."

"And does she have any interesting quirks?"

"Quirks?"

"Yes, you know ... has she ever said anything or done anything that you might consider unusual or strange?"

"Well, not really. She's just kind of a bitch, is all."

Leilani frowned. "I see. Well, why do you think Winston Kuparr is an—asshole, my dear?"

"Well, it's Kuparr Winston, but for one, he called my dad an idiot."

"Oh, he did, did he?" Leilani began writing on the notepad.

"He thinks you're an idiot, too."

Leilani crushed the tip of the mechanical pencil she was using. "What are you saying? Why exactly does he think your father and I are idiots? Does he not support your father's political agenda? My political agenda? Our politics in general?"

"I'll say. He seems to be one of those independent thinkers—not a fan of the nanny state."

"I see. And does he use social media to spread lies and disinformation?"

"Well, probably—I don't really know. He did really embarrass me in front of my coworkers. It made me feel horrible."

"When was this?"

"It was on a layover in Papeete."

"What exactly happened, my dear?"

"Well, the crew was meeting for happy hour. I might have had a little too much to drink, and I maybe didn't feel that great. He insisted on escorting me back to my room. I got sick and threw up. When he joined back up with the rest of the crew that night, he told them that I had thrown up all over him. That was the reason he gave for why he was wearing different clothes. He also told them I tried to come on to him. The next day, everyone kidded me about it. They said that I had probably raped him. It was horrible. There was no safe space for me. I had to work the flight back to Honolulu with all those same people. I wanted to shoot myself."

Leilani rolled her eyes. "Oh, my dear, you poor thing. People like this Winston character make me want to cringe."

"They're terrible. It would serve Kup right if he died in the crash."

Leilani smiled as she tossed her broken pencil into the trash can beside her. "Is there anything else you'd like to tell me about Kuparr Winston, Susan?"

"Uh, no. That's really all I can think of right now. I've only flown with him a few times."

"Okay, well, thank you, my dear. We must have lunch sometime—with Gretchen. *A hui hou.*" Leilani ended the call and opened her laptop.

In seconds, she had pulled up Kuparr Winston's Facebook account. Her breathing intensified. *How are comments like this still getting through the censors? The FTA has got to do a better job with social media.*

CHAPTER TEN

Kona, The Big Island of Hawai'i
07:45 HST, 1 January

Kahealani Winston focused on the coffee maker as Kona coffee began streaming into her "Damonati for Hawai'i" coffee mug. *Kup hates this mug.* She looked at the digital time display on the coffee maker as she pulled her brown hair up and away from her eyes. *He should have texted me by now.*

She sat down at the small wooden breakfast table and breathed in the coffee aroma. She would need to savor every drop; with the baby coming, she had just cut her coffee consumption in half.

The windows beside the breakfast table afforded her a peekaboo view of Kealakekua Bay and the Captain Cook Monument several miles in the distance. She had planned on taking the canoe down to the bay and doing some paddling that morning.

Kup was an Ironman. She found his obsession with exercise to be a bit threatening at times, even though she admired his fortitude. She would swim across the bay with him, but she hated running and biking. Paddling was her preferred method of exercise. It cleared her mind and kept her five-foot-six body in shape. It also kept her connected with the ocean.

The coffee caffeinated away her morning brain fog, which was made worse by her terrible night's sleep. The civil defense sirens used for tsunami warnings had started about twelve thirty but had ended after thirty minutes as confused people along the coastline evacuated *mauka*, inland, away from the coastline. Police sirens had wailed through the night. Fighter jets had crisscrossed the island in search of a perpetrator while *rumors* trickled in from texts and phone calls. The runways at the

Kona, Hilo, and Waimea airports had been destroyed. The ocean floor of the ports in Kawaihae and Hilo had heaved upward, rendering them unusable. The Ironman swim course in Kona was now only fourteen inches deep. *How is Kup going to get home this morning?*

The massive splash of a humpback whale breaching about a half mile offshore held her attention until her cellphone rang.

Kahealani grabbed the phone. She read the display. *Central Pacific Airlines Flight Operations?* "Hello?"

"Good morning. Is this Kahealani Winston?"

"Yes, it is."

"Mrs. Winston, I'm Gerald Napaka, the chief pilot at Central Pacific. How are you doing?"

"Okay, I guess." Kahealani's heart began pounding against her chest.

"Mrs. Winston, I have some bad news concerning your husband."

"Bad news? What … what do you mean bad news?"

"Kuparr's plane is missing."

"Missing?"

"Yes. The last radio contact was with Nadi Control in Fiji. The last position report we have from them was several hundred miles northeast of Vanuatu."

"But everything was fine in Sydney. He called me just before he left for the airport from his parents' house." Kahealani's hands began shaking. "What about radar? Were they being tracked?"

"They would have been over open ocean at the time of the last radio transmission."

"Well, what do you think …" Her voice cracked. "What do you think happened?"

"We really don't know at this time. There have been no distress signals received by SARSAT satellites; however, several governments have started search-and-rescue operations. An aircraft from the Australian Air Force is en route to the area, Fiji is sending patrol ships, and search and rescue aircraft are departing from Hickam and Guam soon. But right now, there are more questions than answers."

Kahealani began blinking back tears. "I don't understand. I mean, airliners don't just disappear."

"Mrs. Winston, I'm sorry to ask this, but have you noticed any strange or erratic behavior by Kuparr over the last few days or weeks?"

"What do you mean?" Kahealani stood up and began pacing across the kitchen floor.

"Has Kuparr been himself? Do you know of any mental issues? Again, I'm sorry to ask you this, but it could be crucial to our investigation into what happened to our aircraft."

"Why are you asking me if he had any—do you think Kup sabotaged the plane?"

"No, I don't. It's just something that we must consider because of the strange nature of the disappearance. It is similar to the Malaysia Airlines Flight 370 from several years ago."

"But Kup would never—"

"Of course not, Mrs. Winston. I had to ask. We have very little to go on right now."

"Do you think everyone aboard is … dead?"

"Look—right now, we just don't know. The Malaysian flight from a few years ago disappeared under similar circumstances, but let's hope for the best."

Kahealani supported herself with her right hand on the breakfast table. Tears dropped into her coffee.

"Mrs. Winston, once again, I'm so sorry. I need to go. Please call me at this number if you can think of anything that might help us. I'll call you as soon as we learn anything new."

Kahealani whispered, "Okay. I … I'll do that." She ended the call and walked through the bedroom into the bathroom. She sank to the floor with her eyes closed and her back against the wall. She rubbed her stomach, thinking of the life forming inside, a life that was now probably fatherless.

Her mind drifted back to the day they had met. He'd been a brash young lieutenant in the Royal Australian Air Force based at Townsville RAAF Base. He and his squadron mates were enjoying an unexpected boondoggle in Cairns because their C-17 had developed a mechanical problem while they were dropping off some cargo at Cairns International Airport. She'd worked in marketing at the Sherwood Cairns Resort, fresh out of college at the University of Hawai'i at Manoa.

She remembered the first time she'd seen Kup. He had pulled his legs together in a cannonball just as he noticed her standing beside the resort pool. The wall of water had shot up from the pool and drenched her and her potential client, who was interested in hosting a corporate retreat at the hotel. The client started yelling at Kup and threatening to punch him in the face. Kup kept apologizing to the man, all the while focusing on Kahealani, who was glaring back at him in her wet business suit. In the end, the client had chosen not to host the corporate retreat at the hotel.

The next day, Kup sent a bouquet of roses that were sitting on her desk when she showed up for work. He stopped by her office wearing his flight suit later that morning to give one last apology.

Soon, they began dating and somehow managed the four-hour drive between Townsville and Cairns. When her Australian work visa was expiring, he'd accepted an exchange position with a USAF C-17 squadron at Joint Base Pearl Harbor-Hickam in Honolulu. She'd transferred to the Sherwood Waikiki.

He had loved being in the RAAF and wanted to make it a career. That would have required them to move back to Australia, and Kahealani wanted to stay in Hawai'i.

Kup chose Kahealani over his career, and when he had finished his commitment to the RAAF, they got married.

Central Pacific Airlines had given Kup a hire date. Kahealani's father had injured himself in a traffic accident soon after, and Kup helped by working their coffee farm on the Big Island. He'd asked Central Pacific if he could push his start date back three months, and they agreed. Two months later, they'd implemented a hiring freeze, which set Kup back a year and a half at the airline.

Meanwhile, Sherwood had promoted Kahealani to the head of marketing for the two resorts on the Big Island. Kup finally left the coffee farm and started training with Central Pacific almost two years after he had been hired.

They'd bought a house above Napo'opo'o on a hillside overlooking Kealakekua Bay. Kahealani loved the house and thought of how happy she had been when she woke up there yesterday.

Her phone beeped, signaling a new text. It was a coworker asking if Kup was aboard the missing flight. Then the phone rang. It was her mother calling.

Kahealani silenced the ringer.

CHAPTER ELEVEN

Northeast of Vanuatu
07:45 VUT, 2 January

Kup blinked as the morning sun illuminated the cloudless sky, the slide raft, the ocean, and the Warden. "Gonna be a bright one today. Silly me left my sunnies on the plane."

Every hour throughout the night, the Warden had eaten something resembling a granola bar from his backpack. For water, the Warden would urinate into the top end of a small metal cylinder about the size of a tennis ball container. Then he would activate the device, and several minutes later, clear water would appear at the bottom.

He'd offered some to Kup, but Kup had declined.

Kup's stomach growled as he watched the Warden eat again. "Time for brekky already? Do you ever not eat, mate? I reckon intermittent fasting for you would be something like an hour and a half."

The Warden shrugged and continued chewing.

Kup envisioned Kahealani's face and wondered if he would ever see it again. He wondered if the slide raft and the skinsuit-wrapped alien sitting across from him would be the last two things he would ever see.

"So, what's the deal with the Spandex suit?" Kup asked.

"Spandex?" The Warden drank from the metal cylinder.

"The skinsuit you're wearing. It looks like something scuba divers wear under their wetsuits. Does it serve a purpose, or are you just trying to make a fashion statement?"

The Warden looked down at his tight suit. "The suit protects me from the climate. It maintains my body temperature correctly in cold or hot weather. It must be tight to perform these functions correctly."

"Oh, that's kinda cool, I reckon."

"It also carries a personal tracker so that Society can keep us safe."

"You keep bringing up this Society. What is it?" Kup asked.

"It is the collective self of us all. It is everything to us."

"And is this Society looking for you?"

"They will be interested in finding the malfunctioning ship and learning what happened. We sent multiple distress signals, but that system was malfunctioning as well. I do not know if the signals went out. After the explosion in the water, I grabbed what I could but forgot to grab a personal beacon. The beacon in the escape pod is at the bottom of the ocean. All I have is the tracker in my suit, but it is not very strong."

"So, you're as screwed as I am," Kup said with a humorless chuckle. "We're two tiny needles in a rather large haystack."

"Haystack? There are no haystacks here."

"Never mind. It's just an expression." Kup watched the Warden pee into his special device. *Am I going to have to drink alien pee water to survive?* "So, what's it taste like, your own piss?"

"It is water that I drink. It tastes like water."

Kup rolled his eyes. "Well, I reckon it may look like water, and it may taste like water, but it's still piss. How long can you survive using that thing? Drinking your own piss?"

"For a couple of your weeks, I believe. It is not quite a closed-loop system because of water loss due to perspiration."

"Well, we're surrounded by ocean. Why don't you just fill that thing with seawater?"

"It is not made to process seawater from Earth. It is made for space travel."

Kup nodded. "So, if I were to pee in it, would drinking water come out of the other end like it does for you?"

"It should. Though we are different, our physiology is similar. Would you like to try it?"

"Oh, hell no."

The Warden nodded as he waited for his urine to be processed.

"And what's up with all your mates from your ship sinking like rocks?" Kup asked. "Not one of them could swim. They thrashed around for a few seconds and then just sank."

"As I told you, we cannot swim. Our bodies are too dense. The ocean ... all bodies of water terrify us. It is almost certain death."

"Well, at least you're not floating around in the middle of the Pacific on a raft. That would be really scary."

"Do not talk of this."

Kup propped his head up and pointed to the sky. "That's weird. There's something in the sky. It's just sitting there. Maybe it's a weather balloon."

The Warden turned his head. "It is not a weather balloon."

"You're right. Weather balloons are … oh bloody—"

"Quickly!" the Warden said as he rolled onto his knees. "There is little time. We must have a Reckoning. We must achieve equity between us before I depart. It is Supreme Law."

"A Reckoning? What the bloody … look! It's descending. It looks just like the—"

"Yes, it is the replacement ship. It will be here soon." The Warden crawled over to Kup and placed his hands on Kup's shoulders.

Kup pulled away from the Warden. "What the bloody hell are you doing?"

"Breathe in the breath of my life."

"What are you talking about?!"

The Warden slammed his forehead against Kup's forehead and pressed their noses together. "Breathe in the breath of my life. We must attain equity."

Kup began shivering. His eyes rolled back.

After several minutes, a large gray triangular spaceship stopped its descent a hundred meters above them.

The only sounds were the wind and the deep-pitched hum emanating from the strange ship above them.

A blinding flash appeared. Kup and the Warden shot apart.

Kup fell against the side of the raft. "Convicts?" *Three islands? Three penal colonies?*

The Warden floated upward toward a dark aperture in the bottom of the ship.

Kup began shaking and hyperventilating. *Three experiments? And if the experiments succeed* … "Bloody hell, it's like what happened to Australia! You can't do this! Not again!"

The Warden disappeared inside the ship.

Vibrations rippled through Kup's body. "No!" His left hand was just centimeters away from a rope hold when he began floating upward. "No! Just leave me here!"

Kup tumbled through the air, kicking his legs and swinging his arms as if he could somehow swim in midair and break the force pulling him upward.

CHAPTER TWELVE

Galveston Island, Texas
15:15 CST, 1 January

The smell of burgers cooking brought Michael Phelps in from his watery pursuit of one particularly obstinate crane. Soaking wet, he bounded up the steps from the yard to the back deck, which stretched out from the living room.

Jerry stood beside the built-in grill of the outdoor kitchen at the north end of the deck. "Michael Phelps, do not—"

Michael Phelps stopped beside Jerry and began shaking. Saltwater flew everywhere, drenching Jerry's shorts and maroon hoodie sweatshirt.

"Bad boy! Bad Michael Phelps!"

Michael Phelps inched closer to the grill as he sniffed the delicacies.

"Oh, yeah, I was going to give you a hamburger patty, maybe one with cheese and bacon on it." Jerry shook his large maroon spatula emblazoned with ATM at Michael Phelps. "But not now."

Daisy walked up the steps and sat beside Michael Phelps, who belted out his best Chewbacca groan. Daisy whimpered.

"Oh, great, teach the new dog how to beg now."

There was a loud thwack from the yard, and Michael Phelps jerked his head to investigate the source. Mikey, an aspiring fifth-grade baseball player, was down below practicing his batting using an automated pitching machine and a batting cage. Michael Phelps had already intercepted and destroyed two foul balls so far that day.

"Mikey, come get your dog!" Jerry yelled.

There was no reply. Mikey's ears were covered by white noise-canceling headphones blasting hip-hop. He wore blue floral board shorts and a Houston Astros T-shirt. His brown hair matched Gail's, as did his study habits. New hair was sprouting on his tan legs, the result of early puberty. He wore shoes as little as possible, which had thickened the skin on the bottom of his feet.

Jerry shook his head and began flipping burgers. He glanced over at the two-pound chunk of Jarlsberg cheese sitting on the dark-green granite counter. *I still need to slice that up for the burgers.*

Jerry's cellphone rang, and he pulled it out of his pocket. It was James Templeton, the managing partner of the downtown Houston office. *James is calling me on New Year's Day? He probably just wants to check on us after what happened last night.*

"Hello, James. Happy New Year."

"Have you seen the news, Jerry?"

"Seen it? I lived it. The entire island is one big shitshow."

"I'm not talking about that. Did you see the news about Central Pacific Airlines Flight 855?"

"No."

"It's missing."

"A plane is missing?"

"Yes. A Central Pacific 777 en route from Sydney to Honolulu vanished last night. No trace. Nothing."

"Wow. Sounds like Malaysia 370 all over again."

"Exactly. That's two hundred fourteen potential lawsuits, and you're our aviation guy."

Jerry's head swiveled as a flash of yellow bounded toward the back stairs. "Michael Phelps! You drop that cheese right now! Drop it!"

"Uh … Jerry, Michael Phelps is at your house?"

"I said drop it!" Jerry began chasing Michael Phelps down the stairs of the back patio and onto the backyard.

The two-pound wedge of Jarlsberg cheese protruded from both sides of his mouth.

"Sorry, James." Jerry panted for several seconds. "No, Michael Phelps is our dog."

"Hmm. That's a rather weird name for a dog. Does he do the hundred-meter butterfly across the bay behind your house?"

"No, but he does about a thousand yards of dog paddling a day. Mikey named … Leave it! Michael Phelps, leave it!" Jerry shook his head. "Michael Phelps, you drop that cheese right now!"

Michael Phelps was well out of range for Jerry to have any hope of catching him and, as such, began devouring the Jarlsberg cheese.

"He's a very bad yellow lab, James, but an outstanding swimmer. Would you like a dog? He's free to a good home."

"No, I've got two already. Back to—"

"Fine! Eat all the damn cheese! You'll be so constipated, you won't shit for a week." Jerry began walking back toward the stairs.

"Ouch. That hurts me just to think about it. Anyway, I think you should take a look at Central Pacific 855 as soon as possible. A lawsuit like this could bring a lot of money and prestige to the firm, not to mention fattening your wallet."

Jerry reached the top of the stairs of the back porch. He glared down at Michael Phelps, who was running a victory lap around the yard with the plastic cheese wrapper flapping up and down in his mouth. "Yeah, James, I'll get right on it." *Glad to see you're so concerned about my family and me.* Jerry reached down into the outdoor mini fridge and grabbed a beer.

"James, did they send out a distress call, mayday, anything?"

"Nothing."

"ADS-B?"

"I don't know what that is, but I didn't see anything about it."

"ADS-B is Automatic Dependent Surveillance-Broadcast. The aircraft broadcasts its position continually."

"Nope. Didn't see that."

"Anything from SARSAT? Search-and-rescue satellites?"

"Nothing."

"Other aircraft or boats? Anything?"

"Jerry, as I said, it vanished. Poof."

"Weird. So, what was their last reported position?"

"Somewhere northeast of Vanuatu—over open water. You really must check it out. It's all over the news."

News? Here's some news: Did you hear Galveston got attacked last night? "How's your family, Jerry? Is everyone okay? It must have been really traumatic for you."

"Yep, lots of stuff on the news, James."

"Let me know what you find out, Jerry. I need to go. We just got to my in-laws' in San Antonio."

So, you can just drive to another city. "Of course, James. Happy New Year."

"Oh yeah, Happy New Year to you. Enjoy your cheeseburgers-no-cheese."

CHAPTER THIRTEEN

Honolulu, Hawai'i
11:45 HST, 1 January

"The food looks delicious, Brian." Senator Damonati took a bite of ahi poke. "Luka sends his regrets that he couldn't make it. He's not feeling well."

"Oh, too bad." Governor Brian Kupule blinked his bloodshot eyes as he stood in the center of the main parlor of the Greek Revival palace built in 1847 that served as the Governor's Mansion. Portraits of past kings and queens of Hawai'i adorned the walls of the antique-filled room. A decorated twelve-foot-tall Christmas tree commanded a far corner. Several television trucks filled the street in front of the mansion, and security held back dozens of reporters outside the grounds.

Leilani smiled. "And the way you've decorated the Governor's Mansion for the holidays is so beautiful."

"Thanks, but it's a little hard to be cheerful. It's been a long day—and night." The dark circles underneath the governor's eyes contrasted with the bright holiday decorations throughout the room.

"I'm sure it has." Senator Damonati sipped champagne. "Any news about Central Pacific 855?"

Governor Kupule shook his head as an aide approached him. "Nothing new, but Hawai'i Island is a mess. They're looting stores left and right over there. I have hardly any National Guard troops to send because they're almost all in Washington right now. The county police are overwhelmed. So, that's my news, but I haven't heard anything new about Central Pacific 855 other than the Australians started searching the last reported position a few hours ago."

Leilani smiled as an aide stopped beside the governor.

The aide whispered in Governor Kupule's left ear. His eyes brightened. "Oh, that's great. When?"

Leilani cocked her head.

Governor Kupule nodded as he said, "Okay, tell them I'll be right there." He turned to Leilani. "Excuse me, Senator, but the Australians have located the survivors of Central Pacific 855." He began walking away with his aide beside him.

Leilani clutched her champagne flute so tight that it almost snapped in two. "That's wonderful news, Governor." She glared at Noa before turning back toward Governor Kupule. "Governor, wait. I need to know more. You must tell me some of the specifics."

Governor Kupule stopped and walked back to Leilani. "Senator, I've told you all I know."

"Do they know if any of the crew survived?" Leilani asked.

The aide looked at Leilani and said, "Uh, the reports are a little confusing. The Australians parachuted several paramedics down to the flotilla of rafts. They're working on a list of survivors. I think I saw that they accounted for all the flight attendants except for one. None of the pilots were among the survivors."

"Well, that is … unfortunate."

"Wait," the aide said. "There was something else about one of the … one of the flight attendants reported that one of the pilots survived the crash but didn't make it to the raft flotilla."

Leilani gritted her teeth. "And what was the pilot's name?"

"Leilani, why is this so important?" Governor Kupule asked.

"Brian, this is a matter for the FAA, and the details surrounding the flight are eerily similar to Malaysia 370. A pilot caused that crash."

"It might have been something like … Winsome," the aide said. "Wisdom, maybe?"

Noa Kim walked up and stood beside Leilani. "Winston? Was it Kuparr Winston?"

"Yes. That's it," the aide said. "Oh, and the survivors also said they had spotted a single raft in the distance alongside the jet. They attempted to paddle toward it, but they eventually lost sight of it. They're hopeful that it might have been the missing pilot—the Winston guy. The Australians are continuing their search for the single raft."

Senator Damonati slammed her champagne flute on a table beside her.

"Did the survivors say why the plane crashed?" Noa asked. "Did they report anything unusual?"

The governor's aide glanced at Noa. "They did report that the plane was flying erratically before it ditched. Oh, and they said all the lights went out. It was completely dark in the cabin."

"I see," Noa said. "Anything else unusual that they might have seen or noticed?"

"Yes. Their cellphones, laptops—pretty much everything electronic went dark along with the cabin lights. The initial report was sketchy. I'm sure our office will receive additional details about the incident once the Australian and US aviation authorities can fully interview the passengers and crew."

Noa nodded. "Thank you. Please keep the senator's office informed of any new developments."

"Of course," Governor Kupule said. "Is there anything else we can do for you, Senator?"

"No. I believe you gentlemen have urgent business to attend to."

Governor Kupule nodded and turned to his aide. "Of course. Let's go."

Noa whispered, "Well, this kinda sucks. At least the survivors didn't report seeing anything."

Senator Damonati turned back toward Noa. "They didn't report seeing anything—yet. We must assume that the other raft will be spotted eventually, and Winston will be on it. He had to have seen something, and when he talks, people will listen. Have Gretchen arrange for us to be picked up in ten minutes from the front of the building instead of the usual spot. Now, follow me."

Senator Damonati walked out the front door and down the sidewalk of the front yard of Washington Place. Noa followed behind her. The gaggle of reporters by the front gate began shouting questions as she approached.

A female reporter shouted, "Senator, it's been reported that the Australians have located the survivors of Central Pacific 855. Do you have any additional information?"

Another reporter shouted, "How many survivors are there, Senator?"

Senator Damonati cleared her throat. "We have not received a number yet. The details are just coming in. It is eerie, however, how similar the circumstances around Central Pacific Flight 855 are to Malaysia 370 from several years ago."

Another reporter shouted, "Senator, the crash of Malaysia 370 was caused by a rogue pilot. Are you saying that a rogue pilot may have caused the crash of Central Pacific 855?"

"Oh, no, I'm not saying that at all. I'm just saying that the circumstances appear … well, they seem suspicious—like the Malaysia 370 crash."

A limousine pulled up in front of the gaggle of reporters.

"Now, if you all will excuse me, I must go. There's much work—"

"Senator! Senator!" a male reporter shouted from the crowd. "What about aliens? There's a rumor going around that the attack on the Big Island is the work of an alien civilization."

Senator Damonati glared at the reporter. "Your job is to investigate the truth and report it to the people. Your job is *not* to parrot some silly conspiracy theory about little green women from Mars."

"But Senator, the Navy and Air Force have both acknowledged the existence of UFOs. And the technologies used in the attacks—what nation on Earth could have done that?"

"In trying and confusing times such as these, it is important that we listen to what our government tells us. I implore the American people to listen to the top minds at our intelligence agencies, not some half-baked twit on the internet. Disinformation is the enemy of democracy. Now, I truly must go." Senator Damonati pushed through the crowd of reporters.

The limousine had stopped, and her driver stood beside the opened right rear door. Gretchen Kupule sat in the left back seat, texting someone. Her brunette bangs hung over her eyes.

Senator Damonati sat in the right back seat, and Noa sat facing her as the driver shut the door. Leilani watched Gretchen's two thumbs fly across the tiny virtual keypad on her phone. "Good grief, Gretchen. Do your thumbs ever get tired?"

Gretchen stopped texting and looked up at the senator. "No, not really." Her thumbs returned to their rapid dance across the phone's keypad.

"Gretchen, please, stop texting. I need to discuss something important with you. I need to know if your sister can be trusted. Do you think she cares enough about our cause to help us? Enough to get"—Leilani looked out the limousine window at the gaggle of reporters—"her hands a little dirty?"

Gretchen looked up from her phone. "Our cause? The only things Susan cares about are sex and money—in that order."

Leilani smiled as she read a text from her phone. "Well, never mind."

CHAPTER FOURTEEN

Vík í Mýrdal, Iceland
12:05 GMT, 2 January

The road made a sharp turn to the right before beginning a steep descent. A rocky cliff rose along its right side. A dusting of snow matched the gray sky, which matched the gray ocean in the distance.

"Is that Vík?" Trevor pointed at a group of buildings a few kilometers ahead that spread along the coast. He sat in the passenger seat of Hildur's gold-colored Škoda.

"Yes, Trevor. It will be so nice after the chaos of Reykjavík." Hildur applied the brakes as the road steepened further. "All the looting and the burning … all the people running around attacking each other … we are not like this."

Trevor laughed. "And I thought you Icelanders were so civilized. Why doesn't the government call in the National Guard?"

"We do not have this. Iceland is a peaceful country. We only have the lögreglan, the police. There is no military except for the Coast Guard."

"So, let's just say—hypothetically, of course—that somebody invades Iceland. Who would defend the country?"

"Well, the Americans would come, and the NATO."

Trevor laughed. "So, my tax dollars should pay for Iceland's defense?"

"Well, it is a silly argument. No one would invade Iceland."

"Really, Hildur. So … what would you call what happened the other night?"

As the road approached the coastline, it veered left. A small sign on the left announced they were entering Vík í Mýrdal. Buildings, all one or two stories, dotted the area. The town itself sat back from a black-sand beach a few hundred meters. To their left, atop a hillside, stood a red-roofed church with a red steeple.

"Let us not talk about this anymore." Hildur slowed down. "I think we should stop by the supermarket. I am not sure how much food I have at my house."

Ahead to their right, multiple flashes of blue light bounced off the white side of the Krónan Supermarket.

"And what is this now?" Hildur said.

"More chaos at a supermarket?" said Trevor. "There's a line of cars trying to get into the parking lot."

"And the lögreglan are here." Hildur slowed the Škoda to a crawl. "I wonder what has happened? Surely, things are not chaos here. Not in Vík."

Hildur joined the line of cars inching their way along the road and into the supermarket parking lot. As a car departed, a policewoman allowed another car to enter. A policeman also guarded the store's entrance.

"I'm getting hungry," Trevor said. "I guess you always want what you can't have."

"The supermarket has plenty of food for everyone. I do not understand why this mad rush. I think the entire town is here."

"They may have food right now, but how will they restock? I mean, can Iceland feed itself?"

"I do not—" Hildur put her right hand over her mouth. "Kolbrún?"

"What? What are you talking about?"

"Look, Trevor. Over by the exit doors."

Two gray-haired ladies were fighting over a package of meat. The lady on the left wore a forest-green parka and blue jeans, and the lady on the right wore a tomato-red sweater, navy yoga pants, and brown hiking boots. Her shoulder-length gray hair flopped back and forth from the meaty tug of war. The policeman who had been guarding the entrance walked over to the ladies and blew a whistle, but the ladies ignored it.

With the policeman distracted, the crowd began pouring into the supermarket. Fists were flying. People were stepping and crawling over each other, trying to enter the supermarket.

"So, Hildur, is *Kolbrún* Icelandic for two old ladies fighting?"

"Kolbrún Gísladóttir is my neighbor. She is eighty-five years of age and lives across the pasture from me."

"And she is one of those ladies fighting over the package of meat?"

"Yes—yes, she is the one on the right in the red sweater. And I believe the lady on the left is Agnetha. She is the minister of the church."

"Minister? Yikes."

"Well, she *was* the minister. I think she retired this year."

Kolbrún reached over and grabbed a chunk of Agnetha's curly gray locks with her right hand. Agnetha lost her balance and fell onto the icy parking lot.

There was a loud screech as the Škoda crunched into a silver SUV in front of them in the line of cars.

Hildur turned her head forward. *"Fjandinn!* I hit that BMW in front of me. I wasn't paying attention."

"You weren't going that fast, Hildur. Probably just a scratch."

"Well, I hope so. I was watching Kolbrún and Agnetha."

Kolbrún smiled as she marched through the parking lot with two reusable shopping bags. She had stuffed both to capacity.

"Well, it looks like Kolbrún won," said Trevor.

"Yes … it is not good to be on her wrong side."

A trim middle-aged man got out of the driver's side of the Mercedes SUV in front of them. He glared at Hildur as he pointed at his rear bumper and yelled, *"Helvítis fokking fokk!"*

"He sounds pissed," Trevor said.

"Yes, but it will be okay. I know him, and this is Iceland. I will just tell him I am sorry." Hildur opened her window. *"Fyrirgefðu, Baldur."*

The man screamed, *"Þú ert að borga fyrir þetta!"*

"He wants me to pay for the damage," Hildur said. "Of course. I have insurance. He needs to relax." She leaned out of the window. *"Rólex, Baldur. Ég er með tryggingar."*

"Rólex?" the man said as he opened the hatchback of the Mercedes SUV and pulled out a sledgehammer.

"Shit!" Trevor started looking behind them. "Let's get out of here."

"He would not—"

"Back up, Hildur! You've got room."

The man started walking toward Hildur's window with the sledgehammer held off to his left side using both his hands. Hildur slammed into reverse and backed up just short of the car behind them. She swung the steering wheel hard left as she shifted into drive, and the Škoda's tires squealed as the car made a hard one-eighty-degree turn. The sledge-hammer slammed into Trevor's door.

"Are you okay, Trevor?"

"Yeah, I'm fine. Shit, what has gotten into people?"

Hildur's hands shook as she drove. "I do not even recognize my town anymore."

She turned right onto Hátún Street, pulled over to the side, and shifted into park. Her hands gripped the steering wheel as her eyes locked on to nothing.

A thirty-year-old white Volvo station wagon stopped behind them and began honking its horn. After seven honks, it pulled up alongside them on the left side.

Trevor looked over at the Volvo. "Hey, isn't that—"

"Kolbrún?" Hildur said as she wiped her eyes.

"Hildur," came a female voice from the Volvo. "*Hver er þessi maður með þér?*"

Hildur rolled down her window. "He is my American friend, Trevor."

Kolbrún dropped her oversized black oval sunglasses down to the bottom of her nose as she studied Trevor. She shifted her attention to the back of the Škoda. "You have returned from Reykjavík? And you have no food?"

Hildur nodded.

"We will eat dinner at my house at eighteen hundred hours. I have lamb chops. *Bless bless.*" Kolbrún sped away.

CHAPTER FIFTEEN

200 Kilometers Above Earth
15:00 GMT, 2 January

Kup lowered his head back down onto the pillow. It was the only body part he could move. He was lying on some sort of bed and covered in sweat. The room smelled hospital sterile; the walls were hospital white. The wall to his left contained a closed doorway. On the wall in front of him, large script resembling Thai characters would translate into "Containment Room 3" if he had needed a translation; he was now fluent in their language. He also knew the basic schematics of the ship he was aboard and its purpose. He didn't, however, know how the systems worked. Those details remained with the Warden. The Reckoning had been interrupted.

Kup looked up at an orange orb, about the size of a chicken egg, floating just below the ceiling. *They're watching me.* The orb pulsated every few seconds. *This ship is part of their plan. This ship will change history—not for the better.*

History had never concerned him much. It was painful, and he had blocked much of it from his memory. He'd felt the subtle prejudgments early in his life; his skin was always a shade off, one way or the other. They would leave him behind; there was always a reason, always an excuse. It was uncomfortable, so he chose to ignore it, just as he had chosen to ignore his nation's history.

When Kup was seven, his maternal grandmother, whose mob hailed from Gundungurra Country, told him stories about the pain, the horrors, and the injustice they had endured as Indigenous people of Australia. Despite having occupied the land for over sixty thousand years, they had become strangers in their own land, overwhelmed by foreigners and foreign technology. These foreigners told them how they should talk, who they should talk to, where they should live, and how they should live. They stole entire generations to reeducate them into a supposedly better way of life, a supposedly superior culture. She had died when Kup was eight. He lost the connection to that past, that history, and that side of his family. He felt disconnected from them, and that part of him became fuzzy. It had happened so long ago.

When he was ten, his paternal grandfather told Kup he had an ancestor who was a convict. The family gossip was that the poor sod had stolen a rooster. Manchester had become overcrowded; there was practically no room for the good people to live, so they shipped off the bad ones. His ancestor had arrived in Van Diemen's Land, an alien in an alien land. Kup had thought the story was cool at the time but hadn't thought much about it in the years since. It had happened so long ago.

And then there was Hawai'i. From Kahealani's family, he had learned about a queen deposed by restless newcomers intent on making their new home like their old home. Their old home needed a set of strategically placed islands in the middle of the Pacific, so it did nothing to return the queen to power and eventually absorbed the islands into the growing country. Of course, back then, Hawai'i had many unwanted suitors. The only real question at the time was if the people would be speaking English, French, Russian, or Japanese.

The old age of imperialism had ended long ago. The new age of imperialism was just beginning—on a far grander scale.

The orange ovoid descended from the ceiling. Seconds later, it transformed into a hologram of the Warden and a platinum-blond female.

"Kuparr Winston, I am the Safety Officer of this ship," the female said. "I believe you already know the Warden—too well, I am afraid."

Kup lifted his head. "What gives you assholes the right to dump a hundred thousand convicts on my island?"

"Interesting," the Safety Officer said. "When we arrived, you and the Warden were experiencing a Reckoning. I see that the Reckoning was at least partially successful. That is unfortunate."

"This human did a great thing for Society by saving my life," the Warden said. "If I had died, our plans would have been delayed indefinitely. The experiments would have failed. Besides this, we experienced inequity between us. Supreme Law required us to have a Reckoning."

Kup stared at the Warden's image in front of him. *If I hadn't saved his life, they would have had to postpone the invasions? The experiments would have failed. Bloody hell, what have I done?*

"Warden, I understand your need to achieve equity and comply with Supreme Law," the Safety Officer said. "However, your actions have forced our—"

"But the Reckoning was interrupted," the Warden said. "Equity was not achieved. In fact, very little was shared. I gained no technical knowledge from him."

"The Reckoning was interrupted because we intervened. And what technical knowledge would you have gained, Warden? How to fly an airplane? A *human* airplane?"

"I don't know anything," Kup said. "Just let me go home. I won't say anything to anybody."

The Safety Officer looked at the Warden. "Warden, can he be trusted? Will he support Society?"

"No. He will not," the Warden said. "He does not see the safety in segregation. He believes all humans are created equal and should be free to follow their own individual paths. He once told someone, 'You gotta do unto others as you would have them do unto you, regardless of their skin color.'"

The Safety Officer glared at Kup.

"He believes government exists to serve the individual," the Warden said. "He does not believe the individual should be subordinated to the collective good of society and government."

"You are antisocial, Kuparr Winston." The Safety Officer frowned.

"He thinks the pursuit of equity is utopian, but he believes its implementation has always resulted in dystopia," the Warden said. "It is sad."

"You can never go home," the Safety Officer said.

"Never go home?" Kup said as he strained against the unseen forces holding him down. "Well, just what kind of a home can I not return to? You people are going to dump a hundred thousand—wait, make that a hundred and five thousand—convicts on my island. The same goes for Galveston and Iceland. What are the people who are already there, whose families have lived there forever, supposed to do? These convicts will overrun them. And then, if these penal colonies are successful, billions will follow. There will be nothing left of us! We'll be wiped out, overrun, overwhelmed. Our lives will be destroyed. Our cultures will be wiped out. How can you do this to Earth? How can you do this to humanity?"

The Safety Officer shook her head. "Kuparr Winston, Society's needs—"

"Society!" Kup yelled. "Screw your Society. You're gonna dump these so-called 'dangerous convicts' here because they have low *Social Scores,* because they don't conform to the racial identities Society has dictated to them, because they think for themselves, because they refuse to segregate themselves according to race? I could go on and on. And these convicts … they're going to be aliens in an alien world. How are they supposed to survive? My people have seen all this before. It's all happened before."

"Kuparr Winston!" the Warden yelled. "Control your thoughts. Do not go further."

"Go further? What are you going to do to me? You can't kill me. What is that … the most supreme of the Supreme Laws?"

"You are correct, Kuparr Winston," the Safety Officer said. "We cannot let you go home, and of course, we will not kill you. We can, however, *Cancel* you."

"Cancel me?" Kup said. "Bloody hell—I didn't think of that. Just let me go! You can track me."

The Safety Officer smiled. "You are antisocial and regressive, Kuparr Winston. You cannot be trusted, and Society cannot take any risks at this point. Of course, according to the Warden, you are also a Mixed and would have to be neutered anyway."

"It is for the best for Society," the Warden said. "You will be remembered for saving my life. You have served the collective whole of us. You will receive a medal of service—after the Cancellation, of course."

"A medal? You're going to give me a medal?" Kup struggled against the invisible constraints that held him to the bed. "I can't believe I jumped in the water with a bunch of sharks to save you, and this is the thanks I get? Why are you doing this to me? What have I done that is so horrible?"

"Kuparr Winston, you did save the life of the Warden, and his death would have resulted in the immediate failure of all three Earth experiments. Now that we have this replacement Command Ship in place, however, we can proceed. Society is eternally thankful for what you did.

However, you are a radical—an unstable, dangerous radical."

"Radical?!" Kup glared at the Safety Officer. "I'm a radical because I believe we should all be treated equally? I'm never going to see my wife again? My unborn child … because you don't like the way I think?"

"Yes," the Safety Officer said. "We must keep Society safe. You will be Cancelled and placed into a *Freedom Vault*. Do not worry, though. As you probably already know, the cryogenic process is painless. You will be free from your subversive thoughts. You will feel safe."

"It is for the best," the Warden said. "You will see. It will all be over soon."

The hologram collapsed back into an orange ovoid of light that ascended back into the ceiling.

Kup began shaking. *If I had just let him drown …*

CHAPTER SIXTEEN

Galveston Island, Texas
14:00 CST, 2 January

Gail Morgenstern stood beside Jerry as he unlocked the gun cabinet in his home office, flipping through multiple pages of social media on her phone. "They're looting Target. They smashed all the windows and are rushing in, grabbing whatever they can."

She ran her left hand through her short brown hair. Between teaching medicine five days a week and being a mother twenty-four-seven, she had little time for frivolities like long hair. "The police are overwhelmed and aren't even trying to stop them."

Jerry nodded. "Well, if the police are overwhelmed, this will keep us safe." He handed Gail her Weatherby shotgun. The shotgun had been a fourteenth birthday present from her father, Dan Koots, an avid bird hunter.

Gail had grown up in Galveston, fishing and hunting with her father. Her mother had died when she was six. At age twenty-two, Gail graduated from Rice University and entered the UT Southwestern Medical School in Dallas, where she met Jerry after he limped into the emergency room following a cycling accident. The romance flourished, and they married nine months later.

The compensation from the lawsuit for the cycling accident paid for their first house, which they purchased for cash in the Houston suburb of Bellaire. After a few years, the University of Texas Medical Branch-Galveston, or UTMB-Galveston, hired Gail as a teaching doctor, and Jerry opened the Galveston branch office for his law firm. They bought the three-story sky-blue house overlooking the bay from Jerry's legal fees after a tragic—and very profitable—regional jet crash in Montana.

Gail took the shotgun with her left hand but remained engrossed in the phone in her right hand. "Now they're hitting the Randalls. Damn, the National Guard is shooting people at Randalls."

"Well, too bad the National Guard wasn't at the Target."

"Jerry, you can't say that. They can't just shoot people."

"The governor declared martial law. I think they can."

While the island itself was descending into anarchy, the airspace above Galveston had turned into a beehive of helicopters. Some were delivering food and supplies; others were delivering soldiers from the Texas State Guard to enforce the emergency martial law declaration signed by the governor. Helicopters from several Houston television stations added to the aerial mix. High above it all, Texas Air Guard fighter jets circled the island, waiting for the return of whoever or whatever had caused all the chaos.

Over what had previously been the Galveston Airport, Texas Air Guard C-130Js had airdropped pallets of food, medical supplies, and, of course, toilet paper. Galveston had enough food to survive for several weeks.

Gail received a text and grimaced as she read it. "They're setting up a triage tent at the medical school. They're asking for volunteers to staff it. Jerry, I think I should go."

"Do you really want to go downtown right now? It's not safe."

"Well, I'm a doctor. I'm needed. And with all classes canceled, what else am I going to do? If I can't teach, I might as well treat people."

"Gail, downtown is complete anarchy right now. How can you stay safe in that chaos?"

"Is it safe anywhere on the island right now?"

Jerry gave Gail a grave expression. She looked back down at her phone. "Besides, it says they have soldiers surrounding the perimeter of the campus. Nobody goes in or out without authorization. So, the campus is probably the safest place on the island."

"Okay, you can go, but only if you let me drive you and only if your dad comes and stays with the kids and the dogs while we're gone."

After Gail's father arrived, Gail and Jerry headed for downtown and UTMB-Galveston. Jerry had his pistol sitting on the center console of Gail's Mercedes SUV. Police sirens wailed off and on, but the beating sound of helicopter rotors intermixed with fighter jets was constant. One mile past the turnoff for the airport, they came to a police roadblock. Gail flashed the officer her medical school ID, and he waved them through.

Jerry's cellphone rang. It was James. Jerry touched the phone icon on the screen in the center console and placed the call on speakerphone. "Hey, James, what's up? Gail's here with me."

"Oh, hi, Gail. Jerry, I booked you a seat on the nonstop flight tomorrow to Honolulu. First Class."

Gail frowned as she shook her head.

"What? Honolulu? Tomorrow?" Jerry shrugged. "James, I can't get off this island, and you want me to fly to Hawai'i?"

"Yes. Have you not heard the news? An Australian Air Force plane located the survivors—a hundred and ninety-eight of them. A Fijian naval ship picked them up, and it's headed to Suva, Fiji. The National Transportation Safety Board and the Civil Aviation Safety Authority of Australia are going to interview all of them. They'll be flown to either Honolulu or Sydney in military transports afterward. You need to be in Honolulu when those people touch down. This case could be a cash cow for the firm."

Jerry shook his head. "James, do you realize what's going on here? We're under martial law."

"Well, that doesn't mean you can't leave."

"People are looting and destroying our Target. Soldiers with machine guns are everywhere here."

"Sounds like a good time to leave. I hear Hawai'i is very nice in January."

"James, come on."

"I'm serious, Jerry. This case could be huge for us. I'm talking hundreds of millions of dollars here, and you're our aviation law guy. We've got to reach those people first."

"But Honolulu? Now? With what's going on here?"

"Yes. Jerry, this has the potential to make us rich beyond our wildest dreams. Hell, after we're done with them, we'll be able to buy what's left of Central Pacific Airlines."

"But James, I can't—"

"Jerry, listen. I've made some calls. A lot of weird shit happened on the flight just before it ditched."

"Weird shit? James, a lot of weird shit happened *here* the other night."

"I know, Jerry. I've heard all about it. But focus on this lawsuit for a minute. Before they crashed, all the power went out in the cabin. Several passengers reported the engines became quiet. Then they started all these crazy maneuvers. And we know that there were no distress calls, no ADS-B, nothing. It sounds so much like Malaysia 370. And get this— according to one of the flight attendants, only one of the three pilots, Kuparr Winston, survived the ditching—who, by the way, is missing now. He wasn't with the survivors that were rescued. Something is just not right here."

"This has all been confirmed?" Jerry asked. "It's not a rumor?"

"Direct from a high-ranking federal official."

"So, it sounds like—"

"Like you better get yourself to Honolulu before all our competitors do. There's one more thing, and it's huge. The American, Canadian, and European passengers are flying to Honolulu in two days. I called in a fa- vor to Senator Damonati to try and get you a VIP pass into the passenger terminal at Hickam."

"You what? No kidding?"

Gail mouthed the word "no."

"No kidding. You'll have the first shot at these poor sops. You'll need to be a little discreet. They'll be processed and reunited with their families. You could have a hectic day or, if things go well, a hectic couple of days. I'll send you a paralegal as soon as I can scrounge one up. This is too easy. You can't say no, Jerry."

Jerry sighed. "What time is the flight?"

Gail shook her head and glared at him. "Jerry, you can't be serious? You're not actually considering going to Honolulu tomorrow and leav- ing us here?"

"It's United Flight 3," James said. "It leaves Intercontinental Airport at 10:05 in the morning. You'll have a lie-flat bed in first class. I also booked you a suite at the Sherwood Waikiki for the next seven days."

"Well, that sounds great," Jerry said. "But how do I get to Intercontinental Airport? There's this thing called Galveston Bay in the way."

"I've chartered a boat. It will pick you up at your dock at six in the morning and take you to a pier in Kemah, where I'll be waiting in a limo. We can stop by your mom's place and check on her on the way if you'd like."

"No! Jerry. No!" Gail said in exasperation. "You can't!"

"I understand your fear, Gail, but this could be huge for you and Jerry," James said.

Jerry pressed the mute button on the screen. "Gail, we can get your dad to stay with you and the kids while I'm gone. I'm sure he'd love it, and he can bring his small arsenal with him."

"Are y'all still there?" James said.

Jerry unmuted the call. "Yes, we're still here."

"Gail, Jerry's our aviation guy," James said. "This case could elevate the reputation of our firm both nationally and internationally, and it is critical for Jerry's future with the firm."

Gail frowned. "Are you threatening us, James?"

Jerry began shaking his head at Gail.

"No, of course not, Gail. But I've spoken with the other partners. We're all in agreement. For one, we have to move fast on this case to get ahead of the competition, and two, this case could be worth many millions. Finally, Jerry's the guy to lead this case for us. It's his specialty." James paused for a second. "Listen, you two, I know things are a little crazy over there right now, but with—"

"A little crazy, James? You think things here are *a little crazy* over here?" Gail slumped back in her seat.

"Okay, a lot crazy," James said. "But I've been told helicopters and small boats are delivering food and supplies around the clock, so nobody is going to starve. Also, did you know the Texas State Guard is going to build a temporary floating bridge across San Luis Pass?"

"And how long will that take?" Gail asked.

"I don't know exactly, but things there on the island should start calming down once people realize they will have food to put in their mouths and toilet paper to wipe their asses."

Jerry turned to Gail and shrugged. He pressed the mute button once more. "He's got a point. Things should start to calm down here."

Gail turned away and said nothing. Jerry took his cellphone off mute again. "James, I'll call you back in a little while. We're driving and need to discuss this."

"Okay, call me. Bye."

Jerry hung up his cellphone. "Gail, I know this is a bad time to leave, but this case could be the biggest, most important opportunity I ever have. This could be a life-changer for me. It could be a life-changer for us. We moved here for your job and to be back in your hometown. I begged the firm to let me open a Galveston office. We also moved here to be near your father, so let's take this opportunity for him to help. Get him to move in while I'm gone."

"So, this is all on me? I owe you this?"

"No, but I'm saying this case is critical to my career and critical to my position with the firm. Not to mention how much money we could make from it."

"Money? We already have a great lifestyle. I'm a doctor. You're a lawyer. We've got an awesome house. We buy whatever we want. How much more money do we need? How much is enough? Are you willing to sacrifice your family's safety for more money?"

"Okay, as I said, it's not just about money. It's about my position with the firm, too. James pretty much said I don't have much of a choice. The partners are insisting that I go—and go now. Gail, please. I need this. I can't keep doing the ambulance-chasing stuff while I wait for some plane to crash."

"Jerry, we've got guns with us right now. I've got a loaded shotgun next to me, and I'm not going hunting. Do you really need to go to Hawai'i? Now?"

Jerry nodded. "Yes. Look, you and the kids can come with me to Honolulu. We could all use a little time away."

Gail shook her head. "I can't leave work right now. The hospital is packed—the emergency room is packed. I can't turn my back on all these people that need me. I have a career, too, you know."

Gail turned her head away from Jerry and stared out the windshield. "All right, I'll call my dad in a little while and see if he can stay with us while you're gone."

CHAPTER SEVENTEEN

200 Kilometers Above Earth
05:30 GMT, 3 January

"Stand up," said the familiar female voice. "They are ready for you."

Kup turned to the left to see the Warden and the Safety Officer glaring down at him. This time, it wasn't a hologram. Both were wearing white skinsuits. Both had identical blue backpacks.

Kup sat up. "Please don't do this! I won't say a word. Please just take me home."

"I will take you to the cryogenic preparation room." The Warden held a flat half-meter-long strip of metal in his left hand. "Now stand up and hold both hands out in front of you."

"You're really going to Cancel me?"

"Yes, of course." The Safety Officer nodded.

"I don't even get a last meal or anything? Not even a last goodbye to my family? This is it?"

"You will come with me now, Kuparr Winston"—the Warden held up a pencil-sized metallic cylinder in his right hand—"or the *tranqtube* can end this now for you."

Kup slid off the cushion. "No, no, I'll go." He outstretched his arms toward the Warden.

"Keep both of your hands out in front of you," said the Warden as he placed the metal strip across Kup's wrists. The ends of the metal strip slowly curved around each wrist to form a cuff. "You may now lower your hands if you wish." The Warden pointed to the open doorway that led to a corridor. "It is this way and to the left. This experience will all be over soon if you cooperate and even sooner if you do not."

"Goodbye, Kuparr Winston. Stay safe." The Safety Officer walked through the open doorway and turned right.

Kup's stomach churned. He felt like throwing up.

The Warden nodded toward the doorway. "It is time."

Kup shook his head as he walked through the doorway into a dim gray oval corridor with a corrugated metal floor. Along the curved walls, closed doorways were spread about a meter apart. "I can't believe you are doing this. I can't believe I saved your life, and you're doing this."

"We will walk in this direction and then take a lift to a lower level." The Warden pointed down the corridor, which was empty.

Kup began walking. "Please, just let me go. I promise I'll keep my mouth shut. I just want to go home." Kup read the Thai-like script above a reinforced doorway on the right side of the corridor. *Emergency Exit? I know there's an escape pod on every level.*

The Warden followed Kup's eyes toward the escape pod doorway. "No, I cannot. No, you will not."

"Bloody hell, just let me go home! I won't hurt any of you. Please, don't Cancel me. I want to see my wife again. I want to see my parents … my friends. I want to finish my life. Please give me my life back—I gave you yours! I just—"

"You will not speak of this inequity," the Warden hissed. "It cannot be—"

"Please."

The Warden stopped. "I cannot."

"Please help me. Please. I'm begging you."

The Warden looked at the tranqtube in his right hand. "I will keep Society safe."

"You both will continue walking!" the Safety Officer yelled as she ate a small cereal bar. She stood at the far end of the corridor, forty meters away.

The Warden looked down the corridor at the Safety Officer. "No, I cannot. We must—"

Kup grabbed the tranqtube with both hands and jammed it into the Warden's right thigh.

The Warden grabbed Kup's wrists as his hundred-and-ninety-kilogram mass collapsed onto the metal grid flooring with a thud that reverberated throughout the corridor. His hands fell to his sides.

Kup stood over the Warden's rigid skinsuit-wrapped body. "That's for my people—*all* my people. I should have let you drown."

"What have you done?!" the Safety Officer yelled.

Kup tossed the tranqtube onto the floor and reached into the Warden's backpack.

"Stop! Stop what you are doing!" The Safety Officer's footsteps pounded the metal floor from thirty meters away.

Kup pulled an orange orb from the Warden's backpack and began running toward the reinforced doorway marked "Emergency Exit."

The Safety Officer was twenty meters away. "Stop! You will stop!"

The reinforced doorway slid open as Kup approached it. A second clear doorway opened a split second later. Sunshine streamed into the corridor, and Kup could see stars and the Earth below through the transparent circular walls on the other side of the doorway. An orange light began flashing from the ceiling of the corridor.

Kup jumped through the portal into a cylinder big enough for three people. The circular walls, floor, and top of the cylinder were transparent except for three small cushions with straps along the wall opposite the doorway.

The sound of footsteps crashing onto the metal floor grew louder and louder as the tempo of the flashes of orange light from the ceiling increased.

The Safety Officer screamed, "You will *not* leave!"

Kup looked around the inside of the escape pod for the orb insertion point. The footsteps were close now. The Safety Officer was only three meters away.

Kup slammed the orange ovoid into a small oval opening in the side of the escape pod. The doorways shut, and an explosive charge ejected the pod downward. Kup shot up to the ceiling.

After the initial explosive ejection, the pod settled into freefall. Kup floated down the pod's wall and buckled himself into the middle of the three sets of straps. What had been blinding sunshine transitioned into a waning twilight. Above him, the triangular shape of the Command Ship receded. Below him, dim, featureless clouds drifted over some portion of the Earth's surface. Kup did not know where or what he was falling toward, only that it was nighttime below.

The Command Ship was a dull star when Kup began to sense his increased weight as the pod decelerated. Minutes later, the Command Ship vanished from view as the escape pod entered some clouds. Snowflakes, illuminated by an unseen moon, streaked past as the electrical charges of St. Elmo's fire enveloped the outside of the pod. Kup strained against the straps from the combined forces of gravity and deceleration.

The pod sank into several feet of snow with a gentle thud. The snow shooting diagonally by the pod obscured two distant red lights.

A small orange light in the pod's ceiling flashed before the clear door slid open. Icy wind and snow blasted into the pod. *I'm back on Earth—somewhere. Somewhere cold.*

Kup looked down at his bare feet and his short-sleeve uniform shirt. His cuffed hands struggled to release the buckle of the restraining strap, and he shivered as he climbed out of the escape pod. His feet sank into the snow, which blunted the razor-sharp edges of the *a'a* below.

CHAPTER EIGHTEEN

Leilani Damonati stood at the railing of the lanai of her condominium. "Luka, I cannot believe Command has decided to proceed without the Peace Squad in place."

Luka shot a melted mouthful of frozen mai tai over the edge of the lanai. "You will have to continue to disinform until the Peace Squad arrives. After that, it won't matter; it will be too late. Until then, aliens do not exist." He reached into the bottom left pocket of his cargo shorts and pulled out what looked like an ordinary smartphone. "Uh oh. This is not good."

"What's not good, Luka?"

"The pilot that was scheduled for Cancellation escaped."

"Escaped? I don't understand. How could he escape from a Command Ship? How did your people let this happen?"

Luka read from his *commblock*. "He attacked the Warden with a tranqtube and somehow got a control orb to operate an escape pod." Luka sucked a mouthful of frozen mai tai through the straw in his drink.

Leilani gritted her teeth. "Luka, put the damn drink down! Where is Winston now?"

Luka swished the mai tai in his mouth as he read. He then launched the contents of his mouth over the side of the lanai once again. "Mauna Kea. The summit of Mauna Kea. They want us to retrieve him and then cancel him."

"Cancel him? We don't have a cryogenic facility down here."

Luka moved the straw away from his lips several inches. "I think they mean your people's kind of cancel."

"Why doesn't the Command Ship send a team to retrieve him?"

"They say they only have a skeleton crew aboard. They cannot spare anyone, and, of course, there's no Peace Squad aboard, so they want us to handle it. 'Retrieve and cancel'—that is what it says. Eventually, we will return him to the Command Ship. In the meantime, he must be discredited."

"Okay, so I can cancel him, but they also want us to retrieve him? From Mauna Kea? How are we supposed to do that? If I were to requisition a military helicopter, it would raise all sorts of questions—uncomfortable questions. What about your transport? Could we use that?"

Luka sucked a mouthful of mai tai into his mouth.

Leilani walked over to Luka, grabbed the tiki-shaped glass, and tossed it over the side of the lanai. "Luka, answer me!"

Luka watched the glass fall twenty-seven floors and into the condominium's swimming pool. He spit what was left in his mouth over the railing. "Your people would eventually detect my transport, especially if we were loitering in the same general area. It is not a good idea."

Leilani began texting. "I need to get Noa in on this. We need to be prepared. If Winston shows up at his house, maybe I can get him here and into custody. I just need a pretext to do so—"

"Just say he raped her."

"What?"

"You said the governor's daughter—"

"Susan Kupule?"

"Yes. You said she was mad because there were rumors about her and Winston. So, make the rumors true. He raped her. You were going to possibly use her to cancel him before he was captured—use her to also get him arrested. More bang money."

"Bang money? Bang for your buck?"

"That is what I said."

"No, it is not, Luka. But let me think … a rape charge? That's a little beyond what she has already agreed to do, but Susan does hate him. I wonder just how much money it will take to make her really hate him?" Leilani began dialing a number on her cellphone.

"Hello?"

"Susan, dear. It's Leilani Damonati again. Sorry to bother you at this late hour, but it's extremely urgent."

"Okay, Senator, but I'm out with some friends. Can I call you back tomorrow?"

"No, you may not. Tomorrow will be too late. Do you remember Noa Kim, my chief of staff here in Hawai'i?"

"Yes, I remember him. He's hard to forget."

"Yes, yes, he is. I need you to meet with him as soon as possible. Where are you?"

"We're at the Grand Hawaiian Bar and Grill."

"Stay put. Noa will be there shortly."

"Uh, okay, Senator. I'll be here. What's this about?"

"Noa will give you all the details, my dear. Just sit tight."

"Okay, Senator."

"Excellent—"

"Is he still single?"

"Noa? Yes, my dear. He's quite single. We must get together for lunch soon. *A hui hou.*"

"Alo—"

Leilani hung up and texted as she spoke. "Luka, what did your people learn about Winston's Reckoning? I know it was interrupted, but just how much of the Warden's mind did he get?"

"They could not tell. That is why he is considered so unsafe. He may know too much."

"Damn. If he has the Warden's technical knowledge … he could ruin everything."

CHAPTER NINETEEN

The Big Island of Hawai'i
20:30 HST, 2 January

Kup crested a small cinder cone and saw a plowed road that led up to the lights to his left. Through the snow, the faint outline of a building became visible. Instead of a roof, it had a large white dome.

Kup wobbled onto the icy road. His legs and feet had become numb extensions of his body. Each step required his complete concentration.

Minutes later, he strained to read a sign illuminated by the red light next to a closed door.

CANADA – FRANCE – HAWAII TELESCOPE
NO VISITORS
MAHALO

Kup spotted a blue Toyota Tacoma pickup truck with Hawai'i license plates parked next to the door. *Am I on Mauna Kea?* He took a step toward the truck, and his right foot spun out on a patch of ice. His face slammed into the road.

He tried to stand, but his numb feet could not get any traction. Using the metal band holding his hands together, he crawled the remaining twenty feet to the door. The overhang above the door had left an ice-free zone, and he was able to stand. He grabbed onto the doorknob to steady himself and tried to turn it. It wouldn't move. Blood from his feet, legs, and nose dripped onto the concrete and froze.

Kup pounded on the door with both fists. He opened his mouth to yell for help, but a dry hiss was all he could manage.

The door opened. A stout middle-aged man stood at the entrance, examining Kup. He wore gray overalls and had a utility belt wrapped around his waist. His graying black hair was greasy and unkempt, as if he hadn't shampooed it in weeks. He held a battery-powered drill in his left hand. His eyes landed on Kup's bleeding bare feet. "What the hell happened to you? Did you get in a wreck or something up here?"

Kup stared at the man as he shivered.

The man eyed Kup's epaulets. "Are you some sort of pilot?"

Kup nodded.

"What … did your plane crash up here?"

Kup shook his head and tried to point with his cuffed hands.

"Did you get arrested?"

Kup collapsed onto the ground.

The man placed the drill on the floor and dragged Kup into the building and into a break room. "Would you like some coffee?"

Kup opened his eyes and nodded.

The man poured a cup of coffee and placed it on the cheap plastic table in the middle of the room. "You need to sit up." He pulled Kup up and onto a chair at the table. "My name is Ikaika. Ikaika Pacheko. I'm the maintenance supervisor for the observatory. Who are you?"

Kup blinked several times and grabbed the coffee mug with both hands. He took a sip of coffee. "Thank you. Thank you for the coffee."

"You're welcome. Now, who the hell are you, and why did you get arrested?"

Kup swallowed hard. "Kuparr Winston. I'm Kuparr Winston." He took a long sip of coffee as he looked around the room. A refrigerator and a small sink were on the far wall. NNN was playing on a small TV in the corner of the room. Along the walls were various photographs of planets, nebulae, stars, and galaxies.

Ikaika studied Kup. "Okay. Now, do you mind telling me why you are walking around the summit of Mauna Kea barefoot in a pilot uniform with these weird handcuffs?"

"I landed up here in an escape pod," Kup said.

"Escape pod?"

"From a UFO, an alien spaceship."

Ikaika rolled his eyes. "Go on."

Kup was relieved he could feel his feet again. "I'm a pilot for Central

Pacific Airlines. We encountered the U—the alien spaceship flying from Sydney to Honolulu, and we ended up ditching northeast of Vanuatu. I—"

"Wait … the Central Pacific crash? You were a pilot on that flight?"

"Yes."

"I think the news said one of them is still missing. Is that you?"

"Well, it must be me. The other two pilots are dead."

"Okay." Ikaika nodded. "So, how did you get here from … ?"

"Vanuatu? We ditched about a hundred miles northeast of the islands of Vanuatu. I would guess it was about three hundred miles west-northwest of Fiji."

"Oh, okay. Fiji. So, how did you get from there to here? A UFO?"

"Yes. They abducted me. I escaped using—"

"The escape pod?"

"Yes."

"And you landed on the summit of Mauna Kea? You couldn't have found a nice warm beach?"

"I wasn't exactly given a choice."

Ikaika rubbed his chin with his thick, calloused left hand. "So, I can't say that I believe in UFOs or all this alien crap, but I can't say that I don't believe in them, either. I do know something weird is going on, and the military says they've encountered things they can't explain, more or less."

He sat back in his chair and looked over at a photo of the Crab Nebula. "So, why'd they do it? I mean, why did this UFO pick you up?"

"They were picking up this alien that I had rescued."

"You rescued an alien? Well, shit. This gets weirder and weirder. How did you do that?"

"His spacecraft was sinking, and he couldn't swim. I jumped in the water and pulled him aboard my raft." Kup emptied his coffee mug.

Ikaika refilled it. "So, this UFO picks up your alien friend and gives you a ride, too?"

"Yeah, basically. That's the story."

"Damn. Crazy shit. But then again, we got a lot of crazy going on right now in the world. Speaking of which, I'm not sure you are aware of it, but this island got attacked, like Galveston and Iceland. There's no way off the island now except by helicopter or those Marine Osprey planes. You're stuck here."

"I live in Kona. I already knew about the attack."

"Did the aliens tell you?"

"The aliens did it."

"No kidding. Damn crazy shit. NNN has been ignoring the whole thing, but there are all kinds of rumors going around saying it was the Russians that did it. I think they're all full of shit. I was outside on my lanai in Waimea with my family on New Year's Eve. I saw the flash of light over the port in Kawaihae. It wasn't the Russians."

"No, it wasn't the Russians. Ikaika, could I borrow your phone? I'd like to call my wife. I want to go home."

"Sure." Ikaika pulled out his phone, unlocked it, and handed it to Kup. Kup dialed Kahealani's number.

"Hello."

"Kahea, it's me. It's Kup."

"Kup? You're alive? Oh my gosh, you're alive!" Kahea cried through the phone. "Are you okay?"

Kup swallowed hard. "I'm okay. Can you come get me? I'm …" His voice began to crack. "I'm at the summit of Mauna Kea, at an observatory."

"Mauna Kea? How did you—"

"Kahea, just come get me."

"I'm leaving right now, but don't hang up. I'm afraid I'll somehow lose you."

"Okay, I can keep talking, but please hurry. Something bad is about to happen—to our island."

"What do you mean? We already got attacked by the Russians. There's already no way on or off the island. Are you saying it's going to get worse?"

"Yes. A lot worse. Aliens—they are real, and they're here. They attacked our island, and they attacked Galveston and Iceland. They're about to dump over a hundred thousand of their convicts on each of the three islands. And none of us, human or alien, can get off the island once they enable the EMP."

Ikaika's eyes widened as he refilled Kup's coffee mug once more.

"What are you talking about, Kup?" Kahealani asked. "What's an EMP?"

"Electromagnetic pulse. It knocks out anything electronic—permanently. Command Ships stationed above each island will create targeted EMP zones around each of their respective islands. Anything electronic passing through these zones will be permanently disabled."

"So, our phones won't work if we pass through this zone and leave the island?

"Phones. Boats. Airplanes. Helicopters. Some antique boats built a hundred years ago might work, but anything remotely modern will be rendered unusable. Nothing in. Nothing out."

"Oh my gosh. This is horrible. Kup, you've got to warn people!"

"Kahea, I just want to sleep. I've had it. There's nothing we can do. If we could somehow sabotage their systems, the experiments would fail, and they would leave. I know that. But we just don't have the technology."

"But we have to try! We have to think of something, Kup."

"Kahea, I need to lay low. Maybe even disappear."

"Disappear?"

"They were going to Cancel me, Kahea."

"Cancel you?"

"Freeze me. Cryogenic sleep. Forever."

"What? Freeze you? We've got to stop them, Kup."

"No, Kahea."

"Kup, you've got to defend yourself, and not just from these aliens. I've been seeing all kinds of things in the news. People are saying you're responsible for the crash. They're saying terrible things about you. You've got to set the record straight. What if I tell them?"

"No, Kahea. Absolutely not. Don't say a word about this to anyone." Kup looked up at Ikaika, who was holding a metal grinder in his right hand as he eyed the metal band across Kup's wrists. "You, too, Ikaika. I've already told you too much."

That night, after Kup had fallen asleep in his own bed, Kahealani wrote an email to every email address she had and made a post on her Facebook page. The email went viral. The Facebook post lasted 2.6 seconds.

CHAPTER TWENTY

Honolulu, Hawai'i
07:00 HST, 3 January

Leilani smiled as Noa took a seat in front of her expansive desk. His eyes were bloodshot red. His tan shirt was wrinkled.

"You look like shit, Noa."

"It was a long night."

Leilani cocked her eyes toward the window as a Central Pacific 737 banked right as it climbed away from Honolulu International Airport. "So, how much did it take for her to agree to our deal?"

"A hundred thousand."

Leilani nodded.

"And I slept with her."

"I see. Her two favorite things, according to Gretchen."

"In fact, I had a difficult time getting away from her so that I could take care of the IT issues at the FBI. She can be a bit mean when she doesn't get what she wants." Noa glanced at himself in the mirror on the far wall. "I do look like shit. My apologies, Senator."

"No apology is needed, Noa. I wish I had ten more Stolings like you on staff."

Noa smiled and flashed his whitened, orthodontically corrected teeth. "Thank you, Senator."

"You said you took care of the IT issues at the FBI. So, everything is in place?"

"Yes, the emails and texts are embedded in the FBI servers. They're also in the email servers, cellphones, and computers of Susan Kupule, Winston, and Winston's wife."

"Excellent."

"Correction. Winston's cellphone is offline and unlocatable. I assume the EMP fried it."

"And Lonnie Yamaguchi is still not at Winston's house?"

"No, Senator. He ended up getting towed off Saddle Road. He's back in Hilo now, trying to rent a car."

"Utterly useless. Another political hire I had to stick somewhere. Who knew I would actually need my Big Island field representative for something important? In any case, we still have no idea if Winston is even alive?"

"Nothing so far."

"Well, let's just hope he's either dead or too terrified to talk. He could ruin everything. A partial Reckoning ... why would the Warden do such a stupid thing?"

"Senator, I've got the FBI set to apprehend Winston tonight if necessary—if he's alive and if we can determine his location. All it will take is a phone call, and he's ours. His past will become what we make it."

"Yes, of course. You know, Noa, with all the trouble you've gone to with this Winston character, perhaps we should make a proper example of him for SB 950. That is, if he's alive, of course."

"Sure, Senator. We could use a scapegoat for the launch of the bill. Paint him as a mentally unstable sexual predator—it would be easy. Make the traveling public feel unsafe with people like him flying them around the country, around the world. They'll be clamoring for the government to monitor people in safety-sensitive positions."

"My thoughts exactly. We could use his case as the impetus to launch the bill a little earlier than we had planned. Are the technical plans in place to begin the social tracking and scoring?"

"All set, Senator."

Leilani stood up from her desk and walked over to the window. "Look at them down there, Noa. Individuals—they aimlessly wander through life without the collective belonging and racial identity of Society. Soon, they'll be clamoring for safety, and their history will be replaced. We will define their future as we define their past."

"Society must advance, Senator."

"Yes, it must, Noa, and it will. Unless, of course, this Winston guy fucks it all up. Make sure that doesn't happen."

"Yes, Senator. Will that be all?"

"There's one more thing, and I hate to even say it—we will need to bring Gretchen in on this. She's bound to hear something from her sister or see some sort of correspondence between all of us. Offer her a big enough carrot, whatever it takes. Threaten her as well. Make sure she's terrified."

"Of course, Senator. I'll get right on it."

"Excellent. And let me know the second you get confirmation of Winston's status."

Noa stood up, left the room, and closed the office door behind him.

Seconds later, a "Damonati for Hawai'i" coffee mug shattered against the other side of the office door.

Noa cocked his head as he heard the muffled voice of his boss. "That bitch! Noa, get back in here! Winston's at his house!"

CHAPTER TWENTY-ONE

Honolulu, Hawai'i
17:00 HST, 3 January

After the long flight, Jerry needed a beer, fresh air, and a view. He plopped his laptop and yellow legal pad onto the beachfront bar at the Sherwood Waikiki resort. In front of him in the distance, surfers rode the gentle blue waves of Waikiki. To his left, Diamond Head jutted its distinct profile out from the line of high-rise hotels that ended at the beach.

Jerry had unpacked and changed into board shorts and a T-shirt. A pair of maroon ATM flip-flops adorned his feet. He signaled the bartender for a beer, opened his laptop, and began reading the plethora of emails concerning Central Pacific 855 that James had sent him while he was airborne on the nine-hour flight from Houston. The circumstances of the crash were getting weirder by the day, as apparently one of the first officers was alive, and his wife had written a mass email claiming that aliens were responsible for the crash. She claimed that aliens were, in fact, responsible for the attacks on Iceland, Galveston, and Hawai'i Island as well. Jerry shook his head as he read.

The bartender laid the pint glass of beer in front of Jerry. "On vacation?"

Jerry took a drink. The cold beer refreshed him as it slid down the back of his throat. "No. I'm here on business." He tapped his large college ring on the bar as he watched a lime-green bikini swagger across the beach with a blond girl and surfboard attached.

"Oh. Where are you from?"

"Huh ... oh, Galveston ... Texas."

The bartender stopped in his tracks. "Galveston! Oh, brah, it's terrible. All those starving people. It's just like the Big Island."

"Well, I left there this morning. I didn't see anyone starving."

"I got a bunch of emails about it, brah. People don't have any food or even basic supplies. It sounds really bad."

Jerry began shaking his head. "Well, as I said, I saw nothing like that. There were people looting and stuff, but I don't think they were starving."

"Looting—oh yeah, I read people were rioting at the Costco in Kona. Like, they were rushing the people at the entryway trying to get in. At Target and Safeway in Kona, people were grabbing whatever food they could carry and running out the doors. They closed the Walmart in Hilo. There was nothing left in the store to sell—or steal. The mayor of Hawai'i Island asked the governor to declare martial law, but he refused. Crazy stuff, man."

Jerry nodded in agreement.

"And nobody has said squat about who did this." The bartender filled a pint glass full of IPA from one of the taps. "You know they know. They just don't want us to know."

Jerry grimaced. "Who do you think did it?"

"Aliens, brah. They did it from outer space. That pilot's wife wrote an email. She says they're gonna invade—any day now."

Jerry shrugged. *Four bartenders here, and I get the chatty conspiracy theorist.* "Aliens? Really? You believe all that?"

"Brah, what country could do what they did?"

"Well, I don't know, but … aliens? Come on, man. There's nothing about this email on NNN, and I can't find anything on social media about it. It's probably just disinformation."

"Brah, I read all about it this morning in the email. And NNN, they just report what the Man wants you to know."

Jerry's cellphone began ringing, much to his relief. It was Gail. The bartender turned away from Jerry to wash some dirty beer glasses.

Jerry answered, "Aloha, dear."

"Enjoying a mai tai, Jerry?"

"Well, actually, I'm having a cold beer right now."

"Awesome. You must be tired after your long flight in that lie-flat, business-class seat. How's the weather?"

"It's beautiful, Gail. Just beautiful. We've got to come back. It's been too long."

"That sounds great, Jerry. In the meantime, we've got a guy bleeding out in our front yard."

"What?"

"Dad shot him."

"Gail, what are you talking about?"

"A guy tried to break into the house. Dad shot him. The police took over an hour and a half to get here. They said they were too busy. Jerry, gangs are roaming the neighborhood. They're everywhere."

"Is everyone okay?"

"Yes, we're all okay. The guy Dad shot isn't doing so well, though. Dad shot him in his right hand and his left knee. He's bleeding really badly. The police handcuffed him to a tree. They gave Dad the keys to the handcuffs and left. They said an ambulance would get here when it got here. I did what I could for him, but the guy is going to bleed out."

"So, somebody tried to break into the house, and your dad shot him?"

"Yes, that's what I've been telling you."

"Okay, tell me what happened. Start from the beginning."

Gail took a deep breath and exhaled through the phone. "We were all sitting in the media room watching a movie with the surround sound blasting. About thirty minutes into the movie, Michael Phelps jumped up and ran out of the room. He started barking and growling from what sounded like the living room. I'd never heard him growl like that. Anyway, Dad and I walked downstairs to see what he was barking at and saw a man had smashed a hole in one of the French doors in the living room. He had his hand through the hole and was trying to unlock the door from the inside."

"And then what happened?" Jerry asked.

"Well, I started screaming for him to go away. Dad had his rifle and aimed it at the man's hand on the doorknob. The man looked at both of us and pulled his hand back through the opening in the window. He pulled out a pistol. Dad shot the pistol out of his hand and shattered the remains of the French door. The man started screaming at us. Dad walked up to the shattered door and yelled at the man to leave. The man started reaching down to the ground to grab his pistol, so Dad shot him in the leg, which sent him tumbling down the staircase. Dad got the man's pistol and held a gun on him while I called the police."

"But is everyone okay?"

"Okay? Yeah, if you're asking if everyone is physically okay, then yes. Of course, Cindy won't stop crying. She's practically choking Michael Phelps; she's clutching him so tight. Mikey has locked himself in his room and won't come out. Jerry, you left your family. You abandoned us here in a crisis."

Jerry sat back and looked out over the blue waters off Waikiki. It was a beautiful, busy, peaceful, and happy scene. People were swimming and surfing. Families were sitting together on the beach. The trade winds were blowing just enough to keep the temperature in the perfect range. Meanwhile, his family was in a war zone, and he had left them. "Gail, I'm so sorry, but I did want you and the kids to come with me."

"Don't put this on me, Jerry. I told you I couldn't leave work right now." Gail exhaled. "You're such an ass, Jerry. All you care about is money and your status."

The bartender pointed to Jerry's beer and mouthed, "Another one?"

Jerry nodded. "Gail, I'm so sorry I agreed to come here. I got so excited about the case and the prospect of what it could mean for me and for my career and all the money I could make. After the governor declared martial law and brought in all the soldiers, I thought things would start quieting down. I thought y'all would be okay. I guess I was wrong."

"Admitting you were wrong will not keep your family safe tonight, Jerry. If Michael Phelps hadn't been with us, the man would have gotten into the house. He could have killed us. He could have killed your kids."

"Gail, I can be on a plane tonight and be back in Houston tomorrow morning. I can charter a boat and be—"

A text popped up on Jerry's phone from James Templeton:

> CPA 855 getting even weirder. Flight Attendant says Kuparr Winston raped her on a layover in Tahiti in November.

"What? Jerry, the damage is done."

The bartender delivered Jerry's second beer.

"You might as well just stay in Honolulu at this point and finish your precious lawsuit."

Jerry jotted down some notes on his legal pad.

"Jerry, hello? Are you there? Talk to me."

A second text appeared:

> Flight attendant says Winston threatened to crash a
> plane if she told anybody.

"Oh shit!" Jerry took a sip of his beer.

"Jerry, what's going on over there?"

A third text popped up:

> Leilani Damonati verified everything so totally
> credible.

"Jerry! What the hell! Talk to me!"

A fourth text appeared:

> Calling Leilani Damonati now I'll let u know what I
> find out.

Jerry put the phone back to his ear. "Gail, I'm just so sorry about all this. I really thought things would calm down there." He jotted down another note on his legal pad. "Gail? Are you there? Gail?"

He pulled the phone from his ear. The call had ended.

CHAPTER TWENTY-TWO

Hapuna Beach, The Big Island of Hawai'i
20:00 HST, 3 January

"So, now they're saying you raped a flight attendant?" Kahealani stood in the middle of their ground-floor hotel room at the Sherwood Hapuna Beach Hotel with her phone in her shaking left hand. "What the hell is going on, Kup?"

Kup sat up from the couch. "What are you talking about, Kahea? I didn't rape anybody."

"People are texting me about it. My parents are texting me about it. Wait … the governor's daughter? You raped the governor's daughter?"

"Susan Kupule says that I raped her?"

"Yes, Kup. She's saying that you raped her. She says you raped her on a layover in friggin' Tahiti. What the hell, Kup?"

"Kahea, I did not—"

"Oh wait … there's more! She says that you threatened to crash a plane if she ever went public about the rape. Oh my God, Kup."

"Kahea, you know I did not—"

"Who am I supposed to believe, Kup? What am I supposed to believe?"

"Kahea, I promise you. I did not rape Susan Kupule. I didn't rape anyone. The aliens … it's all true. It's all real. I—" Kup jumped up from the couch as a spotlight streamed into the hotel room through the sliding glass doors that led to the small ground-floor lanai.

A voice from outside the hotel room boomed, "Mr. Winston, this is the Hawai'i County Police. Please open the door to your hotel room."

A female voice said, "It's him."

Over static, a male voice said, "Copy that. We're standing by for your order."

"Police?" Kup mumbled.

"Mr. Winston, I am Sergeant Miller of the Hawaiʻi County Police," the female voice said from outside the window beside the front door. "I need you to open the door to your room."

Kup turned and faced the front door. "Are you kidding me? What the bloody hell have I done? I didn't rape anybody."

"Agent Perez of the FBI will explain everything to you once you open the door," Sergeant Miller said. "Please comply with my instructions."

Kup peered through the door's peephole. A thirty-something man in a blue FBI T-shirt stood ten feet back from the door in the hotel's open-air hallway.

Kup opened the door halfway.

The man said into his cellphone, "We got him."

The man hung up and walked over to Kup. "Mr. Winston, I'm Agent Perez of the FBI." He flashed his badge at Kup. "You are under arrest for intentionally crashing a US-flagged airliner. You have been determined to be a domestic terrorist, and under the Keep America Safe Act, your civil rights may and will be suspended for a period of seven calendar days from today. I'm going to handcuff you. We will transport you to the Federal Detention Center in Honolulu. There's a Marine V-22 Osprey standing by to take us there. Do you understand what I have told you?"

Kup stood there with his mouth open. "Intentional crashing?"

Agent Perez held up a pair of handcuffs.

"Are you kidding me? This is all bullshit!" Kup shook his head. "Some woman says I raped her and that I was going to crash a plane, and that's it? I'm under arrest and assumed guilty?"

Agent Perez replied, "Mr. Winston, we have evidence that indicates you threatened to crash a Central Pacific aircraft. I have orders to take you into custody. That's all I can tell you at this point. Now, please, Mr. Winston, turn around so that I may handcuff you."

"What evidence? Tell me what evidence you have!"

Agent Perez patted the revolver on his right side. "Mr. Winston, please turn around so that I may handcuff you."

Kup looked back at Kahealani as Agent Perez handcuffed him and read him his curtailed rights. She stood in the middle of the hotel room, shaking her head with her mouth open. Tears streamed down her cheeks.

Agent Perez held out his right hand. "Your cellphone, please, Mr. Winston."

A policeman walked past Kahealani with Kup's laptop in his hands.

"My phone?" Kup said. "It got fried. I tossed it."

Another policeman approached Kahealani. He said something to her, and she handed him her phone and pointed to her laptop sitting on the bedside table.

Agent Perez shook his head. "Of course you did, Mr. Winston. Of course you did." He walked Kup down the open-air corridor to the hotel lobby.

CHAPTER TWENTY-THREE

Honolulu, Hawai'i
07:00 HST, 4 January

The receptionist at Senator Damonati's office pointed to a spot on the couch, and Jerry sat down as instructed. He wore a blue business suit with a small ATM pin on his tie. A flurry of aides and assistants walked past him. Some smiled. Some glared. Some said, "Aloha." Some said, "Good morning."

He had received the text from James at five that morning. Jerry had a meeting with Senator Damonati from 7:20 to 7:35 a.m. at her office. Senator Damonati wanted to meet Jerry in person before she arranged for the VIP pass that would allow him into the passenger terminal at Joint Base Pearl-Hickam. James had said not to be late.

After several minutes, a twenty-something woman approached Jerry. "Good morning, Mr. Morgenstern. I'm Gretchen Kupule, Senator Damonati's aide. She is ready to see you now. Would you like a cup of coffee?"

Jerry stood. "No, I've had five cups already. I can't seem to get enough Kona coffee."

"Well, you better enjoy it while you can. Who knows when the ports on the Big Island will reopen."

Jerry nodded and followed Gretchen into Senator Damonati's office. He paused to gaze at the expansive view of Honolulu Harbor.

"I hope you have more important things to do this morning than stare at boats, Mr. Morgenstern."

Jerry saw Senator Damonati glaring at him from behind a pair of oversized square glasses. She sat at one end of a conference table at the side of the large office.

"Uh, no, sorry, Senator," Jerry mumbled.

Senator Damonati pointed to a seat at the opposite end of the conference table. Noa Kim sat to her right.

"This is my Hawai'i-based Chief of Staff, Noa Kim," Senator Damonati said.

Noa nodded at Jerry as he sat down.

Senator Damonati looked at Jerry. "Mr. Morgenstern, James Templeton tells me that you intend to file a lawsuit against Central Pacific Airlines, and he has requested that I get you access to the passenger terminal at Hickam."

"Yes, Senator. That would be very helpful."

Senator Damonati smirked. "Yes, I'm sure it would be extremely helpful. James also says that you are an expert in aviation law."

Jerry nodded. "Yes, Senator, that is my specialty. I studied—"

"Mr. Morgenstern, getting you access into the passenger terminal at Hickam will require that I pull some strings—call in some favors. I'm sure you understand these things."

"Yes, of course. I would be very grateful."

"Unfortunately, your gratitude is of little use to me or this nation; however, your expertise might prove valuable. Perhaps we can do each other a favor."

"Sure, Senator. Whatever I can do to—"

"Mr. Morgenstern, as I am sure you are aware by now, last week Susan Kupule, a Central Pacific flight attendant and daughter of the governor, confided in me that Kuparr Winston raped her while they were on a layover in Papeete, Tahiti. The incident occurred back in November."

"I have heard that, Senator."

"Furthermore, I am also sure you are aware that the FBI has evidence that Kuparr Winston threatened to intentionally crash a Central Pacific aircraft if Susan Kupule ever reported the rape or confided in anyone. I guess I count as 'anyone.'"

"If he did this, it's horrible, Sen—"

"Mr. Morgenstern, it is horrific what this man did to this poor woman and to the passengers aboard Central Pacific 855."

"Okay, but how can I help?"

"You can help protect the flying public from deviants like Kuparr Winston. That's what you can do, Mr. Morgenstern." Senator Damonati nodded at Noa.

"The senator is sponsoring a bill to protect the traveling public from mentally unstable aircrew like Winston," Noa said. "Senate Bill 950 will force US airlines to track the mental health and social media presence of their aircrew employees—both pilots and flight attendants. It will require the FAA to establish a website where the public can view the mental stability of the people who will be flying them around the country and the world.

"Furthermore, the FAA will develop an algorithm that will evaluate, or score, the mental and social fitness of each aircrew. The flying public will be able to input their airline, flight number, and date of travel. The website will furnish a snapshot of the mental health and stability of their assigned aircrew as well as their social stability score."

"Mr. Morgenstern"—Senator Damonati tapped her right pointer finger on the table—"just as we must keep women safe from sexual predators like Kuparr Winston, we must keep the flying public safe from social deviants like Kuparr Winston."

Jerry nodded. "Okay, but I still don't get what your bill and this FAA website have to do with me."

Senator Damonati sat back in her chair and studied Jerry. "Mr. Morgenstern, you claim to be an expert in aviation law. We are writing a senate bill that will further regulate our aviation industry and protect us all from the likes of Kuparr Winston. Tomorrow, representatives from the National Transportation Safety Board will be meeting with Kuparr Winston here in the Federal Building. I was planning on sending Noa to the meeting; however, while Noa is outstanding at most things, he is not an expert in aviation law. You are."

"Can you really get me into an NTSB meeting with Winston?" Jerry wanted to pinch himself.

Senator Damonati smiled. "Of course I can, Mr. Morgenstern."

"Okay, so what do—"

"I want you to be my eyes and ears in that meeting. I need you to examine what Kuparr Winston did—or claims he did—aboard that plane from a ... well, from a legal perspective."

"Okay, but the survivors are arriving tomorrow morning, too. I—"

"You will have time for both," Noa said. "The NTSB meeting is from seven to eight tomorrow morning in room 213 of this building. The survivors are not scheduled to arrive until ten thirty."

"So, what's your answer, Mr. Morgenstern?" Senator Damonati asked. "Will you help us in our cause? Will you help protect your fellow Americans who are out there every day flying blind, trusting that they don't have a Kuparr Winston upfront piloting their plane?"

Jerry nodded. "Yes, of course, Senator."

Senator Damonati smiled. "Excellent."

"We expect a verbal synopsis of the meeting at exactly eight fifteen tomorrow here in this office," Noa said. "Do not be late for any reason. Your VIP pass for Hickam and the passenger terminal will be waiting for you. We expect a full written report to be submitted by the close of business tomorrow afternoon. This written report must reference SB 950. I will send you a draft version of the bill shortly. Understood, Mr. Morgenstern?"

Senator Damonati stood. Noa stood up and glanced at his watch.

For a split second, Jerry sat in awkward silence before rising out of his seat. "Yes. I'll be here after the meeting to give—"

"You will be here no later than eight fifteen if you want the pass into Hickam," Senator Damonati said. "I do not tolerate tardiness. Oh, and one more thing—you are not to speak to anyone about what Kuparr Winston says in the NTSB meeting. Gretchen will show you out. *A hui hou,* Mr. Morgenstern."

CHAPTER TWENTY-FOUR

Kona, The Big Island of Hawai'i
13:00 HST, 4 January

Kahealani stood in line at Costco, reading her new phone, which was still downloading her bottomless pit of unread emails. Some of the subject lines were supportive, but most were filled with expletives. One email from a friend told her that some talk show host had posted her email address on television.

The asphalt and concrete seemed to magnify the smell of sweat around her. Loudspeakers blared the message that customers could only purchase two food items and four nonfood items per card member. A Hawai'i County policeman allowed one person inside the store as each person left the store. Kahealani had been in line for forty-five minutes already, but she was only halfway through the line, which zigzagged back and forth underneath an overhang.

There hadn't been a line at the cellphone store, and she had purchased a new phone in a matter of minutes.

Kahealani opened the Facebook app out of habit to pass the time; however, Facebook, X, Instagram, TikTok, Snapchat, and Pinterest had deleted her accounts.

The phone started ringing. Kahealani didn't recognize the number, and she declined the call.

The phone rang again with the same number.

Oh, what the hell. "Hello?"

"Kahea?"

"Kup?"

"Oh my gosh, it's so good to hear your voice."

There was silence.

"Kahea? Are you there? Please talk to me."

"Kup, I'm so confused right now. I thought you were dead, and then you called me from Mauna Kea—alive. Then … then all this happened with the governor's daughter—those emails and texts. Did you rape her, Kup? Did you? I have to know the truth."

Several people in line turned their heads toward Kahealani.

"Kahea, I promise you, I did not rape her. I didn't rape anyone. I promise."

Tears began pouring from Kahealani's eyes. "And the airplane—did you crash it, Kup?"

"Kahea, of course not. I would never do anything like that. I haven't lied to you about any of this. I don't understand why Susan Kupule is going after me. Please, believe me. Do you really think that I'm capable of rape and going kamikaze with an airliner?"

"I don't know who to believe anymore." Kahealani wiped her eyes. "Where are you, Kup?"

"I'm in the Federal Detention Center in Honolulu. It's next to the airport. They let me call you, but I think they're listening."

"Kup, those texts they say you sent me—I don't remember them. I never …" Kahealani wiped her eyes. "Kup, I'm trying to believe you. I'm trying to make sense of all this. Why is this woman saying that you crashed the plane? Why would she say you raped her if you didn't actually rape her?"

The people in line around Kahealani were now openly staring at her. Some moved away from her.

"Kahea, I don't know why she's doing this. I know she doesn't like me. I think she's mad at me from that night in Tahiti, but … but to accuse me of rape … I mean—"

"What happened that night in Tahiti, Kup? You've got to tell me." Kahealani's hands shook as she held the phone to her ear. "You've got to tell me everything."

"Sure, Kahea. Of course. We had a long, forty-eight-hour layover in Papeete. The entire crew met for drinks before dinner at the resort where we stayed. Susan—well, everyone seemed to enjoy themselves, but Susan was pissed when she showed up. She had been slamming down some fruity rum drinks for quite a while already. Anyway, we were making plans to all go out to dinner someplace when Susan ran over and began spewing her brains out all over some poor bush. I went over to help her. She stopped spewing and wiped her mouth with the napkin I brought her. She thanked me."

"And then?"

"At that point, everyone got up to go to dinner. Susan said she felt sick and needed to go back to her room. I said I would take her back to her room and catch up with everyone else at the restaurant."

"You took her back to her room?" Kahealani asked.

"Yes. I took her to her hotel room and put her in bed. She asked for a Coke. I got her a Coke from the minifridge, and when I turned around, she was naked in the bed."

"Shit, Kup. Did you leave the room then?"

"I know I should have. Instead, I walked over to her bed and opened the Coke for her. She said, 'Did I say I wanted a Coke? You must have misunderstood me.' I backed away. I said I had to go."

"So, you left the room then?"

"No—again, I know I should have. She called me an asshole for leaving but then started heaving, like she was going to vomit all over again. I put my hand over her mouth and dragged her to the toilet. Her spew shot all over my shirt and shorts. After I got her to the toilet, I left. She kept screaming obscenities at me as I was leaving. I was covered in her vomit, so I went back to my room to shower and change clothes. I caught up with the rest of the crew at the restaurant about forty-five minutes later."

"Did you tell anyone else what happened?"

"The people at the table noticed I had changed clothes and started giving me shit about Susan and me having sex. I was getting ribbed left and right. Finally, I told them I had changed clothes because she had barfed all over them. Everyone kept giving me a hard time the rest of the night, and I think they gave Susan a hard time the next day as well. She was mad at me for telling everyone that she had thrown up on me."

"And this happened back in November?"

"Yes."

Kahealani began shaking her head. "Why didn't she bring these charges right after it happened? Why now? Why didn't you tell me about all this? Why, Kup?"

"Kahea, I don't know. I guess I thought it was just easier to keep quiet and let it all go away. I didn't think—I knew I didn't do anything wrong. I was just trying to be a good bloke that night. I was trying to help. I was trying to do the right thing, honestly, Kahea. I never asked for any of this. I don't know where all this shit about me crashing the plane came from, either. I wish I could give you an explanation for all this, but I don't understand what's happening to me. I mean, I'm abducted by aliens, and the next thing I know, people are accusing me of rape and intentionally crashing an airplane."

"Kup, those emails about crashing the plane—they're all over NNN, and they're addressed to me from you. There are also some emails addressed to you from me. There are texts from me to you on NNN. I know I didn't send them. I know I didn't write them."

"I know, Kahea. The FBI showed me copies of the emails and texts."

"My phone, Kup, is blowing up with texts and emails. They're horrible. My friends and family are telling me I need to divorce you. Total strangers are saying they hate me. They say I should go to prison too because I knew you were going to crash that plane, and I did nothing to stop you. Those texts and emails I supposedly sent you make me sound like I'm crazy, like I've lost my mind. Sherwood is suspending me without pay. Some talk show host said I was a disgrace to women everywhere and that I should be run out of the country—like I could go anywhere even if I wanted to."

"I'm so sorry you're caught up in this too."

"What the hell did I do, Kup?"

"I don't know what to tell you. I feel the same way."

"Kup, I don't remember getting any emails or texts like that. I *know* I didn't. I would have freaked out." Kahea glanced up. She had only about a hundred yards between her and the store entrance. "And I sure as hell didn't write any of them."

"Kahea, they're obviously bogus."

"I know that. I know they are fake. I … but who would do such a thing? And why? Why, Kup?"

"Kahea, I don't know, but your beloved Senator Damonati keeps coming up. She seems to be pushing this. In any case, I don't see any way out. The powers that be have already determined my guilt, and I've got no defense even though I did nothing wrong. Hell, I can't even get a lawyer for another six days."

Kahealani put her left hand over the side of her mouth. "Kup, I'm trying to believe you. I want to believe you, but I just don't know who I can trust. Everything is so—"

"Please, Kahea, you're all I have. You're my entire life. Please help me. Please go public with all this. It's the only way now."

"Kup, they threatened me."

"Who threatened you, Kahea?"

"A man came inside the hotel room after the FBI took you away. His name was Lonnie something. He said he was Senator Damonati's field representative for the Big Island. He said if I ever denied any of the charges publicly, they would come for me, and I would be arrested too."

Kahealani walked a few steps forward. "Kup, I'm scared. I—" Kahealani pulled the phone from her ear. The screen was dark. She tapped on the screen, but nothing happened.

The line started backing up. People were shouting at each other. Kahealani pressed the button to turn the phone back on, but the screen remained blank.

The line exploded forward, carrying Kahealani with it. People behind Kahealani were pushing forward, pressing her into the people in front of her. The mob in motion couldn't stop.

Kahealani glanced down and saw a bloodied police badge as she stepped on a man's face.

PART TWO

'OPALA

CHAPTER TWENTY-FIVE

Eyjafjallajökull, Iceland
11:30 GMT, 5 January

It was almost noon, and the sun had risen above the horizon as a few high cirrus clouds broke the purity of the blue sky. Unending snow-covered glaciers extended to the north, while south of them, the whiteness of the glacier fell away to a horizon of blue ocean many kilometers away.

Thirty minutes ago, the tour group had exited the monster truck, which resembled a boxy fifteen-passenger van with eight oversized tires. While the monster truck was street-legal, it performed best on the heavy snow of the glacier.

They had hiked atop the glacier along a worn pathway of packed snow. Hildur recognized a quick photo opportunity and stopped along the trail. She was leading ten stranded American, British, and Canadian tourists. Trevor was one of the Americans, but he was along for free.

Hildur pointed to a snow-covered peak in the distance. "That is the Eyjafjöll Volcano. It rises to a height of one thousand six hundred fifty-one meters, and the crater is four kilometers across. When it last erupted in 2010, its ash cloud caused many disruptions to air travel between North America and Europe. We are thankful it is sleeping right now. The glacier we are walking on is Eyjafjallajökull, the ice cap of Eyjafjöll."

The tourists took in the view, and many snapped selfies with their phones. They had decided to continue with their scheduled ice cave tour while they worked out the logistics of getting home, and Hildur was more than happy to lead the tour. With the runways at Keflavík Airport destroyed, it looked like it would be a very bleak tourist season for her business.

After a few moments, Hildur pointed down the trail. "Let us continue. The mouth of the cave is just ahead."

The entrance to the cave appeared to be nothing more than a scraggly hole in the side of a rather jagged section of the glacier. Inside the cave, however, the ice shimmered in Hollywood-fake translucent hues of blue. The ice at the bottom of the glacier, compressed by thousands of years and thousands of kilograms, contained very little air, giving it a bluish color.

They walked along the ice floor for the first thirty meters until the cave made a bend to the left. Hildur halted. A wall of smooth white ice blocked the entire cave.

Trevor, following closely behind Hildur, whispered, "This wasn't here the other day. What do you suppose caused this?"

Hildur whispered, "I do not know. I do not understand."

Dr. Charles Billingsley, a tourist sporting a ski hat adorned with the Union Jack covering his thick, curly gray hair, walked up to the ice wall. "What the bloody hell? Is that it? We hiked all this way, and that's all there is to this cave?"

Hildur stepped back and turned to Charles with her mouth open.

Charles raised his voice. "Your bloody website says this cave goes back over three hundred meters. What have we gone here—maybe forty meters? I'd say forty-five, at the most."

"Mr. Billingsley, this is something new," Hildur said. "Last week, the ice cave went all the way back, three hundred meters. Something has happened."

"Well, what happened then? This is shit."

Hildur shrugged her shoulders. "I do not know. Perhaps some water flowed for a while, but later refroze and sealed off the cave here."

"Well, I've never seen water flow and freeze into a wall before."

Trevor began touching the ice and studying it. "It's so smooth. It's perfect," he whispered to himself.

"Neither have I, but I promise you this was not here last week," Hildur said.

Charles shook his head. "I believe we're due for a refund of some sort."

A loud thud echoed through the cave.

A middle-aged woman from Toronto, Jean Blankenship, cocked her head. "What was that?"

Charles Billingsley walked a few steps toward the mouth of the cave. "It came from out there." The pinging of his crampons increased in cadence as he trotted out of the cave.

Hildur gave Trevor a worried glance.

The surrounding ice shuddered and cracked as another thud reverberated through the cave.

"Fjandinn!" Hildur shuddered. "We need to go back. Everyone, begin walking back out of the cave, please."

Jean Blankenship asked, "Are we in danger? Is the volcano erupting?"

Hildur shook her head. "No. Do not worry. We should be okay. But let us move on out of the cave now, please."

The group began walking back toward the mouth of the cave while Charles Billingsley ran toward it.

Charles froze when he exited the cave. "Bloody hell!"

Hildur called out from behind the group, "What is it? Why have you stopped?"

Charles turned back to the group, who were still fifteen meters inside the cave. "I'm not sure what is going on out here. There's something in the sky, a vertical cylinder of some sort. It's massive—several kilometers away. It appears to be ejecting some type of metallic disk. The disks—these giant, spinning disks—are coming out of the bottom. They have parachutes."

The group began pouring out of the cave. A lady from Denver started screaming.

Hildur exited the cave and, for several seconds, stood speechless as she stared at the sky.

"What should we do?" Charles asked. "That thing is moving toward us!"

"Quickly, everyone," Hildur said. "We must get back to the monster truck. Go as fast as you can!"

"It's happening," Jean Blankenship said. "Just like that woman in Hawai'i said it would in her email."

Hildur shot Jean a confused look. "Everyone, run as fast as possible! Your crampons will still give you traction on the snow."

The group began running as fast as they could with their crampons on their boots—except for Trevor, who kept stopping to look at the strange object in the sky.

Hildur stopped. "Trevor, what are you doing? We must go! That … that thing is dropping those disks. We must get past them!"

Trevor nodded and began trotting as fast as his crampons would allow.

The cylindrical object in the sky continued moving toward them and continued ejecting metal disks. It would soon pass over and in front of them if they didn't hurry.

Ahead of Hildur, the group had stopped. Hildur yelled, "Keep going! We—"

Hildur saw that Jean Blankenship had fallen, and Charles was helping her stand. Jean began walking with a limp.

"Fjandinn," said Hildur under her breath. "Everyone, keep running! Trevor and I will assist Jean."

The rest of the group began running again. The object in the sky was close now and emitted a low-pitched hum. It was several hundred meters off to their right and moving left. It would pass in front of them.

Charles yelled, "There's a gap between the disks. There's a chance—"

"We're not going to make it!" said the lady from Denver, who stopped running.

Charles grabbed her by her arm and yelled, "Bloody hell, we're not!" He began running with the lady in tow but shook his head as he glanced up at a disk spiraling down. Parachutes slowed its descent and spin rate. "That one won't land on us, but the next one—that one is going to be close! Run, everyone!"

The object was now above and in front of them.

Another disk spun out of the bottom and began spiraling down over the trail in front of them.

Charles yelled, "We can make it! We can get to the other side. Just keep running!" He looked back at the group behind him. Hildur, Trevor, and Jean Blankenship were a hundred meters behind. Jean was limping.

The lady from Denver once again stopped. She began screaming, "It's too close! It's going to crush us!"

Charles looked up at the massive disk descending upon them. "Oh, bloody hell, you're right. Everyone, start running back to the cave!"

Everyone reversed their direction and began running back toward the cave—everyone except the lady from Denver. She stood in the middle of the trail, staring upward at the metallic disk.

Charles yelled, "Come on! You're going to be crushed if you just stand there!" He grabbed her arm, but she wouldn't move. "Come on, you stupid twit! Do you want to die?"

The lady started walking.

Charles yelled, "Run!"

The group had now caught up and passed Hildur, Trevor, and Jean.

The disk was a few hundred meters above them and blanketed the sky.

Charles ran with the lady in tow, who began running and screaming at the same time. Loose snow began blowing outward from the center of where the disk would land. Ahead of them, the group had stopped and looked back. They were clear of the disk's path.

Hildur yelled, "Hurry, keep running! You are close!"

The disk was about fifty meters above the ground when Charles and the lady vanished from view in a miniature blizzard of blowing snow as the air was forced out from underneath the disk.

Seconds later, the ground shook. Parachutes floated to the ground and disappeared into the layer of billowing snow.

CHAPTER TWENTY-SIX

Eyjafjallajökull, Iceland
12:20 GMT, 5 January

The snow had cleared, and Charles was bent over, grasping his knees with his hands. He gasped for breath. Behind him, the metal disk rose two meters above the ground. Above him, the massive object in the sky continued moving toward the southeast.

Hildur yelled, "Where is—"

"Gone. She's bloody gone. She fell. I tried to reach for her. I couldn't see her with all the snow."

Hildur shook her head and turned away from the disk. In the distance, toward the northwest, the disks had formed a broken line that disappeared beyond the horizon. Beings were streaming out of these disks and onto the glacier. When she turned to look back at Charles, she noticed a tall, redheaded woman staring down at him from the top of the disk. She wore a red skinsuit.

The redheaded woman said, *"Vatn? Mig vantar vatn."*

"What is she saying?" Charles asked.

"Water. She wants … water?" Hildur glanced back toward the mouth of the cave. They were at least five hundred meters away.

Charles began backing away from the disk.

The tall woman was joined by several tall beings, both male and female, all redheads and all wearing red skinsuits. They began talking and pointing at the group of humans in the snow below.

"Oh, bloody hell," Charles said. "Who are these people?"

"They're convicts," said Jean Blankenship. "These disks are full of convicts. We should get inside the ice cave."

Hildur looked at Jean and then back at the strange people atop the disk. "Convicts?"

The group atop the disk had grown to over a hundred. Many started yelling, *"Vatn! Mig vantar vatn!"*

"I am not sure what is happening here or who these people are," Hildur said as she scanned the horizon. "Please now, everyone, back to the cave."

A male jumped down from the left side of the disk and disappeared into the snow. He began screaming.

Charles ran toward Hildur. "I'm all for getting inside the bloody cave, but then what do we do?"

Hildur watched another male jump from the disk onto the packed snow and ice of the trail. He stood up and began walking toward her.

"I do not know, but we cannot stay out here," Hildur said. "Run!"

Once everyone was back inside the cave, Hildur pulled out the two-way radio from her backpack. Her hands shook as she selected the frequency monitored by ICE-SAR, the Icelandic Rescue Service. Multiple voices were talking over each other in Icelandic on the radio.

A tall, muscular man wearing a solid red skinsuit appeared at the entrance to the cave. Even though he had bent his head to the left, his thick, unruly auburn hair rubbed against the ceiling of the two-meter-high cave entrance. On the left chest of the skinsuit, there was a black outline of Iceland.

Hildur dropped the radio, which made a dull thud when it hit the ice. Frantic voices in Icelandic continued to talk over each other from the radio's speaker.

The man listened to the voices on the radio as he studied each person in the cave. He turned his head toward Hildur. *"Vatn? Mig vantar vatn."*

Hildur nodded and dropped her backpack to the floor.

The man approached Hildur, stopping centimeters from her face. *"Vatn?"*

Hildur's hands shook as she pulled out a bottle of water and handed it to him.

He took the bottle and began studying it. *"Hvernig næ ég vatninu úr ílátinu?"*

Hildur narrowed her eyes. *"Hvað?* Do you speak English? You unscrew the lid."

"What's he saying?" Charles asked. "He's never opened a bloody bottle of water before?"

The strange man walked over to Charles and shoved the bottle of water in his face. "Yes. That is what I am saying. You open it."

Charles took the bottle and did as instructed. He handed it back to the strange man, who began gulping the water.

The man finished the bottle and tossed it onto the ice. *"Vatn. Ég þarf meira vatn."*

Hildur turned to the group. "He wants more water."

The strange man said, "Yes. I need more water, please."

Charles grabbed his water bottle, opened it, and handed it to the man. "So, where exactly are you from?" Then he raised his right eyebrow. "And who is your bloody tailor?"

The man chugged the entire bottle of water in seconds. "You have food? We are hungry. This planet is not home." He tossed the empty bottle onto the ice.

Charles picked up the empty bottle. "Planet? What the … are you saying you're a bloody alien?"

Jean muttered, "Told you so."

"Yes. Food. We need food now. Please, I have so much hunger."

Hildur handed the man a candy bar.

He examined and unwrapped the candy bar. "What is this?" He held the candy bar up to his nose. "No nutrition. We need real food. We do not store the calories in our bodies." He pointed at Jean Blankenship. "Like her."

Hildur took a step forward. "The chocolate bar is all we have. It will give you energy, at least."

The strange man took a bite of the candy bar and chewed.

"So, back to this planet thing," Charles said. "Why did you come to Earth?"

"It was not our choice. We have a low Social Score. We are convicts. Many thousands like us are being brought here."

Hildur backed away. "What did you do?"

"Individually, I was without work for too long and not contributing to Society. It gave me a low Social Score. Society got rid of those of us with low Social Scores."

"What is a bloody Social Score?" Charles asked.

Jean Blankenship leaned back against the ice wall. "Their government ranks each citizen based on how much they support their society."

Everyone turned to stare at Jean, who said, "As I said, this guy's wife in Hawai'i wrote an email about all of this. She said her husband had told her this was going to happen."

"You knew about this?" Charles asked. "You knew this was going to happen, and you didn't tell us?"

Jean nodded. "Well, I didn't know it was going to happen today and right here. I also didn't think it was real. Somebody sent me the email. The guy was that pilot from Hawai'i—the guy that raped the flight attendant and crashed the plane—not exactly a credible source. Anyway, he predicted these aliens were going to dump a hundred thousand convicts each on Iceland, Galveston, and the Big Island of Hawai'i, all the places that were attacked. I thought it was just some internet conspiracy crap and forgot about it. But I guess maybe it's true."

The female who had first stared down at Charles from the disk appeared at the mouth of the cave. Her tight red skinsuit emphasized her tall, lean figure and muscular breasts. She leaned her head over to the left to avoid hitting the top of the cave entrance. Her steel-gray eyes focused on each person in the cave as she extended her right hand, palm flattened and facing up toward the humans. The four fingers beside her thumb were of equal length. *"Ég er þyrstur og svangur."*

"She is thirsty and hungry," Hildur said. "Someone give her water and a candy bar."

Charles handed the woman a water bottle and a candy bar. "Do you have a name?"

"English," the female said. "Yes, okay. I am a *Red.*" She grabbed the water and candy bar from Charles. "Yes, we need water and food. We must eat continuously. Please."

"That's your name?" Charles said. "Red?"

"Red is who I am—what I am. My individual name is Es-mar."

"Well, Es-mar, you're not exactly what I was expecting for a bloody alien invasion," Charles said.

"We are not invaders. I am not here by my choice. We are con—"

"Vatn og matur!" screamed a male with waist-length reddish-orange hair from the mouth of the cave as he broke off a meter-long icicle and pointed it at Trevor.

"He wants water and food also," Hildur said.

Twenty more men and women wearing identical red skinsuits poured into the cave. They all had red hair, and they all were too tall and too muscular. They began yelling in unison, *"Vatn og matur!"*

The small mob walked deeper into the cave as the tour group of humans retreated.

"Toss them whatever water and food you have," Hildur said.

The humans began rummaging through their backpacks and pockets, tossing what food they could at the aliens. A feeding frenzy ensued as the aliens fought over the meager offerings.

The humans continued retreating deeper into the cave, but the mob followed them like an unsatisfied pack of wolves—until the humans came up to the wall of ice.

The aliens were now face-to-face with the humans.

Es-mar approached Hildur. "You will get more water and more food. And no more chocolate candy."

Hildur looked around her tour group to see if anyone had anything else to give out. "We gave you everything we had. We do not have any more to give you."

Es-mar grabbed Hildur by the throat with her right hand and lifted her off the ground. "You will give us more food and water."

Hildur started choking and gasping for breath. "I said … we—"

Trevor pounced on Es-mar, and she fell onto the ice with Trevor on top of her. Hildur fell to the side, gasping for air.

A male alien grabbed Trevor and slung him into the wall. "The gravity is low here," he said. "I like this." He turned to the group of humans. "You will give us more food and water now."

Trevor slid down the wall of ice and collapsed. The male alien with the icicle walked over to Trevor and smiled. He held the point of the icicle a few centimeters above Trevor's chest, over his heart. He turned to Hildur and asked, "Is this the correct location of the heart?"

Es-mar stood back and glared down at Hildur.

Hildur climbed onto her knees. In a raspy voice, she whispered, "Stop this. I will take you to a place with more food and water … it is all I can do."

Es-mar continued glaring at Hildur. "You will take us to get more food and water. Now." She turned her head and stared at the quivering group of humans huddled together.

Hildur nodded and stood back up.

Trevor still lay crumpled on the ice floor, and Hildur ran over to him. She pushed the icicle out of the way. Trevor stirred and opened his eyes.

Es-mar focused her steel-gray eyes on Hildur. "What are you doing? Leave him. We will go now."

"Can someone help me with Trevor?" Hildur asked.

Several human men grabbed Trevor and began carrying him out. After a few moments, he could walk on his own. Hildur led the humans out of the cave, and the group of aliens followed them.

As they emerged, the sun was approaching its highest point of the day. It would only provide four and a half hours of daylight that winter day. The group began hiking back along the trail at a good pace behind Hildur.

Hildur knew that what they were about to do had risks, but they had no choice. When they reached the metal disk, she stopped and turned around to face the group. "We will now have to hike around the disk on fresh snow and unknown ice. Everyone, please stay in a single-file line behind me—step where I step. Be careful. There could be hidden crevasses underneath the snow."

Hildur eased her right foot into the deep snow and sank to her knees. She did the same with her left foot and waved to the group. "Okay, let us go."

The group began the slow hike around the right side of the disk. Every few minutes, Hildur would stop and look back to check on everyone.

After about twenty minutes, they rounded the disk, and Hildur saw the monster truck in the distance sitting at the trailhead. *We are close,* she thought.

Hildur stopped to check on the group behind her. One alien, the one called Es-mar, was walking several meters outside of the group's footsteps. Hildur was about to yell at Es-mar to get back in line until she felt around her throat with her right hand.

She turned back and continued her slow hike toward the trail.

The sun sat low in the sky when Hildur finally planted her feet back on the trail, a wave of relief rushing through her. She turned around to check on the group. Es-mar was walking straight to the monster truck, cutting the corner through untracked snow. She was at least thirty meters from the group.

Hildur began helping the first group of humans onto the trail and telling them to keep walking toward the monster truck, which was about three hundred meters away at this point.

A woman screamed. Hildur stopped and turned her head back to check on the group. "What happened to … the female that was walking way over there by herself? She said her name was Es-mar."

The group of humans shrugged their shoulders. The aliens gave no response and continued walking toward her.

"Hjálp!" said a muffled voice out over the snow. *"Vatn. Hjálp!"*

"Fjandinn!" Hildur scanned the snow for footprints. She yelled, *"Hvar ertu?* Where are you?"

The muffled voice said, "Water! I'm in water!"

Hildur shook her head. She couldn't pinpoint the voice. She began walking toward the muffled cries, easing each step into the snow. "Keep talking. I am trying to find you by your voice."

Ahead, she saw a set of solitary footprints trailing off in the snow. Hildur turned and headed for the spot where the footprints ended.

The muffled voice in the snow had stopped.

Hildur approached the hole in the snow and probed the edge of the crevasse with her right foot. She peered over the edge.

Es-mar shook in slush up to her shoulders. She looked like someone having an epileptic fit.

Hildur grabbed a section of rope from her backpack, tied a loop in one end, and tossed the loop down the hole. "Can you grab the rope and put the loop under your armpits?"

Es-mar ignored the rope.

Hildur screamed, "Es-mar, you must take the rope!"

Es-mar reached for the rope with flailing arms. After seven attempts, she was able to grab the rope and hold it above her head.

"Now place the rope under your armpits," Hildur said.

Es-mar thrashed as she lowered the rope around her.

"I'm going to pull you out," Hildur said. "Okay?"

Es-mar's head shook as her body convulsed in the slush.

Hildur stepped back a few meters from the crevasse and began pulling as hard as she could.

It wasn't enough. Es-mar was three times heavier than Hildur.

CHAPTER TWENTY-SEVEN

Galveston Island, Texas
12:00 CST, 5 January

Gail walked outside onto the back porch to water her flowers. The familiar noise of fighter jets was absent. Whether the quiet calmed her or unnerved her, she wasn't sure. *Everything is fine. I'm just worn out.*

Glances turned into stares, and water soon spilled out of the flowerpot and onto her shoes. "Dammit," she said as she tilted her watering jug up.

A sense of normalcy had returned. The Texas State Guard was busy building a temporary floating bridge to reconnect Galveston to the Texas mainland via San Luis Pass. Panic buying had subsided, and the roving patrols of police and the Texas State Guard had brought the looting and crime under control. She had had a long phone conversation with Jerry, and her anger at him had subsided.

Daisy and Michael Phelps played in the yard below with Mikey. Mikey threw an old baseball into West Bay, and Michael Phelps leaped into the water and retrieved the baseball over and over. Daisy watched from beside the staircase leading up to the back porch.

Gail's phone rang. It was her father, Dan Koots, who had driven into town to get their ration of groceries.

"Hey, Dad."

"Have you seen it?"

"Seen what, Dad?"

"The UFO in the sky. It's over San Luis Pass right now, headed your way."

Gail raised her head as she walked toward the far corner of the porch.

The water jug fell to the floor.

A metal cylinder floated in the southwestern sky. A cap topped the cylinder, like some giant floating mushroom, and disks shot out of the bottom as it moved across the sky.

"Oh my God, Dad." She squinted.

"Yes, and it's ejecting disks out of the bottom. The disks are parachuting down. That thing looks just like some of those videos on the internet from Iceland. I told you we would be next. You better get the kids and dogs inside. Those *people* will be on the ground in no time."

The sound of jet engines came from the west. Gail glanced out over West Bay, trying to spot the jets.

"How long until you get back here?"

Sirens began wailing across the island. Gail struggled to hear her father over the phone.

"I'll be home in about five minutes. Until then, get everyone inside the house and lock all the doors."

A loud alarm began erupting from Gail's cellphone. It was from the Galveston County Civil Defense. A message said multiple observers had reported an unidentified object over San Luis Pass moving northeast and urged all residents to take shelter.

Gail tried to say goodbye to her father, but he had already hung up the phone.

In the distance, disks floated down by parachute.

Gail looked down at Mikey in the yard below. "Mikey, you and the dogs need to come into the house!"

"Aww, Mom. Why? I'm not hungry."

"You all have to get into the house right now. Do not argue with me!"

"It's not fair. Cindy gets to play at the neighbor's house, and I can't even play with the dogs."

"Cindy!" Gail dropped her cellphone. "Oh, crap."

The noise from the jet fighters, which had been getting louder and louder, stopped.

Gail scanned the sky for the jets but couldn't see them. "Get yourself, Daisy, and Michael Phelps in the house right now, dammit!"

Gail's hands trembled as she reached down for her cellphone.

Mikey climbed the back staircase, pounding each step. Daisy and Michael Phelps followed. As they reached the porch, two explosions, seconds apart, emanated from the southwest. Two dark smoke clouds rose from the ground.

"Oh my God!" Gail fumbled for the favorites list on her phone. "Why did I agree to let her go next door?"

Mikey watched the black plumes of smoke rising from the ground. "Mom, what were those explosions?" He turned his head to the southwest. "What's that thing in the sky? Crap, Mom, is it like Iceland? Are we being invaded like Iceland?"

"Take the dogs inside. I need you to lock all the doors and windows. Do not—I repeat, *do not* go outside without my permission. Understood? I'm going next door to get Cindy."

Mikey nodded. "Okay, Mom. I'm on it." He opened the door, and the dogs followed him inside.

Gail looked back at the object in the sky. It was getting closer every minute, and the disks kept popping out of the bottom. "Cindy!" She texted her neighbor as she ran through the house and out the front door.

Mikey was checking the doors and windows on the middle floor of the house when a civil defense alert sounded on the television. He glanced at the television as a banner flashed across the screen saying to seek shelter. What they needed to take shelter from wasn't clear.

Gail was dragging Cindy across the street when Dan's blue Dodge Ram pickup pulled into the driveway.

Cindy was sobbing. "Mom, what's happening? Are the Russians coming from the sky?"

"Let's get inside, sweetie. We'll be okay inside." Gail glanced at her father, standing in front of the truck and peering skyward. He held a paper sack full of groceries. "Dad, come on!"

Dan, wearing Levis, a collared white short-sleeve shirt, and brown roper boots, began shuffling toward the stairs. "Damndest thing I've ever seen." He climbed the stairs behind Gail and Cindy, running his right hand through his thinning brown hair.

Gail and Cindy rushed through the front door. Dan stopped on the front wraparound porch of the house and studied the object. He yelled, "I think it's going to be close! I would guess it will be a little east of us when it goes over."

Gail stood at the open door. "Dad, get in here now."

Cindy screamed, "Grandpa, get in the house!"

The UFO emitted a whirring noise as another disk came spinning out of the bottom. It appeared to be almost overhead but offset to the east of them.

"I'll get inside in a second. I've never seen anything like this."

Michael Phelps walked outside onto the porch and started barking at the sky. Daisy remained at the doorway.

Gail stood at the open door with Daisy. The metallic disk spun counterclockwise as it fell from the sky. Multiple parachutes opened above it, slowing its rotation and descent.

Dan had seen enough. He made his way inside and waited for Michael Phelps before deadbolting the front door.

Gail stood back several feet from the door. "Do you think we're safe here, Dad?"

"I think so. It looks like the disk will land to our east, but I'll get the sailboat keys in case we need to run out the back. God help those people over there in those houses, though."

The disk landed on a subdivision, a convenience store, and a miniature golf course. Through the front window, they could see people fleeing from crushed houses and cars as a thousand hatches on top of the disk opened all at the same time.

Gail gasped and put her left hand over her mouth. "Oh my God."

Heads and bodies began popping up from the disk. All the heads were covered in thick brown hair.

"Mommy, why are they here?" Cindy asked. "And why did they land on all those houses?"

Beings dressed in solid brown skinsuits began streaming over the edge of the disk and into the neighborhood.

"Close the blinds." Dan reached down and placed his right hand on the holster of his Beretta pistol. "Everyone in the guest bathroom, now."

They all filed into the guest bathroom in the middle of the second floor, one of the few rooms without a window. It contained a bathtub, toilet, and sink and was a tight fit for the six of them. It had become the designated safe room from the human mobs roaming Galveston. Gail's shotgun stood in the corner beside the toilet.

Once they were inside the guest bathroom with the door locked, Dan kneeled beside Cindy. "Cindy, you keep Daisy quiet, okay?" Cindy nodded. "Mikey, you keep Michael Phelps quiet, okay?" Mikey nodded.

Long minutes of relative quiet passed before glass shattered some-where in the house. Footsteps pattered about, and voices spoke in an unintelligible language. Cabinets were being opened. Glasses broke on the floor. The sounds all seemed to come from the kitchen.

There were sounds of eating and drinking for several minutes. The room became quiet as the doorknob of the guest bathroom started shaking.

Someone was trying to get in, and it was more than Michael Phelps could take. He leaped out of Mikey's arms and lunged at the bathroom door, growling and barking at the unseen intruder on the other side.

There was a male voice from the other side of the door. "Where do you keep the rest of your food and water? I am the Doctor. We must have food soon, or we will perish."

Gail and Dan looked at each other. Dan shook his head.

"Tell us now, or we will make you tell us." Splinters of wood flew into the bathroom as a fist smashed through the door above the door-knob. A hand consisting of four fingers of equal length and a shorter thumb began unlocking the door from the inside.

Michael Phelps bit down on the intruder's hand. The voice on the other side began screaming. Michael Phelps's snout slammed against the door as the intruder attempted to pull his hand back through the hole. Orange-colored blood oozed down the side of the door.

Cindy screamed, "Leave Michael Phelps alone!" She jumped up and began pulling him back from the door.

Michael Phelps relaxed his grip on the alien's hand, and the alien pulled it out of the hole in the door.

Dan grabbed the shotgun, stuck it into the hole, and began firing at multiple angles. There was the sound of more glass breaking and screams on the other side of the door, and then the sound of footsteps radiated from all around the house.

Moments later, it was quiet.

Gail turned to Dan and whispered, "Do you think they're gone?"

Dan bent down and closed one eye as he peered through the hole in the door with the other. "I don't see anybody. The place is a mess, though."

Gail took a deep breath. "What should we do?"

Dan stood back up. "Michael Phelps and I will go out into the living room. Y'all stay in here until I say it's clear."

Gail nodded.

"Take this." Dan handed the shotgun to her and unlocked the door with his left hand. The Beretta was in his right.

As Dan cracked the door open, Michael Phelps jammed his snout through the opening and pushed the door open. He walked out into the living room and began sniffing the floor. Dan followed him out the door and shut it, then began examining the room.

They had shattered the front bay windows. Several cabinets in the living room were open; their contents spilled out onto the floor. They had emptied the kitchen of food. Both the refrigerator and freezer doors were open and revealed two empty compartments. The pantry door was also open. The only things left in the pantry were some paper plates and a box of trash bags.

Dan walked over to the front window. Outside on the street, beings in brown skinsuits walked in random directions. Most were eating, drinking, or trying to break into houses.

Dan walked over to the guest bathroom door and knocked. "Gail, I think it's okay for y'all to come out now. Whoever broke into the house must have gotten what they wanted and moved on. It looks like they only took food and drinks. All the expensive stuff is still here."

Gail, Mikey, Cindy, and Daisy walked out of the guest bathroom and into the living room.

Gail put her hand over her mouth as her cellphone pinged, showing she had received a text.

Dan shot her a dirty look.

She put the phone on silent and read the text from her next-door neighbor:

> There are two men in your bathroom!!!!
> I'm looking right at them now! I think
> one of them got hurt. They're bandaging
> a hand, I think. I'm in our master bedroom.
> Where are u? Are y'all okay?

Gail gasped and handed the phone to Dan after another text came through:

> They're leaving the bathroom!!

CHAPTER TWENTY-EIGHT

Galveston Island, Texas
12:20 CST, 5 January

Dan handed the cellphone back to Gail and whispered, "Get everyone to the sailboat right now. Here are the keys. I'll be right behind y'all. Untie the boat and start the engine."

Gail nodded. She grabbed Mikey and Cindy and herded them out the back door, carrying her shotgun in her left hand. Daisy followed Cindy out the door, but Michael Phelps stood beside Dan and uttered a low, guttural growl.

Gail was halfway to the boat dock when there was a loud thud and a muffled scream behind her. She swiveled her head. On the back porch, an alien with long brown hair was sitting on top of Dan, punching him in the face with his right hand.

Gail stopped and turned around. "Dad!"

Michael Phelps pounced on the alien and bit down on his right arm. The alien jumped up and slammed Michael Phelps against the wall. Michael Phelps released his grip and slid down to the floor.

The alien turned and stared straight at Gail.

Gail grabbed Cindy's hand and started running again. "Run, Cindy!"

Mikey had already untied several mooring ropes, and Daisy was inside the cockpit, which occupied the aft third of the forty-five-foot sailboat. The back of the cockpit had a two-foot-wide gap with steps that led back to a swim platform. A two-and-a-half-foot-wide metal steering wheel and control center occupied the aft half of the cockpit. The forward two-thirds of the sloop contained the cabin, and the deck over the cabin had several windows and hatches. The mast rose from the deck just forward of the center.

Gail leaped onto the dock. She turned around and lifted Cindy into the boat's cockpit. The alien was about fifty feet away and closing.

Gail laid her shotgun on the dock as she fumbled for the ignition key of the sailboat's diesel engine.

The alien was thirty feet away when she turned the key to start. The cold diesel struggled to start. After several seconds, Gail turned the ignition back to the off position. *We're not going to make it.*

Gail turned the ignition again, but again, the diesel engine wouldn't start.

Footsteps thundered across the dock.

"Dammit!" Gail pounded on the instrument panel with her left hand as she rotated the key back and forth between START and RUN. "Start, you piece of shit!"

The alien was on the dock now, eyeing the bow of the sailboat.

She reached for her shotgun, but it was still sitting on the dock, out of reach.

Gail turned the ignition key to start once again. This time, the reluctant diesel turned over and continued running. Gail slammed the throttle into reverse, and the forty-five-foot sailboat began backing out of the dock.

It was too late.

The alien leaped onto the bow of the boat, which dropped a foot and a half before bobbing back up. He stood up and glared into Gail's eyes as he grabbed the mast with his left hand to steady himself. His shoulder-length brown hair billowed across the black outline of Texas on the upper left chest of his brown skinsuit. Orange blood dripped onto the white fiberglass deck.

"Mikey, you and Cindy get inside the cabin right now!" Gail screamed as she pushed herself toward the back of the cockpit.

Michael Phelps sprang onto the dock.

The alien, well over six feet tall, examined the sailboat's cockpit.

Mikey jumped up and began spinning the dials on the combination lock that secured the entrance to the sailboat's cabin.

The alien began walking aft as the sailboat's bow slid past the last few feet of the dock.

Yellow flashed from the left as Michael Phelps jumped onto the alien and bit down on his right hand. The alien fell onto the starboard rail, and Michael Phelps clamped down on his neck as they tumbled over the starboard side of the sailboat.

Cindy stood up and hung her body over the starboard side. "We can't leave Michael Phelps! That man is going to kill him!"

Gail put the boat into neutral after it had backed away about twenty-five yards from the dock. She glanced over the starboard edge. There was water shooting everywhere as the alien swung his arms and legs in every direction. Through the spray, Gail could see Michael Phelps with his jaws clamped down on the back of the alien's neck.

Cindy called out, "Michael Phelps, let go! Swim over here!"

Michael Phelps seemed to pause at the command but continued clamping down. The alien was gasping for breath as he convulsed and thrashed in the shallow water.

Gail screamed, "Michael Phelps, come!"

Michael Phelps released his grip on the alien's neck and began swimming toward the back of the boat.

The alien continued his violent churning in the eight-foot-deep water, even though he was just ten feet from the dock and fifteen feet from the seawall.

Michael Phelps arrived at the back of the sailboat and placed both front paws on the swim platform. Mikey reached down and heaved the lab's butt out of the water. Michael Phelps leaped into the sailboat's cockpit and began licking Cindy's tear-covered face.

The water beside the boat flattened as the alien's body disappeared and sank to the bottom.

Gail collapsed into the driver's seat of the boat at the aft port corner of the cockpit. Her hands shook.

The sound of distant jet engines came from the west, from the mainland.

She turned her head back toward the house. Dan was limping toward the dock. He was about twenty yards away. About thirty yards behind him, fifteen or so aliens were in pursuit.

Dan looked back and increased his pace as best he could, but the limp slowed him down.

Gail jammed the sailboat's diesel into forward and began steering the bow back toward the front of the dock. "Dad, hurry!"

The mob of aliens was gaining on Dan as he stepped onto the dock.

They were now only about fifteen feet behind him. The bow of the sailboat was still ten feet from the end of the dock.

He's not going to make it, Gail thought.

Dan reached the end of the dock and turned back. An alien was five feet from him and reaching his left hand out to grab him. The sailboat's bow was still seven feet from the dock—too far for Dan to jump.

Dan dove into the water. The alien behind him stopped at the end of the dock, refusing to jump into the water after him.

The momentum of the mob of remaining aliens pushed the lead alien over the edge of the dock and into the water, only four feet from Dan. Dan began swimming away while the alien thrashed his arms in and out of the water. The alien was three feet from the dock and eleven feet from a swim ladder.

Fourteen aliens stood on the dock and observed the alien man in the water churning around.

Dan swam to the swim platform at the back of the sailboat and lifted himself into the cockpit. Gail put the engine in reverse and backed away. As she did so, the violent spray of water subsided as the alien slid underwater. One alien stood on the dock shaking his bandaged right fist at Gail while the other aliens walked back toward the house.

The jets were loud now. Gail looked up. Four F-22 Raptors were flying in extended trail formation, headed for the strange object that now appeared to be hovering over downtown Galveston. As the jets headed out over the bay and approached the island, three of the four went silent.

The fourth jet turned away from the island and began circling over the Texas City Dike.

Dan collapsed onto a cushion in the cockpit beside her. His nose was bleeding, and he had a large cut on the right side of his mouth.

Gail looked back up at the sky. Three parachutes popped open, followed by the sound of three distant explosions. The UFO was turning to the east. As it flew over the island's eastern tip, it started falling, and its forward motion slowed. Gail lost sight of it.

Gail grabbed her cellphone and opened the NNN app to get some news about what was going on.

There was nothing.

The constant *tocotocotoco* sound of an approaching helicopter came from the west, from the mainland.

Her mind was pinging in a hundred different directions. She needed to talk to someone, needed to go somewhere, and needed to figure out what to do.

The helicopter was close now and only about fifty feet above the water.

Gail dialed Jerry's number and waited for him to answer. It rang five times and went to voicemail. Gail started screaming into her phone, "Aliens, Jerry! They're here. They're real! Same thing as Iceland. All the rumors are true. These disks came down—these mobs are all over the neighborhood. They broke into our house. Michael Phelps attacked one of them. They've got orange blood! We escaped in the sailboat, but I'm afraid to go back to the house. What's the name of the company in Kemah that did the work on the boat last year? I can't remember the name. Call me. Text me. I think I'll go …"

The beating of the helicopter's rotors changed into a soft whirring sound as it autorotated. Gail turned her head and dropped the phone into the driver's side drink holder as the orange-and-white helicopter plopped into the bay and flipped over onto its side. The calm water exploded as the helicopter's rotors fragmented into a maelstrom of shrapnel.

Gail sat motionless. Mikey grabbed her arm. "Mom, the helicopter."

Gail nodded, and she shifted the sailboat's engines into forward. She turned the boat around and steered toward the sinking helicopter as fast as the forty-five-foot cruiser would go.

She would rescue the rescuers.

CHAPTER TWENTY-NINE

Honolulu, Hawai'i
08:35 HST, 5 January

Sitting at the far end of the long wooden table in the conference room of the Prince Kuhio Federal Building, Jerry finished writing "near midair with large gray triangular object—UFO?" on his legal pad. He glanced at his phone. Gail had left him a voicemail earlier; it would have to wait until the hearing was over.

After each new revelation from Winston concerning UFOs and alien invasions, the NTSB investigator would nod and write down some notes. Several times, he would crack a slight smile.

The investigator focused his questions on the system failures and malfunctions of the 777 and the steps performed by the crew leading up to the ditching. He ignored any questions dealing with aliens or invasions or the rumors and conspiracy theories about what had just happened in Iceland only hours ago, as the FTA had officially called the photos and videos on the internet before they disappeared.

Jerry began forming the verbal synopsis he would give Senator Damonati when Winston mentioned something he called a Reckoning. *This guy is completely wacko.*

Jerry's cellphone vibrated once again. He glanced down and saw a text from James Templeton:

> Crazy stuff going on in Galveston right now. How are Gail and the kids doing?

Jerry held his phone in his lap and opened the NNN app. It showed nothing about Galveston.

Next, he opened a social media app. There were a few posts about Galveston; however, almost all the videos and photos had been replaced with notices about violence and disinformation.

Jerry started continually refreshing the app, and occasionally, he would catch a post that remained up for several seconds before it was removed. These short-lived posts showed spinning metal disks parachuting down from the sky. Mobs of strange men and women in tight brown skinsuits roamed neighborhoods, searching for food and water. They were looting homes and stores all over the island. Some residents had placed food and drinks outside in their front yards, hoping the mobs would take the stuff and move on. Sometimes it worked, but sometimes it backfired and made those homes targets.

What the hell? Is this real? Jerry looked at Winston across the table as he discussed the flight control system of the 777. *Is this guy for real?*

The interrogation ended, and Jerry left the conference room. He glanced at his watch. He had fifteen minutes to get to Senator Damonati's office. He began walking toward the elevators. In a hallway, he stopped to listen to Gail's voicemail. *Orange blood? They escaped in the sailboat?*

Jerry got into the elevator and headed up to the top floor. He dialed Gail's number, but the call went straight to her voicemail. Dan's number did the same. He tried texting them both. Both texts indicated they were undelivered.

Jerry watched a video emailed to him from one of his neighbors that showed a massive cylindrical object floating over Galveston. It looked like a vertical tube and appeared to be spinning. Metal disks were spiraling out of the bottom and floating down to the ground by parachute. The email said it was just like Iceland.

What the ... Iceland? And now Galveston? Is Winston right?

Jerry searched for news about Iceland on NNN. Again, there was nothing.

The elevator doors opened, and Jerry sat down in a chair in a small waiting area. He called everyone he could think of in Galveston who might know anything about Gail and his kids. The few who answered sounded frantic and scared. No one knew anything about his family, though.

Gail said they had escaped in the sailboat.

Jerry looked up the number for the Coast Guard in Galveston. The call was automatically transferred. A male voice answered, "US Coast Guard Air Station Houston. This is Ensign Gallegos. How may I help you?"

"Hello, my name is Jerry Morgenstern. I'm calling from Honolulu."

"Yes, sir?"

"I'm trying to find my family in Galveston. I received a voicemail from my wife—"

"Sir, I'm sorry to interrupt, but it's complete chaos in Galveston right now. We can't help you. I suggest you contact the Galveston Police. We're swamped here. I'm sorry, but I need to go."

"Wait, don't hang up! I think my wife and family are on our sailboat somewhere. My wife's not answering her cellphone. Can you at least check and see if there have been any reports about a lost sailboat? The boat is the *Legally Mine*. It's a Catalina 45."

"Wait … *Legally Mine*. You said *Legally Mine?*"

"Yes."

"We've been tracking that boat by helicopter. It's in Galveston Bay under sail and appears to be headed toward Kemah. We've been unable to hail the sailboat by radio."

Kemah. She's heading for our old boat slip. They had kept the sailboat at a slip in Kemah when they lived in Bellaire. "Oh, thank God. Does it appear everyone is okay?"

"Yes, as far as we can tell. Mr. Morgenstern, the reason we're tracking that sailboat is that it has six of our crewmen aboard. The sailboat rescued them after their helicopter crashed. A news helicopter witnessed the rescue from a distance and reported it to us. It took us a while to be able to overfly the sailboat because of the no-fly zone around Galveston Island that was just implemented."

"No-fly zone?"

"Yes. We've lost multiple military and civilian aircraft as they approached the island, both rotor and fixed-wing. We've also had several ships lose power as they approached. As I said, the situation is chaotic and changing rapidly."

It's all true—just like he said, Jerry thought.

"Mr. Morgenstern, I have your cellphone number. I'll call you as soon as I learn anything more about your wife and family."

Jerry took a deep breath. "Thank you. Thank you very much."

The call ended. Jerry's phone said 8:10. *Shit! I need to talk to Winston about all this before they take him back to his cell.*

He glanced down the hallway toward Senator Damonati's office.

Jerry got up and pushed the down button on the elevator. After the doors opened, he ran to the conference room, which had a five-foot-high window across its entire length. Winston was alone in the room, shackled to the table. A guard was posted at the entrance, and Jerry told the guard he had left something in the room. After conferring with Agent Perez, who was standing ten feet away talking on his cellphone, the guard unlocked the door.

After the guard closed the door, Jerry leaned over the table toward Winston. "The metal disks. The alien mobs. Iceland. Galveston. So far, everything you said would happen has happened."

"Sorry, mate, they told me not to say anything to anybody while I'm unsupervised, but yeah, it's all happening. The Big Island is next."

"An alien mob attacked my family in our home this afternoon in Galveston. They apparently escaped in our sailboat. They're almost to Kemah, on the mainland."

"They were able to escape by sailboat? Interesting."

"Interesting?" Jerry raised an eyebrow.

"The EMP. They sailed through the EMP."

"EMP? I don't know about that. They've set up a no-fly zone around the island. A bunch of planes and helicopters have crashed." *Could this guy be for real? He's been right about everything so far.* "Mr. Winston, let's say everything you said so far is—"

Winston vanished from Jerry's view as the room became an opaque gray void.

Jerry's knees buckled, and he fell to the floor.

CHAPTER THIRTY

Vík í Mýrdal, Iceland
18:45 GMT, 5 January

The lights of Vík spread out below as the monster truck struggled to top the crest of the last hill on the drive back. They had loaded it well beyond its certified capacity. It seemed to groan as it trudged uphill. The slow speed, the slow hike around the metal disk in the deep snow, and the extra hour it had taken to rescue the female alien had pushed their arrival into the early night.

Her tour group of ten humans and the twenty-two aliens they had encountered in the ice cave had overwhelmed the monster truck. Some aliens were inside; others were on the roof. Another ten were holding on to the sides.

Shadowy figures could be seen off to the left, and occasionally, the monster truck's headlights would illuminate beings in red skinsuits walking along the road.

Several texts popped up on Hildur's phone. The first one said that giant metal disks had landed in a line from the crater of Eyjafjallajökull to a point two kilometers north of Vík. Another text showed a video of two British fighter jets from the *HMS Prince of Wales* flaming out and crashing as they approached Reykjavík Harbor. A third text reported that a mob of strange people had looted the Krónan Supermarket. There was no food or any beverages left in the store. Another said these weird people had broken into their house looking for food.

Hildur also had a voicemail from her father, Einar, and one from Kolbrún, who had seen strangers breaking into Hildur's house. Kolbrún said she was sitting in her living room with her hunting rifle if Hildur needed anything.

The female alien who had fallen into the crevasse was semiconscious and lying on the floor. Hildur had not been able to pull her out by herself. It had taken her plus four human men to get her out of the crevasse. None of the other aliens with them had seemed interested or concerned at the time.

Trevor had recovered and was sitting beside Hildur as she drove. He couldn't stop talking about all the technologies they had witnessed.

Hildur's house sat at the end of Hátún Road. She'd bought it because it offered a commanding view of Vík, the ocean, and the mountains. She had also built an addition to the home that served as the office and meeting point for her tourist business.

The monster truck's headlights illuminated her house and office as they approached. Three windows were shattered, and the front door was open. Empty food containers were strewn about on the snow of her front yard. Below, in the town of Vík itself, the lights of several police cars flashed from multiple locations while spotlights from two helicopters probed from above.

Hildur pulled up to the designated parking spot for the monster truck and switched off the engine. The aliens clinging to the roof and sides hopped off and ran into her open house and office. They came back outside after a few minutes and started walking toward Kolbrún's house. A gunshot echoed across the pasture, and the alien closest to Kolbrún's house collapsed. The aliens backed away and walked down the street toward Vík.

Hildur climbed out of the monster truck and stared at her ransacked house.

Es-mar, the female Hildur had rescued, climbed out of the monster truck and stared at Hildur. The other aliens jumped out and began running toward Hildur's house. The humans aboard walked toward their rental cars. They had all decided to drive to Reykjavík as fast as possible after Hildur had told them there was an evacuation order in effect.

Es-mar walked over to Hildur and grabbed her by the shoulders. "I am sorry for what I did. I need to discuss this with you alone."

"Hildur, I'm going inside," Trevor said. "Where's your first aid kit? I need to replace these bandages."

"Under the kitchen sink," Hildur said. "I am so glad you are okay."

Trevor nodded and continued walking.

Hildur tried to pull away from the alien, but her grip was too firm. "Why are you holding me like this? What do you want with me?"

"You saved my life. It does not make sense to me."

"Well, I know I should not have. I should have left you to die there. I told everyone to walk single file in my footsteps, but you chose to walk alone, far away from my footsteps. You endangered not just yourself but the entire group by doing that."

"Yes, I have always had a problem following directions—conforming to the group. It is why I am here. I was a *Seer*, a social engineer, but my projects were constantly malfunctioning. I eventually realized that our approach was inherently wrong and unnatural. We were predestined for failure. I spoke up about this publicly. It is why I have such a low Social Score and why they sent me here."

"This is why you were sent to Earth?"

Es-mar nodded. "Yes. There are many like me as well. Nevertheless, I owe you a debt, and I must repay this debt. We must bring ourselves back into balance; we must experience equity. We must have a Reckoning before we can move on."

Hildur grimaced. *What is she talking about? Is she going to give me something? I could use a martini.*

"The Reckoning will make our minds even. It will make us equal. You will know all of me—I will know all of you. You must breathe in the breath of my life as I will breathe in your life."

Hildur frowned. "I do not know ... I—"

"Hildur, I cannot leave until there is a Reckoning between us. There is no danger, even between species. It is a natural process. In time, humans will learn the practice, I am sure."

Es-mar looked Hildur straight in the eye and said, "Place both of your hands on my shoulders, as I have done to you."

Hildur put her hands on the alien woman's shoulders. Es-mar drew Hildur's forehead against hers. She squeezed her nose against Hildur's. "Breathe. Breathe in the breath of my life."

Hildur took a deep breath. "Why are you—"

"Do not talk. Breathe. Breathe in the breath of my life."

Hildur took another deep breath.

"Hildur! Stop!" Trevor yelled as he ran out of the house. "She's a convict. Do not do this!"

Hildur and Es-mar both lost consciousness, but the two remained standing with their foreheads and noses pressed together and both hands clenching each other's shoulders.

Trevor stopped five meters from them. "Oh, crap … this can't be good."

CHAPTER THIRTY-ONE

Honolulu, Hawai'i
09:00 HST, 5 January

Jerry sat up against the back door of the cargo van. The air smelled sweet and inviting, like a donut shop—except they were moving. There was road noise. Shelves lined both sides of the interior and held cartons of fresh-baked malasadas and loaves of Hawaiian sweetbread. Winston was looking out of the windshield a few feet in front of him.

"What the hell happened?" Jerry asked as he blinked his eyes. "Where are we?"

Winston turned his head away from the windshield and faced Jerry. "Those two kidnapped us." Winston pointed with his left hand toward the driver and passenger seats of the van. "As best I can tell, we're on the H1 Freeway."

Two tall blond men were sitting in the front of the van. Both wore Hawaiian shirts, and both were eating malasadas from a container between the driver and passenger seats.

Jerry sat up against the side. "Who are they?" He loosened the maroon tie around his neck and unbuttoned the top button of his collar.

"I'm guessing they work for the Warden. Guards or something."

"The Warden?"

"The guy in charge of the Hawai'i penal colony."

Jerry shook his head. "Penal colony? Are you saying they're aliens? Like what you talked about in the interrogation?"

Winston smirked. "Yes. They're aliens."

"Why did they kidnap us? What do they want from us?"

"They kidnapped me. They want me. I'm not sure why you're here, mate. Wrong place, wrong time, maybe."

"Okay," Jerry said. "So, what do they want with you?"

"They want to freeze me. They call it 'Cancelling,' but it's a little more severe than our type of canceling."

"They want to freeze you?"

"Yeah. I mentioned it in the interrogation, but the NTSB investigator wasn't that interested. I reckon you weren't that interested, either."

"Oh yeah, I do remember you mentioning that they wanted to Cancel you."

"Oh well. It couldn't be much worse than dealing with the FBI, Senator Damonati—and you. What exactly is it that you do for Senator Damonati?"

"I … uh. I was just representing her office. She wanted me to …"

"Just tell me, mate. I'm going to be frozen soon enough. I'll be a threat to no one."

"She wanted me to report back my impression of what you did aboard the aircraft from a legal perspective."

"Legal perspective? So, you're a lawyer?"

"Yes. My specialty is aviation law."

Winston began laughing. "Wow. So, somebody creates a bunch of bogus emails that get me arrested by the FBI, and then Senator Damonati sends her bloody aviation lawyer to spy on my NTSB interrogation. Get stuffed, mate. The same goes for your boss, Senator Demon."

"She's not my boss. Are the emails really fake? I mean, who would do such a thing, and why?"

"Yes, they're fake. Look, I have no idea why Susan Kupule and Senator Damonati are coming after me. I mean, I know Susan Kupule is pissed off at me, but I was only trying to help. To say that I raped her? Why would she do that? You got any ideas?"

Jerry shook his head.

"Well, I thought you might know since you're the senator's lawyer—excuse me, errand boy."

The alien in the passenger seat glanced at Winston and Jerry and began talking to the driver in another language.

Winston listened to them and then looked back at Jerry. "They're going to dispose of you."

"Dispose of me? You speak—"

"Their language?" Winston nodded. "They took you by mistake. I guess you weren't supposed to be there when they showed up. They also screwed up the dosage. We should still be asleep."

"Okay, but what do they mean by 'dispose of me'?"

"Dispose, dump, whatever. They're not going to kill you."

"Are they going to freeze me?" Jerry asked. "Like you?"

The alien in the passenger seat said, "Shut up. You talk too much."

"We're being followed," Winston said. "They're trying to lose whoever is following us. It sounds like there is some sort of rendezvous on the windward side of the island. I assume they'll dump you before then."

"Rendezvous?" Jerry said. "With whom?"

"A transport ship. They're taking me back up to the new Command Ship over the Big Island. The cryogenic facility is up there."

"You've got to escape," Jerry whispered as he pulled out his wallet and took out ten hundred-dollar bills and a business card. "I want you to take this."

"Huh? A thousand dollars and your business card are going to help me when I'm in their Command Ship? What, am I supposed to post bail and call my lawyer?"

Jerry shook his head. "You said they're going to dump me somewhere, but maybe you can escape from them before the rendezvous. Maybe you could hide out somewhere."

"Great. So, I manage to somehow escape from these aliens, and then I call Senator Damonati's lawyer so he can have the good senator relay my location to the FBI."

Jerry took the wad of cash and the business card and held them in front of Winston. "Just take it."

"We're on the H3 Freeway now," Kup said as he gazed out the windshield.

"I don't work for Senator Damonati," Jerry said. "I was just doing her a favor by attending the NTSB interrogation. I don't know why, but I believe you. Everything you've said, as crazy as it sounds, has come true."

The cargo van began decelerating.

"Hurry," Jerry said. "Take it."

Winston turned to Jerry and took the cash and business card. "Does this mean you're my lawyer now?"

"No, it doesn't, but call me if you escape."

The cargo van slowed to a crawl, and they heard a single click from the back door. Multiple horns started blaring from the cars behind them.

The alien in the passenger seat swiveled his seat around to face them. He wore a turquoise Hawaiian shirt adorned with *humuhumunukunukuapua'a*. He stood, but the cargo van's interior height of seventy-six inches forced him to hunch over. Grabbing Winston by the neck and lifting him off the floor, he turned to Jerry and said, "The door is unlocked now. You must deplane."

Winston started choking.

Jerry stood at the backdoor of the van and looked back at Winston and the alien. *Deplane?*

The alien smiled at Jerry. "You will deplane now while we're going slow. We can speed up if you would prefer."

Jerry opened the back door of the cargo van and jumped through the doorway. He fell onto the asphalt of the H3 Freeway, rolled for several feet, and stopped in front of a yellow Honda Fit. The elderly lady following them screamed as she swerved into the right guardrail. She was only going ten miles per hour.

Jerry stood and surveyed himself. He had only a few minor cuts. He turned to see the back door close as the cargo van sped away. *Kama'aina Bakery?*

The elderly lady in the Honda Fit rolled down her window. "Why did you jump out of the bread truck? You made me wreck my car!"

Jerry turned back toward the Honda Fit and shrugged his shoulders.

A black Suburban with government license plates stopped beside Jerry. Agent Perez hopped out and opened the back passenger door. "Get in. Get in now, Mr. Morgenstern."

CHAPTER THIRTY-TWO

Vík í Mýrdal, Iceland
19:10 GMT, 5 January

Hildur stood in front of the television in her living room with the remote in her right hand, flicking through multiple channels, looking for news about the invasion. The Reckoning had given her a completely different view of what was happening. The invaders were here against their will, the excess citizens of a planet well beyond its carrying capacity. They had resided at the bottom rung of society because their "Society" had given them low Social Scores. These aliens had received low Social Scores because they were repeatedly noncompliant with the greater goals and greater good of Society. They were not typically violent; they just disagreed.

"Hildur. Hildur, *hleyptu mér inn. Ég er með kjötsúpa,*" said the muffled voice of Kolbrún from outside.

Hildur turned to Trevor, who stood beside the door. "Can you let Kolbrún in? She has *kjötsúpa.*"

"*Flýttu þér. Áður en einn þeirra sér mig með mat.*"

"And she's worried they're going to see her with food." Hildur rolled her eyes as she switched channels.

Kolbrún walked through the living room holding a Crockpot with both hands. A rifle was slung over her left shoulder. She put the Crockpot on the kitchen table. "Come to the table now, Trevor. I have made here kjötsúpa if you are hungry."

"What's kjötsúpa?"

"Kjötsúpa is lamb stew," Hildur said. "It is Kolbrún's specialty."

Kolbrún smiled as she pulled several bowls from Hildur's cupboard. "Hildur, you are watching television?"

"I have been trying to find some news about the invasion. There is nothing about it on any of the channels. Not the Icelandic stations. Nothing on the BBC, Deutsche Welle, or NNN. How could all these news channels not be covering what has happened to us?"

Kolbrún shook her head. "There is nothing in the news about this invasion. They do not care about us."

"Well, the British are coming," Trevor said.

"Yes," Kolbrún said as she placed several bowls on the table. "I have heard this. The NATO is helping us. I have also heard there is an EMP around Iceland. Trevor, you are the scientist. What is this EMP? Why does it make the planes fall out of the sky, and the ships lose all their power and drift into the rocks?"

Trevor sat at the table. "Well, when you make a radio transmission, you create a fluctuating magnetic field that travels outward through the air in all directions. When this fluctuating magnetic field hits a conductor, like an antenna, it creates a corresponding fluctuating electrical current that can be decoded as information. These magnetic fields and corresponding electrical currents are low energy, so they don't create any damage. But if we were to intensify the energy of such a magnetic field, like what would happen if you exploded a nuclear bomb, the resulting electrical currents created in any conductor encountered by this magnetic field would be strong enough to fry any sensitive electrical components. Semiconductors are especially sensitive, and the effect would be like a power surge in your electrical wiring. There can also be man-made nonnuclear EMPs generated, and there are weapons that do just that. Several years ago, I worked on an EMP weapons project at my lab."

Kolbrún sat down at the table. "So, this EMP targets airplanes and ships?"

"Well, no. It doesn't target them, but it does destroy the semiconductors that run the various computer systems installed in modern aircraft and ships. Many years ago, these EMPs would not have been such a big deal, but today, we run everything off semiconductors. So, aircraft that encountered these powerful EMPs became very difficult-to-control gliders because they were forced to use backup cables and hydraulics and had no propulsion. Some were able to glide and land. Others were able to glide into the water. Others became uncontrollable and crashed."

Hildur asked, "And the same for the ships? They lost their controls and engines as well?"

Trevor nodded. "Yes, although it's not quite as serious for a ship. It won't sink from an EMP, but it will lose most of its control and power systems. And of course, the newer and more modern the ship, the more vulnerable it is to the EMP. The same goes for aircraft."

Es-mar peeked her head around the corner of the hallway as she ate a small cracker.

Kolbrún reached for her rifle. *"Farðu út!"*

Es-mar backed herself up against the wall as Kolbrún jumped up from her seat and pointed the rifle at her.

"Nei!" Hildur screamed. *"Nei,* Kolbrún. *Hún er vinkona mín!"*

Kolbrún clicked the safety off the rifle and rested her index finger against the trigger. *"Farðu út!"* The rifle followed Es-mar as she walked toward the front door.

"Hún er vinkona mín!" Hildur screamed as she jumped up from her seat and grabbed the barrel of the rifle. "I said she is my friend. Ask Trevor if you do not believe me."

"Friend? She will steal what little food you have."

"No, Kolbrún. She will not. I know her thoughts. She will not take anything from us." She faced Es-mar as she pointed the barrel of the rifle at the floor. "Es-mar, please sit at the table. Kolbrún has made kjötsúpa for us. She would like very much for you to have some."

Kolbrún clicked the safety back on the rifle. "Very well. She may eat with us if you insist, but I do not trust her." Kolbrún marched back into the kitchen with her rifle slung over her left shoulder. She eyed Es-mar as she walked past her. *"Fjandands geimverur."*

"They are not damn aliens." Hildur shook her head as she sat back down at the table. "Kolbrún, something happened between me and this girl here. We understand each other. I understand their world."

Kolbrún returned with an extra bowl and stirred the contents of her Crockpot. "Well, all I have seen are mobs of them all looking for food. They try to break into my house and get my food. I do not like them."

"I understand, Kolbrún, but put yourself in their shoes," Hildur said. "They were brought here against their will. This is a strange place to them. They are simply trying to survive."

Kolbrún replaced the lid on the Crockpot. "Well, I am trying to survive as well—on a small pension. I cannot afford to feed a bunch of convicts from another planet."

"How did you know they are convicts, Kolbrún?"

"I have received emails from people in town. They are saying they are convicts. They have been sentenced to spend the rest of their lives—"

Hildur jumped up from the table. "Email? We will use the email!"

"Use email for what, Hildur?" Trevor asked.

"To let the world know what is going on here. There is no news reporting. I have seen a few posts on social media, but they seem to disappear soon after they are posted. I do not understand why, but everything about the penal colony is being blocked—except personal email. The world needs to know what is happening to us. We must make a video and tell the world the truth."

Trevor shook his head. "Are you sure that's a good idea, Hildur? I mean … could it make you a target?"

"Trevor, I understand them. I understand their world. The Reckoning has given me this insight. I will make a video. We will send it out to everyone I know. Hopefully, it will go viral. I must tell the world what I know."

"I really think this is a bad idea, Hildur," Trevor said. "If news about what is happening here is being suppressed, somebody is doing it for a reason, and that somebody might not be too happy with your video."

"Nonsense, Trevor. Iceland is a free country. I will make the video now." Hildur sat down in front of her desktop computer, which sat in an alcove of her living room.

She began recording. "Hello. My name is Hildur Einarsdóttir. I operate ice cave tours at Eyjafjallajökull. I am speaking to you today from Vík, Iceland, because all the news stations are ignoring what is happening here, and the world needs to know.

"Earlier today, Iceland was invaded by aliens. I experienced this invasion with my very own set of eyes from Eyjafjallajökull. Many here in Vík are saying that these invaders are violent and that they are running around in angry mobs stealing food. Some have also said that these invaders are convicts disposed of here by their home planet's government. This is all true; however, it is not the whole truth.

"I experienced what these aliens call a Reckoning. I shared my mind equally with a female alien who I rescued from an ice crevasse. I know her mind. I know their world. While it is true that they are all convicts, most are not guilty of violent crimes. They were sent here because their planet was becoming overcrowded, and their Social Scores were too low. They were disposed of here not because they committed some violent act but because they did not conform to what Society dictated for them.

"Society, or their Society, is attempting to social engineer itself into what it calls 'The Great Society,' but these convicts got in the way. Their offenses ranged from publicly disagreeing with Society's policies to attempting to take part in an interracial sexual relationship.

"Society divides itself into three races. An individual's race defines that individual, and the individual can have no identity that does not conform to his or her racial norms. Furthermore, interracial relationships beyond acquaintances are strictly forbidden.

"There are rumors that other groups of convicts have been sent to Earth. There are rumors that a place in Texas was also attacked, just like Iceland. I do not know this for certain, and there is nothing on the news about this.

"Now, I will speak about these alien convicts. I have seen them act as an angry mob, and I have seen them act with kindness as individuals. Please, if you encounter one of them, put on their shoes. They have been removed from their loved ones and from the only world they have ever known. They were brought here against their will and dumped onto the glacier.

"I do not know how many are here, but it must be several thousand. Some are what we would call medical doctors, journalists, scientists, and engineers. They have very advanced technical knowledge and could be of great use to us here on Earth.

"If you are seeing this video, I ask you to please forward it to as many people as possible. I also ask that if you encounter an alien, please try to understand what they are experiencing. You must know that they are simply trying to survive on an alien planet."

Hildur ended the recording and pasted the video file onto a new email. She copied her entire email address book and hit Send. The email soon went viral.

CHAPTER THIRTY-THREE

Honolulu, Hawai'i
09:20 HST, 5 January

It darkened inside the cargo van as they entered the Tetsuo Harano Tunnels through the Ko'olau Mountains. Kup raised his head just enough to see out of the windshield. Ahead, two police cars blocked both eastbound lanes of the tunnel. The speedometer read seventy-six miles per hour.

He flattened himself on his stomach on the cargo van's floor.

Gunfire erupted, and glass shattered seconds before the bread truck slammed into both police cars. The impact knocked Kup against the backs of both the passenger and driver seats, but the bread truck continued down the road, although at a slower speed.

The alien in the passenger seat was slumped over with his head on the dashboard. Thick orange blood dripped onto his left knee and coagulated. Thick orange blood also dripped from the driver's head onto the yellow hibiscus print of his lime-green Hawaiian shirt.

It brightened inside the cargo van, and Kup sat up. Through the windshield, the H3 Highway snaked left along the steep sides of the Ko'olau Mountains. The cargo van was headed to the right.

Kup shook the driver's shoulder. "Are you okay?"

He didn't respond, and they began accelerating as they went downhill. Small guardrails lined both sides of the elevated road. They offered little protection from a deadly fall along the near-vertical, jungle-covered mountainside to the valley floor below.

"Are you okay? Can you drive?" Kup shook the driver's shoulder once again. "We're going to go over the side. Turn us left!"

Kup reached forward, grabbed the steering wheel with his left hand,

and tried to steer to the left. "Let go!"

They started wobbling left and right as Kup and the driver fought for control.

"Let go of the steering wheel, dammit! You're going to kill us both!"

The driver turned his bloodied head and attempted to focus on Kup's hands.

Kup turned left so hard that the right wheels lifted off the pavement, and they almost rolled over. They missed the right guardrail by a few inches.

"We're going too fast. Hit the brakes!"

Another big curve appeared ahead to the right. They were still going too fast and accelerating even more as the road lost elevation.

"Slow down, dammit!"

The automatic transmission had a manual shift mode. Kup reached down to the gearshift with his right hand and switched to manual mode. The transmission indicated it was in fifth gear.

He began turning to the right. The wheels on the left side lifted off the pavement.

Kup slammed the gearshift into fourth gear. The engine started whining, and the RPM indicator shot up.

He shifted into third. The engine whined louder, but the tires on the left side settled back onto the pavement.

He shifted into second, and the engine revved even higher in response. The speedometer showed thirty-five and was slowing.

The cargo van lurched as he shifted into first gear. He eased further to the right, causing the right side to scrape along the guardrail. The cargo van slowed down even more. He applied more pressure to the steering wheel, and the cargo van screeched to a stop.

Kup's left hand shook as he opened the driver's side door. He unbuckled the driver's seat belt and nudged the driver's shoulder to the left. The driver tumbled out of the seat and onto the pavement.

Kup squirmed into the driver's seat. He reached down and shoved the alien's legs clear of the door, then glanced back along the left side of the cargo van to see if anyone was following them. *I'm in a bread truck?*

A black Suburban emerged from a bend in the road. It was the only vehicle on the road. "Bloody hell." *That's got to be a government vehicle.*

Kup slammed the door shut. He put the transmission back into automatic mode and shifted into reverse, then backed away from the guard-rail, shifted into drive, and sped away. He shook his head after glancing at his passenger. *I'll really blend in driving around in a bread truck with a dead alien in the right seat. At least his shirt won't stand out.*

Kup swung to the right and onto the exit ramp for the Likelike Highway. He glanced at his side mirror. *Damn! They took the exit, and they're gaining on me. Where can I go?*

He entered traffic and began honking his horn and squeezing in between cars. The black Suburban weaved in and around the traffic as it closed in on him.

He swung into the right shoulder and accelerated as he entered Kaneohe. The tires squealed as he turned right onto Kamehameha Highway. *I've got to get off the main roads.*

In the side mirror, Kup saw a moving van had trapped the Suburban. Kup sped up, hoping to increase the distance between them.

He looked down at the orange coveralls he was wearing, with "Federal Detention Center – Honolulu" plastered across the front. *Could I be any more conspicuous?*

Kup examined the wardrobe of the dead alien in the passenger seat. The khaki cargo shorts and turquoise Hawaiian shirt appeared wearable.

A road sign for the Pali Golf Course appeared ahead and to the right. He turned right onto the road. *Please don't be a dead end.*

The two-lane road ended in a parking lot beside the two-story tan clubhouse of the golf course. The knife-edged green of the Ko'olau Mountains in the distance formed the backdrop.

Kup pulled into a stall in a remote corner of the parking lot. He swiveled the passenger seat around and, after multiple attempts, pulled the dead alien to the floor. As fast as he could, he changed into the dead alien's clothes. Kup found a wallet containing several hundred dollars in the front right pocket of the cargo shorts. Poking out of a clear pocket on the side was a Hawai'i driver's license. *Luka Hill?* He tossed the wallet through the shattered driver's side window and shoved Jerry's cash and business card into the right front pocket of the shorts.

Soon, he was back on Kamehameha Highway in the turquoise Hawaiian shirt covered with humuhumunukunukuapua'a. The dead alien was lying in the back of the van, wearing only his navy boxer shorts adorned with orange and yellow pineapples. The prison jumpsuit was stashed in a rubbish bin with "OPALA" written across its flapper door.

Kup looked ahead as Kamehameha Highway came to a dead end at the Pali Highway. *Left or right? Which way?*

The traffic turning left was shorter, so Kup got into the left turn lane. Soon after turning onto the Pali Highway, Kup turned right onto the Kalaniana'ole Highway toward Waimanalo.

Kup continued looking in the side mirror for the black Suburban or even a standard police car. He knew he had to get out of the bread truck somewhere; he just didn't know where that somewhere should be.

Kup passed Waimanalo Beach Parks. *I could park the bread truck here,* he thought. *But then what?*

He saw a sign for Makapu'u Lighthouse Road. He needed somewhere to dump the conspicuous and probably stolen bread truck. Soon, he would be in Hawai'i Kai and on the eastern edges of Honolulu.

Kup turned left and headed down a short road that ended at the paved trailhead leading to Makapu'u Point Lighthouse. The spots of splattered orange blood blended into the burnt-orange interior and weren't too noticeable.

Kup got out of the bread truck and closed the door, opting to leave the keys in the ignition. *Maybe somebody will steal this thing.*

As Kup walked to the trailhead, he passed several tourists. None gave him a second look. The cash and business card were in the right front pocket of the cargo shorts.

The paved trail had climbed from fifty feet to two hundred eighty-five feet in a southwest direction when Kup stopped to look around. To the southeast, the faint outline of Moloka'i rose from the horizon. Toward the north, the trail climbed to over five hundred feet, where it came to a dead end at Makapu'u Point. Directly below, the Pacific Ocean met a rocky shoreline that formed a series of cliffs rising to where Kup stood. Toward the northwest, Kup could see cars parked along the road that led to the trailhead. He could also just make out the bread truck half a mile away.

Around him, quite a few people and dogs enjoyed the trail. Very few of them were serious hikers, and Kup blended in well. The anonymity gave him time to think. *I could borrow someone's cellphone and call Jerry. I could tell them I dropped mine over one of these cliffs while taking pictures. That's believable. Jerry could pick me up back at the trailhead.*

Kup started scanning people as they approached from below and above his spot on the trail. About twenty feet away, he spotted a young couple taking selfies with the ocean in the background. He began walking toward them but stopped when a police siren started wailing in the distance.

Kup's heart began pounding.

The police car's flashing lights were moving northeast along the Kalaniana'ole Highway, just south of the turnoff for the Makapu'u Point Lighthouse Trail.

Please don't turn.

The police car slowed and turned right onto the access road leading to the trailhead. It slowed down and pulled alongside the parked bread truck.

CHAPTER THIRTY-FOUR

Honolulu, Hawai'i
10:30 HST, 5 January

Kup stood frozen, staring at the police car in the distance, his only exit now blocked. There were no other access points. He began running north toward Makapu'u Point, away from the police. What he was running toward, he wasn't sure.

Why is all this happening to me? I didn't ask for any of this. To Kup's left, the rocky landscape strewn with cactus and kiawe trees plunged to the lower switchback, leading back to the trailhead. To his right, cliffs dropped to a rocky shoreline. There was nowhere to go but forward. *Why are they doing this to me? I just want all this to end.*

The police siren stopped.

Kup kept running as the trail kept climbing. About fifty feet to the right, a couple had veered off the paved trail and were heading down a rocky trail toward the ocean below. Kup followed and soon passed them, scrambling down the trail toward a series of tidepools where ten people were swimming.

At the tidepools, Kup took off his turquoise shirt, wadded it up, and stuffed it underneath a large rock. He shed his flip-flops and jumped into the water. *Jerry's business card! You idiot!*

But the cool water felt good and, for an instant, gave him peace.

Kup pulled himself out of the tidepool and reached into his pocket for the business card, which was embossed plastic. It was waterproof—and expensive.

He slipped on his flip-flops and began walking along the rocky shore-line with the ocean to his left and rising cliffs to his right. His turquoise shirt remained wadded up underneath the rock.

The going was slow along the rocks compared to the paved trail, especially wearing thin prison flip-flops. The saltwater spray from the crashing waves kept him cool beside the rocky cliff, but his tongue flopped up against the dry roof of his mouth in search of any last bit of saliva.

His feet and legs ached, and he chose a flat area to sit for a few minutes. In an endless cycle, the waves crashed upon the rocks and shot spray about twelve feet into the air. Twenty yards to his right, the rocky coastline rose up and formed a small cliff about fifteen feet above the water, which fluctuated from dark blue to turquoise to sea green. Directly in front of him, the outline of Moloka'i remained on the distant horizon, and beyond Moloka'i lay the island of Maui. Beyond Maui lay the Big Island and Kahealani.

Kup rested his forehead on both of his palms. He propped his elbows on his knees and thought about jumping in the water one last time and swimming until he couldn't swim anymore.

Another wave crashed against the rocks. He heard a faint but familiar male voice in the distance. The Warden wasn't speaking English, but Kup understood him perfectly. *He found my shirt? It had a tracker in it? He thinks I might have jumped in the ocean there. Who is he talking to?*

The *tocotocotoco* sound of an approaching helicopter somewhere in the distance drowned out the Warden's voice.

Kup stood up and scanned the rocky coastline. Behind him, sheer cliffs were pockmarked with pocket caves. He heard the Warden's voice again. It was louder now.

Kup ran across the rocks and examined a small cave about ten feet deep. The floor was sunken several inches and covered with stagnant water. The opening was just big enough for him to crawl through, but the interior was much larger. It took several seconds for his eyes to adjust to the darkness. A'ama crabs, their black shells blending in with the dark interior, mostly scampered out of his way, but some were crushed beneath his flip-flops.

"Kuparr Winston," said the not-so-faint voice of the Warden just as a wave crashed.

Kup's heart pounded against his chest.

The Warden stood twenty feet away at the peak of the small cliff as he scanned the surface of the ocean. He wore hiking boots, shorts, and a dark-green Hawaiian shirt. The grip of a tranqgun stuck out of the right pocket of his shorts. He held a commblock in his right hand; its connected earpiece and mic were in his right ear.

He's directing the search for me. They're all headed this way—all of them.

The Warden turned around and scanned the rocky cliffs. He paused for several seconds at each cave entrance, including Kup's.

He turned back and faced the ocean as he pulled a small thermal scanner, about the size of an oversized smartphone, from his left front pocket. He began scanning the ocean surface from left to right, followed by the coastline, cliffs, and caves to Kup's right. The thermal scanner would soon be pointed directly at Kup's cave, directly at Kup.

Kup pulled back from the cave entrance and pressed himself against a sidewall of the cave, out of view from the cave entrance. His heart felt like it would jump out of his chest.

Seconds of silence turned into minutes.

The Warden began talking.

Kup eased himself toward the cave entrance to hear better. *He thinks he may have found me? In the ocean?* Kup peeked out of the cave entrance.

The Warden still stood on the small cliff with the thermal scanner in his left hand. Both the scanner and the Warden were facing the ocean.

Kup crawled out of the cave and ran toward the Warden.

When Kup was five feet from him, the Warden spun around and faced Kup.

Kup squatted into a ball.

The Warden pulled the tranqgun out of his pocket with his right hand, and the commblock fell to the ground. "Stop, Kuparr Win—"

The impact with the Warden felt like hitting a brick wall, except the brick wall lost its balance and gave way. The Warden fell backward over the small cliff. The tranqgun and thermal scanner flew ten feet skyward before following the Warden and Kup into the ocean.

The cool ocean enveloped Kup and stopped his descent eight feet under the water. He opened his eyes. With his unfocused, underwater vision, he saw a flat, sandy bottom two feet below his left flip-flop, which had somehow managed to stay on his foot. Ten feet in front of him, rocks rose straight up to the small cliff he had just tumbled over, and ten feet to his right, rocks rose to a ledge about four feet deep. Rapid clicking sounds from a nearby pod of spinner dolphins indicated a discussion of the sudden human intrusion. To his left, a small whitetip reef shark scurried out of view. In every direction, aquarium-worthy fish mostly went about their business.

Kup kicked toward the surface but went down to the sandy bottom instead as four fingers of equal length clasped around his ankle. He spun his head around and saw the Warden kneeling on the sand.

Kup looked into the Warden's eyes. *He's terrified.* Kup tried to pull free of the Warden's grip but soon realized it was futile. *He's got at least five minutes of air left in his lungs. I'd be lucky to have two.* Kup spun himself around and placed his hands on the Warden's shoulders. He pressed their foreheads together. His eyes rolled back.

After a minute and a half, Kup needed air. His subconscious broke off the Reckoning, but it had lasted long enough. The Warden had agreed to the deal—his life in exchange for Kup's escape.

The Warden, now fully conscious like Kup, released his grip on Kup's right leg.

Kup surfaced, took three large breaths, and dove back down. He grabbed the Warden's left wrist with his right hand and began pulling him to the surface. The Warden was too heavy, and Kup was physically spent. He pulled the Warden sideways and began swimming underwater. The Warden stood and walked along the sand, following Kup toward the rock ledge that was to their right.

Kup stuck his left hand into a large crack in the rock wall and pulled himself and the Warden upward and onto the sand of the four-foot-deep ledge. The Warden collapsed onto his knees. The top of his head was less than a foot below the surface.

Kup stood and took a huge breath as he looked down into the water. "Oh, come on, really? Stand up, you twit." Kup reached into the water, grabbed the Warden's right wrist, and pulled upward.

The faint *tocotocotoco* of a helicopter became fainter.

The Warden's head pushed above the surface as he stood up. He gasped for air as a small wave crested over his head. "Help me!"

Kup put his right hand underneath the Warden's right armpit and walked him to an outcropping of rocks. "Come on, mate. It's just a little water."

With considerable effort, the Warden pulled himself onto the rocks.

Kup walked to the edge of the shallow ledge. In the distance, one of his prison flip-flops bobbed on the surface. Well beyond that was the hazy outline of Moloka'i. *It's too late for the Big Island. There's not enough time.*

The sound of the helicopter was growing louder again.

Kup glanced back toward the Warden and nodded before returning his gaze to Moloka'i. *Eyjafjallajökull. He's worried about Eyjafjallajökull.*

He took a deep breath and dove into the water.

CHAPTER THIRTY-FIVE

Kealakekua Bay, The Big Island of Hawai'i
12:00 HST, 5 January

Kahealani Winston floated in her canoe in the middle of
Kealakekua Bay and ate the avocado sandwich she had brought
for lunch. The avocado was from a tree in their yard, and she
had baked the bread herself. A hundred yards away, a pod of spinner
dolphins continually jumped out of the water and spun. No one knew
why they did it. The best explanation seemed to be because they could.

Kahealani had paddled out across the bay from the small pier at
Napo'opo'o, which was on the south end of Kealakekua Bay, below her
house. The bay was her special place. According to legend, Kealakekua
was a shortened version of *Keala Ke Akua*—the Pathway to God.

Kahealani couldn't fly to O'ahu to see Kup. The FBI wasn't telling
her much and had even threatened her if she attempted to interfere in
their official investigation. Out of fear, she had avoided contacting the
press.

As for the press, there had been rampant speculation on social media
that what had happened to Iceland and Galveston might also happen to
the Big Island; however, NNN had treated the rumors as disinformation.
Either way, with her life in turmoil, she didn't care what happened next.

The surrounding water was full of semisubmerged snorkelers who
didn't seem to care either.

She looked up at the sky when she noticed the nonstop noise of
fighter jets from the previous few days was gone.

She stopped chewing when she heard three explosions seconds
apart somewhere to the south. After several more seconds of quiet, she
shrugged and continued eating.

She thought about how she had volunteered for the campaign of Senator Damonati the previous year. When she reached out for help from Senator Damonati's staff that morning, they told her the senator believed the best course of action was to let the FBI investigation run its course. They said there was nothing the senator could or would do for Kahealani, but she thanked her for her previous support.

A male snorkeler treading water beside Kahealani took off his mask and began staring past her.

Kahealani turned her head to the side. There was a commotion aboard the hundred-passenger catamaran to her right. Everyone seemed to be looking and pointing at something. She paddled to spin her canoe further to the right and strained her head to get a better view.

Kahealani dropped her paddle into the water. A massive UFO consisting of a vertical cylinder topped by a much wider cap floated toward her. The ship was spinning counterclockwise as it paralleled the coastline slightly inland.

By now, more and more snorkelers were treading water, watching the object. A metal disk spun out from the bottom of the UFO. Several parachutes inflated, and the disk floated down out of sight. Kahealani began paddling back toward Napo'opo'o, and one by one, snorkelers began swimming back to their boats.

Within minutes, the object was almost above her but inland from where she was. She watched a disk disappear into the brush south of Napo'opo'o. It landed with a dull thud. She stopped paddling as another disk spun out from the bottom of the UFO and tumbled end over end. It eventually righted itself, and when it did, it was directly overhead.

Kahealani began paddling with all her strength. Screams rippled across the bay. Boat engines were revving up all around her. Several wakes tossed her canoe. She paddled as hard as she ever had in her life.

The sky darkened overhead as the massive disk shadowed the sun. She had to keep paddling. There were more screams and cries for help from people in the water as boats roared past them.

A whoosh of wind blew past Kahealani, followed by the sound of water ejecting skyward. Seconds later, a five-foot wave raised the back of her canoe and spun it around. She stopped paddling.

The end of the disk rose from under the water about twenty yards in front of her, and water spilled over the sides as it emerged. The opposite end of the disk angled up and appeared to have dropped onto land on Kaʻawaloa, which was on the north side of the bay.

On top of the disk, clear hatches popped open, and out of those hatches popped not quite a thousand heads. The side of the disk nearest Kahealani started sinking while the side of the disk on land tilted upward. Bodies began scrambling onto the surface of the disk as water poured into the disk on the side that was sinking.

In less than a minute, the massive disk began sliding down the steep coral-encrusted walls of Kealakekua Bay. Where there had been hundreds of human snorkelers floating in the water minutes before, there were now almost a thousand panic-stricken beings from another planet. The water churned as they struggled to stay afloat after waking up in an alien world after a long cryogenic sleep.

The now familiar tsunami warning sirens along the coast of the island began blaring. Kahealani assumed they were warning the island of something else.

Hundreds of unintelligible screams and cries for help echoed against the four-hundred-foot cliffs that formed the east side of the bay. She had one small canoe. There wasn't much she could do for them, but she still paddled over to help those that were closest.

There were fewer and fewer screams, and the water became calmer.

Kahealani's canoe flipped over. She opened her eyes underwater and saw bodies thrashing about all around her. She kicked her legs and stroked her arms to the surface. A foot struck her forehead. She surfaced and watched her canoe submerge under the weight of ten alien bodies, all wrapped in tight white skinsuits.

She swam back to the small pier at Napoʻopoʻo. Each time she stopped to catch her breath, there were fewer and fewer screams, fewer and fewer cries for help.

Kahealani walked toward her white Jeep Wrangler in the parking lot. It was a short drive home. Police sirens wailed in the distance. *Everything he said has come true. Everything they've said is a lie.*

She reached down to grab the key hidden under the back bumper. She wasn't alone.

A female voice from behind her said, "Excuse me, but do you have any food? I am hungry."

Kahea stood up and turned around. A tall blond woman about her same age stood about five feet from her. She was wearing the same white skinsuit as the people she had seen drowning in Kealakekua Bay. The skinsuit accentuated her slim, muscular figure. She was over six feet tall.

Kahealani's mouth gaped open. She wasn't sure if she should run; she wasn't sure if she should help. "Uh … I have some pineapple. You can have that." *They all seemed so helpless in the water, but this one is on land.*

"Yes. I am hungry. I have not eaten in a long time."

Kahealani reached into the back seat of her Jeep and handed the woman her Ziploc bag of cut pineapple.

The woman took the Ziploc and studied it. "Thank you, but how do I open the bag?"

Kahealani glanced at the bag. *You don't know how to open a Ziploc?* "You slide the little red thing at the top to the other end."

The woman's skinsuit bore an outline of the Hawaiian Islands on the left side of her chest. She opened the Ziploc bag, took out a chunk of pineapple, and began chewing. "This is delicious. May I have more? I am so hungry."

"You may have it all."

"Thank you. Thank you so much." The strange woman began eating the remaining pineapple as fast as she could swallow it.

Kahealani thought of what Kup had told her. "So, you are an alien? An alien convict?"

The strange woman stopped eating. Her eyes darted left and right. "Yes. We are not of this planet." She looked down at the ground. "And yes, we have very low Social Scores."

"We?"

"Yes, all of us wearing these suits. Our world ran out of room for us. I believe you have an expression—we were 'culled from the herd.'"

"And what did you do? I mean, why were you chosen to be sent here?"

"I became self-centered, self-righteous. I had grown to believe I knew better than Society what was best for my children."

"What?" Kahea shook her head.

"Well, I am what you would call a medical doctor. One of my children developed a serious medical condition. Society decides who will receive treatment and when. The wait for treatment was very long. I feared for my child's life, and I treated him myself. He reported me to the authorities, who charged me with *Social Deviation*. My Social Score dropped, and Society selected me for *Transport*."

"Your child reported you to the authorities?"

"Yes, it increased his Social Score. I am very proud of him. I also have a daughter and a male partner, and I will not see any of them again."

"That is so sad," Kahealani said. "I'm so sorry to hear all this."

The strange woman nodded and ate another piece of pineapple. "It is beautiful here."

Kahealani nodded. "So where are you … where are all of you supposed to live now that you're here? I mean, you all arrived in these big disks with nothing?"

"We do not know. This is our prison. Society taught us English and Hawaiian and some general facts about Earth and its plants and animals. They also told us about this island. It is 10,430 square kilometers in area and is the largest island in your country, the United States. Its highest peak is Mauna Kea, at 4.2 kilometers above the ocean surface. The current estimated population of the island is 216,894 humans and 105,000 convicts. The island experiences eleven of the thirteen climates of Earth and is surrounded by the Pacific Ocean. This ocean will kill us."

Kahealani grimaced. "Why will the Pacific Ocean kill you?"

The woman turned her head away. "It is impossible for us to swim."

Kahealani thought back to the frantic thrashing of the aliens she had seen in the water.

The strange woman ate the last chunk of pineapple. "Thank you for the plant. Do you know where I can get more? I am still hungry."

"I don't have any more food with me, but let's walk over here to this tree. It has some delicious fruit called lychee."

The strange woman followed Kahealani to the lychee tree. Kahealani picked several lychees and showed the woman how to peel them.

The strange woman gathered several lychees and placed them in the Ziploc bag. "Thank you for the … pineapple and for showing me the lychee tree."

"You're welcome." Kahealani turned away and began walking toward her Jeep. Halfway back to it, she stopped and turned around toward the alien woman. "Where will you go?"

The woman pulled half a lychee out of her mouth. "I do not know."

Kahealani glanced at her Jeep.

The alien woman took another bite of lychee.

"Who are you?" Kahealani asked. "Do you have a name?"

"I am a *White*."

"Your name is ... White?"

"My individual name is En-gatha. You would pronounce it *en-gat-ha*. But I am a White."

"Okay, well, En-gatha, would you like to come to my house? I live up the hill there." Kahealani pointed up the hillside to the east. "I have food there."

"Yes. I would like that."

Kahealani grabbed her keys and showed the woman how to buckle her seatbelt, then started driving up Napoʻopoʻo Road to her house. They passed several individual aliens walking along the road in both directions, foraging among the plants along the road. They didn't seem interested in Kahealani and En-gatha.

Kahealani turned left onto Kanele Street.

Kahealani's neighbor, Jim Akana, yelled from his yard, "Kahea! Are you okay? Why do you have one of them in your Jeep?"

Kahealani turned toward Jim, whose clothes were dripping wet. "It's okay, Jim. She's okay—even polite."

He pointed at the angry mob stuffing themselves in Kahealani's front yard. "Well, *they're* not polite."

Kahealani looked at her house across the street. In her yard, she recognized her Crockpot in one alien's hands. She had been cooking beef stew that morning.

"Sons of bitches surrounded me in my front yard, demanding food," Jim said. "I tried to fight them off, but they chased me into the backyard. One of them grabbed me by the throat and threw me into the damn swimming pool! Here's the weirdest thing—they all surrounded me in the pool, like they were waiting for me to die or something. I thought one of them was going to jump in the water and drown me, but not one of them would get in the water. Then a couple of them went around the house, smashing the windows. They ate every bit of food I had in the house."

Kahealani had counted eight broken windows in her house when an alien reached down, grabbed a football-size rock, and hurled it at a sliding glass door.

CHAPTER THIRTY-SIX

"Iceland?" Jerry glanced down at his Rolex Submariner and yawned. *How can he just keep talking?*

Kup sat in a large recliner in the corner of Jerry's suite, sipping a Lavaman Red Ale. He wore a brand-new blue golf shirt emblazoned with the emblem of Hawai'i Kai Golf Course, which he'd bought with the cash still sitting in his cargo shorts pocket. He also sported a brand-new pair of white spikeless golf shoes and black footies. He had swum ashore at Alan Davis Beach and hiked along the Kai Iwi Shoreline Trail, ending up on the Hawai'i Kai Golf Course. After he'd made his clothing purchases, the cashier had allowed Kup to use the phone.

"The key to disarming the EMPs is in Iceland."

"Okay, care to embellish?"

"Each island is a penal colony and has a Command Ship emitting an EMP down over it. The aliens can shape the EMP, and it's narrow at the top and wider at the bottom, like a cone. The cone is configurable, though. They can shape the bottom to conform to the shape of each island. The problem is, everything electronic underneath the EMP would be permanently disabled, and I guess they don't want that for whatever reason." Kup took another sip of beer.

"Go on."

"So, what they did was place a second EMP in the ground on each island that is exactly out of phase with the Command Ship's EMP. The ground-based EMP cancels out the Command Ship's EMP, like a pair of noise-canceling headsets."

"I'm a lawyer, not an engineer," Jerry said. "How do noise-canceling headsets work?"

"They sample the ambient noise with a microphone and emit a sound exactly out of phase with the ambient noise. The ambient noise gets canceled out, more or less."

Jerry nodded. "Okay, I understand, I guess. The ground-based EMP cancels out the airborne EMP—but wouldn't that cancel out the EMP everywhere?"

"So, here's the deal. The ground-based EMP is a hemisphere instead of a cone."

"Huh?"

"Think of it like half a bubble or like a giant circular dome. This bubble covers the entire island but doesn't fully extend to the top or sides of the EMP cone from above. It fades out at a certain point, and a band is left where the EMP from above is unaffected. If you pass through this band in either direction, it will destroy everything electronic. But within the ground-based EMP bubble, everything works normally. Inside the narrow EMP band or shroud, however, you're screwed."

"So, how big is this band?"

"It varies from as narrow as eight hundred meters to almost three thousand meters. The width is different for each island."

"Meters?" Jerry asked.

"Yes, they use something similar to our metric system."

Jerry shrugged. "Okay, so I understand the electromagnetic pulse and the system they're using, but I still don't understand why you need to go to Iceland."

"Because they don't do anything independently, including engineering. So, instead of each island having an independent electromagnetic pulse system, they're all joined together collectively with a central Command Ship that sits over Hawai'i. The central ground controller, however, is unmanned and buried in an ice cave in Iceland. It controls the other two ground controllers via the Iceland Command Ship and satellite relays. They're using our satellites to do this, by the way. The Warden had voiced concerns about the vulnerability of the emitter in Iceland, but Command ignored him."

"Command?"

"The central military authorities."

"Gotcha. So, what's the vulnerability?"

"The ground-based electromagnetic pulse emitter in Iceland has a manual override where you can control the ground-based emitters in Galveston and Hawai'i remotely."

"Okay, and what does that get you?"

"If I manually override the controls of the ground-based EMP emitter in Iceland, then I can reconfigure its EMP emitter—and the emitters in Galveston and Hawai'i—and raise the electromagnetic pulse to each Command Ship, destroying each Command Ship's electric systems. I can take out all three Command Ships."

Jerry sat back in the recliner next to the sliding glass door. "Damn. You got all this information from your Reckoning thing?"

"Yes. It sounds crazy, but I know what the Warden knows. I received all this technical knowledge of their systems. The Warden is an expert; he helped design the system. He is also the head of all three penal colonies. This plan is my idea, though. I mean, the Warden didn't tell me to go to Iceland and destroy their Command Ships, but he was concerned about this vulnerability."

"Okay, so let's say you're successful, and you destroy all these EMPs. Won't they just come back and rebuild the system? Won't they just come back for you?"

"No, they won't. The island penal colonies are experimental. That's why they're in different climates, why the islands are different sizes, and why they have different population densities. They're looking for the best places, the best islands—however, they're also looking for the best planet to dump their excess citizens. Earth is their first choice, but there are many others available. If all the penal colonies fail, the entire experiment fails, and they will move on to planet number two. If the penal colonies are successful, however, there will be more—lots more—and then the nonconvicts will come. *Billions* of them."

"Billions?"

"Yes, billions. Earth will be overrun by their technology and overwhelmed by their culture. We'll become second-class citizens on our own planet. Our culture, our language—hell, even our past—will be erased. We'll all be reeducated into Society—their Society. It's all happened before. I reckon I never really gave a damn about my family's history or my nation's history, but now I know I can't let that history repeat itself."

"All right, Kup. So then all you gotta do is head over to Iceland and find this EMP thingy and reprogram it. Wait, where is the EMP thingy in Iceland, anyway?"

"Hidden in an ice cave under Eyjafjallajökull."

"Huh …" Jerry stood up. "The girl in Iceland. I saw a video she made. She does ice cave tours in—Eyeyawhatever you just said."

Kup jumped out of the recliner. "Eyjafjallajökull? Bloody hell! Show me the video, Jerry."

"Sure. You know what? I think she also experienced the Reckoning thingy like you." Jerry grabbed his iPad. After a few seconds of manipulation, he found the video and handed the iPad to Kup.

"How did you get this video, Jerry?"

"One of my friends back in Houston emailed it to me. Not sure where he got it from."

Kup viewed the video. "Her name is Hildur Einarsdóttir. She has had a Reckoning—with a convict. Shit, Jerry. She's the key. She can get us into the ice cave under Eyjafjallajökull."

"Us?" Jerry frowned. "There's no—"

"Jerry, the aliens hid the EMP emitter in the ice cave under Eyjafjallajökull and sealed it off with a wall of ice about a meter thick. This Hildur lady can take us there."

"Stop saying 'us.' How are you—how are you going to cut through a meter of ice?"

"I'm working on that. We could melt it or drill through it with an auger, maybe."

"Okay, so all *you* have to do is cut through a meter of ice in an ice cave in Iceland and reprogram the EMP thingy. Easy, right?" Jerry rolled his eyes. "But let me ask you this: How is a guy who's about to be on the FBI's Most Wanted list going to get off *this* island? And how are you, or anyone for that matter, going to pass through the EMP shroud you say surrounds Iceland?"

"We'll sail through it, Jerry."

"Sail through it? Sail to *Iceland?* From where?"

"I'll show you." Kup began manipulating Jerry's iPad. "Your wife was able to sail through the EMP shroud. That's how she got to …"

"Kemah?"

"Yes, she was able to sail through the EMP shroud that surrounds

Galveston Island and get to Kemah, which is on the mainland. She's inspired some people. I read this news story on a spare computer at the golf course they let me use while I was waiting for you."

Kup handed the iPad back to Jerry, who began reading the Worldwide News article.

"Isn't this one of those conspiracy websites the FTA is always warning us about?" Jerry said.

"Just read the damn article, mate."

> Faroe Islands Ferry Company Organizes Rescue Operation
>
> By William McGurn
>
> Skál Lines of Tórshavn, Faroe Islands, announced this morning an ambitious plan to bring much-needed supplies to the people of Iceland.
>
> Company officials said they were inspired by seeing the private sailboats in Galveston, USA, ferrying supplies across the No-Transgression Zone surrounding Galveston Island. They got the idea to do the same thing using their combo passenger/vehicle ferry, the *Sissal*.
>
> They plan on station-keeping the ferry outside of the Iceland No-Transgression Zone and will use a fleet of small daysailers sailed by volunteers to bring supplies into the port of Seyðisfjörður on the west coast of the island nation. The daysailers will return to the ferry with any refugees who would like to leave Iceland.

The company has obtained 30 small sailboats that will be loaded onto the *Sissal*, currently in port in Hirtshals, Denmark. They will also install two small cranes to lift the sailboats in and out of the water.

Skál Lines is seeking volunteers with sailing experience to join them on the rescue mission. Volunteers can embark on the *Sissal* in either Hirtshals or Tórshavn.

The *Sissal* will depart Hirtshals at 16:00 on 8 January and Tórshavn at 14:00 on 10 January.

Interested sailors can call the Skál Volunteer Hotline in the Faroe Islands at +298 34 68 68 or email them at volunteer@ skallines.com

"This is our ticket to Iceland, Jerry. We volunteer to sail one of those small sailboats."

"Volunteer? *Us?* This is your deal, your problem," Jerry said. "Why do I need to go?"

"*My* problem? Yeah, my island just got inundated, but what about your island? What about Galveston? Bloody hell, do you even give a damn about your hometown? I mean, not everyone's family can just hop in the family sailboat and sail away to safety. Don't be such a wanker, Jerry."

"I can give you some money, but—"

"And furthermore, I don't know how to sail. And you've got resources I don't. I'm a wanted man. I need your help to do this. Please."

"But Denmark?" Jerry asked. "Can you even get to Denmark from Hawai'i by the eighth, Kup?"

"Well, technically, yes. Flying commercially, we'd have to leave in the morning to get to either Aalborg or Copenhagen to arrive by—"

"In the morning? Are you out of your mind?"

"Possibly. Look, Jerry, Denmark by the eighth would be tight, but the Faroe Islands by the tenth would be doable. Plus, it will give you more time to obtain my fake passport."

Jerry walked over to the suite's safe, pulled out a wad of hundred-dollar bills, and walked over to Kup. "Here's two thousand dollars. I've heard enough. I've done enough. Now get out of here."

CHAPTER THIRTY-SEVEN

Honolulu, Hawai'i
10:00 HST, 6 January

Jerry stood at the railing of the lanai of his suite. The trade winds tossed his hair as he studied the airline's app on his phone. Gail and the kids were on time and would land in a few hours. Dan and the dogs were staying at Dan's sister's house in Houston.

For Jerry, success drove his life. Money drove his life. He would drive the nicest car, live in the nicest house, sail the nicest sailboat, and become the expert in aviation law.

But everything was now up in the air.

His career-capping lawsuit against Central Pacific was obviously bogus, and he'd broken the law many times over the last two days. His career might already be over.

Galveston had been taken from him. His home and his hometown would never be the same. It had been inundated by beings that would overrun the island, overrun the city, overrun everything he had known. Its residents would have no choice but to adapt and accept their new place in the new Galveston.

The videos from home kept replaying in his mind. Some of the people were his friends and neighbors. Hundreds more were strangers. *Kup said if the penal colonies are successful, more and more of them will come here. Eventually, there will be billions of them.*

Jerry could not kick the images out of his mind, but he had been able to kick Kup out onto the street. At least he'd given him some cash to get a hotel room.

There will be billions more of them if we don't do something.

And now Senator Damonati and Agent Perez were on their way there to meet with him. They had given no reason for the meeting.

He watched a family of four run into the waves below. *I could lose everything. I could lose everything either way.*

James Templeton's distinctive chime emanated from Jerry's cellphone.

Damn. James, now?

"Aloha, James."

"Holy crap, Jerry! I just heard about what happened to you yesterday. Are you okay?"

"Yeah, I'm fine. I got a few scratches. That's all."

"Any idea who Winston got to spring him from the FBI? And why did they take you along?"

"No idea to both questions, James."

"Oh my gosh, this makes Winston and Central Pacific look terrible. We're gonna make bank on this lawsuit, Jerry. By the way, how are things going with the lawsuit? I've lined up a paralegal for you. How many survivors have you signed up?"

"The lawsuit is moving along, but I haven't signed anyone up."

"What?"

"I got kidnapped yesterday, remember."

"Jerry, you gotta move on these people while the experience is still fresh in their minds, while they're still hurting, and while they're still in Honolulu! We don't make money off people who aren't hurting."

"Sure, James. I'll get back to it. As I mentioned, I was a little busy yesterday jumping out of a moving bread truck."

"Oh yeah, are you sure you didn't injure yourself? It wouldn't be a bad thing if you showed up in court all bandaged up from being dragged along on Winston's escape attempt."

"Attempt? James, Winston didn't attempt to escape—he was kidnapped."

"What?"

"You heard me, James. He was kidnapped."

"By whom?"

"Aliens."

"Aliens? Really? You're starting to sound like Winston."

"I'm talking about the same aliens that invaded Galveston. And Iceland. And Hawai'i Island. Those aliens, James."

"Jerry, why would these aliens want to kidnap Winston?"

"Because he knows too much."

"Winston knows too much? Jerry, he's a maniacal pervert who crashed an airliner."

"James, did you see the email from Winston's wife? Everything she said was going to happen has happened."

"No. I don't know what you're talking about."

"James, Winston knew about all this before it happened. His wife made an email before Galveston was invaded. He's been right so far about everything."

"Jerry, I do not like where you're going with this. You need to get ahold of yourself and get back on track with this lawsuit. I think you may have a concussion from falling out of that bread truck."

"James, I know this all sounds crazy, but I think Kup—I think Winston may be innocent. I don't think he crashed Flight 855. I think his not-so-crazy-anymore story about the UFO near miss is true. It's the only explanation that makes any sense."

The doorbell for the suite rang.

"Jerry, have you lost it? Do I need to fly out there myself and take over the lawsuit?"

"James, I've got to go. I'm meeting with Senator Damonati and the FBI. I'll call you later."

"Okay, but Jerry—you watch what you say to Damonati. You better not screw this up for the firm."

The call ended as Jerry opened the hotel room door.

Agent Perez stood in the doorway. "Hello again, Mr. Morgenstern."

"Please come in, Agent Perez." Jerry stood aside from the door. "Any word on Winston's location?"

Agent Perez shook his head as he walked past Jerry and into the hotel suite. "No, he's still missing. Honolulu Police found the stolen Kama'aina Bakery cargo van at the Makapu'u Lighthouse Trail with the dead whatever in the back."

"Dead whatever?" Jerry closed the door behind him.

Agent Perez shrugged. "I think you know what I mean."

"May I ask what this meeting is about, Agent Perez?"

"No idea, Mr. Morgenstern. Gretchen Kupule, Senator Damonati's aide, summoned me here." Agent Perez grimaced and opened his mouth to speak again, then looked away from Jerry toward the sliding glass doors and lanai.

Jerry motioned toward a dining room table made of koa wood in the center of the suite. "Please sit down. Can I get you anything to drink?"

"Yes, I could use some water. Thanks." He took a seat at the table. "Nice room you got here, Mr. Morgenstern."

Jerry handed Agent Perez a cold bottle of water. "Call me Jerry."

"Thanks, Jerry. Lucas."

Jerry sat down at the table. "So, Lucas, you don't know what Senator Damonati wants?"

Lucas shook his head. "No idea. But when Senator Damonati says to do something, you better do it. She had the former special agent in charge of the district office here fired because he refused to do her bidding. My superiors gave me strict orders to give her whatever she wants."

Jerry received a text from Gretchen Kupule. They were walking down the hallway, and he needed to have the door already open when they arrived.

Jerry walked over to the door and opened it. Seconds later, Senator Leilani Damonati entered the hotel room. Her eyes were puffy. She gave a cursory nod to Jerry as she passed by.

Gretchen Kupule followed her, carrying a large briefcase. She managed to text someone at the same time. Noa Kim nodded at Jerry and closed the door behind him.

Agent Perez stood up. "Senator."

Senator Damonati glared at Agent Perez and took a seat at the head of the table. She glanced back at Jerry. "I'd like some water also, Mr. Morgenstern."

Gretchen walked over to the table and placed a notepad and pen in front of the senator. She then took a seat beside her.

Jerry handed the senator a bottle of water, placed three more bottles of water in the center of the table, and sat down.

Senator Damonati took a drink of water and cleared her throat. "Thank you for meeting with us, Mr. Morgenstern. We seemed to have missed you for our previously scheduled meeting yesterday at eight fifteen."

Jerry nodded. "Uh, I couldn't—"

"It was unfortunate that you got ensnarled in Kuparr Winston's escape, Mr. Morgenstern. It would be—"

"Escape, Senator?"

"I believe, Mr. Morgenstern, that I was still speaking. As I was saying, it would be helpful if you could provide the FBI, who obviously need all the help they can get, and my office with any insight as to where Kuparr Winston might be hiding—after his obviously pre-coordinated *escape*."

"Okay, well, I—"

"Furthermore"—Senator Damonati cleared her throat—"we would like to know exactly what happened just before you exited Winston's escape vehicle, Mr. Morgenstern."

Senator Damonati took another sip of water.

Jerry took a sip as well. "Okay, well, the two guys up front in the bread truck started talking in some foreign language I didn't understand. It didn't sound like any language I could recognize. Winston seemed to understand them and said that they were going to dispose of me—that they had picked me up by mistake. Winston said that the aliens—"

Senator Damonati slammed her bottle of water down on the table. Droplets of spit-infused water landed on the table, magnifying the brown grain of the koa wood. "Please, Mr. Morgenstern." Senator Damonati's bloodshot eyes glared at Jerry. "I will not hear any of this rubbish. Please do not spread disinformation."

Jerry sank in his chair. "Well, Winston said they were aliens. I don't know … they did look a little weird."

"So, Mr. Morgenstern, you believe Winston? You believe a sexual predator that purposefully crashed an airliner full of innocent passengers?"

Jerry looked outside the sliding glass doors at the Pacific Ocean. "Of course not, Senator. I … was merely reporting to you what Winston said to me."

Senator Damonati leaned forward toward Jerry. "I see. And what exactly is your opinion of the mental state of Kuparr Winston from a legal viewpoint, the viewpoint of an expert in aviation law?"

"I believe Kuparr Winston is not of a sound mind and has no business operating a commercial airliner." Jerry exhaled.

Noa Kim said, "Mr. Morgenstern, did Winston mention anything yesterday about where he was going?"

"He said he was going up to some spaceship to get frozen."

Noa shook his head. "That's not what I meant. Did he say where he was going—where he would hide? Where would he go if he got away?"

Senator Damonati glared at Noa. "What Noa means to say is that if, in Winston's mind, he was being kidnapped, did he say where he might go if he escaped?"

"Look, I'm a little confused," Jerry said. "He said nothing to me about escaping or hiding somewhere. We really didn't talk that much or that long. The whole thing was a little frightening, frankly."

Senator Damonati sat back in her chair. "It is unfortunate that you learned nothing yesterday, and it is unfortunate that the FBI"—Senator Damonati again turned her glare to Agent Perez—"allowed Mr. Winston to escape from federal custody and now haven't a clue as to where he might be hiding. I have spoken with the special agent in charge about the district office's incompetence. He has assured me they will locate Mr. Winston soon; however, his escape only further proves his guilt. Since you claim Winston said nothing about where he was going, did he say anything about how he had raped Ms. Kupule? Did you learn anything from him that would bolster the rape and sexual harassment case against him?"

Jerry shook his head. "No. He never even mentioned it."

"I see. Well, it is a shame a busy woman like me must do the FBI's job for them, but I will ensure the safety of the women on this island and women everywhere from monsters like Winston, just as I will ensure the safety of the flying public from pilots like Winston." Senator Damonati stood up. "Our society will become safer and better, Mr. Morgenstern. Our society will become great. That is inevitable."

Noa and Gretchen began gathering their things and stood.

Jerry and Agent Perez stood as well.

Senator Damonati handed Jerry her half-empty water bottle. "If you think of anything, or your mind becomes clearer, you will please contact Gretchen or Noa, Mr. Morgenstern."

Jerry took the bottle and nodded. "Of course, Senator. I have their numbers in my phone."

Senator Damonati began walking toward the door of the suite. *"A hui hou,* Mr. Morgenstern."

Gretchen ran ahead to open the door while Noa trailed behind Senator Damonati.

Jerry looked over at Agent Perez, who was standing at attention as the hotel door slammed closed.

"What the hell was that?" Jerry said. "And why were you even here?"

Agent Perez sat down. "I was here as punishment for losing Kuparr Winston."

Jerry shook his head. "No shit. It's like she blames you personally. Did she not hear what happened? Does she think somebody broke Winston out of custody? And what about the 'great society' crap?"

Agent Perez looked away from Jerry and gazed at the blue Pacific through the wall-to-wall sliding glass doors of the suite.

Jerry studied Agent Perez. "Are you okay? Is something bothering you besides the scolding from Senator Nutjob?"

Agent Perez turned back to face Jerry. "I learned something earlier today. Something disturbing. I'm not sure what to do or who to tell."

Jerry sat back. "Okay. You can trust me. I'm a lawyer."

Agent Perez laughed. "Yeah, right."

"Agent Per—Lucas, everything about this is disturbing. Maybe we can help each other understand some of this."

Agent Perez cleared his throat. "Okay. So, you were alone with Kuparr Winston yesterday. You saw who or what kidnapped him. Do you still believe he intentionally crashed Central Pacific 855?"

Jerry raised his eyebrows. "Before I answer that, tell me what you learned earlier today. What happened?"

"I believe I received two texts from Senator Damonati's aide by mistake. I got them about thirty minutes after I got the text summoning me here for this meeting."

"From Gretchen Kupule?"

"Yes, her."

"Okay, what did the texts say?"

"The first one said they needed to destroy the original file with the altered emails in case the wrong people found it."

"Altered emails? Damn. Do you think they were talking about Winston's emails?"

"Yes."

"No shit? This is huge."

"But it effectively disproves your case against him."

Jerry nodded. "True, but ... well, I'm not so sure about my case now, anyway. And what did the second text say?"

"It said they needed to keep a close watch on Susan Kupule because of how much and how often she drinks. They were concerned she might talk too much about the *fake* rape charges."

"They trumped up those charges, too?" Jerry said.

Agent Perez opened his mouth to speak but stopped short. He turned back and gazed out at the Pacific again. After a few seconds, he turned back and faced Jerry. "Look, Mr. Morgenstern—"

"It's Jerry."

"Look, Jerry, all my life, all I ever wanted to do was be an FBI agent. I wanted to get the bad guys and find the truth. That text, though—I don't know. It kinda blew me out of the water. I don't think I know who the bad guys are, who the good guys are, or if anybody is good. So, I'm asking you, since you were with him during the whole escape incident—do you think Kuparr Winston intentionally downed Central Pacific 855?"

"No."

"No?" Perez cocked his head.

Jerry sat back in his seat. "Lucas, we both saw the blood of the guy that Kup dumped onto the highway yesterday. You know he isn't human. Surely the FBI or the police have done a pathology report on him."

"Somebody high-up classified the pathology report. I can't access it."

"That's interesting."

"And the district office is under incredible political pressure to prosecute Winston, but the evidence—other than those texts and emails—is just not there. The NTSB is acting all weird, too, and now I get these texts from Damonati's aide. You know, my neighbor texted me earlier that my house in Kona was ransacked by—"

"Aliens?"

Lucas nodded. "Yes. My house got looted, and the mobs emptied my freezer. They shattered several windows. My neighbors are terrified. But with the no-fly zone, I'm stuck here chasing dead ends."

"Dead ends?"

"I feel like every time I start to get on the right track, Senator Damonati screams, 'Squirrel!' and I'm sent to investigate some dead end. To make matters worse, they expect me to turn the dead end into meaningful evidence. And then yesterday, you two vanished from the interrogation room. I was standing ten feet from the door. How did those two guys get into the room, and how did the four of you get out?"

"I can't answer that."

"Look, Jerry. I saw what happened with my own eyes, but my superiors are painting this as an escape attempt by Winston."

"I can assure you that it wasn't an escape attempt. We were kidnapped. They just grabbed me by mistake."

Lucas nodded. "I believe you. We need to right this wrong. I need to do something to help the people on the Big Island."

Jerry stared down at the table. *"Not everyone's family can just hop in the family sailboat and sail away to safety."*

"Oh, what the hell." Jerry shook his head. "I need a fake passport—or at least a stolen one."

"What?"

"You said you wanted to do something to help the people on the Big Island, and I'm guessing you know of some pretty unsavory characters around here."

"Why do you need a fake passport?"

"I don't. Kuparr Winston does."

CHAPTER THIRTY-EIGHT

Vík í Mýrdal, Iceland
21:00 GMT, 6 January

"Hildur, *opnaðu dyrnar,*" said a male voice outside the house.

Hildur jumped up from the living room couch. "Papa?"

"Your father made it?" Trevor asked.

Hildur paused on her way to open the front door. "Yes, he must have made it through the alien mobs. I told him to stay at my uncle's house, but he is stubborn." She opened the door and hugged her father. "How was the drive from Grindavík? I have been so worried for you."

"Hræðilegt. Af hverju ertu að tala ensku?" A tall man with light-gray hair walked into the living room and eyed Es-mar and Trevor sitting on the couch. "Oh, I see now why you speak English." He turned his head toward Hildur. "I watched your video. Even now, as I see her with my own eyes, I still cannot believe you have one of them in your house."

Hildur sat down on the futon. "Trevor, please meet my father, Einar Ólafsson."

Trevor stood up and shook Einar's hand. *"Gaman að hitta þig."*

Einar smiled. "It is nice to meet you too. I like *you*." Einar turned to Hildur. "I approve of your new boyfriend, Hildur."

"And Papa," Hildur said, "this is my good friend Es-mar. She already knows you, though."

Einar glared at Es-mar as he sat down on the oversized chair opposite the couch. "My daughter tells me you are not to be feared, but on the drive back home today, my car was attacked by ... I was attacked by aliens like you. They were just like you. There were hundreds of them.

All crazy. And the yelling. *'Matur! Matur! Gefðu okkur mat!'* I had no food with me in my car to give them. They began pounding on my car, smashing the windows, and tearing off the side mirrors. I was afraid for my life. But here I sit in my daughter's living room, talking to you. You, who are the same as the mob that attacked me. So, forgive me if I do not embrace you as my daughter suggests in her video."

"Papa, do not—"

"I am sorry for this, Einar," Es-mar said. "Please forgive us. We are in an alien world. We are afraid. We are hungry." She looked down at the floor. "We are confused."

Einar shook his right pointer finger at Es-mar. "People are saying you are convicts. Dumped here in our country. Your society discarded you because you were rubbish for the rubbish bin."

"What you say, Papa, is true," Hildur said. "Very rude, but true. They are convicts, but very few of them are real criminals. They were dumped here by their Society because they disagreed with it." Hildur pointed at Es-mar. "She is an engineer but disagreed with Society's engineering plans."

Einar looked from Hildur back toward Es-mar. "So, you are a convict because you opposed your society as an engineer?"

"Yes. I was a Seer, a social engineer." Es-mar looked Einar in the eye. "I was given a low Social Score because I did not support the goals of Society, the new engineered Society. I tried to, but the programs never worked correctly. Everything I was taught proved to be false when I actually tried to apply it. Eventually, I realized that you cannot engineer a society, but this is heresy. My Social Score was so low, I was threatened with Cancellation but was—"

"Cancellation?" asked Einar. "Oh yes, Hildur has mentioned this. They freeze you like a halibut in the market."

"Well, yes. This worked for many years, but now our planet has become so overcrowded that almost all the Freedom Vaults are full, which is why I am here. The Seers created Transport. Only the most unsafe will now be Cancelled. The rest of us with low Social Scores will be transported to Earth. Transport is the final phase of Society's plan for the Great Society."

"They are trying to engineer a Great Society?" Einar asked.

"It wasn't always this way on our planet," Es-mar said. "My grandmother told me sagas of the times long ago. Our world was moving toward racial blindness and equality. Our engineers had made incredible technical advances. We had limitless, clean energy. We developed rapid space travel. Advances in medicine advanced our longevity, and eventually, our planet became unbearably overcrowded. There was conflict. The engineers turned their attention to society. Our technical advances stalled as scientific truth became driven by the Seers. Today, our technology is unreliable, and our Society is a nightmare."

"I have heard a similar story before," said Einar. "History repeats; the children do not learn from the mistakes of the parents."

"It started with the children," Hildur said. "They all had to go to the toilet together. No one could finish until everyone was finished. No one could receive a grade higher than another. Everyone studied the same things. Competitive sports were banned. The goal was equity."

"What's wrong with equity?" Trevor asked. "I mean … everyone being the same and having the same things is a worthy goal. No jealousy, nothing to steal because you've got the same stuff everyone else has."

"And no individuality," Es-mar said. "It's a world where there's one color, or in our world, it was all white, red, or brown. Encounters with someone of another race came to be viewed as threatening and unsafe, and so the *Great Segregation* began. The three races were segregated and returned to their three home continents. Interracial sexual relations were banned, all in the name of safety and equity. I still had many friends who were Whites and Browns. I had a boyfriend who was a Brown. My family and I were moved to a place far away. Our individual names and identities were subordinated to our race, which was then subordinated to the greater society. The individual was valued by how well they conformed to their racial norms and how well they supported the greater society. This was measured by their Social Score. Eventually, our society became Society. Those who opposed Society were labeled as regressive. Many lost their jobs; many became outcasts. Some even committed suicide."

"And the convicts?" Einar asked.

"The convicts came next," Hildur said. "Society's actions created tension and opposition amongst the nonbelievers, the troublemakers, and those who were regressive and resistant to change and to the progress that Society promised and represented. There was crowding and homelessness, as those with low Social Scores were shunned and unable to work. The economies of the three continents began to fail, and Society had trouble housing and feeding its citizens.

"Society needed more land or fewer citizens. Their solution was Cancellation, which was initially just a social program whereby Society could silence its noncompliant citizens through the media and social media. As Society evolved, the term came to mean cryogenic freezing and permanent storage, permanent silence."

"You might as well just kill someone," Einar said. "It would be easier."

"Society is highly progressive," Es-mar said. "Execution, or capital punishment, was banned centuries ago."

"And Cancellation is not capital punishment," Trevor said. "It is not murder. It is simply a way to prevent unsafe disinformation from being fed to the masses and creating unsafe situations."

Einar looked at Trevor. "How are you so well-informed of these things? Did you also have this Reckoning?"

Trevor shook his head. "No, I've just heard these two discuss all this. That's all."

Einar nodded. "Okay, Es-mar. You were saying they could not freeze enough citizens, so they sent them all here?"

"Yes. They announced Transport. They decided to purge the lowest members of Society, the citizens with the lowest Social Scores, so that the remaining citizens would have more room to live. At the same time, Society's average Social Score would rise, and the Great Society would finally be achieved."

"This Great Society you talk of." Einar shook his head. "Similar things have been attempted here on this planet. Hitler, Stalin, Mao, Castro—they all removed millions from their societies to achieve this so-called 'great' or 'perfect' society." Einar's back stiffened. "My grandmother was born in—"

"Berlin," said Es-mar. "She was born in the days of the Weimar Republic. She watched her country change. She watched it turn on itself and turn on her and her family. She opposed Hitler and the National Socialists. At first, it was the mobs of Brownshirts—the political hacks sent out to harass the nonbelievers into conformity. Then came the SS and the camps built to purge society of its weakest elements, all in the name of building the great society, the thousand-year *Reich*, racially purged of the scum at the bottom of society. Your grandmother survived Dachau."

"My grandmother barely survived Dachau."

"Only to return to the Soviet-occupied sector of Berlin," Es-mar said.

"Yes, and she had lost everything," Einar said. "Her family no longer existed. All she wanted was a new start, but unfortunately, she couldn't keep her mouth shut. She protested. The budding intellectuals of the DDR, so eager to build a new and socialist Germany—their new great society based on equity—labeled her a reactionary and a fascist. Her new society flung her to the bottom. The *Staatspolizei* watched her. Her neighbors watched her. Life became dangerous. She fled to West Berlin days before the wall was built."

"So, she escaped her second encounter with a great society by just a few days," Es-mar said.

"Yes," Einar said. "My grandmother's story is burned into my memory."

"And so it is burned into Hildur's memory," said Es-mar.

"So, you truly know my daughter's mind as your own?"

"Yes."

"Then I will embrace you as my own daughter. It is my hope that, in time, this alien place will not seem so alien to you."

CHAPTER THIRTY-NINE

Honolulu, Hawai'i
21:00 HST, 6 January

K up sat on the bed of his motel room, which had a stunning view of the parking garage across the street. Though technically in Waikiki, it had been years since the four-story cinder-block building had graced the pages of any tourist brochures—or websites. The previous night, it had taken Kup about thirty minutes to acclimate to the combination of cigarettes and mildew. The short, curly black hairs on the sheets, however, were a different matter. He had slept in his clothes on top of two large bath towels he had placed on top of the bedspread. On the bright side, the receptionist took cash and didn't ask a lot of questions.

That morning, he had bought the T-shirt, shorts, underwear, and flip-flops he was wearing in addition to five burner phones. Of the five phones, one was a smartphone. The other four were cheap flip phones. He had paid cash for everything.

He dialed Kahealani's cellphone number on one of the flip phones. "Come on, answer."

On the fifth ring, Kahealani said, "Hello?"

Kup tried to talk.

Kahealani repeated, "Hello? Who is this?"

Kup started crying. "You're … you're okay?"

"Kup? Where are you? The news … they say you escaped from federal custody. What's going on?"

"Kahea, I can't talk long. I can't tell you where I am, and I can't tell you what I'm doing. I just called to tell you I love you and to see if you're okay."

"Kup, I love you too. I'm so worried about you."

"I'm okay. How are—"

"Kup, I'm so sorry … I'm so sorry I doubted you. Everything you said—"

"It's okay, Kahea. It's okay. How are things over there? I haven't seen anything about the Big Island on NNN."

"Kup, things are terrible here. Our house got looted. They stripped all our fruit trees bare. All the stores got looted by people last week, and they got looted again by the alien mobs. Kup, I'm worried about having enough to eat."

"Kahea, I've got fishing gear and two spearguns in the garage. You grew up fishing and spearfishing with your dad."

"Yeah, I thought about that, but what if an alien mob comes by and takes whatever I catch?"

"Just wade into the water, Kahea. They won't follow you into the water."

"Okay … I guess I could go fish from the tidepools. Also, the mobs have cleared out of the Kona side of the island since they stripped it clean of anything to eat. They're fanning out toward Hilo and Waimea now, where there's still some food left. In Waimea, a mob mauled a live cow."

"That's terrible, Kahea."

"Kup, people are saying we're going to run out of food. Even with all the farms and fruit trees and fish we have, we're still going to starve. Because of the FAA's no-fly zone and the Coast Guard's no-transgression zone, people are saying we only have a week or two of food left on the entire island."

"Kahea, please be strong. I'm going to fix this. I can't tell you how right now, but I will get our old lives back. I will see our child born."

"Kup—"

"I have to hang up now. I love you."

"Kup, wait, don't hang up!"

Kup pressed the End button on the cheap flip phone and tossed it into the sink, which was full of water.

One down, four to go.

He grabbed the second flip phone and dialed the reservation number for Cave Tours Iceland listed on their website. A recording in Icelandic and English announced they were currently closed. Kup hung up the phone.

Kup glanced over at the muted television. NNN was currently displaying a photograph of his face. He had joined the FBI's Most Wanted list.

Great. My finest moment.

He watched the rest of the news segment, followed by excerpts from Susan Kupule's press conference earlier. She warned people on Oʻahu to be diligent with a sexual predator like Kuparr Winston on the loose.

Nothing about the Big Island? Or Galveston? Or Iceland?

Kup typed "bbc.com" into the smartphone's browser. *Nothing?*

He typed "Galveston invasion" into the search window of the web browser. The top hit was a news story on *Alternativ Zeit*, a German conspiracy news site. Kup selected the English translation. The article reported that private sailboats were ferrying food and supplies to private docks in Galveston, providing a lifeline for the fifty thousand residents of the island.

Kup typed "Iceland Invasion" into the search window next. A news report from *The British Reporter* popped up, and Kup clicked on the story. The prime minister of Iceland had implemented a state of emergency due to roving bands of aliens along the South Coast as far west as Höfn and as far east as Selfoss. Officials estimated the aliens would be in Reykjavík within a day or two. Food supplies were becoming scarce as large-scale looting occurred with the influx of 105,000 aliens among the island nation of 365,000 inhabitants. Resupply efforts had been stopped because of the no-fly and no-transgression zones surrounding the island. Officials were estimating they had two weeks' worth of food left.

The burner phone he'd used to call Cave Tours Iceland rang.

Kup looked at the phone number. The country code was 354, Iceland.

Kup answered the call. "Hello?"

"*Halló.* This is Cave Tours Iceland. Did you call? Are you interested in an Ice Cave Tour?"

"I'm looking for Hildur Einarsdóttir. I believe this is her company."

"Yes. I am Hildur Einarsdóttir."

Kup sighed. "Ms. Einarsdóttir, I believe you experienced a Reckoning with an alien convict. I, too—"

"You misunderstand them. They are here against their will. They are only trying to survive."

"Yes, I watched your video about the convicts, but I'm talking about something else. I also experienced a Reckoning. I know how to free Iceland."

"Free Iceland? I did not learn this from *my* Reckoning," Hildur said.

"My Reckoning was with the Warden of the three Penal Colonies. He has technical knowledge of their entire EMP system. Your Reckoning was with a convict. She would not have had this technical knowledge."

"Well, yes. I would think not, Mr… . ?"

Kup paused.

"Hello? Are you still on the phone?"

"It's Winston. Kuparr Winston."

"Winston? You are the rapist?"

"Ms. Einarsdóttir, I did not—"

"And you are the pilot. The pilot that crashed the airliner in the Pacific?"

"I didn't do either of those things. I promise you."

"But the news reports—"

"They're all lies."

"I would like to believe you, Mr. Winston, but it is difficult. Perhaps you—"

"Ms. Einarsdóttir, Iceland—or more specifically, the ice cave under Eyjafjallajökull—is the key to freeing all three islands that were attacked and are now isolated from the world."

"Eyjafjallajökull?"

"The aliens placed an EMP emitter deep within the ice cave in Eyjafjallajökull and shut off the cave with a wall of ice. If I—"

"The ice wall? You know of the ice wall? The new ice wall?"

"Yes. The aliens installed the ice wall only a few days ago. Anyway, if I can get to that EMP emitter, I can manually override the whole alien EMP system and bring down all three of their Command Ships. This will free up the islands and allow air and ship traffic to bring in supplies once again."

"This is a lot of information, Mr. Winston. I can take you to Eyjafjallajökull ice cave, but how will you get to Iceland?"

"I'm working on that."

"And once inside the cave, how will you penetrate the ice wall? The ice could be thick."

"The ice wall is about one meter thick."

"One meter? I suppose we could use my father's auger to drill a hole, but the hole will be not so big—maybe twenty centimeters across."

"Could we use heaters as well?"

"I am afraid heaters would not work. There is no electricity available there, and we will have to hike about a kilometer in the snow to reach it. My father's auger, however, does not need electricity; it uses petrol."

"What if we used the auger to cut multiple holes in a circle? We could then punch out the circle. Would that work?"

"I do not know. I can call my father and check on his auger. Otherwise, I can buy one in Reykjavík. No one has looted augers, only food."

"So, are you saying you will help me?"

"Yes, I will take you to the ice cave in Eyjafjallajökull. But first, you must fly to Iceland, Mr. Winston, which is not possible."

"Call me Kup, and like I said, I'm working on getting to Iceland. But thanks for agreeing to help."

"Yes, of course, Kup. You will call me Hildur."

"Okay. Thanks, Hildur."

"Kup, I agree we must stop these alien penal colonies. If they are successful, there will be more convicts, and then the nonconvicts will come. Our world will no longer be ours."

"Thank you, Hildur. I'll call you back with our plans for getting to Iceland. Thank you for agreeing to help."

"Kup, so you did not rape that woman?"

"No."

"And you did not crash the plane?"

"No."

"Very well. I believe you."

"Thanks, Hildur—thank you. It feels so good to hear you say that."

"Goodbye, Kup. I will await your phone call and additional instructions."

"Goodbye, Hildur."

Kup jotted down Hildur's cellphone number before he hung up. He turned the burner phone off and tossed it into the sink with the first phone.

Two phones down. Three phones to go.

Kup used the third burner phone to volunteer himself and Jerry for the Iceland rescue mission aboard the *Sissal*. He was told to bring exposure gear and arrive at the dock in Tórshavn no later than 13:00 on the tenth. The *Sissal* would depart at 14:00 with or without them. Room and board aboard the ferry would be complimentary.

The third burner phone's purpose in life was complete, and so it met the same fate as the first two. Kup had one left. It was a long shot, but he had no one else.

PART THREE
FRELSUN

CHAPTER FORTY

Over Yakutat, Alaska
18:30 Alaska Standard Time, 9 January

Jerry gazed out the window of the Gulfstream G5 as the private jet banked to the right over a narrow strip of Alaska. The lights of Yakutat gave way to the dark vastness of the Yukon Territory forty-nine thousand feet below them. He tapped the right armrest with his bare ring finger. *I can't believe we're doing this. I'm so screwed.*

He wore a nondescript white polo shirt, khaki pants, and brown loafers. Underneath it all, he wore a pair of maroon-and-white boxers with the ATM logo. Kup had insisted that they blend in as much as possible.

He was scared and sad at the same time. Repeating the goodbyes with his family had been terrible. Not being able to tell them any details had made things worse, but he couldn't risk them knowing where they were going or what they were doing.

Jerry studied Kup's face. The seats faced each other in club-style seating. "You know, I like you better without the cheesy mustache. You should make that permanent."

Kup frowned. He had shaved his mustache and dyed his hair a light-brown color. He was now a close enough match for the picture of Melvin Reynolds Ferguson—well, a tan Melvin Reynolds Ferguson, anyway.

"So, how long until the Fergusons realize the passport is missing?" Kup asked.

"Who knows? The guy said they were on vacation in Maui until to-morrow. As expensive as that passport was, you'd think we would have a little more time left on it."

"Oh, come on, the passport was cheap compared to this thing." Kup pointed around the cabin of the G5.

"Don't remind me."

"When do you expect your boss will notice the credit card charge for this?"

"Getting fired is the least of my worries."

Kup laughed. "Welcome to my world. At least you're not a domestic terrorist and a bloody rapist."

"I'm just aiding and abetting a domestic terrorist and rapist—so much better." Jerry smirked as he looked out the window. "Kup, I've been wondering about what happened on New Year's Eve. How did they do it?"

"How did who do what?"

"The harbors. The airports. The causeway. How'd they do what they did? I saw everything firsthand in Galveston. There was a cruise ship heeled over onto the Strand right next to my favorite beer joint. I walked right under someone's balcony—I could touch it. I walked on the seafloor next to the landing for the Bolivar Ferry; my knees didn't even get wet. The seafloor was hard and shiny. Word is, it's pure aluminum. I drove by the airport. The runways and taxiways were just gone; they vanished. There was nothing there but packed dirt. And last but not least, the causeway. The old railway bridge and the bridge across San Luis Pass were gone too. So, how did they do all that? You've got the Warden's mind; you've got to know."

"I know, but I can't say that I fully understand it. I can't even say that the Warden fully understands it. He was trained to operate the equipment, but his understanding of the physics involved was limited."

"Okay, so give me the limited lawyer version," Jerry said.

"Well, they use something called quantum electrodynamics to rearrange the structure of molecules at the atomic level. They call it a Quantum Transubstantiater. It takes matter in one state and turns it into a particular element in another state. So take, for example, the runways in Galveston. The runways are composed of a bunch of different materials like steel and concrete, so there are all kinds of different molecules, but they are all in a solid state. The device basically turns all the solid matter within a defined space—which would be the runway itself—into a specific element that must be a gas in its present state. Specifically, that gas was argon. Similarly, it turned the seawater within the defined space of Galveston Harbor into a particular element in a solid state. They chose aluminium."

"So, the rumors are true, but why argon and aluminum?"

"I think it had to do with the target element's density. They try to get it relatively close to the density of whatever it is that they are transforming. It uses less energy, I believe. Argon is a denser gas, so its density is closer to the material in concrete. It's also harmless. Aluminium is strong but relatively less dense than other metals, so its density is closer to that of seawater. It will also be difficult to dredge a harbor full of aluminium. Lithium was considered, for example, but ultimately rejected because it is so light that it floats in water. In any case, the target material cannot be a compound; it must be a single pure element."

"So pure argon and pure aluminum?"

"Yes. The Quantum Transubstantiater performs the transformations at the molecular level layer by layer, kind of like how a 3D printer deposits each new layer on top of the old one, except it happens very fast, in microseconds."

"So, what happens if it's making seawater into aluminum and it encounters something already solid, like steel?"

"The first layer of steel molecules is transformed into hydrogen, and a large amount of energy is released in the form of an explosion. It's a side effect of the process."

"Hmmm ..." Jerry stared out the jet's window. "Okay, so this thing is turning water into aluminum layer by layer in the harbors when it encounters the keel of a cruise ship and turns it into hydrogen. So, why are all ships heeled over on the new shallow aluminum seafloor? Does that make any sense to you?"

"Actually, they were surprised by this also, although they're not really into boating. The reports indicate that the explosions that occurred as the layers of the keel were transformed into hydrogen lifted the ships continually above the rising seafloor. The keels remained intact because only the first few layers of molecules were transformed, and the keels themselves are very thick."

"Oh ... and as for the causeway ... the people that were sitting in the Chevy Tahoe that I saw are—"

"Argon."

"Damn."

"Mate, if you'd been a minute earlier, you'd be argon right now too, floating around somewhere over the Gulf of Mexico. I'd say you're one lucky man."

"Well, I'd say Daisy is one lucky dog."

"Daisy?"

"The Weimaraner I told you about, the one in the Tahoe."

Kup nodded.

Jerry closed his eyes and tried to go back to sleep, but he kept envisioning himself as a noble gas drifting over the Gulf of Mexico. He was lucky to be alive, yet he felt far from it.

CHAPTER FORTY-ONE

Mikey and Cindy had just finished dinner and gone into the bedroom to watch television when the hotel suite's phone rang.

Gail answered the phone, "Hello?"

"Is this Gail Morgenstern?"

"Yes, it is."

"Mrs. Morgenstern, my name is Gretchen Kupule. I am Senator Damonati's aide. The senator would like to meet with you."

"With me?"

"Yes, ma'am."

"I don't understand. Why does she want to meet with me?"

"She will explain everything in person. Is five minutes enough time for you?"

"She wants to talk with me for five minutes?"

"No, she will be at your door in five minutes. Please have the door open for her arrival. She's a very busy woman."

"What?"

"Thank you, Mrs. Morgenstern. We'll see you shortly."

"Wait. What? My kids are ... hello? Hello? Are you there?" Gail put the phone back on the receiver. *What the hell? Five minutes? Jerry said he met with her.*

Gail walked into the bedroom. "Kids, I'm going to have a meeting with someone. I need you two to stay in here and be quiet. Okay?"

Mikey and Cindy both nodded. Between the lazy river, the pool, and the beach, they were exhausted.

Gail looked in the mirror and messed with her hair. *I've never met a senator before.*

The doorbell rang. Gail shook her head. *That was five minutes?*

When Gail opened the door, a twenty-something woman said, "Mrs. Morgenstern, I'm Gretchen Kupule. Nice to meet you. The senator will be here momentarily. Please standby for her arrival."

"Uh, okay," Gail said. "Nice to meet—"

"Dr. Gail Morgenstern." Senator Damonati said as she approached the doorway. "Aloha. It is so nice to meet you. You are just as beautiful as Jerry said you were."

Gail blushed. "Jerry said I was beautiful?"

"Yes, of course he did."

"Well, thank you, Senator. It is very nice to meet you, too. Please, come in."

"Mahalo. And please, it's Leilani to my friends." Senator Damonati pointed back toward Noa, who stood behind her. "And this is Noa Kim, my Hawai'i-based chief of staff. Of course, you've already met Gretchen."

Noa looked past Gail at his image in the mirror in the hallway. "It's a pleasure to meet you, Dr. Morgenstern." He turned back toward Gail and smiled.

"Nice to meet you too." Gail stood aside as the three walked into the suite. "Please, everyone, have a seat. Can I get anyone something to drink?"

"I'd love a glass of cold Chardonnay to enjoy that beautiful sunset." Senator Damonati paused beside Gail's phone, which was sitting on the dinner table amongst a pile of tourist magazines.

"I have sauvignon blanc," Gail said. "Will that be okay?"

Senator Damonati shrugged. "Yes. That will have to do. Nothing for Gretchen and Noa, my dear. But please join me on your beautiful lanai for the sunset."

"Sure." Gail walked into the kitchenette to pour the wine.

Senator Damonati eyed Gail's phone as she whispered in Noa's ear on her way to the open sliding glass doors. She paused and turned back toward Gail. "Tell me, Gail. Have you ever seen a green flash?"

Gail poured the second glass of wine. "No. I can't say that I have."

"Well, the conditions look excellent for it." Senator Damonati stepped out onto the lanai. "And your view, my dear—it's outstanding. How kind of Jerry to book all of you in this beautiful suite."

Gail walked out onto the lanai and handed Senator Damonati a glass of wine. "Well, it's Jerry's law firm that's paying for it."

"Yes, of course, my dear. I'm glad to see that my dear old classmate James Templeton treats his team so well. *Okole maluna,* my dear."

Gail clinked her glass of wine against Senator Damonati's glass. "Bottoms up."

"The sun is almost down, Gail. Look for the green flash in the last few seconds before the sun completely disappears beneath the horizon."

The last few rays of the sun bent from yellow to green.

Senator Damonati turned to face Gail. "Did you see it?"

"Yes. I sure did." *Well, that was neat, but what does this woman want?*

"Excellent. Well, now that we've taken care of that, let us sit down with Noa and Gretchen. I am sure you are wondering why I am here."

Gail nodded as she walked inside. "Yes, Senator. I certainly am."

Gretchen was sitting on the couch, texting. Noa stood beside the dinner table as he zipped his leather messenger bag closed.

After sitting down on the couch beside Gretchen, Senator Damonati said, "Gail, your husband was performing some work for my office. We've tried to contact him several times today, but he hasn't responded. We're concerned. Is he okay?"

"Yes. He's fine."

"Oh, good. When did you last speak to him?"

"This morning. He said he was going away for a couple of days. It had something to do with the lawsuit he's working on—you know, the Central Pacific crash."

"Yes. I'm familiar with your husband's lawsuit." Senator Damonati placed her wine glass on the coffee table and glanced at Noa. "You said he was going away? Where exactly has he gone, my dear?"

"He didn't tell me."

Noa walked over and sat down on the loveseat to Gail's right.

"You don't know?" Senator Damonati glared at Gail. "Your husband says he's going away somewhere for a few days, and you're telling me you don't know where that somewhere is?"

"Yes, he said it was best if I didn't know where he was going. I admit it's a little strange, and it does bother me. But this whole week has been bizarre."

"Did he leave Oʻahu?" asked Noa.

"As I said, I don't know. He didn't tell me."

Senator Damonati cleared her throat. "Gail, do you think your husband left Hawaiʻi?"

Gail shrugged. "I told you, I don't know. I just don't know. He was very secretive about it all."

"When exactly did your husband depart, Dr. Morgenstern?" Noa asked.

"It was around ten this morning when he left the hotel. What's going on? Did Jerry do something wrong?"

Senator Damonati placed her right hand on top of Gail's left hand. "I don't know, Gail. You tell me."

Noa began typing into his phone's browser.

Gail said, "Senator, I've—"

"It's Leilani, my dear, please." Senator Damonati squeezed Gail's hand.

"Leilani, I've told you everything I know. What's going on? Is Jerry in some sort of danger? I mean, everything is just so strange right now with the alien invasions."

Senator Damonati began laughing. "Please, my dear. You don't actually believe in that nonsense, do you? You're a medical doctor."

"Believe it? I lived through it. I saw the disks with my own eyes. I don't know why the media is ignoring what happened. Why is that, Senator? Why is there a complete news blackout about what's going on in Galveston?"

Senator Damonati stood up. "Dr. Morgenstern, you will let my office know the minute your husband contacts you."

Noa and Gretchen both stood and began walking toward the door.

Gail stood up. "You need to tell me what this is all about. Why are you so interested in where my husband is?"

Senator Damonati smiled, walked over to Gail, and grabbed both her hands. "Gail, this is a beautiful suite, and I am sure your two children are enjoying their time here. It would be so unfortunate if something happened."

"If something happened? What are you talking about? What would happen? Are you threatening my children?"

"Oh, of course not, my dear. Just make sure that you keep Gretchen or Noa updated on any new information about your husband. I'm sure your children will be fine then—as long as you comply."

Senator Damonati released Gail's hands and began walking toward the door.

Gail raised her voice. "Comply? Comply with what?"

Senator Damonati gritted her teeth before smiling. "Comply with whatever I request of you. Do so, and you will continue to be a mother to your children. Everybody wins."

"Continue to be a mother?" Gail's lips quivered. "You bitch! If you even touch one hair of one of my kids' heads—Senator Damonati or Leilani or whatever the hell you want me to call you—I will come after you! I swear, I'll kill you! I'll fucking kill you!"

Noa glanced up from his phone. "Got it."

Senator Damonati smiled. "Gail, my dear. Are you familiar with the term *domestic terrorist?*"

"What?!" Gail began shaking.

"A hui hou, Dr. Morgenstern." Senator Damonati followed Gretchen out the door.

Noa shook his head and whispered in the senator's ear as she passed by him.

Senator Damonati stopped and said, "Make the call."

Noa nodded and slammed the hotel door behind him.

Gail began shaking. *What the hell is going on here? Why ... where is Jerry? Why the hell wouldn't he tell me where he was going?*

Gail sat down. *And was she actually threatening us? A senator?* She glanced at the closed bedroom door. She jumped up, walked over to the door, and opened it. Mikey and Cindy were both asleep on the bed.

I need to talk to James. Maybe he knows what's going on. Gail walked over to the dinner table. *My phone was right here. Where's my damn phone?*

CHAPTER FORTY-TWO

Vágar Airport, Faroe Islands
09:00 GMT, 10 January

Jerry was sitting on the left side of the Gulfstream G5 as the jet descended toward Runway 30 at Vágar Airport. The rising landscape, illuminated by the morning twilight, slid by as the jet turned left over an inlet. "The mountains are too close, and they're above us."

Kup smiled. "I remember this approach from years ago in the C17. It was a little tricky. You follow an inlet and then make a hard left turn on short final to line up on the runway. The runway sits in a saddle between the mountains. I guess it was the only stretch of level land they could find."

Jerry shook his head.

"Oh, and there's water on each end of the runway," Kup said.

"Great. Thanks for letting me know."

At about six hundred feet of altitude, the pilot cranked the G5 to the left. Jerry gave Kup another nervous glance. "We're turning? Now?"

Moments later, Jerry breathed a loud sigh of relief as the G5's main wheels touched down.

Kup's heart, however, pounded against his chest as the jet's thrust reversers activated. *There's no turning back now. Have the authorities already reported the passport stolen? Are the police waiting for me inside?*

The G5 slowed down to taxi speed and backtaxied on the runway to the terminal. The pilot had said they would need to go through the arrival hall to go through customs like arriving airline passengers. Kup watched passengers ascend a staircase up to an Atlantic Airlines Airbus A-320 as the G5 turned right onto the short taxiway to the ramp and the modern glass-and-steel terminal building. *No police yet.*

The G5 came to a stop in front of the passenger terminal on the opposite end of the A-320. Light snow covered the hills surrounding the airport. Earlier, the pilot had said the temperature was −2°C outside. Kup was still wearing the khaki slacks and short-sleeve shirt Jerry had bought him in Waikiki. They were the warmest clothes he could find, but at least he had on socks and closed-toed shoes. They'd be able to buy a coat and sweater soon enough.

The pilots were planning on spending the night and flying to Stavanger, Norway, the following day to pick up some oil executives. They had arranged their own transportation to Tórshavn. Jerry and Kup had never told the pilots what they were doing in the Faroe Islands, and the pilots knew better than to ask.

The copilot opened the door of the G5, and cold air blasted into the warm cabin. Kup began shivering. An airport worker greeted them and welcomed them to the Faroe Islands before he directed them to the arrival hall in the terminal.

At the terminal entrance, Jerry opened the door for Kup. "Well, here we go. Let the adventure begin."

Kup put his right hand on the passport that rested in his left chest pocket. *Yeah, here we go.* His heart was still pounding against his chest as he walked through the doorway into the customs room. He was carrying a small duffel bag and realized how few possessions he had with him now. Jerry at least had a briefcase and a roller bag.

The Faroe Islands are a self-governing territory within the Kingdom of Denmark. While Denmark handled foreign affairs, the islanders maintained independent trade and customs policies.

They approached the one open customs lane. The female agent behind the glass motioned them over. "*Góðan morgun.* Good morning. Welcome to the Faroe Islands, gentlemen. Your passports, please."

Jerry handed his passport to the customs agent.

Kup glanced up at a video camera mounted above the customs booth.

"Sir, your passport, please." The customs agent stared at Kup.

Kup stared at the camera. *Oh, bloody hell. They're filming me.*

"Sir?"

Jerry glared at Kup. "Melvin, give her your passport."

"Yes, of course." Kup placed the passport through the opening in the glass.

"Thank you. Now, you will each need to fill out these forms." She handed over two forms and opened both passports to the photo page.

Why couldn't we have come someplace busy? We're the only people in here.

"Mr. Ferguson, where will you be staying here in the Faroe Islands?"

"What?" *She's looking right at me.*

"Where will you be staying here in—"

"The Hotel Havnia in Tórshavn." He had stayed there years ago when they had diverted to Vágar in the C-17.

"The Hotel Havnia?"

"Yes." *Please let that place still be around.*

"Very well." The agent examined Kup's passport as she held it up alongside Kup's face.

Kup feigned a forced smile and began filling out the customs form in front of him. *Shit. Shit. Shit.*

When Kup looked back up, she was holding Jerry's passport up in front of him. The agent took Jerry's customs form and stamped it. "And what is your purpose for visiting the Faroes, Mr. Morgenstern?"

"Uh … we're …"

"Business or pleasure? You did not mark it on the form."

"Pleasure." Jerry smiled.

The customs agent studied Jerry's face for several seconds.

"We're looking at a yacht to purchase," Jerry said.

"Please enjoy your stay. We do not get too many tourists here this time of year."

The agent handed Jerry his passport and took Kup's customs form.

"Ah. I see you live in Hawai'i. That explains your tan, Mr. Ferguson." The agent stamped Kup's form and handed him his passport. Kup took it and put it back in his chest pocket, next to his pounding heart.

The customs agent motioned them through. "Good luck with the search for the yacht, gentlemen. Good day."

They both nodded and walked toward the exit doors, which opened automatically as they passed through. Kup took a deep breath as they did so.

Several minutes later, they were in a Volvo SUV taxi driving through the Vágar Tunnel, which was almost five kilometers long and connected Vágar Island with Streymoy Island under the Vestmannasund Strait.

A full hour after landing, Jerry and Kup arrived at the SMS shopping center, where they went on a warm clothing shopping spree. They also purchased two dry bags for the passage to Seyðisfjörður over the last bit of the North Atlantic, and Jerry converted his US dollars into Faroese krónur to minimize their credit card trail.

Not that it mattered much when you'd already entered a foreign country with someone with a stolen passport.

CHAPTER FORTY-THREE

Honolulu, Hawai'i
07:10 HST, 10 January

The hair on the back of her neck stood up as Gail watched the sunrise over Waikiki from the lanai. She looked back inside. Mikey and Cindy were watching cartoons on their iPads. They had never adjusted to the time change. *We need to get out of here. Maybe a walk on the beach would be good.*

She had made reservations for the afternoon flight to Houston on her laptop an hour ago, but the afternoon was still hours away.

Minutes later, they were trotting down the hallway toward the glass elevator, which triggered Gail's fear of heights but delighted Mikey.

The elevator departed the thirty-first floor and began descending into the man-made valleys of Waikiki. Gail kept her eyes closed.

Cindy said, "I wonder what all those police cars are doing at our hotel."

Gail looked down at the hotel entrance, now twenty-six floors below them. She counted four police cars and a large van.

Passing floor twelve, she could read "HPD SWAT" on the side of the van. Her heart began pounding.

Passing floor six, she saw Noa Kim talking into his cellphone beside a limousine. Their eyes locked on each other. Noa began shouting something and pointing up at the elevator. Senator Damonati eased out of the back of a limousine. She looked up and waved at Gail.

Eight armored and armed police officers disappeared under the hotel's entryway.

Passing floor four, Gail slammed her palm against the second-floor button. The button lit up, and several seconds later, the elevator's doors opened onto the second floor.

"Come on!" Gail said. "We need to run."

Mikey pointed at a sign above the elevator buttons. "Uh, Mom. This isn't the right floor for the beach. It says so right here to use the lobby floor."

"Just get out of the elevator, Mikey!" Gail grabbed Cindy's left hand and began running down the hallway. "Where are the damn stairs? We need to go down the stairs."

"Mommy, I'm scared," Cindy said. "What's going on?"

Gail knelt. "Cindy, I need you to be very quiet and do exactly what I tell you. Okay?"

Cindy nodded, but tears began streaming from her eyes.

Mikey said, "I'll find the stairs, Mom." He began sprinting down the hallway.

Gail began running behind Mikey with Cindy at her left side. She rounded a corner and saw the main bank of eight elevators.

Mikey, now twenty feet in front of them, opened a doorway and motioned for them to follow. "Stairs, Mom."

Gail was ten feet from the doorway when she heard a ding from one of the elevators. Seconds later, an elevator door began to open, and a male voice said, "It's them!"

Gail glanced toward the elevator as she ran through the doorway to the stairwell.

The same voice yelled, "Stop, Dr. Morgenstern! Do not endanger your—"

The doorway to the stairwell slammed shut.

Gail, Mikey, and Cindy scrambled down the stairs.

"We've got to get out of the hotel," Gail whispered. "Go out the back, toward the beach."

"Why are the police chasing us?" Cindy asked. "What did we do?"

Mikey opened the door. "It looks clear. I don't see any police."

Gail squeezed Cindy's hand. "I don't know, sweetheart, but everything's going to be okay. This is all a big mistake."

Mikey opened the door further. "Come on. The beach is down this hallway and to the left."

Gail nodded as she and Cindy entered the lobby and followed Mikey down a hallway. She heard the door slam behind them.

Mikey disappeared around the corner.

Ahead of her, Gail heard a man's voice yelling, "Stop!" When she rounded the corner, she saw a hotel security guard chasing after Mikey. The guard's left hand was over the earpiece in his left ear. He glanced backward and noticed Gail and Cindy.

The guard stopped and faced Gail and Cindy while talking into the microphone attached to his earpiece. He held out both hands, palms out, toward Gail. "Dr. Morgenstern, please stay right where you are."

Mikey yelled, "Mom!"

Behind Gail, the sound of footsteps grew louder. In front of her, the security guard stood in the middle of the hallway.

Gail froze. "Mikey! Run!" She bolted left with Cindy in tow and entered a small coffee shop that was part of the hotel. They had eaten breakfast there one morning on the coffee shop's lanai, which looked out over the children's pool.

She ran into a middle-aged man carrying three coffees to go. The man fell, and hot coffee shot across the small coffee shop. His screams competed with the yelling from the security guard now chasing after them.

Once outside on the lanai, Gail dragged Cindy between tables of people disturbed enough to look up from their phones.

The security guard's voice yelled, "They're right there! The boy was headed out the beach exit."

Gail and Cindy ran around the last table and headed to the right of the oval-shaped children's pool. The beach was fifty feet away.

Multiple pairs of footsteps pounded the tile floor behind her.

A male voice behind her yelled, "Dr. Morgenstern, this is the Honolulu Police SWAT Team. I need you to stop right now where you are!"

Gail glanced over her shoulder and saw two policemen in full black armor. Each was carrying a semiautomatic rifle. Gail faced forward and yelled, "Run, Cindy! Run as fast as you can!"

Cindy began crying. "I can't go any faster! I need to stop, Mommy."

"Stop, Dr. Morgenstern!" said the same male voice from behind. "You're creating an unsafe situation for your children."

When Gail leaped onto the sand of Waikiki Beach, she felt Cindy's hand slip from her grip. She stopped and turned around. Cindy was ten feet away, face down in the sand, and crying. An armored policeman was over her, reaching down to help her up. Another armored policeman stood behind Cindy with his semiautomatic rifle pointed at Gail.

"Don't shoot my mother!" screamed Mikey.

Gail cocked her head and saw Mikey twenty yards farther down the beach. She began shaking.

The policeman holding the rifle said, "It's over, Dr. Morgenstern. You and your children need to come with us."

"What … what have we done?" Gail said as she struggled to catch her breath. "Why are you chasing us? I don't understand any of this."

With Cindy back on her feet, the other policeman approached Gail. "Please turn around, Dr. Morgenstern. I need to handcuff you."

Gail stood there shaking. Her head swiveled back and forth between Mikey and Cindy. She offered no resistance to being handcuffed as she mumbled, "Why?"

The policeman pointing the rifle at Gail said, "Dr. Morgenstern, you have been designated a domestic terrorist by the Federal Bureau of Investigation. As such, we are taking you into immediate custody for transfer to the FBI. Agent Perez of the FBI will explain things to you. Do you understand what I have said?"

Gail shook her head. "I don't understand any of this."

A policewoman in a regular HPD uniform walked up and took Cindy's hand. "Cindy, I'm Officer Nohea. We're going to walk with your mother back through the hotel, okay?"

Cindy looked back at Gail and then up at the policewoman. Tears streamed from her eyes.

Mikey, flanked by two policemen, approached Gail and said, "Mom, what is going on? What did you do?"

Gail, Mikey, and Cindy were escorted back through the hotel lobby and out the front entrance. Shocked onlookers photographed and videoed the procession.

A man in an FBI T-shirt spoke into his cellphone beside a black Suburban with government plates. He hung up the phone and approached Gail. "Dr. Morgenstern, I am Agent Perez of the Federal Bureau of Investigation. You threatened a United States senator with murder, and you are believed to be involved in and withholding relevant evidence in connection with the terrorist attack on Central Pacific Airlines Flight

855. As such, you have been labeled a domestic terrorist, and as such, your legal rights are being suspended for seven calendar days starting today. Your children are being removed from your custody until further notice. Your belongings on your person, in your hotel room, and in your home in Texas are now the property of the federal government."

"I want to call a lawyer," Gail said.

"Your husband is a lawyer," said Senator Damonati, standing beside her limousine parked fifteen feet away. "Why don't you call him, my dear?"

"You'll be given court-appointed legal representation in seven days, Dr. Morgenstern," Agent Perez said. "I am obliged, however, to tell you that should you divulge your husband's location immediately, the federal government is willing to lessen the charges against you."

Gail faced Senator Damonati. "I told you I don't know where Jerry is." She looked at Agent Perez. "I'm not a terrorist! I'm a doctor. I'm a mother. I don't know where my husband is. I don't … why are you doing this to me?"

"I'm following orders, Dr. Morgenstern," Agent Perez said. "That's all I'm doing."

Senator Damonati's smile waned into a frown. "Gail, my dear, the FBI is doing this because you are a danger to society. And what kind of a mother puts her children in such an unsafe situation?"

Gail began shaking again. "I'm not a bad mother. I … he didn't tell me … G5. I heard him say something about going to the G5."

Senator Damonati glanced at Noa Kim, who began typing into his phone. "G5?" she asked. "Where exactly is G5, Gail?"

Gail shrugged.

Senator Damonati walked several feet toward Gail. "Is G5 some sort of code for a meeting location? A hiding location, perhaps? Gail, my dear, tell us. Think of your children."

"I don't know where G5 is. I only overheard him mention going to it; I promise you. Please, let me go."

Noa Kim whispered in Senator Damonati's left ear. She nodded and said, "Perhaps a few FBI interrogation sessions will improve your memory, Dr. Morgenstern. Agent Perez, you will keep me apprised of any new developments."

Agent Perez nodded.

"*A hui hou,* Dr. Morgenstern," Senator Damonati said as she returned to her limousine. "If there's anything I can do to help, please let me know. Noa would be happy to cancel those reservations for Houston for you since it would appear you'll be constrained for a while. Oh, and rest assured, I will check on your two children from time to time. I'm sure the state will take excellent care of them—no matter where they eventually end up."

Agent Perez motioned for Gail to climb into the backseat of the Suburban. "Please, Dr. Morgenstern. As I said, I'm only following orders. I'll try to make this as painless as possible for you."

Gail watched Mikey and Cindy depart in separate police cars before she climbed into the Suburban.

Agent Perez's cellphone rang as he slammed the Suburban's door shut. It was Agent Hetman, the special agent in charge of the Honolulu Field Office.

"This is Agent Perez."

"Hetman. Did you learn anything from Morgenstern's wife? Any bones we can toss to Damonati? Maybe get her off my back for a while." The volume on the phone was loud enough for Gail to hear both sides of the conversation.

"Uh ... she said she overheard him saying he was going to G5."

"G5?"

"Yeah, any idea where that would be? Maybe a codename for someplace?"

"Well, I have heard of a jet called a G5."

"A jet?"

"Yes, a big fancy private jet," Agent Hetman said. "A few years ago, we intercepted a Mexican drug lord in one down on the Arizona border."

"So maybe—"

"So maybe Winston flew away on a G5, Agent Perez. Maybe Morgenstern helped him. That's where I'd start looking. Who knows, maybe Morgenstern went with him. It is a little weird how he just disappeared after getting caught up in Winston's escape."

"Is Morgenstern a suspect at this time, sir?"

"No, he hasn't broken any laws that I'm aware of. I'm not sure why Damonati is going after his wife. Look into the G5 thing and let me know what you find out."

Yes, sir."

"And by the way, I saw where HPD reported two stolen passports this morning. The report is being forwarded to the State Department. It could be—"

"Two passports? Stolen?" Agent Perez clenched his teeth.

"Yes, that's what I said. Two passports were reported stolen. It could be nothing, or there could be a connection to Winston. He would need a passport to travel internationally—preferably not his own."

Gail watched Agent Perez take a deep breath and close his eyes for several seconds.

"Agent Perez, is everything okay?" Agent Hetman asked.

"Yes, of course, sir. I'll look into the passports and the private jet as soon as I get back to my office."

CHAPTER FORTY-FOUR

The North Atlantic
20:00 GMT, 10 January

"Number five. That's us." Kup pointed at a dark wooden table ahead and to their left.

Jerry and Kup plopped their Gull beers down on their designated table in the *Sissal's* bar after stuffing themselves at the buffet. A large, burly man with bushy grayish-blond hair and a beard to match was sitting at the same table at the spot marked with a number six. He nodded at them.

The mood in the room was one of camaraderie and a sense of purpose as the volunteers prepared to receive the briefing on the rescue mission.

Kup took a drink from his beer after he sat down. He looked around the room. "It's like we're in the bloody hall of Vikings."

The bearded man across the table said, "You are English?"

Kup smiled. "Australian, but I live in Hawai'i now. Name's Melvin Ferguson, mate."

"My name is Agnar Jákupsson." The man slammed his liter of beer down on the off-white plastic table and shook Kup's hand. "But my friends will refer to me as Aggi."

Jerry's eyes lit up. He beamed at Agnar. "My name's Jerry, Jerry Morgenstern."

Agnar wiped beer foam from his beard with his left hand as he reached out to Jerry with his right. "It is nice to meet you."

Jerry's manicured hand disappeared inside Agnar's thick and calloused hand. "Nice to meet you, too. Gotta love your nickname."

"Ah, an American. Well, it is wonderful that you two came all this way to help our cause. My wife is stuck in Iceland. She was visiting her family when the attack occurred. I hope to bring supplies in and my wife out."

"Wow," Jerry said. "Well, good luck. I know how tough it is to have family behind the Zone. My wife and family were stuck behind, but they sailed away in our boat."

Agnar squinted at him. "Galveston?"

Jerry nodded. "Yes, she was the first one."

Agnar pushed back from the table. "Good for her. I am so glad she escaped. It is not so good, the situation in Iceland. The people, they keep trying to stay ahead of the aliens, but the aliens keep spreading out, looking for food. An island of three hundred fifty thousand people in an instant gets another one hundred five thousand mouths to feed. The governments are powerless to do anything. We must take matters into our hands, like your wife did."

"You can say that again," Kup said.

Agnar took a gulp of beer. "And why did you two decide to join the rescue operation?"

Jerry and Kup looked at each other.

"After my family made it out okay, I felt like I needed to help other families stuck behind the Zone," Jerry said.

Agnar took a sip of his beer and closed one eye. The other eye pointed at Jerry. "But you could have done this in Galveston, yes? Why come all the way to Iceland?"

"Well … uh … it seemed like the people in Galveston were doing okay with all the sailboats from around Houston. I wanted to help the people of Iceland, who are more isolated."

Agnar stroked his beard. "But the people on the internet say the situation in Galveston is worse. One hundred five thousand aliens inundated an island of only fifty thousand humans. And the island is also only forty-three by five kilometers, tiny compared to Iceland. The news report I read gave them only a couple of days before the food supply is depleted. And the sailboats can only transport so much with the US Coast Guard restricting the traffic flow because they are worried about the aliens escaping to the mainland USA."

Jerry eyed his Rolex. "When are they going to start the presentation?"

Agnar shrugged. "I watched a video from Galveston of people running out into the surf and standing in waist-deep water while they ate.

They say these aliens are like cats, terrified of the water. It's not possible to do that in Iceland. Well, I guess it is possible, but it would be painfully cold, the water."

"Crazy times." Jerry took a long gulp of beer as he tried to think of something to change the subject. "So, Agnar, you—"

"Aggi, please, my new friends."

Jerry smiled. "So, Aggi, you said your wife is from Iceland. Where are you from?"

"I live in the village of Klaksvík in the Faroe Islands."

A voice came over the loudspeaker. "Ladies and gentlemen, we are ready to start the briefing. Because we have people from many countries here, I will speak in English. Hopefully, everyone has taken their seats at their designated spots, which correspond to your boat number and the order in which we will launch you.

"In the morning, we will launch boat number one at nine fifty-five, which is the official start of morning twilight. We are experiencing short days, so we must maximize the daylight we have. Now, if you will, please look at the screen here."

A large screen displayed a satellite view of Iceland. The speaker pointed to a spot on the east coast. "Seyðisfjörður is here." He moved his hand to a spot on the ocean to the east of Seyðisfjörður. "We will be here, fifteen kilometers due east of the Icelandic coastline. The EMP zone is three kilometers wide and is between nine and twelve kilometers from the coastline. This red band here represents the EMP zone. Our friends in Seyðisfjörður, who sailed back and forth with a Faraday bag and some sacrificed electronics, tested the EMP zone yesterday."

The speaker pointed to a red dot between the coastline and the EMP zone. "At the rendezvous point, we will have a group of volunteers from Seyðisfjörður in motorized boats. As you are aware, the ferry port and terminal in Seyðisfjörður are not usable. So, the plan for you volunteers will be to launch from the aft opening of the vehicle deck at your designated times. You will sail Fareast 18s, which were donated by Danska Sejl in Copenhagen.

"We stripped them of all nonessential gear and all electronics and loaded the cabins with food and supplies for Iceland. We will give each of you a small waterproof Faraday bag. You will place your electronics and handheld radio inside the Faraday bag before crossing the EMP zone in both directions. You can use the radio in an emergency; however, you must know that if you remove it or any other electronics from the Faraday bag while in the EMP zone, they will be rendered unusable.

"You will sail eight kilometers from the ship, through the EMP zone, and then on to the rendezvous point. A motorized boat will signal you with three flashes of light when it is safe to remove your radio from the provided Faraday bag. They will contact you by radio and maneuver to your position. You will tie up to them and then transfer the supplies over to them. If there are any refugees aboard the motorized boats, you will bring them back to the ship.

"Now, we estimate the sailboats will average eight kilometers per hour, so it should take you about one hour to sail to the rendezvous point. If we allow thirty minutes for the transfer at the rendezvous point, the round trip should take approximately two and a half hours."

Kup whispered in Jerry's ear, "How far past the rendezvous point is the town of Seyðisfjörður?"

Jerry whispered back, "The town is at the end of that long fjord with the same name as the town. The fjord looks to be about fifteen kilometers deep. So, it should take us about three hours total to sail from the ship all the way to the town of Seyðisfjörður."

CHAPTER FORTY-FIVE

Honolulu, Hawai'i
17:00 HST, 10 January

Agent Perez listened to the voicemail from HCF, the Honolulu Control Facility, for the third time. He jotted down the list of destinations of the seven G5 jets that had departed O'ahu the previous day.

Phoenix, AZ

San Jose, CA

Vancouver, BC

Montrose, CO

Vágar, Faroe Islands

San Diego, CA

Sacramento, CA

He circled Vancouver and Vágar and glanced at the old-fashioned clock mounted on the wall of his temporary office on O'ahu. It read five minutes past five p.m. *I could use a beer. Canada or the Faroe Islands? Unless they just stopped on the mainland and headed somewhere else. I need to report this, but if ... why does the FAA have to be so efficient?*

Before he left, Perez scanned his messages to check for anything new. A message popped up about the stolen passport of Melvin Reynolds Ferguson. The message's header displayed its journey through multiple European and American bureaucracies before making its way to the Honolulu Field Office.

The message contained a video from Vágar Airport Customs, Faroe Islands. Perez's right hand quivered as he clicked on the video. Kup's wide-eyed face stared at the camera. He had shaved his mustache and lightened his hair, but it was undeniably Kup.

Nothing about Jerry? I guess he didn't go with Kup. Where is he?

Perez closed the video and the message. He looked at the Dell computer tower sitting on the floor beside his desk and at his unopened bottle of Gatorade. He took the Gatorade bottle and poured its entire contents onto the computer. Forty-five seconds later, the computer emitted a hissing sound, and the screen went blank. *That thing was ancient anyway.*

Perez called the IT Office and left a message that he had accidentally spilled some Gatorade on his computer. He locked his office door and walked down the hallway toward the building exit. *I could really use a beer now.*

"Agent Perez?" It was Karl Hetman's voice.

Perez stopped and turned around. "Yes, sir?"

Hetman slouched beside the doorway to his secretary's office. His belly indicated an ongoing battle between beer, aging, and physical fitness. Beer and aging were winning. "Can you come into my office, please?"

"Of course." Perez walked back down the hall to Agent Hetman's office.

Hetman motioned to the chair on the other side of his desk. "Please sit down."

Perez sat down. His heart was pounding.

"I have some concerns about the pace of the Winston investigation that I'd like to go over with you, Agent Perez."

Perez nodded. *Like, maybe why is Winston in the Faroe Islands?* "Okay."

"Agent Perez, have there been any updates that I'm not yet aware of?"

"Updates? No, sir."

"Nothing?" Hetman looked into Perez's eyes. "Any lead on the G5 Morgenstern's wife mentioned?"

"No, sir."

"How hard have you questioned her, Agent Perez?"

"Well, sir, I was planning on—"

"Have you used the special protocols for domestic terrorists?"

"No, sir, not yet. I thought—"

Hetman held up his right hand with his palm facing Perez. "Agent Perez, once again, do you have any updates on Kuparr Winston or Jerry Morgenstern? Anything?"

Perez shuffled his feet. "No, sir." A drop of sweat rolled down from his left temple onto his left thumb. "My computer is down."

"Down? When did this happen?" Hetman opened his laptop.

"Earlier. A few minutes ago."

"Huh." Hetman flipped the laptop around so that Perez could view the screen.

"Please press the Play arrow, Agent Perez."

Perez didn't have to. He recognized the video, but he pressed Play anyway. "What is this?" His right foot began tapping the floor as the video began playing in front of him.

"This is a video from customs at Vágar Airport in the Faroe Islands," Hetman said. "The individual you see used the stolen passport of Melvin Ferguson. That individual is Kuparr Winston."

Perez opened his mouth.

"But you knew that already, Agent Perez. The logs show you viewed this video ten minutes ago. Apparently, your computer was working then. I've been waiting for you to storm in here with this discovery. Instead, I had to ask you point-blank if there was anything new, and you point-blank lied to me. Agent Perez, what is going on here?"

Perez sat speechless.

"But wait, there's more, Agent Perez. I received a phone call a few minutes ago from a Ms. Hoʻolina at the FAA. She said she left you a voicemail this morning but hadn't heard back from you. Seven G5s left Oʻahu yesterday. It turns out one of them was headed to the Faroe Islands."

Perez swallowed hard but didn't say anything.

"So, I repeat, Agent Perez—what is going on here? Why didn't you report any of this to me?"

Perez reached for his phone and pulled up the texts from Gretchen Kupule, alluding to the manipulated emails. He slid the phone across the desk over to Agent Hetman.

Hetman squinted to read the text messages and pulled the cellphone up to his face.

The senator wants you to be at a meeting with J Morgenstern this am at his hotel room Sherwood Waikiki.

Okay. I'm available.

The meeting will be at 10 am sharp. Suite 31081. Don't be late!!!!

Okay. I'll be there. See you then.

We need to go ahead and get rid of the file with the altered Winston emails. The senator is concerned about the wrong people getting their hands on them.
Also keep a close eye on my sister. She drinks a lot. If she starts blabbing to someone about the fake rape charges, we r screwed.

Hetman put the cellphone back on the table. "What the hell is going on, Agent Perez? Who sent you these texts?"

"Gretchen Kupule."

"Senator Damonati's aide?"

Perez nodded.

"And the governor's daughter?" Hetman asked. "And the texts implicate the governor's other daughter?"

"Yes, and yes."

"Scheissballs, Agent Perez!"

"Agent Hetman, I believe the charges against Kuparr Winston are not only false but are also fraudulent."

"Fraudulent? You do realize that these texts would also implicate Senator Damonati."

"Yes, sir."

"Do you realize how powerful she is?"

"Yes, sir."

Hetman laid the phone back down on the table. "Why didn't you come to me with these texts earlier?"

"I don't know. I guess I … lost faith … I wasn't sure who to trust."

"Are you positive these texts are from the senator's aide?"

"I'm positive."

Hetman shook his head. "Damn. I've got six months until I retire, and all I wanted to do is stay clear of Senator Damonati. Well, never mind that, Agent Perez."

"Sir, I—"

"You know I need more evidence and more time to go after Senator Damonati. And she's been bugging the hell out of me about Winston."

"And what about Winston?" Perez asked.

"Winston?" Hetman looked up at the ceiling and then back at Perez. "I'll notify Headquarters of the video and its connection to the stolen passport and Kuparr Winston. FBI Headquarters will reach out to the legal attaché in Copenhagen, who will reach out to law enforcement in the Faroe Islands. Of course, it's the middle of the night in Europe right now, so things may take a while. I won't, however, notify Senator Damonati about the video—not yet, at least."

Perez sat motionless, staring out the window.

Hetman broke the silence. "Why the Faroe Islands? Why did they go there?"

"I have no idea, Agent Hetman. Wait—you said 'they'? 'Why did *they* go there?'"

"Morgenstern went through customs at the same time as Winston. They're together."

"No shit."

"Something you'd like to tell me, Agent Perez? Like what they plan to do in the Faroe Islands?"

"No idea, sir. Will that be all?"

Hetman sat back in his chair and stared at Perez. "No, that will *not* be all, Agent Perez. I'm taking you off the case until I can—"

"But sir, it—"

"I need a little time to sort this shit out, Agent Perez. You slow-rolling the investigation and then lying to me hasn't exactly helped your cause."

Agent Perez nodded slowly. "I understand. Will that be all, sir?"

"No, it won't. I want you to get to Susan Kupule. Since they're so worried about her blabbing, see if you can get her to admit to filing the false rape charges. That would go a long way to restoring your credibility—and your career. You can use the special protocols."

Perez stood up. "I'll figure out a way to make that happen, sir." He reached over the desk to retrieve his phone.

Hetman placed his hand on it. "This cellphone is mine now."

"But it's my phone. You can't keep it."

"Yes I can, and yes I will."

CHAPTER FORTY-SIX

The Iceland No-Transgression Zone
10:00 GMT, 11 January

Kup shuddered when Jerry opened the hatchway onto the vehicle deck of the *Sissal* as cold arctic air rushed into the warm climate-controlled passageway.

Laid out before them in neat rows were sailboat after sailboat sitting on trailers. A ramp led to a second level filled with multiple rows of sailboats sitting on trailers. The sailboats were already rigged and loaded, and a small tractor was pulling Sailboat 5's trailer over to the crane at the back of the ferry.

Through the cavernous opening in the aft of the vehicle deck, a line of small sailboats trailed off in the distance to the west. White cliffs etched the horizon and the eastern coast of Iceland.

The large digital clock on the wall showed 10:55. Their launch time was in five minutes. The sunrise would not occur for another eleven minutes, but at northern latitudes, sunrises and sunsets were gradual, time-consuming events.

The official plan was to reach the rendezvous point on the other side of the Zone around noon. After transferring the food and supplies to the motorboats from Seyðisfjörður, they would sail back to the ferry and arrive around 13:30. Instead, Jerry and Kup planned on sailing past the motorboats and into Seyðisfjörður. If everything went as planned, they would reach the town of Seyðisfjörður before sunset, which would happen at 16:04.

The ocean was calm, with a reported swell of half a meter. A northerly wind at twelve knots was forecast for the next several hours, along with some high cirrus clouds.

The ship's crew were now hooking Sailboat 5 to the straps attached to the two cranes. One crane would lower the aft end while another would lower the bow. The aft straps were clipped to two newly installed metal rings at each corner of the back of the sailboat. The forward strap was clipped to a single metal ring installed at the bow.

Standing to the left, against the wall, was Agnar Jákupsson. He waved as Jerry and Kup approached. "Great day to go sailing."

Jerry smiled. "Yes, it's beautiful out there, Aggi."

Agnar laughed. "Yes, it could be quite a bit more treacherous. We are quite lucky today." He glanced at Sailboat 5. "Well, it looks like they are ready for you two. Good luck."

Kup reached over and placed his gloved hand on the side of the sailboat. The cold wind attempted to cut through both his drysuit and the layers of clothing underneath it.

Jerry raised his left leg over the starboard rail and dropped it on the fiberglass floor of the daysailer.

"Wait!" said a male voice from behind them. Jerry paused and turned his head toward it. "Stop! Are you Mr. Jerry Morgenstern and Mr. Kuparr Winston?"

Kup froze.

The captain of the ferry stood ten meters away from them. He wore a white long-sleeve shirt with epaulets and black slacks. He seemed impervious to the cold. His second-in-command and two security officers stood beside and behind him, wearing heavy coats.

Kup stared at them, frozen like a deer in headlights.

Agnar looked at Kup. "Who is Kuparr Winston?"

Jerry glanced at Agnar and looked down at the floor. Kup looked back toward the open ocean and the cliffs of Iceland in the distance.

The captain, first officer, and two security guards stopped two meters from Jerry and Kup. The captain said, "I am Captain Arnfinsson. I asked if you two are Jerry Morgenstern and Kuparr Winston. We received a request from the Faroe Islands Police to check and see if we had these two men aboard."

Jerry and Kup both stood there, unsure of what to say to the captain.

"I am the captain of this vessel. You will answer my question, please."

Kup shrugged. "I'm Kuparr Winston."

Captain Arnfinsson studied Kup's face. "And are you traveling under the name Melvin Reynolds Ferguson using a stolen American passport?"

Kup nodded.

Captain Arnfinsson turned to Jerry. "And may I assume you are Jerry Morgenstern?"

Jerry nodded.

"Gentlemen, you will come with me." The captain motioned for them to follow him. The two security guards fell in behind them. Agnar stood against the wall with his mouth open.

Captain Arnfinsson instructed the crew to unhook Sailboat 5 and move it to the side. They would skip this boat for now. He turned and walked back toward the hatchway that led to the interior of the ship.

They followed the captain through the ship's interior until they came into a small meeting room. Captain Arnfinsson motioned for them to sit down at the small wooden table in the center of the room. The second-in-command of the ship entered and stood in the corner while the two security guards stood outside the closed door.

Captain Arnfinsson sat down at the table opposite Jerry and Kup. "Mr. Winston, I am told that you are a fugitive from the American federal police. I am also told that you stole a passport, traveled to the Faroe Islands illegally, and then boarded my vessel to volunteer for a rescue effort for Iceland. These are strange times, but your story makes little sense. Can you please explain why you are aboard my ship and why you felt it necessary to use such extraordinary measures to be a part of our voluntary effort here?"

Before Kup could answer, Captain Arnfinsson turned to Jerry. "And you, Mr. Morgenstern, have committed no crime other than traveling with a fugitive. The American Government is putting enormous pressure on the Danes, who are putting enormous pressure on the Faroese."

He looked at Jerry and then at Kup. "So, gentlemen, tell me why you are here."

Kup took a deep breath. "We're here to save Iceland, Galveston, and Hawai'i Island."

Jerry raised his eyebrows.

Captain Arnfinsson studied Kup's face. "Continue."

"I know how to bring down the EMP system that controls the no-transgression zones around each island."

Captain Arnfinsson narrowed his eyes. "You know how to do this? Why have you not shared this information with the American military?"

"Why?" Kup laughed for a split second. "Because I've been in government custody since aliens rescued me from the plane crash that the same government is accusing me of causing. I've apparently done all kinds of terrible things, and my guilt is a foregone conclusion. So, I decided that if I was going to do this, I'd have to do it alone."

Captain Arnfinsson glanced over at Jerry.

"With a little help from my mate here," Kup said.

"Okay," Captain Arnfinsson said. "Tell me why you and only you can disarm the EMP."

"I shared the Warden's *Ha*—I mean, we had a Reckoning. That's the term they use."

"Reckoning? What is this, and who is this Warden?"

"Sorry," Kup said. "The Warden is in command of the three penal colonies—an alien, of course. He's a technical expert on their systems. A Reckoning is a mind coupling, a complete sharing of two minds so that they are brought into balance. They achieve equity. I know everything about him; he knows everything about me. As for me, I gained technical knowledge of the entire alien EMP system, and I learned about an engineering vulnerability that concerned the Warden. He had tried to persuade his superiors to address this vulnerability, but they ignored him. If they learned that I was trying to exploit it, I'm sure they would harden the vulnerability, which is why as few people as possible can know about this. They monitor all media."

"So, this vulnerability is in Iceland?"

"Yes. And this rescue mission seemed like our only opportunity— the only way to get through the EMP to Iceland."

"But the daysailers are not going all the way," Captain Arnfinsson said as he tapped the table with his thick right pointer finger. "They are not going to Seyðisfjörður itself. They will be stopping well short."

"We had planned on sailing all the way," Jerry said.

"Past the rendezvous boats?"

"Yes," Kup said.

Captain Arnfinsson glanced at his second-in-command for a second.

Kup looked around the room. "Besides the four of us here, only our contact in Iceland knows this information."

Captain Arnfinsson sat back in his seat. "If you disarm the EMPs that are around each island, what happens next?"

Kup cleared his throat. "The islands will be open again, but the alien convicts are here to stay. The transport ships were built for a one-way journey only and have already been destroyed."

"If I had heard this story two weeks ago, I would have thought you belonged in a mental institution, but today I …" Captain Arnfinsson scratched his head as he looked over at his first officer again. "The Faroese authorities asked if you two were aboard. I have not answered them yet. I will need to confer with my first officer in private on this matter. Please excuse us."

Captain Arnfinsson stood and motioned for the first officer to follow him out the door.

Once the doorway was closed and they were alone, Jerry turned to Kup. "So that was your Hail Mary?"

"My what?"

"Your Hail Mary. You know, a Hail Mary pass. In football."

"Football? Oh, American football. I'm not that familiar with it. It's pretty new to me."

Jerry smirked. "It's when your team is out of time and out of options. The quarterback throws the football up in the air in a wild hope that somebody from his team will catch it and run down the field and make a touchdown. Kind of a last-hope effort, a shot in the dark."

Kup nodded. "I reckon at this point, it's all we have."

"Yes, it is, I guess. I wonder where Gail will live with her hometown uninhabitable and her husband imprisoned. Speaking of which, I hope they send me to one of those federal prisons for white-collar criminals."

CHAPTER FORTY-SEVEN

Honolulu, Hawai'i
00:30 HST, 11 January

Agent Perez smiled as his breathing quickened. *Oh, damn. She's a lot prettier in person.* Sweat formed on his forehead. Her social media posts indicated Susan Kupule liked to go to the Grand Hawaiian Bar and Grill. She liked to go there a lot—almost every night she was in town, in fact.

So, Agent Perez had gone to the Grand Hawaiian that night, too, hoping she would show up and drink too much—and talk too much. The new special protocols for domestic terrorists made his job easier, a lot easier. Speech was no longer free. In fact, speech itself could be a crime.

He had planted himself on a barstool at the long koa wood bar opposite the entrance and nursed a Fire Rock Pale Ale while he waited.

Soon enough, Susan arrived with two girlfriends. Their short, skin-tight dresses caused a stir amongst the patrons as they entered the bar. Susan's blue dress was the shortest and tightest of the three.

Agent Perez swallowed the bottom fifth of his beer, hoping the alcohol would offset his sudden loss of self-confidence. *Shit. What if she blows me off? This has to work. I'm screwed if it doesn't.*

He thought back to when he had been getting ready to go out for the night. He had stood in front of the mirror in his hotel room as he secured the minuscule Bluetooth microphone to the inside of his shirt collar. He had gotten a haircut earlier that day, and the barber's hair gel still held his close-cropped black hair in place. He had splashed on some newly purchased cologne and slipped on a new pair of black leather OluKai flip-flops.

The three women started the night off with a round of tequila shots.

A bit later, Perez ordered a round of mai tais from the bartender and walked over to Susan Kupule's table. "Ladies, I see you all need refills."

Three sets of blurry eyes focused on him and the four drinks he was carrying.

One of Susan's friends tossed her shoulder-length auburn hair back as she took one of the drinks. "Why, thank you, sweetheart. Have a seat." She motioned for Agent Perez to sit down at the empty seat at their table, which happened to be next to Susan Kupule.

Perez sat down.

Susan winked at Perez. "So, what's your name, mai tai man?"

"I'm Miles. Miles Nicodemus," Perez said, using the name of his ex-brother-in-law.

"And does Miles live on Oʻahu, or is he visiting?" Susan drained a good inch of the mai tai in one sip.

"Visiting. I'm here for a medical conference." Perez's ex-brother-in-law was an orthopedic surgeon.

Susan smiled. "Oh, you're a doctor?"

"Yes. Orthopedic surgeon."

"How interesting." Susan inched closer to Perez.

Perez took a tiny sip of his mai tai and reached into his right shorts pocket to activate the Bluetooth microphone in his collar. "Uh … you look familiar. Like I've seen you on TV."

"TV? Oh, you might have seen my press conference with Senator Damonati."

"Senator Damonati? Oh, yeah, the Hawaiʻi senator. Wait … I remember now … a pilot raped you. I'm so sorry you went through that." Perez slid back from Susan. "Please forgive me. I didn't realize—"

"It's okay, honey." Susan finished her mai tai. "I'm fine."

"Fine? I don't know … I mean … I should leave."

Susan glanced left and right. "Listen, I made the whole thing up with the pilot. Senator Damonati is paying me a hundred grand to do it. It has something to do with her campaign or some new law she wants passed."

Perez smiled. "Ah, I see. So … you're okay?"

"Never better, but don't tell anyone. That's our little secret, okay?"

"Sure. My lips are sealed."

"Now, how about buying me another drink, Doctor Miles?" Susan gently squeezed the inside of his right thigh with her left hand. "I could use a little *mileage* tonight."

CHAPTER FORTY-EIGHT

The Iceland No-Transgression Zone
12:00 GMT, 11 January

Kup had never been so cold or so enchanted in his life. They were sailing along on a broad reach at six knots and were being escorted by a pod of about twenty orcas. The details in the snow-clad cliffs that formed the opening to the fjord of Seyðisfjörður became more defined with each passing minute, and the sun was reaching the peak of its five-hour trek across the northern sky.

Three motorboats were close now—only about a hundred meters away. One of the motorboats signaled them with three flashes of light.

A large orca swam alongside Kup while he hiked out on the upwind side of the sailboat. For several lingering seconds, the orca rolled over and looked Kup straight in the eye.

Jerry tweaked the sails as the wind picked up. He yelled, "Open the Faraday bag and turn on the radio!"

Kup smiled at Jerry. "In a second. This killer whale is looking right at me!"

Kup pulled himself into the cockpit and opened the watertight Faraday bag. It was almost impossible with the thick, watertight gloves he was wearing, so he pulled the gloves off. His hands soon stung from the cold spray shooting up from the bow. In less than twenty seconds, he opened the Faraday bag, pulled out the waterproof handheld radio, closed the bag, and put his gloves back on.

Kup placed both gloved hands under his armpits, hoping that might help them warm up.

Jerry laughed. "So, turn it on. See if it made it through the EMP."

Kup pulled his hands out from underneath his armpits and began fumbling around with the radio. After several attempts, he moved the switch to ON.

There was nothing but silence for several seconds until a male voice came over the radio. "Sailboat 5, this is Motorboat 2. Please continue with your present course. We will maneuver alongside you and raft up together."

"What should I say?" Kup held the radio in his right hand.

"Don't say anything. Just ignore them."

A blue-and-white tugboat began speeding toward them.

"We're going to have to say something eventually," Kup said. "We can't outrun them."

The blue-and-white tugboat was now abeam them on their starboard side. As it went past, it started a wide turn to its starboard side and pulled in behind them.

The voice on the radio returned. "Sailboat 5, we will maneuver to your port side. When we tell you, you will luff your sails. Be ready to catch our lines. Sailboat 5, do you copy?"

Kup raised his eyebrows. "They'll be alongside us any second now. We can't just keep ignoring them."

"Okay, talk to them," Jerry said.

Kup nodded and pressed the push-to-talk button. "Motorboat 2, this is Sailboat 5. We intend to continue sailing to Seyðisfjörður. Do not raft up with us."

There was silence over the radio. Kup eyed the approaching tugboat. "What if they force us to stop?"

Jerry shrugged. "Well, I guess you'll have to tell a sixth person on this planet why you're so intent on getting to Iceland."

The voice returned to the radio. "Sailboat 5, it is not possible to sail all the way to Seyðisfjörður. You will luff your sails and take our lines. Captain Arnfinsson of the *Sissal* has ordered you to do so. We will take you to Seyðisfjörður after the transfer has taken place. We have several refugees aboard that will sail Sailboat 5 back to the *Sissal*. It will be better for you this way."

Kup smiled. "Yes! We should be in Seyðisfjörður in under an hour."

Jerry nodded and began loosening the ropes to the sails so that they swung into the wind and began fluttering. Seconds later, they were catching ropes that were flung over by the crew of the tugboat, now only a meter away on their port side.

Twenty minutes later, three refugees aboard Sailboat 5 pushed off from Motorboat 2 and headed eastward back out to sea toward the *Sissal*. Motorboat 2, full of food and supplies, turned westward and entered Seyðisfjörður fjord at a speed of fifteen knots.

Forty minutes later, Kup spotted a tall blond girl kissing a tall blond man on a rocky beach. *That's got to be Hildur and Trevor. Nobody else is out there.*

Kup whispered to Jerry, "No police. That's a good sign."

Jerry nodded. "But you know the authorities in the Faroes have called their buddies in Iceland by now. Captain Arnfinsson said he would delay his reply to the Faroese authorities until we were past the motorboats. It's only a matter of time."

"I don't know," Kup said. "I would guess the police here might have their hands full with other, more critical stuff than a fugitive American."

"Well, let's hope so."

After the tugboat beached itself, Jerry and Kup grabbed several loads of supplies and carried them to an open truck bed. They thanked the captain and crew and walked over to Hildur and Trevor.

Everyone shook hands as a blue-and-white SUV with flashing blue lights approached them. "Lögreglan" was plastered on the side.

Kup's heart was once again racing.

CHAPTER FORTY-NINE

Near Höfn, Iceland
18:00 GMT, 11 January

Three hours and fifty minutes after they had politely thanked the policewoman in Seyðisfjörður for the warning about the approaching alien mobs and had loaded up in Hildur's fully charged Škoda, they passed the intersection for Highway 99 to Höfn. One kilometer past the intersection, the strobe lights from a police car parked on the shoulder illuminated several orange cones. Hildur began slowing.

Jerry glanced through the windshield. "Why is there a roadblock, Hildur?"

"Because of the aliens. They are ahead."

As Hildur slowed the Škoda to a crawl, the policeman held his right hand up, indicating for her to stop. He walked over to her window as she rolled it down.

The policeman studied Hildur and Trevor first before glancing into the backseat. He seemed to fixate on Kup as he said, *"Þú getur ekki farið þá leið. Ég þarf að snúa þér við."*

Kup turned away from the policeman's stare. *Shit. He must be asking about me.* "What does he want, Hildur?"

"He says we cannot go this way. He wants us to turn around."

The policeman nodded. "Yes, you cannot continue. It is not safe. You must turn around."

"I am so sorry, officer." Hildur smiled at the policeman as she slammed her foot down on the accelerator and steered into the opposite lane. The Škoda shot around the police car, reaching one hundred kilometers per hour in just over four seconds.

Kup swung his head around, expecting the policeman to pull out a gun and start shooting. Instead, the policeman pulled out his cellphone and took a picture of the back of Hildur's car.

Kup faced forward again. "Are you sure he wasn't looking for me?"

Hildur shook her head. "No. As I said, he just wanted us to turn around."

"Will he call ahead to another policeman?"

"It is possible, but I think not likely," Hildur said. "The police, they are so overwhelmed right now. They are not so used to the chaos. We have, at most, one murder a year in the whole country and very little crime. The policeman had to report the incident—that will be the end of it. He has more important things to deal with than us. Besides, I told him I was sorry."

Kup shook his head. "Well, that's the second roadblock I've run in a week."

Jerry looked ahead through the windshield. "So, if the police are trying to keep people out, how bad is it up ahead, Hildur?"

"We should encounter the band of the alien mobs in a few kilometers. They are looking for food. If we can get through this band, things should be calm the rest of the way to Vík. In the areas that have already been cleaned out, there are very few aliens still around, and most of them are individuals or small groups. These seem okay, almost polite. It is a strange part of their social makeup. They act horribly in large groups but are quite timid when alone. Anyway, once we get to Vík, things should be all right. There are only a few aliens there. Many people in Vík have taken these aliens into their homes."

"In fact …" Trevor said. "Hildur has one staying at her house right now—if Kolbrún hasn't shot her yet."

"Wait, you've got an alien staying at your house?" Jerry asked.

"Yes, of course. I experienced the Reckoning with her. She was an engineer. I feel sorry for her."

Jerry squirmed in his seat. "And who is Kolbrún?"

"Kolbrún is my neighbor. She is a widow. She can be a little bit overprotective sometimes. I think she gets lonely."

Trevor looked back at Jerry. "Just don't piss her off."

Hildur laughed. "Yes. She carries a rifle now, sometimes a shotgun. It depends on her mood. I have always attempted to be with her good side."

"Damn," Jerry said. "I'll be on my best behavior around her."

Hildur slowed the Škoda as she pointed to a cheerful red-and-white farmhouse illuminated by the waning twilight and puny crescent moon. A mob of about a hundred aliens was smashing its windows.

"Look," Hildur said. "An alien mob is there. I would guess the residents have already left the house and taken their animals with them. We should start seeing more of the mobs now—maybe for the next twenty or thirty kilometers, I think."

Two minutes later, they crested a hill, and the Škoda's headlights lit up a line of aliens covering the road. Instead of braking as the car descended along the road, Hildur sped up and began honking her horn.

The line of aliens ahead didn't budge.

Jerry grabbed the back of the seat in front of him. "Shit! You're gonna kill a few of them and us at the same time!"

Hildur clenched her hands on the steering wheel. "It is the only way. If we stop or slow down, they will destroy the car."

"But there must be two hundred of them up ahead!"

"Please make sure that your seatbelts are fastened," Hildur said.

They were only about a hundred meters away from the first aliens in the line. The speedometer was pegged at 200 kilometers per hour.

"Bloody hell," Kup said under his breath. "I'm glad I'm in the back seat."

Trevor put his hands on the dash and lowered his head. "This worked on the way out … I hope it works again."

They were now only fifty meters away from the mob.

"I can't believe we're playing chicken with a mob of aliens," Jerry said as he pressed his forehead against the back of the front passenger seat.

Hildur tucked her head down as she continued to honk her horn.

With just a few meters to spare, the alien mob split apart and separated, with half going to the left and half going to the right. They created a narrow lane in the middle, leaving not quite enough space for the Škoda to pass through. The passenger-side mirror encountered some unseen body part and spun away from the car.

Seconds later, they were clear of the mob.

They all breathed a sigh of relief and relaxed.

As they rounded a curve in the road, a furry gray mass flashed in front of them before bouncing onto the hood of the Škoda and slamming into the windshield. Chunks of broken glass and blood flew back from the windshield onto Hildur and Trevor. Hildur rolled down her window and stuck her head halfway out so that she could see. The Škoda began slowing, but Hildur drove several kilometers farther until they were well clear of the alien mob. She stopped beside an intersection.

Everyone hopped out of the Škoda and surveyed the damage. Except for the shattered windshield, the Škoda would be okay. The sheep, however, was dead.

Jerry and Kup began tugging on the sheep's two front legs while Trevor and Hildur yanked on the sheep's head. The body slid halfway across the shattered windshield.

Kup stopped pulling when he noticed a mob of about thirty aliens walking toward them from the other road. "Aliens!" He jumped back from the car. "We've got to get out of here."

The other three stopped pulling to see what Kup was talking about.

Hildur grabbed the sheep. "Quickly! Remove the sheep. Let them see it. Toss it behind the car."

Everyone started pulling on the sheep. It began sliding along the windshield once again.

Kup looked back toward the approaching mob. "They're getting closer. Pull!"

The alien mob was only about fifty meters away when the sheep slid off the car and fell to the snow-covered asphalt.

"Drag it over there, behind the car!" Hildur ran around the front of the car. "Make sure they see it."

She jumped into the driver's seat. "Get in! Hurry! They are close."

Jerry, Kup, and Trevor dragged the dead sheep back behind the car. Trevor slipped on the ice as all three released their grip on the sheep.

Kup glanced at Trevor's face, drenched in blood. "Are you okay, Trevor?"

"Yeah, I'm okay." Trevor wiped blood from his forehead as he stood.

Jerry headed for the left back door as Kup jumped into the back seat from the right. Trevor, however, kept fumbling for the passenger door.

Hildur looked across the car at Trevor. "Trevor! Hurry, get in the car!"

"I can't see; I'm bleeding. Help me!"

Kup looked out the back window. One alien had pulled ahead of the pack. He was only twenty meters away. Kup jumped out and shoved Trevor into his seat. He turned around and froze.

The alien who had run ahead was standing in front of the dead sheep, only two meters from Kup. *"Kindurnar era okkar!"*

Kup held on to the open door. "What is he saying?"

The mob of thirty was closing in.

Hildur yelled, "Tell him '*Já.* ' Get in the car! He wants the sheep."

The alien turned and faced the approaching mob. He turned back toward Kup. *"Kindurnar era okkar!* The sheep is ours! "

Kup nodded. *"Já!"* He turned and jumped into the car. Hildur slammed her foot on the Škoda's accelerator, and they shot forward.

Kup turned to look out the rear window. The mob had encircled the dead sheep.

CHAPTER FIFTY

Vík í Mýrdal, Iceland
08:00 GMT, 12 January

Kup awoke to the smell of coffee. He had slept on a futon in Hildur's small living room. In the kitchen, Kolbrún was busy preparing breakfast. Her rifle was by her side.

When they'd arrived the previous night, Kolbrún had been sitting on the couch in Hildur's living room with her rifle held in her lap. Her attention seemed to alternate between the television and Es-mar, who was sitting on the futon. Kolbrún had eventually returned home but had promised to be back in the morning with breakfast. She still had quite a stash of food that several aliens had died trying to steal.

Kup stood and began folding his sheets.

Kolbrún walked over to the coffee maker and said, *"Góðan daginn."* She grabbed the coffee pot and held it out toward Kup. *"Langar þig í kaffi?"*

Coffee? "Yes, please. And good morning to you too, Kolbrún." *I think she was asking me about coffee.*

"Íslensku." Kolbrún grimaced as she grabbed a coffee mug and began pouring.

She held a small carton of milk. *"Mjólk?"*

Kup glanced at Kolbrún's rifle, propped against a kitchen cabinet. *"Já."*

Kolbrún smiled and held up a jar of sugar. *"Sykur?"*

Kup shook his head. *"Nei."*

Kolbrún beamed as she bounded out of the small kitchen and into the living room. She handed Kup the mug of *kaffi* and the carton of *mjólk*.

Kup took the coffee and poured milk into it. *"Takk."*

Kolbrún nodded her approval and returned to the kitchen with the milk carton.

Kup sipped the coffee. *Well, that pretty much exhausts the Icelandic I learned in the car yesterday. Thank God she didn't shoot me for mispronouncing something.*

Hildur walked into the living room and smiled at Kup. "Good morning. I hope you slept okay on the futon?"

Kup returned the smile. "Good morning. Yes, I slept great."

Hildur nodded and walked into the kitchen. She poured herself a cup of black coffee and began arguing with Kolbrún in Icelandic. It seemed to Kup that Hildur wanted to help Kolbrún with the breakfast, but Kolbrún would not have it. She kept shooing Hildur away and saying, *"Nei."*

Hildur walked back into her living room and sat down in the chair opposite the futon. "Kolbrún is preparing us a typical Icelandic breakfast of *hafragrautur* and *skyr*. She hauled it all over here early this morning."

Kup took a sip of coffee. "Sounds delicious. I think."

Hildur laughed. "It is oatmeal and Icelandic yogurt. She has some jam and homemade bread as well."

"Well, I could use a bit of tucker. I haven't eaten since the ferryboat."

"You may need to get used to the hunger. Food is getting scarce. As you saw, they have looted all the stores in Vík. There is nothing left. The mobs are spreading out farther and farther along the south coast of Iceland. They are expected to reach Höfn late this evening. Going west, the mob is in a line from Selfoss to Sólheimer. They are saying the mob is moving slower going west because that direction is more heavily populated, but they could still reach Reykjavík in a matter of days. The Coast Guard and police have tried to stop them, but they are overwhelmed. There are simply too many mobs and too few police and Coast Guard."

"What about the Icelandic military?"

"We have no military—just the police and Coast Guard. They've also tried to move the food out of the stores and warehouses ahead of the mobs. This has worked so far, but they are still looting the stores and breaking into houses. There has been talk of trying to give the alien mobs food so they will stop the looting, but with the no-transgression zone, we cannot get enough food for the alien mobs and the Icelanders. Many are now saying that the alien mobs will circle around the interior on the east and west coasts and meet up somewhere along the north coast. When that happens, there will be nothing left for us, and we will have nowhere to go. Unless, of course, you can eliminate the EMP, as you claim."

"Hildur, if you can get me to the cave and through that ice wall, I can eliminate the EMP. When did you say that your father was bringing the auger?"

"He should be here any minute with the auger."

"And the auger works? He tested it?"

"Yes, he says he tested it yesterday. It works fine. He is also bringing two fifteen-liter tanks full of petrol."

Kup nodded and took a sip of coffee. "How's Trevor?"

"I think okay. The cut to his head was not deep."

There was a loud knocking at the front door. A male voice said, "Hildur, *hleyptu mér inn. Hurðin er læst.*"

Hildur walked to the door. "I forgot it was locked, Papa. I guess there is no longer a need to lock the door with all the mobs gone."

Einar walked into the living room and eyed Kup, sitting on the futon. He turned his head toward Hildur. *"Er þetta maðurinn sem þú varst að segja mér frá?"*

Hildur nodded. "Yes, Papa, this is the man I told you about, but English, please." She turned to Kup. "This is my father, Einar Ólafsson."

Kup stood up. "Nice to meet you, sir. Thanks for bringing us the auger." *Why do I feel like Obi-Wan Kenobi just walked into the house?*

Einar nodded at Kup. "You can stop the EMP? This is true?"

Kup gave Hildur a look of disapproval. "Yes. I can. But please, the fewer people that know about this, the better our chance for success."

Einar shrugged. "Who would I tell? I am just an old man in a small village." He turned to Kolbrún and the huge spread of food on the table. "Kolbrún, where did you get so much food?"

Kolbrún stopped what she was doing. "I have a secret hiding place, Einar."

"You also have a not-so-secret gun."

"Well, what is a little old lady to do?" Hildur shrugged. "Will you join us for breakfast, Einar? I have made hafragrautur."

Einar nodded. "Yes, I have not eaten in a day and a half. Hildur, should I load the auger and petrol in the monster truck?"

"Yes, Papa. Kup and I will help you."

Kup, Hildur, and Einar went outside and loaded the auger, petrol cans, and the remaining supplies in the monster truck. When they returned, Es-mar, Trevor, Jerry, and Kolbrún were crammed around the small kitchen table with plates set for each of them. Einar, Hildur, and Kup joined them and sat down to eat breakfast.

Kup looked at everyone around the table. "Can we go over our plan one more time to make sure that we are all on the same page?"

Everyone nodded but Einar, who said, "I thought the less I knew about this craziness, the better."

"It's okay," Kup said. "Just don't say anything to anyone else, and for sure, don't put anything out on social media."

Einar laughed. "Do I look like a social media person?"

Kup shrugged. "I don't know. I'm just saying they're out there, listening and watching everything. Trust no one."

Einar pointed a finger at Kup. "Well, you have to trust someone." He turned to Kolbrún. *"Hafragrautur er ljúffengur."*

"English, papa," Hildur said. "Do not be rude."

"The hafragrautur is delicious." Einar smiled at Kolbrún. "I have now told you twice."

Kolbrún smiled. *"Takk,* Einar."

Hildur shook her head.

Kolbrún rolled her eyes and stuck her tongue out.

Kup cleared his throat. "So, we leave here at nine thirty and should arrive at the trailhead by eleven. Then we hike to the cave entrance." Kup glanced at Hildur. "And we should get there by around noon, correct?"

Hildur nodded. "Yes, that is correct—if everything goes as planned."

"Okay, so around noon, we hike inside the cave—a distance you estimate to be about fifty meters—until we come to the wall of ice across the rest of the cave. It is my understanding that this wall of ice is about one meter thick. We'll begin drilling through the ice with Einar's auger. The plan is to drill multiple holes in the ice wall in a circular pattern. We'll space the holes so that they are almost touching. The ice should break away in a big chunk that we can push through to the other side. Once we—"

"I keep hearing 'Einar's this' and 'Einar's that,'" Einar said. "How many of you have operated an auger? Why is Einar not going along on this expedition?"

Hildur said, "Papa, we ..."

Einar looked at Hildur as he held a spoonful of *skyr*. "Yes?"

Kup shrugged. "Why not? We could use Einar's experience, and there's plenty of room in the monster truck, right?"

Hildur nodded. "Well, yes, there is room, but—"

"Good, then." Einar smiled. "It is settled. I will accompany you all to Eyjafjallajökull and the ice cave." He swallowed the *skyr*.

Hildur glanced over at Es-mar. "I think she should go, too. Since we will be dealing with alien technology, I think we should have an actual alien along with us."

"But the hole in the ice with the water—what if I fall in again?" Es-mar said.

"As long as you follow directly behind me, you will not fall in, Es-mar. I will promise you this."

Es-mar frowned. "I will do this thing if you need me."

"Very well," Einar said. "Es-mar will go with us. You were saying, Kup?"

Kup cleared his throat. "Uh, yeah. Once we break open a hole big enough for us to pass through, we'll make our way to the EMP emitter."

"Do you need any special tools to operate the EMP emitter?" Trevor asked.

Kup shook his head. "No, but there is a very specific sequence of actions that I must perform in a precise order, or the device will lock down for one hundred fifty minutes."

"And you know these sequences cold?" asked Trevor.

Jerry pointed to Kup's head with his right pointer finger. "Yes. They are embedded in his brain—literally embedded. He's a walking, talking alien encyclopedia."

Trevor frowned and faced Kolbrún. "Kolbrún, that was delicious. Can I help you clean up?"

"No," Kolbrún said. "No one will help me. You all have a very important duty to perform today. This little thing I have done this morning is my small contribution to saving my country and to saving my world. I have made each of you a sandwich to take with you to Eyjafjallajökull. You will need food to keep your strength up. I will make two more sandwiches for Einar and the alien girl now that they are going too. Now, everyone, please go and prepare yourselves for your journey. *Bless bless.*"

Kup stood and walked into the living room, past the muted television. A phone number for the lögreglan was listed below a video featuring his face at the customs office of Vágar Airport.

CHAPTER FIFTY-ONE

Honolulu, Hawai'i
23:00 HST, 11 January

Agent Hetman glanced down at his ringing cellphone as the elevator doors closed. "Senator Damonati?"

"This should be interesting," Agent Perez said as he pressed the button for the eighteenth floor. He was back on the Winston case; however, Agent Hetman would maintain complete control of the newly opened Damonati case.

"Yes, Senator. What can I do for you?"

"I assume, Agent Hetman, that you still do not know where they are; otherwise, you would have already called me."

"Are you talking about Winston and Morgenstern, Senator?"

The elevator doors opened, and Hetman began walking along the open-air corridor.

"Of course I am, you useless moron. Some ferryboat captain reported that they were—I repeat, were—on his ship. He apparently just realized this a few hours ago. Do you know where they are now, Agent Hetman?"

"Obviously not," Hetman said as he stopped at apartment 1815's front door.

"Iceland."

"Iceland? How on Earth did they get through the … why Iceland? Why would they go to Iceland?"

"They sailed to Iceland, Agent Hetman—in little sailboats. Don't worry, though. My contacts at the State Department have already been in direct contact with the Icelandic authorities. You might as well put me on salary since I seem to be doing your job for you. This was just a courtesy call, or maybe I was just curious to see just how incompetent you are."

"Well, thank you for the compliment and for contacting the Icelandic authorities, Senator. That's one less phone call I will have to make. Speaking of phone calls … do you mind holding for a minute or two? I have someone here who may wish to speak with you."

"Hold? You want to put me on hold? Just who do you think—"

Hetman pressed Mute on his phone and knocked on the door.

Forty seconds later, Gretchen Kupule opened the door. She stopped texting when she noticed Hetman's FBI badge hanging around his neck. "Uh, can I help you?"

Agent Perez stepped forward and said, "Ms. Kupule, we have evidence that you are involved in a plot to undermine and interfere with an official investigation of the National Transportation Safety Board. Furthermore, we have evidence that you have aided and abetted Senator Damonati and your sister in making false and fraudulent accusations of rape. We are taking you into federal custody. Please hand over your cellphone and laptop computer."

Hetman held his right hand, palm up, toward Gretchen. "Your cellphone, please, Ms. Kupule."

Gretchen dropped her cellphone into Hetman's hand like she was saying goodbye forever to her best friend. "My laptop … it's on the kitchen table. Wait … I want to call my boss. I want to call Senator Damonati about all this."

Hetman smiled. "Of course, Ms. Kupule. No problem. In fact, I have her standing by on my phone." Hetman pressed the Mute and Speaker buttons on his phone. "Senator, I have you on speaker. There is someone here who would like to speak with you."

"How dare you put me on hold, Agent Hetman! Your career is over! I don't care—"

"Uh, Senator …" Gretchen leaned over Hetman's phone. "I'm not sure what—"

"Gretchen?" Senator Damonati said. "What are you doing with Agent Hetman? What is going on?"

"Uh, they knocked on my door. They say they are going to take me into custody. They say I aided and abetted you. They told me they want my … my cellphone and my laptop. I'm not sure what I should—"

"You listen to me, Gretchen! Do not—I repeat—do not give anything to the FBI. I want you to throw your cellphone and laptop over the rail! Hell, throw yourself over the rail, too, while you're at it!"

CHAPTER FIFTY-TWO

Eyjafjallajökull, Iceland
11:00 GMT, 12 January

The sky was lightening as the monster truck climbed up and onto the eastern slope of Eyjafjallajökull. In fifteen minutes, the sun would rise and end the hour and ten minutes of morning twilight. The streak of good weather had ended, and light snow was falling.

Everything was coming together, but Kup couldn't get the video from Vágar Airport out of his mind. *They know I'm here.*

Hildur had just announced that they were only five kilometers from the trailhead. She was driving the monster truck, with Trevor sitting up front in the passenger seat. Kup was in the passenger compartment, seated in the first row next to Jerry. The first row of seats faced backward in a club-type seating arrangement. Einar and Es-mar were in the second row.

Einar observed Kup for a few minutes and said, "The news report on the television—it worries you?"

"Yes. I hadn't thought about any law enforcement since Hildur ran the police roadblock yesterday. It seemed like I had finally vanished beyond the reach of the FBI."

Einar nodded. "The American Government can be quite influential. But the news report said that the lögreglan was looking for you, which means they don't know where you are. They also lack the time or resources to devote to finding you. I am sure the reports are just to put on a show for the American Government, to make it look like they are doing something. I have not seen the police in Vík for several days. They are busy with the evacuations ahead of the mobs and with the mobs themselves, of course. I still know some people in the police force. I spoke with some of them about the current crisis. They are overwhelmed."

"Well, I hope so. But you never know."

"Ah, so true. You never know what life will bring. A few weeks ago, I was an old widower living out the rest of his life in a quiet seaside village. Today, I am going to drill a hole in an ice wall so some American can save my country from aliens." Einar chuckled to himself as he gazed out the window at the vast expanse of white.

"Actually, I'm Australian."

Einar looked at Kup. "Oh. I did not know this."

"Yeah, I grew up in Sydney—married an American, though. We live in Hawai'i now—or lived in Hawai'i. She's still there. Stuck behind the Zone."

"Ah, stuck, you say? So, it is the Big Island of Hawai'i?"

"Yes."

Einar nodded. "So, you must save your island as well as mine."

Kup pointed at Jerry. "And he's from Galveston. But his family escaped in a sailboat."

Einar studied Jerry. "Ah, an Aussie Hawaiian and a Texan. Excellent. And we will all save our island homes together."

"I know it's crazy …" Kup pointed to his window. "But this place reminds me so much of Hawai'i Island with the volcanoes and the fields of a'a and pahoehoe lava beside the ocean. The stark beauty of it all. Except it's covered in white instead of green."

Einar nodded. "I have heard this before. I have always wanted to visit Hawai'i. If you are successful today, perhaps I will make plans to travel there before I am too old."

Kup smirked. "Well, if I am successful, you will be welcome in my home. Of course, I will probably be locked up in some federal prison somewhere."

Jerry laughed. "And I'll be your damn cellmate."

Hildur turned her head toward them. "We are getting close to the trailhead now. It is only a few hundred meters ahead."

A large metallic disk covered with several centimeters of snow filled Jerry's window. Einar pointed to it. "It is a crime what they did to the land. Dumping these giant disks on the glacier." Einar frowned at Es-mar.

"I am sorry my people did this," Es-mar said. "It was not my doing."

The monster truck stopped, and Hildur said, "We are here."

Jerry opened the door. The cold, dry air sitting atop the glacier swept into the warm interior.

One by one, they filed out of the monster truck. The snow crunched beneath their feet. Everyone besides Einar strapped a backpack full of supplies and a pair of crampons to their backs.

Einar took the auger and strapped it across his back. He also took a fifteen-liter can of petrol in each hand.

Kup shook his head. *What is up with the old people here? My parents would have already fallen three times just trying to get in and out of the monster truck.* "Einar, let one of us carry the petrol cans."

Einar shrugged.

"I'll take them," Trevor said as he took the petrol cans from Einar.

Hildur walked to the start of the trailhead. "I will lead the way. Once we get to the disk, we will hike around it in a clockwise direction. Es-mar will follow behind me in my tracks. I do not care about the order after her, but everyone must follow the established footprints when we hike around the disk. Once we get to the trail on the other side of the disk, you may hike freely as long as you walk on the established trail."

Hildur looked each of them in the face. "Okay, so let us go now."

"Go ahead without me," Trevor said. "I need to take a leak. I'll catch up. I know the way."

Hildur nodded. "We will wait for you at the disk when you have finished leaking, Trevor." She began walking along the trail toward the gray disk three hundred meters ahead of them. Everyone but Trevor filed in behind her.

When Es-mar reached the disk, she stopped and stared at the narrow trail that led along the circumference of the disk. "I do not know if I can go forward. The water is beneath the snow."

"Do not worry," Hildur said. "We will follow the tracks where we came the other day. As long as we stay in those tracks, we will be okay. There will be no water today."

Es-mar sighed. "I do not know this to be true, but you know that it is. I will go."

Hildur took a careful step to the left and placed her foot down on an established footprint.

Es-mar traced Hildur's footprints step by step. Trevor, who had only minutes before caught up with the group, followed in Es-mar's footprints. Kup, Einar, and Jerry followed Trevor.

About halfway around the disk, Einar broke the group's silence. "So, tell me this, Kup—if you are successful today in disarming the EMP, what happens next?"

Kup tried to hide his heavy breathing. "What—what do you mean?"

"I mean, once you disable the EMP and the runways and piers are rebuilt, we can come and go from the island as before. We can import and export food and supplies as before, but with the aliens here, can we return to how our lives were?"

"Well, that's a good question. Society built these disks and the ships that transported them here for a one-way journey. The alien convicts are here to stay."

"So, the alien convicts are here to stay, but currently, they are trapped on the three islands. Perhaps the rest of the world does not want the EMP shroud to go away. They might not like it that these aliens can leave the three islands and disperse throughout the world. I read that some have already snuck onto the mainland of Texas aboard people's sailboats."

Kup stopped in his tracks and turned to Einar. "I guess I had never considered that some people would want the aliens contained, even if it meant imprisoning innocent humans."

Einar nodded. "I mean, without their funny tight red suits, they look a lot like us, especially us Icelanders. It will be like trying to contain a nasty virus once you eliminate the barrier of the EMP shroud. There will be nothing to stop them from spreading out all over the world."

Kup began hiking again. *Is he right? Am I doing the right thing here?* The stories from his grandparents flooded his thoughts with long-dormant memories. *If I don't act … if the penal colonies are success-ful … No, not again. Never again.* Kup stopped walking and faced Einar. "I have no choice. We must live free. *All* of us, together equally." Kup pointed at Es-mar. "Including her."

Einar nodded. "Very well then. I will stand with you for Iceland. For Earth. For our freedom, our liberation, our *frelsun*."

Hildur stopped and looked behind her to check on everyone.

Trevor glanced at his watch and scanned the clouds while they wait-ed. Kup caught up to Trevor, and the group hiked on as a whole.

Hildur called back, "We are almost back to the trail! Only about thirty more meters."

The snow stopped, and blue sky peeked through several breaks in the clouds. Hildur announced they had reached the trail once again, and one by one, they stepped onto the hard-packed snow.

Hildur pointed to a peak in the distance as she pulled her phone out of her pocket. "That is Eyjafjöll. Let us hope it continues to sleep while we are here." She grimaced as she read a text.

Einar stopped alongside her. *"Er allt í lagi,* Hildur?"

She shook her head and whispered something in his ear.

"What is it?" Jerry asked. "What are you two talking about?"

Hildur looked at Jerry. "Kolbrún says that the lögreglan came to my house and knocked on the door. Then they came to her house and asked if she knew where I was. They said they had received an anonymous phone call that I was harboring the two American fugitives. I received this text fifty-one minutes ago. I never heard the ding, and we are now out of cellphone range."

CHAPTER FIFTY-THREE

"**W**e have arrived at the entrance to the ice cave," Hildur said as she untied her crampons from the back of her backpack.

Kup was only a few meters from the mouth of the cave when he swiveled his head toward the southeast and scanned the cloudy sky one last time. Trevor glanced at his watch and shook his head.

Einar looked at the mouth of the cave in front of him. "Well, let us get inside now."

One by one, they attached crampons to their shoes and filed inside the cave behind Hildur. The crampons clinked as their spikes bit into the ice.

Jerry rubbed his gloved right hand along the cobalt-blue ice that formed the walls of the cave. "This is beautiful. How are these ice caves formed?"

Hildur talked as she walked. "Well, technically, we should call this cave a glacier cave. Water that has melted on the surface in the summer seeps into the glacier and forms rivers underneath it. These rivers of water carve out the cave. It is typically too dangerous to come in here in summer. In wintertime, the ice does not melt so much, and it is safe to walk through the cave."

"And why is the ice so blue?" Jerry asked.

Hildur stopped and pointed to a translucent blue chunk of ice that jutted out from the side wall. "Over thousands and thousands of years, the weight of the glacier compresses the ice and forces the air out. This lack of air within the ice causes the ice to refract various shades of blue. Also, algae trapped within the ice can sometimes give it a greenish color."

Hildur continued walking and rounded a turn in the cave to the left. "And here, we have reached the ice wall. Notice that it is white. It is new ice."

Kup walked up and placed his right glove across the white wall of ice in front of them. He guessed the height of the cave at this point was about three meters.

The Warden had been on the other side of the wall; thus, so had Kup's mind. He faced Hildur. "The EMP emitter is about a hundred meters past this wall."

Hildur nodded.

Trevor stood back from the group and stared back at the mouth of the cave.

Einar rubbed his glove over the ice wall. "You are sure this is a meter thick, Kup?"

"Yes."

"Well, it is a good thing we have the extra petrol. You never know how hard the ice is until you start drilling." He lowered the auger down to the floor. "So where should I make the first hole?"

Kup pointed to a spot on the ice wall about a meter above the floor and to the left of the center of the wall. "Start here. I think the wall is a little less thick around this area."

Einar nodded. "Okay, here we go." He pulled the starter rope on the auger, which roared to life. Shards of ice began shooting away as the auger bit bore into the ice.

Einar paused the auger. "The ice is not very dense and has a lot of air pockets in it. We are lucky. The auger is cutting through quite well."

The auger took about five minutes to break through the ice. Einar pulled the bit out and shut down the auger. "Well, let's have a look at what's on the other side."

Kup was already on his hands and knees and began peering through the hole, which was about thirty centimeters wide.

Hildur squatted behind Kup. "Do you see it?"

Kup moved his head around to observe from several angles. "No, it's a little too dark in there, and it's a little too far away."

He looked up at Einar. "Let me give the auger a try. Why don't you take a break?"

Einar handed the auger to Kup. "Be my guest."

Kup took the auger from Einar. It was heavier than he expected. *This guy is a workhorse. He seems to thrive with all this.*

Kup started the auger and placed the bit to the left and up from the first hole. The two holes would touch each other when he finished drilling. Kup switched the bit on, and after about seven minutes of drilling, the auger broke through the other end of the ice wall. Kup pulled the auger out, turned it off, and set it on the ice floor. His arms ached.

This time, Einar was on his hands and knees. "You have done a good job for your first time with the auger. The hole is straight, and there is a nice overlap between the two holes. Who would like to try next?"

Hildur reached down and grabbed the auger. "I would like to try it." Six minutes later, she had cut a third hole in the ice.

Trevor grabbed the auger next and aimed it at a spot beside Hildur's hole. It bit into the ice but continually slowed down.

Trevor stopped the auger. "This part of the ice must be really hard."

"Push harder," Hildur said. "You've got to put your weight into it."

"Perhaps you should just watch, Trevor," Einar said.

"I would like to try the auger," Es-mar said as she grabbed the auger from Trevor. She cut the fourth hole in two minutes and forty-seven seconds.

Jerry cut the fifth hole in just over eight minutes. Two hours later, they had drilled twelve holes in a circle. Everyone except Trevor took turns with the auger. The cutout in the ice was hanging by a ten-centimeter-wide piece of ice at the top. The last hole in this piece would cause the cutout to come crashing down. At least, that was the plan. Of course, after that, they would have to push the chunk of ice through to the other side. They hoped it would slide across the ice without too much effort.

Einar reached for the auger. "We should have enough petrol in the auger to cut the last hole, but I will add some from one of the cans just to be safe." Einar grabbed the funnel and unscrewed the lid of one of the petrol cans. "There is water in the petrol!"

"How could there be water in the petrol, *pabi?*" Hildur asked.

"I do not know. I checked these just this morning." Einar unscrewed the lid of the other can of petrol. "This can is the same. It has water in it also." He grimaced as he shook his head. "We will have to conserve what petrol we have in the auger already."

Einar positioned the auger against the ice wall.

Es-mar grabbed Einar's arm. "Stop."

Einar glared at her.

"Do you hear the noise?" Es-mar cupped her hands over her ears.

The other five cocked their ears. A faint *tocotocotoco* echoed inside the cave.

Trevor started running toward the mouth of the cave. "I'll go have a look."

Hildur nodded. "Yes, I hear it. We must hurry."

Kup strained his ears to listen. "A helicopter? That's a bloody helicopter!"

Hildur yelled, "Trevor, do not let anyone see you!"

Einar grabbed the auger and started it. "I will drill as fast as I can, but it will use up the petrol faster." He hoisted the auger up to the last bit of ice and began drilling.

After a couple of minutes, Trevor came walking back, panting. "A helicopter landed on the trail outside the cave entrance. It says 'Landhelsomething' on the side."

"Landhelgisgæslan?" Hildur asked.

"Yes, that's it."

"It is the Coast Guard," said Hildur. She turned back toward Einar. *"Flýttu þér, faðir!* Hurry up!"

"Yes. I will hurry." Einar bore down on the auger.

Kup walked around the bend in the cave and peered toward the cave entrance.

There was a thud, and the ice beneath Kup's feet cracked. He ran back to the ice wall. The chunk of ice had fallen and was now blocking the hole. They had to push it through.

Einar set the auger down on the ice as everyone else began pushing on the ice chunk. Even with crampons, they were having trouble getting traction.

Kup signaled for everyone to be quiet, or at least as quiet as possible, while heaving against the chunk of ice.

There were muffled voices in the cave.

Seconds later, a male voice said, "Hildur Einarsdóttir, *ertu hérna? Þetta er lögreglan."*

Hildur mouthed, "The police."

Kup looked down. The chunk of ice had moved about five centimeters.

"Kuparr Winston," the same male voice said. "Are you here? This is the police."

Kup looked down again at the hole in the ice wall. The gap had widened to eight centimeters. He whispered, "Push."

"Jerry Morgenstern. Are you here?"

The ice chunk slid twenty centimeters.

Kup whispered, "One last push."

The ice chunk slid another five centimeters, and the opposite end crashed onto the ice floor on the other side.

The rapid clinking of crampons slamming into ice echoed through the cave.

Kup felt through the hole with his right hand. The chunk of ice was sitting at an angle, blocking the hole. There was a gap, but it was only fifteen centimeters wide.

"Stansa!" yelled the same male voice. "Stop!"

Kup turned his head toward the voice. Two men wearing steel-gray uniforms, black berets, and black combat boots stood six meters away, staring at them. The yellow six-pointed star of the lögreglan adorned their berets. Over their gray uniforms, they wore black Kevlar vests that held extra ammunition, radios, and knives. Each man had an MP5A3 submachine gun slung across his chest, and each rested his right hand beside the trigger. Their left hands held the barrels, which both pointed at the ground. Holstered Glock pistols hung from their right hips.

Everyone froze.

"Víkingasveitin?" Hildur asked.

CHAPTER FIFTY-FOUR

Eyjafjallajökull, Iceland
15:30 GMT, 12 January

"Yes, we are the Viking Squad," said the shorter man on the right. He was clean-shaven with short black hair and wore his beret low across his forehead. He turned to Hildur. *"Hvað ertu að gera hér?* What are you doing here?" His brown eyes studied the hole in the ice wall.

They all looked at each other, but no one said anything.

The man on the left had close-cropped blond hair and was much taller. His face and eyes had a hint of an Asian ancestor somewhere in his family tree. He noticed Es-mar, who was chewing a granola bar. He pointed his submachine gun at her chest. "What is this convict doing here?"

"No!" Hildur said. "Put your gun down. She is harmless, and she is ... my friend."

"You are Hildur Einarsdóttir?" the man asked.

"Yes, of course," Hildur said. "Put the gun down."

The man lowered the MP5A3 to his chest. "Very well." He looked at Kup. "I am Inspector Halldór Grímsson. You are Kuparr Winston?"

Kup eased himself out of the hole in the ice. "Yes. That's me."

"And you are Jerry Morgenstern?"

Jerry nodded.

The man looked at Trevor. "And you are Trevor Ringlund, correct?"

Trevor nodded.

"We are members of the Echo Squad of the Special Unit of the National Police Commissioner," Halldór said. "My colleague here is Inspector Sandur Helgason. The two of you"—he pointed at Jerry and

Kup—"have entered Iceland illegally. And you, Mr. Winston, are also responsible for the crash of an airliner and the rape of your coworker." Halldór patted the barrel of his machine gun with his left hand. "We are under orders to take the two of you into custody. Before we do this, however, we must frisk all of you for any weapons."

"What?" said Sandur. "Why are—"

"You will frisk the convict, the old man, and Hildur. I will frisk the other three. That is an order, Sandur."

Sandur shook his head as he began frisking Es-mar.

When Sandur frisked Hildur, she said, "Aliens invaded our country. It is in total chaos, and you are spending your time chasing these two Americans?"

"I am only following orders, his orders," Sandur said. "Please cooperate."

Halldór demanded Trevor empty his pockets and took additional time screening him. When he had finished, he focused his piercing blue eyes on Hildur. "Yes. We are under orders. We will, all of us, comply with those orders." He turned back to Kup and Jerry. "The helicopter is waiting for us outside the cave entrance. You both agree to come with us?"

Kup stared at the hole and nodded.

Sandur squatted down and peered through the hole. With his machine gun resting on his knees, he reached up with his left hand and adjusted his beret. "Before we go, you will tell us what you are doing in this ice cave. Why have you drilled this hole in this wall of ice here?"

No one answered.

Halldór glanced down at the hole in the ice wall. "We do not have time for this. We must go now."

"To save Iceland," Kup said with a shrug. "To save your bloody country. To save this whole damn planet from being colonized. That's what we're trying to do."

Sandur stood up and planted both feet wide apart. "What do you mean by this?"

Kup looked at Sandur. "On the other side of this ice wall, about a hundred meters farther into the cave, is the emitter that—"

"Enough, Mr. Winston," Halldór said.

"Behind this wall of ice"—Kup glared at Halldór—"is the emitter that controls the EMP shroud surrounding Iceland. If I can get to it, I can destroy it. I can also destroy the EMP shrouds around Galveston and Hawai'i Island."

"How do you know this?" Sandur asked.

Kup took a deep breath. Then he retold the story about the rescue of the Warden and the Reckoning as Halldór handcuffed him.

Sandur studied Kup's face. "I read your wife's email. She told of the alien invasion before it happened."

Kup nodded. "Yes, she tried to warn people, but I think it just got me arrested."

"How long will this process take, the dismantling of the EMP?" Sandur asked.

Halldór handcuffed Jerry.

"Not long. Not long at all." Kup reached down, grabbed the auger with his handcuffed hands, and started jamming the end of the auger into the gap between the edge of the hole and the chunk of ice they had pushed through. "We're so close. Let me finish this, please."

Halldór stepped forward. "You will stop this, Mr. Winston. Stop what you're doing!"

Kup strained as he tried to pry the ice chunk off the ledge of the hole. "We're too damn close!" Vapor shot from his mouth.

Halldór switched the MP5A3's trigger group from SAFE to SINGLE ROUND, producing a noticeable click. He pointed the submachine gun at Kup's back. "Stop what you are doing, Mr. Winston. Stop it right now."

Kup looked back at the barrel of the gun but held on to the auger.

Hildur walked up to Halldór. "*You* stop what *you* are doing! You walk around with a machine gun, which you have pointed twice now at my friends. This is not my country. This is not normal."

Halldór scowled. "Nothing about our country is normal now, but we will adapt."

"Adapt?" Hildur grabbed the end of Halldór's gun with her left hand and pointed it at her chest. She hissed, *"Skjóttu mig!"* She pointed at Kup with her right hand. *"En slepptu honum!"*

Halldór glanced at Kup. The MP5A3 remained pointed at Hildur's chest, but Halldór pulled his finger from the trigger. "I will not shoot you, Hildur Einarsdóttir, and I cannot let Kuparr Winston go. I have my orders."

Kup dropped the auger on the ice. "No. Stop it. Put the gun away." He walked over to Halldór.

Halldór pulled the gun back from Hildur's chest and flipped the trigger group back to *SAFE*. "Walk ahead now, Mr. Winston. We will follow." He placed the MP5A3 back across his chest.

Sandur put his hand out in front of Kup's chest. "Wait. You did not answer my question. How long would it take for you to dismantle the EMP?"

Kup shrugged. "I don't know for sure, but I would guess about twenty or thirty minutes. That would be once I get to the emitter, which isn't happening." Kup shook his head as he walked toward the cave entrance.

Sandur turned to Halldór and whispered, *"Láttu hann klára."*

Halldór replied, *"Nei."*

Hildur walked up to Halldór. "Yes. Let him finish!"

Halldór shook his head at Hildur.

"What have you got to lose if you let him try?" Hildur said. "If you deny him the chance, you will condemn all of us—all of Iceland. You will condemn the whole world."

Kup had rounded the bend and was now out of sight of the group.

Halldór turned to Hildur and Sandur. "We have our orders. We will follow them." He faced Jerry. "Mr. Morgenstern, please come with us to the helicopter."

Jerry turned to Hildur. "Well, we tried."

He turned back to Halldór. "What's the penalty for entering Iceland illegally?"

Halldór shrugged. "I do not know."

"Okay." Jerry nodded. "Are the prisons in Iceland nicer than prisons in the States?"

Halldór turned and started walking behind Jerry. "I do not know. I have never been inside a prison in America."

Jerry and Kup walked out of the mouth of the cave as the bottom of the sun touched the horizon. Halldór and Sandur were right behind them. Sandur walked two meters to the right of Halldór.

Ahead of them, sitting in the middle of the trail, was a white Airbus H225 helicopter with the blue and red stripes of the Icelandic flag. It was about forty meters away. Its rotors began spinning. Through the windshield, the pilot waved his left arm for them to hurry. The instrument console hid his right arm.

Sandur yelled, *"Af hverju er hann að flýta sér svona?"*

The pilot was once again waving his left arm for them to hurry. Sandur's and Halldór's radios crackled with his voice. *"Skildu þá eftir. Við verðum að fara núna. Það hefur orðið annað þyrluslys!"*

Sandur and Halldór looked at each other.

The pilot started waving both arms for them to hurry and said over the radio, *"Við höfum fengið nýjar pantanir!"*

Kup and Jerry both stopped and faced Sandur and Halldór.

"What's going on?" Jerry asked.

"There has been another helicopter crash," Sandur said. "They keep getting too close to the Zone. The pilot says we have been ordered to leave you two here."

"That's great!" Kup said. "Unlock our handcuffs."

Halldór glanced at his watch and then up at the sky. He pulled the Glock from its holster and pointed it at Kup's chest. "Get down on your knees, Mr. Winston. You as well, Mr. Morgenstern."

Jerry and Kup both dropped onto their knees.

"Halldór, *hvað ertu að gera?"* Sandur asked as he turned and faced Halldór.

Jerry jumped as the sound of a single gunshot echoed across the glacier.

Sandur fell backward and landed in the snow with a soft thud after the bullet from Halldór's Glock slammed into his Kevlar vest.

In an instant, Halldór's Glock was once again pointed at Kup's chest.

"This was not supposed to happen this way, but unfortunately, I am given no choice," said Halldór. "Goodbye, Mr. Winston. You should have just let them Cancel you."

Jerry jumped once again as a bullet flew past him, and the sound of another gunshot blasted across the glacier.

Halldór's Glock flew through the air and disappeared into the snow a split second before he himself landed on the snow.

Halldór rolled over onto his stomach and pointed his MP5A3 at the pilot, who was standing in front of the nose of the helicopter.

A bullet from the pilot's gun grazed Halldór's right ear.

The pilot's head exploded onto the shattered windshield of the helicopter as a three-second burst of bullets flew from Halldór's machine gun.

The helicopter's rotors made a whooshing sound as they decelerated.

Halldór stood up. Blood dripped from his right hand onto the snow as he aimed the MP5A3 at Kup. His right hand had a slight quiver as he began to squeeze the trigger.

"Halldór! *Nei!*" Sandur yelled as he fired multiple rounds into Halldór's Kevlar vest. The MP5A3 fired ten rounds at the sky before it landed in the snow a few centimeters from Halldór's left shoulder.

"Ertu orðinn brjálaður?!" Sandur stood and pointed the Glock directly at Halldór's forehead. *"Hvert ertu?!"*

"What the hell is going on?!" Jerry yelled. "What did you just say?"

"I asked him if he had gone crazy." Sandur's eyes remained fixed on Halldór. "I asked him who he was."

Halldór's breathing became labored. "No, Sandur, I am not crazy. I am simply following orders." A red-colored hole formed in the snow beneath his right hand.

Black smoke billowed from the helicopter.

"It does not matter, Mr. Winston," Halldór said as he leaned up and reached for the MP5A3 with his bloodied right hand. "They will be here—"

"Stansa!" Sandur screamed. *"Stansa!"*

Halldór lifted the MP5A3 off the snow.

"Nei, Halldór!" Sandur screamed as he fired three bullets into Halldór's right hand.

The MP5A3 fell back onto the snow. Sandur kept his Glock aimed at Halldór's forehead as he walked toward him.

Halldór once again raised his head. Blood gushed from the fragments extending from his right wrist. He looked over at Kup. *"Samfélagið verður ... Samfélagið verður að sækja fram."* He reached for the MP5A3 with his left hand.

Sandur fired a single bullet into Halldór's forehead.

CHAPTER FIFTY-FIVE

Honolulu, Hawai'i
06:00 HST, 12 January

The line of cars backed up for half a mile on the H1 freeway toward Honolulu International Airport. Senator Damonati sat in the back right seat of the black stretch limousine, which would occasionally speed up to ten miles per hour, but something closer to zero was more typical.

She held her iPhone in her right hand, studying an airline app. *What are all these people doing on the freeway at six in the morning, and how am I supposed to know how to work this stupid app?* "James, or John, or whatever the hell your name is, can you not go any faster? If I miss this flight, the next flight I can take is sold out in first class. That means I will have to fly economy. I don't fly economy. You need to fix this!" She gritted her teeth as a white Ford F-150 sped by her window. *I can't believe they couldn't find an available transport. I have to fly on an airplane—an airliner! And where in the hell is Noa?*

"Senator, I'm doing the best I can. There must be a wreck up ahead. By the way, my name is Joseph, ma'am."

Senator Damonati watched a gray Toyota SUV pass by through her window. "James, why are you letting people pass us? Get in front of them."

"Uh, yes, Senator. I'll try," Joseph said.

The limousine lurched into the lane on their right. A blue BMW sedan stopped beside them to avoid a collision.

"That's more like it, James. Shit, if I have to fly economy with all those … *people*."

A police siren started wailing from somewhere behind them.

Senator Damonati arched her head to look behind the limousine before she texted Noa for the eighth time that morning.

The police sirens grew louder. Two Honolulu Police Department vehicles snaked their way through the traffic.

"Step on it, James!" Senator Damonati said as she dialed Noa's number. "Drive over in the damn median if you have to!"

The two police cars straddled the limousine on the left and right. A black Suburban with US Government plates pulled in behind the limousine.

From behind them, a voice from a loudspeaker said, "This is the FBI. Pull over into the right shoulder as quickly and safely as possible."

"James, you will do no such thing," said Senator Damonati. "We need to get going, not stop!"

"Senator, it's the FBI. I gotta pull over."

"You will not stop!" Senator Damonati strained her head forward. "You will not pull over to the shoulder!"

A second black Suburban pulled in front of the limousine. Its rear window opened, revealing a machine gun attached to a serious-looking man.

The voice from the loudspeaker said, "You are surrounded. If you do not pull over into the right shoulder immediately, we will force you to do so."

The limousine driver inched his way to the right, across two lanes of traffic, and into the right shoulder of the freeway. The police car on the right gave way as the limousine entered the shoulder.

"If this is Hetman's doing …" Senator Damonati glared back through the rear window of the limousine as they came to a stop.

Agent Hetman got out of the back seat of the black Suburban behind them.

Hetman stopped beside Senator Damonati's window.

After several long seconds, she opened the window. "Agent Hetman, I hope you know what you're doing. I am going to miss my flight because of this circus. I do not like missing flights."

"Senator, I need you to please step out of the vehicle. We are taking you into federal custody."

Senator Damonati leaned her head out of the open window. "Do you have any idea who and what you are messing with? You obviously are doing this on your own without proper authorization."

"Senator, I'm following the special protocols—the special protocols you pushed through Congress. I don't need authorization." Hetman pulled the gun from the holster hanging on his left side. "Don't make this any more difficult than it already is. I'm asking you to cooperate and comply with my request."

"Do you think I'm afraid of your guns? You think I am just a United States senator. Well, I am much more than that." Senator Damonati slammed the limousine's door into Hetman's crotch. She stood and glared up into his eyes. "You may question me. You may arrest me. You may detain me, Agent Hetman, but it won't make any difference in the end."

Agents wearing Kevlar vests and holding semiautomatic machine guns stationed themselves at the front and sides of the limousine. Agent Perez stood beside the open door of the Suburban.

"Senator, please turn around," Agent Hetman said. "I need to handcuff you."

Senator Damonati turned her back to Agent Hetman. "This is pointless, Agent Hetman. Pointless."

"Senator, where is your assistant, Noa Kim?"

"It's a workday, Agent Hetman," said Senator Damonati. "Where do you think he is?"

Hetman handcuffed her. "Well, he's not at your office, and he's not at home." He led the senator to the open Suburban door. "We have evidence that Noa Kim manipulated official FBI data within official FBI servers at your direction. You have been determined to be a domestic terrorist; as such, your civil rights will be suspended for—"

"As if I give a damn about my civil rights." Senator Damonati stopped beside the door and smiled at Agent Hetman. "They will come for me, and when they do, they will come for you as well."

CHAPTER FIFTY-SIX

Eyjafjallajökull, Iceland
16:25 GMT, 12 January

Sandur reported the deaths of the pilot and Halldór over his radio. After a pause lasting several seconds, the agitated voice on the other receiver replied that it would be a while until the Coast Guard could spare another helicopter. There were no additional questions about the circumstances that had led to the deaths. In the new normal, there was no normal.

Sandur unlocked Jerry's and Kup's handcuffs and motioned for them to go back inside the cave. "You two continue what you were doing," he said.

Bewildered but relieved, Jerry and Kup walked back inside the cave. Kup paused about five meters in and looked back at Sandur, who was standing over Halldór's body. Northern lights, relatively dim in the evening twilight and framed by the cave's entrance, danced pale green above Sandur's head.

Jerry paused but continued walking.

"Inspector Helgason!" Kup yelled. "Help me save your country. Help me save our planet."

Sandur took a deep breath and nodded. He looked up at the sky and began walking toward the entrance of the cave. A shaft of dim purple curved across the sky.

As Sandur entered the mouth of the ice cave, Kup illuminated a ridge of sea-blue ice with his flashlight. "Inspector Helgason, did—"

"Please, at this time, I am not sure that I can be an inspector or what I should inspect. Just call me Sandur."

"Okay, sure. And call me Kup."

Sandur nodded.

"Inspector Grimsson said something in Icelandic just before he died," Kup said. "What did he say?"

"It was something about advancing society," Sandur said with a shrug.

Kup began walking again. "Did you know Inspector Grimsson well?"

"Halldór was like an older brother to me. I took an oath to protect the people of Iceland. Halldór took the same oath. Nothing makes sense anymore."

"His blood was red, wasn't it?" Kup asked. "I saw it. It was red."

"Yes, of course. Why would you—"

"What the hell?" Jerry said as he rounded the bend in the cave several meters ahead. "Kup, get over here!"

Kup and Sandur's crampons created a clipped cacophony as they bit into the ice in rapid succession. Seconds later, they rounded the bend in the cave. Einar, Hildur, and Es-mar lay on the floor, illuminated by Jerry's flashlight. Blood had pooled and frozen to the left of Einar. The auger lay beside his feet. Fragments of material from his coat were scattered about the ice.

Sandur placed his right index and middle fingers beneath Einar's left chin. "There is no pulse." He nodded toward Hildur and Es-mar. "The other two are breathing." He placed his right index finger across his lips and whispered, "Where is the other man that was with you?"

Kup dropped to his knees and peered through the opening in the wall of ice. He looked up at Sandur and shrugged.

Sandur grabbed the Glock-17 pistol from the holster on his right hip and handed it to Kup. He gave Jerry a large knife.

Jerry looked at the knife. "Why do I get the knife?"

Sandur whispered, "Sorry, Kup is more valuable. Flashlights off." He slid through the hole in the ice wall. Once on the other side, he motioned for them to follow.

Jerry shook his head, switched off his flashlight, and crawled through the hole. Kup followed him.

Sandur flipped the MP5A3 trigger mode from SAFE to RAPID FIRE and motioned for them to follow. He eased each crampon into the ice floor as he walked.

The floor was strewn with brown pebbles that amplified the sound of their steps. Adrenaline seemed to amplify the sound of their breathing—even the blood pulsating through their veins.

After about twenty steps, Sandur turned to Kup and whispered, "How much farther?"

Kup glanced backward at the blackness behind them and shrugged.

Sandur nodded and began walking again. Jerry followed behind Sandur. Kup followed Jerry.

They rounded a bend and saw a dull glow ahead.

After rounding another twist in the ice cave, they could see the EMP emitter thirty meters ahead. A low-pitched hum drowned out the clinking sounds of their footsteps.

The emitter was a light-gray horizontal cylinder flattened from the top into an oval shape four meters wide and two meters tall. The surface appeared to be eggshell-smooth and emitted a dim, white light that filled the cave with a simulated twilight. It rested on two aluminum posts that extended deep into the ice floor. There were no visible control panels.

Sandur stopped. He turned his head back toward Jerry and swallowed hard. His eyes were wide open.

Kup mouthed, "Do not touch it."

Sandur and Jerry nodded.

Sandur continued his slow, deliberate walk toward the EMP emitter. When he was five meters from the end of the emitter, he signaled to Kup to go on the left side. He would walk along the right side. He signaled for Jerry to stay where he was.

Jerry rolled his eyes.

Kup walked along the left side of the emitter, searching for the palm reader that would activate the control panel. He scanned the ridges and crevices of the cave. Halfway down the length of the emitter, which turned out to be about fifteen meters, Kup found what he was looking for. It was a pale-orange oval about thirty centimeters tall and fifteen centimeters wide. He continued walking to the end of the emitter.

Sandur crouched down, looking underneath the emitter back toward Jerry. He stood up and shrugged.

Kup whispered, "I found the controls. I'm going to start the process."

Sandur nodded and signaled with his fingers that he would walk back along the right side toward Jerry.

Kup nodded and walked along the left side to the palm reader. He placed the Glock he had been carrying on the ice beside his left foot, stood up, and placed his right hand onto the orange oval. A three-dimensional hologram appeared behind him. It depicted the Earth, which was thirty centimeters in diameter, with three spacecraft—one positioned above Iceland, one above Galveston, and one above Hawai'i Island. The EMP cones pointed down from the three spacecraft, and the EMP bubbles hovered over each island.

Fifteen centimeters below the image of Antarctica was a three-centimeter-tall, one-and-a-half-centimeter-wide orange ovoid. Kup grabbed the ovoid and flung it into the air beside the hologram of the Earth. A thirty-by-fifteen-centimeter rectangular hologram centered itself at Kup's eye level. It was comprised of multicolored lights and symbols that resembled Thai script.

Kup smiled and took a deep breath. With his left index finger on the orange light at the top left of the hologram, he swiped the entire hologram down with his right hand. The hologram flashed orange thirty times. As it returned to the previous display, the hologram depicting the Earth began pulsating.

Kup nodded. He reached over to the portrayal of the EMP bubble that sat over Hawai'i Island. With his thumb and index finger, he began raising the EMP bubble to the Command Ship depicted over Hawai'i Island.

"Sandur!" Jerry yelled.

Kup froze as the silence of the cave returned.

A single click came from the direction of Jerry's voice.

"Uh, Kup," Jerry said. "Trevor's here."

Kup squatted down and looked under the emitter. Sandur was lying on the ground on the other side of the emitter, about ten meters away. Jerry's khaki cargo pants and hiking boots were visible at the end of the EMP. To the right of Jerry's pants were Trevor's faded blue jeans and camouflage hiking boots.

Trevor rounded the corner of the EMP and glared at him. "I'd move away from the control panel—and don't even think about reaching for that pistol."

Trevor held the MP5A3 in his right hand and had it pointed toward Jerry. He shoved a tranqtube into his front left pants pocket. "Yeah, thanks to Sandur, I traded up. Now you, stand up."

Kup studied Trevor's olive-colored skin, light-blond hair, and two-meter height as he stood.

"Walk toward me," Trevor said. "Your friend Jerry is in a very precarious situation right now."

"Trevor, are you … are you one of them?"

Trevor laughed. "You mean, am I an alien? Hell no. I'm half Norwegian, half Cherokee. At least that's what they told me. I was taken from my parents when I was a baby and sent to a place we called the Orphanage."

"Orphanage? Who took you?"

"The same people who took poor Inspector Grimsson when he was fresh out of the womb." Trevor looked over at the EMP emitter. "The same people that built this fine piece of machinery. The same people who are on their way here as we speak."

"How could I not know about this … Orphanage?"

"The Warden wouldn't have known. It's a secret program, but there are thousands of us Stolings. Society must advance, Kup. We will all do our part for the greater good. They sent me to observe Hildur because she operated tours of this ice cave. Just observe—no contact with Society, a sleeper. Those were my orders. I was told they would contact me if they needed me. Don't call us; we'll call you. Well, when I heard your plans for the EMP emitter, I couldn't take it anymore, so I called the lögreglan. They took forever to get here. I thought they had blown me off, but then, to my surprise, Inspector Grimsson showed up and slipped a tranqtube in my pocket. He told me to make sure the three on the front side of the ice wall stayed on that side of the ice wall. Einar became increasingly difficult to deal with. He single-handedly pushed the chunk of ice over onto its side. I tried to get the tranqtube on him, but he started swinging that stupid auger in my face. You gotta do what you gotta do sometimes. Anyway, then all hell broke loose outside of the cave, and Sandur took out Inspector Grimsson. Not sure what all that was about."

Kup squinted. "Wait, you saw—"

"Yep. From the entrance of the cave. Not what I was expecting. At that point, I decided I had to get my game face on."

Kup reached up with his right hand toward the holographic image of the EMP bubble over Hawai'i Island.

Ten rounds from the submachine gun slammed into the ice ten centimeters from Jerry's feet and reverberated across the cave. Kup pulled his hand back.

"Shit!" Jerry screamed.

"Jerry?" Kup said. "Are you—"

"He's okay, Kup. I missed. I won't miss next time. Oh, and don't think I'm bound by Supreme Law. I'm not one of them—I'm one of you. Now, get away from the control panel. Or do the needs of the many outweigh the needs of … Jerry? Come on, Kup, he's just one man. He's a small sacrifice to free the hundreds of thousands trapped on three islands. What's it going to be, Kup? Jerry or Hawai'i Island? Jerry or Galveston? Jerry or Iceland?"

"Kup," Jerry said through gritted teeth. "I'd like to be brave and tell you to proceed, but I didn't ask for any of this shit. I want to see my wife and kids again. Hell, I want to see my damn dog again."

"I'm going to count down from ten, Kup," Trevor said. "If you're not on your knees five feet in front of me with your hands behind your head by the time I say 'one,' Jerry will have at least five bullet holes in him. I know; I know. One is all it takes, but the trigger on this thing is a little touchy. So, here we go. Ten."

Kup looked down at the Glock beside his left foot.

"Nine."

Kup reached for the hologram with his right hand for a split second but pulled his hand back.

"Eight."

Kup took a step toward Trevor.

"Seven."

"Come on, Kup!" Jerry said as he stared at the barrel of Trevor's gun.

Kup was still seven meters away from Trevor.

"Six."

Kup took half a step forward but stopped.

"Fi—"

A gas engine roared to life. Trevor turned his head, jumped, and began shaking seconds before chunks of his stomach spiraled outward and splattered onto the walls, ceiling, and floor. The red tip of the auger blade shot out ten centimeters from his shredded coat before Trevor fell face-forward to the ground. His body shook as the auger continued boring into the ice floor.

Hildur stood behind Trevor. She looked at Kup and Jerry and began to tremble.

Jerry walked over to the auger, turned it off, and lifted the MP5A3 from Trevor's lifeless hands.

"He killed Einar ..." Hildur looked down at Trevor's lifeless body, now anchored to the floor. "He killed my father."

"What happened?" Jerry asked.

"He attacked Einar with the auger. Es-mar and I tried to stop him, but he poked us with a tranqtube. I lost consciousness. When I woke up, my father was dead. Es-mar was breathing but would not wake up."

Kup walked to Trevor's body and kneeled beside him. Fresh, warm red blood flowed onto the ice. The edges of the pooled blood began freezing and solidifying. Kup looked over at Sandur's body. "What happened to him?"

"Trevor jumped on his back from the top of the emitter and poked him in the neck with a metal cylinder," Jerry said. "It all happened so fast."

Kup reached into Trevor's left pant pocket and retrieved the tranqtube. He twisted one end half a turn clockwise. "I'm going to try to revive Sandur." He stood and walked over to where Sandur lay.

Hildur ran her right hand over the right side of her neck. "You are going to jab him with that?"

Kup held the tranqtube in his right hand and squeezed. "Yes. I set it to revive a human ... I think."

Kup kneeled beside Sandur. With his left hand, he felt the right side of Sandur's neck.

Then he felt a vibration.

"Do you hear the hum?" Hildur asked.

"Yes," Jerry said. "And the cave ... the cave is vibrating."

Kup shook his head. With his right hand, he jabbed the tranqtube into the side of Sandur's neck. "We've got to—"

A split-second blinding flash of light appeared in both the ceiling and the floor of the cave twelve meters away from Kup.

Sandur grabbed Kup's right wrist as he studied the tranqtube.

Where the flash of light had been in the ceiling, dim moonlight shined through an oval-shaped hole eight meters long and four meters wide.

Jerry's flashlight illuminated the walls of newly cut ice on the sides of an oval hole in the floor that was also eight by four meters. The hole in the floor was four meters deep. Slush began oozing up from the bottom.

Hildur was on her knees beside the hole in the ice. "Above us! There is a spaceship—a round spaceship!"

"A Peace Ship?!" yelled Kup.

"Yes!" Hildur began sliding backward, away from the hole.

Kup pulled his wrist free from Sandur's grip, shoved the tranqtube in his right pocket, and ran back around the EMP emitter to the palm reader. "Jerry, check on Sandur! I've got to hurry."

Jerry laid the machine gun on the ice as he kneeled beside Sandur.

A second momentary flash occurred. Three aliens dressed in red skinsuits, black boots, black gloves, and gunmetal-gray helmets floated down through the hole in the ceiling and landed in the slush of the oval hole in the floor. Each helmet had a small orange oval on the front. The slush covered their knee-high boots. All three aliens looked down at the slush, then up at Hildur.

Hildur stood and backed away farther from the hole in the floor. "Hurry, Kup! They are here!"

Kup slammed his right palm onto the orange oval spot on the emitter. The holograms had vanished.

Jerry helped Sandur stand and handed him the machine gun.

The alien soldiers walked to the side of the hole. They all looked down at the slushy water, which had risen to their waists. One by one, they each pulled out small metal rods and inserted them into the ice.

The hologram of Earth reappeared behind Kup.

The alien soldier closest to Hildur hoisted himself onto a rod just below the top edge of the hole.

"They're climbing out of the hole!" Hildur yelled. "Hurry!"

Sandur stood beside Hildur and pointed the machine gun at the nearest alien. He squeezed the trigger, and twenty rounds bounced off the alien's skinsuit and helmet.

A second alien was now within a meter of climbing out of the hole as the hologram control panel appeared in front of Kup.

Sandur fired the machine gun for ten seconds at the second alien's helmet and chest. Bullets ricocheted and lodged themselves into the walls and ceiling of the ice cave.

The closest alien planted a rod vertically on the ice floor just outside the hole and hoisted himself up so that his helmet was level with the floor. He looked down at the rising slush, which would soon reach the top of the hole, and grabbed another rod with his left hand.

Sandur jabbed the end of the barrel of the MP5A3 into the ice around the vertical rod. "Nei!" A torrent of bullets ripped into the ice, and the alien fell backward into the slush. His right hand held a metal rod with a chunk of ice attached. He thrashed and screamed in the slush as he sank to the bottom of the hole.

Sandur looked over toward Kup. The hologram of Earth was pulsating. He pointed the machine gun at the ice surrounding the highest metal rod of the second alien and fired another stream of bullets. The second alien thrashed and screamed as he sank to the bottom of the hole.

The third alien had planted two vertical rods and pulled himself up and over the edge of the hole.

Sandur squeezed the trigger again, but no bullets fired. "I am out of ammo already. Where is my Glock?!"

The alien soldier stood up and began walking toward Kup. He shook slush from his arms and legs as he walked.

"Kup still has the Glock!" Jerry yelled as he began running toward Kup.

Kup reached down and slid the Glock across the ice toward Jerry.

Sandur threw the MP5A3 onto the ice as Jerry grabbed the sliding Glock.

The alien soldier pulled out his tranqgun and fired it at Jerry. The *microndart* navigated itself through multiple layers of clothing and embedded itself into Jerry's chest.

Jerry fell to the ice, paralyzed from the neck down.

Sandur grabbed the Glock from beside Jerry and fired multiple rounds at the alien.

A stray bullet bounced off the alien's chest and grazed Jerry's left thigh as the alien turned and aimed the tranqgun at Sandur.

Sandur fired the Glock for the last time. He needed to reload.

The alien fired the tranqgun. The microndart knocked Sandur to the ice floor as it embedded itself into the Kevlar of his vest.

Sandur shoved the Glock into the holster on his right hip.

The alien soldier stopped to inspect his tranqgun.

Sandur stood up and tucked his head down into his chest. He yelled,

"Frelsun!" as he ran toward the alien soldier.

The alien soldier looked up from his tranqgun as Sandur slammed into his stomach. The two rolled into a ball and slid across the ice into the slush-filled oval hole.

"What's happening?!" Jerry yelled. "Can somebody help me? I can't move."

Hildur ran to the edge of the hole. Sandur and the alien were both on the floor of the hole, immersed in slush. The alien was thrashing around as Sandur pried his helmet off. Sandur punched the alien in the face repeatedly.

Kup yelled, "I got Hawai'i and Galveston! I just have Iceland left to do."

An intense sound wave blasted into the cave from the oval hole in the ceiling.

Hildur began screaming.

Small bits of ice fell from the top of the cave.

Jerry yelled, "What the f—"

Kup put both hands over his ears as he dropped to his knees.

The hologram of the Earth continued pulsating.

CHAPTER FIFTY-SEVEN

andur surfaced in the slush-filled hole and yelled, "Kup, did you finish?"

He swam through the slush and hoisted himself onto the ice beside Hildur's unconscious body. Slush fell from his uniform.

Jerry was lying on the ice, face down, several meters away. Blood trickled from his nose and left thigh onto the ice and froze. Kup was lying on his back underneath the two holograms.

Sandur ran to Kup and kneeled beside him. "Kup, did you finish?"

The pulsating hologram of Earth depicted only one Command Ship. It was over Iceland.

"Wake up!" Sandur said as he felt underneath Kup's jaw for a pulse.

The two holograms began pulsating faster.

Sandur felt the side of his own neck, reached into Kup's right pocket, and grabbed the tranqtube.

His eyes darted between the flashing holograms and the tranqtube.

Sandur jabbed the tranqtube into the left side of Kup's neck and tossed it onto the ice.

Kup blinked several times and grabbed Sandur's left arm with his right hand. He let go, pressed his thumb and forefinger together, and spread them wide apart.

"What are you doing?" Sandur asked. "What do I need to do?"

"Spread the bubble." Kup continued pressing his thumb and forefinger together and then moving them apart. "Hurry! It's pulsating rapidly. It is going into shutdown mode."

Sandur moved his head closer to Kup. "What?"

"Spread the bubble."

"What do you mean?" Sandur glanced over toward the opening in the cave's ceiling. "What is that?"

A one-meter-tall black ovoid floated above the slush-filled hole.

Kup turned his head. "Oh bloody hell! It's a *Peace Drone!*" He turned and focused on Sandur's face as he took his right hand and pointed it at the EMP bubble over Iceland. "Use your fingers. You've got to raise the EMP bubble to the Command Ship. Hurry!"

The black ovoid began floating toward them.

Kup pressed his right thumb and forefinger together before easing them apart and stretching them as far apart as he could. "Do it now!"

Sandur reached toward the image of the EMP bubble with his thumb and forefinger and began spreading them apart as Kup instructed. The EMP bubble responded to his fingers and rose toward the depicted Command Ship.

The Peace Drone was twelve meters away when it began spinning.

Sandur continued spreading his fingers until the bubble touched the Command Ship.

The Peace Drone was only five meters away.

"Finish it," Kup said. "Just a little farther!" He looked at the Peace Drone three meters away. "If that thing touches us …"

As Sander spread his fingers another centimeter, the EMP bubble rose above the Command Ship.

The Command Ship, the EMP cone, and the EMP bubble all vanished from the hologram. Five seconds later, the hologram of the Earth vanished. The hologram of the control panel shrank into an orange ovoid a few centimeters tall.

The Peace Drone stopped spinning and dropped to the floor of the cave.

"I think you did it." Kup took a deep breath. "You did it."

"Let us hope so," Sandur said.

Kup opened his eyes wider. "You're wet. You must be cold."

Sandur reached down and grabbed Kup's left forearm. "I am fine. Now get up. We must revive the other two. What knocked all of you unconscious?"

The ceiling above them shuddered and creaked as chunks of ice fell to the cave floor.

Sandur dove under the emitter and pulled Kup along the ice beside him. "What was that? Are they coming back?"

Kup shook his head. "No. It's over. The Peace Ship that was hovering above us—I assume there was a Peace Ship hovering above us—lost its command."

"So … ?"

"So, I reckon the ship dropped onto the glacier above us."

The chunks of ice stopped falling from the ceiling. Sandur and Kup crawled out from underneath the emitter.

Kup grabbed the small orange ovoid and tossed it toward the wall of the cave. A blank rectangular hologram appeared.

"What are you doing?" Sandur asked.

"Just making sure it's dead. The emitter still has power, but without its command, it has no brain. It's brain-dead."

Sandur nodded. "Why did you have me manipulate the hologram? What did that do?"

"The hologram was kind of like a three-dimensional touchpad. You use pinches, swipes, and spreading motions to manipulate and control the EMP signals. When we raised the EMP ground signal up to each Command Ship, the ground EMP knocked out the Command Ship's electronics."

Sandur nodded. "We need to revive those two," he said as he looked at Jerry and Hildur lying on the ice. "I believe you need this." He picked up the tranqtube from the ice floor and handed it to Kup. "I assume I used it correctly since you are standing in front of me."

"Yes, you did," Kup said as he grabbed the tranqtube and walked over to Hildur. "And it's still set to Human Revive." He punched the tranqtube into her neck.

Hildur's eyes fluttered. "Did you do it, Kup? Did you destroy the EMP?"

"I did," Kup said as he kneeled beside Jerry.

Hildur tried to stand but collapsed back onto the ice. *"Fjandinn!* I am so weak."

Sandur pulled her up and held onto her. They walked slowly toward Jerry.

Kup jabbed the tranqtube into the right side of Jerry's neck.

"Help me!" Jerry said. "I can't move. I can't feel my legs!"

Kup studied the tranqtube for several seconds before jabbing it into Jerry's neck a second time.

"Shit!" Jerry yelled. "My leg! What the hell happened to my leg? It hurts like hell!"

Kup helped Jerry to his feet.

"There is a medical kit in the helicopter," Sandur said as he studied Jerry. "Your leg was merely grazed. It is not serious."

"Well, it sure as hell feels serious!" Jerry said as he began limping. Dried blood was caked over his swollen lips and nose.

Sandur turned to Kup. "We should be going now. I will need dry clothing soon."

The four of them began walking toward the ice wall and the cave entrance.

"So, Kup, this Warden that you mentioned, where is he now?" Sandur asked.

"He's probably dead," Kup said. "I saved his life twice, only to kill him in the end."

Sandur shook his head.

Jerry stopped and looked over the oval hole in the ice with the three lifeless bodies. The bodies and the slush that surrounded them would be frozen solid soon.

Sandur grabbed his MP5A3 from the floor and slung it over his right shoulder. He stood in front of Hildur. "You are okay? No major injuries?"

Hildur looked at Trevor's rigid body on the floor and shuddered. "I am okay, but I would like to go home."

Sandur loaded the Glock with a new magazine and motioned for the other three to follow him back toward the wall of ice and the mouth of the cave. "I will make a radio transmission when we are outside of the cave and arrange a helicopter to take us to Reykjavík. There will be many questions."

"Sandur, what will happen to us now?" Jerry asked as he limped beside him. "Will we still be facing extradition and prison charges?"

Sandur shrugged. "I do not know. I would guess it will depend on what kind of world we find when we exit this cave."

"It has to be better than the world we left when we entered," Kup said.

They rounded a bend in the cave. The ice wall was thirty meters ahead. They walked slowly to match Jerry's limp.

Sandur said, "So tell me, you two. Will they not be back? They cannot be too happy with what we have done."

"No, I don't think so," Kup said. "The Warden was told that if all three penal colonies failed for any reason, they would move on to the next planet."

"And you believe him?"

"I am him—at least mentally," Kup said.

"And the convicts?" asked Sandur.

"They're here to stay. They're ours now."

"I see," Sandur said. "So, what now for us? What now for them?"

"What do you mean?" Kup said.

"Now that the EMP shrouds are gone, transportation to the three islands can be restored, and hopefully, things can return to normal. Except—"

"Each island has a hundred thousand aliens on it?" Kup smiled.

Sandur nodded. "What do we do with all of them? How do we assimilate them into our society? Do we keep them on the islands, or do we let them move throughout the world? Do we give them equal rights?"

"Kup and I know their world," Hildur said. "We know their inner being. Outside, they appear to us as aliens, but inside, we are the same. They are us in different packaging, but even the packaging isn't that different."

Jerry laughed. "So we're red M&Ms, and they're green M&Ms, but we're both milk chocolate on the inside?"

Kup nodded. "I guess you could say that. The challenge for us"—Kup slid for a second on the ice—"will be to see the good in the individual aliens and ignore the psychotic madness of the mobs. The convicts were sent here against their will because they offended the greater mob. As a world, we must not prejudge them. We cannot become a worldwide mob."

"Heavy stuff there, Kup," Jerry said. "And I thought you just wanted me to help you save the planet—or save three islands on the planet. By the way, should I send my future medical bills to you for reimbursement? I anticipate some pain and suffering."

Kup rolled his eyes.

One by one, they crawled through the small hole in the ice wall. On the other side, Es-mar was still lying on the ice, unconscious. Kup pulled the tranqtube from his pocket and adjusted the revive setting. He kneeled beside her and pressed it into the left side of her neck.

Hildur kneeled beside Einar's cold body. Sandur kneeled beside her and put his arm around her shoulders. "I am so sorry for what happened to your father, Hildur. It is hard. My mother died two months ago from cancer."

"I am sorry to hear that about your mother." Hildur shook her head. "My father was such a good man. I am such an idiot. I brought Trevor into my house."

Kup helped Es-mar to her feet.

Sandur pulled a green bandana from his pocket and handed it to Hildur. "Please, use this for the tears."

Hildur took the bandana and wiped her eyes.

Sandur asked, "How did you meet this Trevor?"

"He took my ice cave tour. He seemed so nice, so intelligent. He said he was headed to a physics conference in Stockholm. It was all a lie."

"You cannot blame yourself, Hildur. We all make the best choices we can at the moment. *Við erum bara mannleg.*" Sandur cocked his ears as the muffled *tocotocotoco* of helicopter rotors echoed through the cave. "A helicopter has already arrived. We must go now."

Hildur stroked Einar's hair. *"Já. Við erum bara mannleg."* She stood and took a deep breath. "We are only human."

EPILOGUE

Eyjafjallajökull, Iceland
13:55 GMT, 19 September

Sandur Helgason squeezed Hildur Einarsdóttir's hand as they entered the ice cave. Today was a day for celebration. After nine months, Hildur's company had finally received approval from the government to resume tours of the ice cave.

They had driven back to Vík that morning from Reykjavík after the meeting with the permitting agencies the previous day. The previous night, they had a celebration dinner with Es-mar and her new boyfriend. Es-mar had just been appointed professor of political science at the University of Iceland, where she would head the newly formed Department of Alien Integration. Es-mar's new boyfriend was part of a team at the university that had just announced a self-sustaining, energy-positive fusion reactor capable of supplying the entire country's electrical grid. Of course, Iceland, with its abundance of geothermal energy, didn't necessarily need the reactor, but the rest of the world did.

In the ice cave, the area with the emitter was still off-limits to everyone except the technology extraction teams. Hildur's permits, however, would allow her to bring tourists up to the security barrier erected thirty meters away. Two members of the Víkingasveitin would be posted at the barrier at all times. Sandur was now in charge of the special detail. He had moved in with Hildur the month before.

Society's engineers had erected a diversion channel inside the cave to safely divert any summertime water flow away from the emitter and away from the ice cave in general.

With Keflavík Airport scheduled to reopen in a week, Hildur's ice cave tours were sold out many months in advance. While inbound tourism to

Iceland was about to boom, leaving Iceland was still tightly regulated. It required a lot of paperwork—and it required proof you were human. The consensus at the UN was that Iceland's aliens were Iceland's problem.

The UN, however, had a different take on Iceland's UFO. Nations across the world were demanding, but not receiving, access to the crash site located on Eyjafjallajökull. There were four additional crash sites on the glacier from escape pods that had fallen through a rising EMP and plummeted to the surface. The Peace Ship had dropped onto the glacier from a height of only two meters. It had been transported intact to a Coast Guard hanger in Reykjavík months ago using every helicopter the Landhelgisgæslan had. It was currently undergoing operational testing.

Hildur stopped walking, placed her hands on Sandur's shoulders, and pulled their foreheads together. They breathed deeply and entered a state of semiconsciousness for two minutes.

Awakening back to full consciousness, Sandur looked at Hildur's stomach and smiled. His hands shook as he rubbed her belly. *"Við munum nefna hann Einar."*

Hildur smiled and nodded. A single tear slid down her left cheek.

They would name him Einar—Einar Sandurson.

***

Galveston Island, Texas
16:55 CST, 20 September

The *Legally Mine* turned eastward into the onshore wind that blew across the flat water of West Bay as Gail spun the large metal wheel at the back of the cockpit. As the sails luffed, she engaged the auto-furling system and started the new diesel engine to motor the remaining hundred yards to the dock at the back of their house. Mikey stood at the bow, holding the bowline. Michael Phelps watched four cranes in the shallows. He sat in the cockpit with Jerry, Cindy, and Daisy.

Dan stood at the end of the dock, waiting for them with a tall gentleman in a brown cowboy hat, Wrangler jeans, and cowboy boots.

Mikey tossed the bowline to Dan as the Catalina 45 slid alongside the dock. The tall man beside Dan reached out and grabbed the aluminum bowsprit to slow the boat's speed. His four main fingers on each hand were all the same length. The scar on his right hand was still visible and matched the outline of Michael Phelps's jaw.

"Hi, Doc," Gail said. "I'm so glad you could join us for dinner."

Michael Phelps leaped off the boat and ran to Doc, his tail wagging. There were no hard feelings from the day Doc had smashed his hand through the bathroom door trying to unlock it, trying to get to them, trying to find more food.

Doc reached down and hugged Michael Phelps. "You know we never turn down food."

Gail and Doc were cochairs of the newly formed Department of Advanced Medical Technology at UTMB-Galveston. Together, they would announce the next day in a press conference that their team had *discovered* the cure for cancer.

Jerry cleated the stern line. He had been in Austin for several days serving on the governor's task force for what people were calling the "Border Wars." What had started as a trickle became an alien flood when the Texas State Guard finished the temporary floating bridge across San Luis Pass connecting Galveston Island to San Luis Island and the Texas mainland. The four contiguous states to Texas had established border checkpoints on the major highways and roads, and Mexico had sent hundreds of *federales* to reinforce the northern border. The TSA banned aliens from traveling on commercial airlines. The response of the federal government was that Texas aliens were a Texas problem.

Meanwhile, the spat between the governor and the president over access to the Command Ship's crash site in the middle of Campbell Bayou on the mainland had morphed into a full-blown political crisis.

***

Kona, The Big Island of Hawai'i
14:35 HST, 21 September

Kup cradled his new baby girl as he smiled at Kahealani, who was resting in her hospital bed. He had barely made the delivery, having been in Honolulu only hours before at a meeting with Governor Kupule.

The Army Corps of Engineers had repaired the first 3,500 feet of Runway 17 at Kona International Airport. C-17s landed hourly, dispensing a few people and a lot of food, but leaving Kona—and the Big Island in general—was still difficult. The application for a flight to Honolulu aboard a military transport was almost thirteen pages long and required proof that you were human. Civilian flights off the island were still banned. Other than the food airlift, the federal government offered little assistance to the over one hundred thousand new residents of the Big Island; it was a Hawai'i problem.

The previous week, researchers at the newly formed Department of Advanced Propulsion at the University of Hawai'i at Hilo had announced a new antigravity propulsion system that promised to revolutionize air and space travel. Kup, now a regent in the University of Hawai'i system, had been present for the announcement.

The Hawai'i Command Ship had slammed into the northwestern flank of Mauna Loa. All eight escape pods were still attached and unused. The federal government had taken possession of a few pieces of the wreckage. Things happen when they happen in Hawai'i.

Kup had been hailed as a hero by many in Hawai'i, Australia, and around the world. Shortly after the Command Ships had come tumbling down, there had been calls for the governor to appoint him to take Senator Damonati's vacant seat. He had declined but agreed to work with Governor Kupule on alien integration. He was starting to develop a very high and favorable political profile, and there was talk of him running for governor in the next election cycle. He was still on leave from Central Pacific Airlines.

Kup glanced up at the television in Kahealani's hospital room. NNN was reporting that, despite a massive disinformation campaign including a multitude of false allegations that had resulted in her expulsion from the senate, Leilani Damonati was leading in the polls in the November election for Hawai'i senator. She had been released from federal detention several months ago when all charges against her were dropped.

Kahealani asked Kup if he would go get a nurse. She wanted some more ibuprofen. Kup nodded and proudly walked out of the room and down the hall with his baby girl in his arms. At the nurse's station, he looked down at a white coffee mug with dried coffee stuck to the inside. The side of the mug said:

> Damonati for a *Safer* Hawaii
> Damonati for a *Safer* America
> Damonati for a *Safer* World

Milton Keynes UK
Ingram Content Group UK Ltd.
UKHW051831160724
445364UK00012B/130/J

9 781963 102451